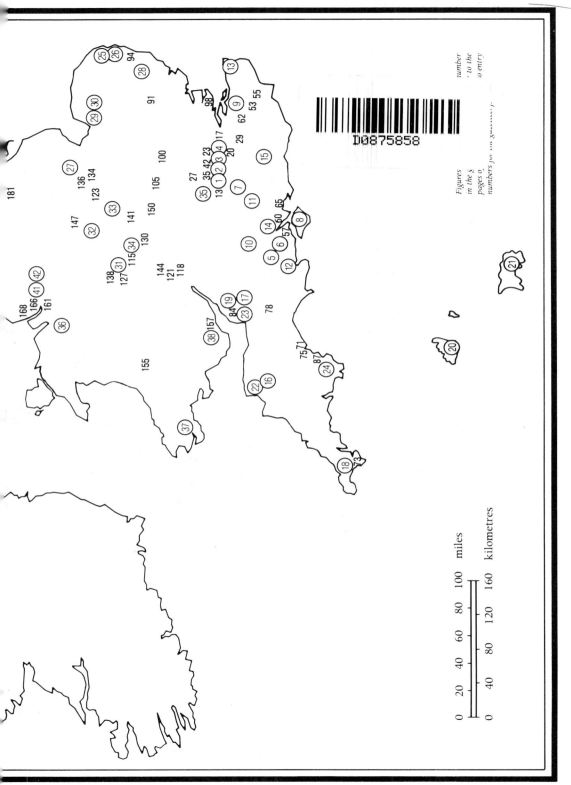

number
to the
pages o
numbers for the gazetteer.

Figures
in the g
pages o
numbers for the gazetteer.

0   20   40   60   80   100 miles

0   40   80   120   160 kilometres

A Guide to the Transport Museums of Great Britain

A Guide to the Transport Museums of Great Britain

JUDE GARVEY

PELHAM BOOKS
LONDON

To my wife Lesley
and my daughters Alexis and Belle

First published in Great Britain by
PELHAM BOOKS LTD
44 Bedford Square
London WC1B 3DU
1982

Garvey, Jude
  A guide to the transport museums of Great Britain.
  1. Transportation museums—Great Britain
  —Directories
I. Title
629.04′074′02   TA1006.G/

ISBN 0 7207 1404 4

Filmset and printed in Great Britain by BAS Printers Ltd, Hampshire
Bound by Dorstel Press Ltd, Harlow

CONTENTS

FOREWORD
by Sir Peter Allen

When the massive bundle of galley proofs of this book was dumped on my desk with the request for a foreword within ten days I said to myself, 'I'm not going to read that lot' – but I did.

And that in itself is proof, I think, that this is a book of quality, enjoyable to read *as a book* and not just a work of reference to be looked at before going to visit one of the museums or collections described. Far from being just a catalogue, it is well written, full of information about the history of the place visited and its relics – who built what, who designed that, who owned the other.

Several things strike me as remarkable about this book and the first is the extraordinary volume of knowledge which Jude Garvey imparts to us. True, he was Director of the Transport Trust for some five years, but the research needed to put this book together strikes me as prodigious. Nor is it all facile praise, though he finds a great deal to admire; some trenchant criticisms emerge now and then and it is often clear where his personal affections are engaged, as in the case of the Windermere Steamboat Museum, for example.

The second remarkable thing which stands out from this book is that an extraordinarily large number of preserved relics of all kinds survive in this country. The Transport Trust has no less than 211 affiliated preservation societies and the railway preservation groups total 131 members. In this book alone Garvey has covered, and very thoroughly, 52 museums and lists another 54 awaiting description. So it must be that the number of preserved items must run into thousands and we can be thankful for it.

Thirdly, it is remarkable how recent all this development is. Most indeed nearly all of the 200-odd museums, societies and collections have been put together in the last twenty-five years, and a large proportion in the last ten. Transport preservation must be one of the most spectacular growth industries of this quarter-century.

A Model A Ford of 1930, viewed from the replica garage at the Lakeland Motor Museum. Photo:
Lakeland Motor Museum.

ACKNOWLEDGEMENTS

Compiling this book has been an undertaking of great interest and enjoyment. It would not have been possible without the help of very many people throughout Great Britain and Ireland. Museum curators, archivists, private owners, club secretaries and members have all responded with enthusiasm to requests for information and photographs. I am very grateful to them all. With regard to the text I owe a debt to Professor Jack Simmons of the University of Leicester who started me off on the right track, to Ruth Baldwin my editor at Pelham for her advice and patience and to my secretary Claire Beauchamp who deciphered and typed the manuscript. All errors of fact and grammar are mine.

I would like to thank the following for providing photographs and for giving or obtaining permission to reproduce them: John Bagley, Michael Barker, Julia Bird, C. M. Booth, Robert Bracegirdle, Mrs J. Bradshaw, John Bradshaw, Neill Bruce, G. Cassidy, Mike Cavanagh, K. Cormack, Lord Cranworth, Ann Emmerson, R. J. Evans, David Firn, T. F. Fitch, Ray Fixter, Keith Fordyce, W. A. Gilbey, Oliver Green, Guy Griffiths, Lt Cdr D. K. Hale RN (Rtd.), Janet Hales, Jack Hampshire, J. P. Heeley, Edward Hine, A. J. Hirst, M. J. Hodgson, Stuart Holm, Stewart Howe, Graham Hunter, Joan Innes-Ker, Capt. Peter L. Jones RN (Rtd.), Brian Lacey, Len Lovell, R. G. Manders, Peter Mann, David Matthews, William Meredith Owens, J. Millard, Peter Mitchell, G. M. Moon, John Moore, M. J. Mutch, F. J. Neal, Douglas Nye, Dr E. S. Owen-Jones, Capt. R. H. Parsons RN (Rtd.), Lt Col C. E. Penn, Group Capt. W. S. O. Randle CBE AFC DFM RAF (Rtd.), Judith Richards, P. Robinson, Philip Scott, Michael Seago, David Senior, Bert Sharples, E. W. Shaw, Louise Sidebottom, Alastair Smith, Michael Stammers, J. D. Storer, Ursula Stuart Mason, Clifford Taylor, Peter Van der Veken, Michael Ware, T. P. Webb MBE, Vanessa Wiggins, Sally Wood.

Since this book went to press, the following museums have closed down: Banham International Motor Museum p. 91–3, 219; Pembrokeshire Motor Museum p. 224; and Ramsgate Motor Museum p. 215.

I
LONDON

BL HERITAGE MOTOR MUSEUM

THE BL HERITAGE MOTOR MUSEUM is situated in the grounds of Syon House on the banks of the Thames and close to a lively section of the Grand Union Canal. The 55-acre grounds also contain a conservatory, an aviary, an aquarium and a butterfly house. Both house, the interior of which was designed by Robert Adam, and grounds, landscaped by 'Capability' Brown, are open to the public.

For many years the estate housed the London Transport Collection until its move to Covent Garden in 1980. In the same year the BL Heritage Collection, as it was then known, moved from Donnington Park to Syon and became the BL Heritage Motor Museum.

The museum's collection is unique amongst many fine collections of vehicles owned by motor manufacturers throughout Europe. It represents not just one or two major interests, but is built up of vehicles from a vast number of companies which created the bulk of the British motor industry, including Austin, Morris, Wolseley, Rover, Riley, Trojan, MG, Triumph, Jaguar, Daimler, Swallow, Lanchester and the Leyland organization. It is the good fortune of the museum that many of these companies had the foresight, over the years, to preserve some of the more notable of their products. The old Wolseley company preserved its first and second three-wheelers and also the first four-wheeled car that it built. Leyland and Thornycroft saved their first steam vehicles, and Daimler preserved several fine examples of their craftsmanship, as did Austin, Morris and Rover. These form the basis of the museum, but there are twenty-five British marques on display from the earliest Wolseley of 1895 to the Metro and

the Jaguar XJS of today. Over three hundred cars are in the collection of which about a hundred are on display at any one time.

The collection is set out in one long and wide hanger-like building with a separate single-storey building to house temporary exhibitions. The first impression, on entering the museum, is one of confusion as the visitor is faced with a bewildering display of cars packed tightly together. With so rich an assembly of exhibits and so many stories to tell, there are obvious problems of emphasis and the use of space. The vehicles occupy most of the floor area and there is little room left for the display of background material to help the visitor understand the relevance of the exhibits or the history they are there to illustrate. The very complexity of the collection has brought its own problems, but with patience and a careful reading of the catalogue visitors will soon become aware of what a treasure-house the museum is and begin to seek out their own interests.

The earliest car in any collection is always one for particular attention and here in the form of the 1895 Wolseley is a very special vehicle. Designed by Herbert Austin, who later went on to found his own motor-manufacturing empire, this is the very first car to be produced by the Wolseley company. Frederick Wolseley, whose early engineering interest had been in manufacturing mechanical sheep shearers in Australia, had come to England to take an interest in the embryonic motor industry and employed Austin as his designer. Their first effort was this little rear-engined tri-car displaying a marked similarity to the French Bollée car of the same period. To the modern eye it looks like a mixture

The 1904 Rover 8hp single-cylinder car was the company's first motor-car design. This 1907 version is in the BL Heritage Motor Museum at Syon Park, London. Photo: BL Limited.

of wheelchair and motor cycle, preserving the hazards of both. The driver faces forward, steering with a tiller mechanism, and the passenger faces aft. It was the only one built and was replaced the following year by another Austin design. This was also a three-wheeler but reversed the earlier configuration by having a single wheel at the front instead of the back. Generally, it was a significant advance on the first machine and Austin himself, during the course of its development, drove it from Birmingham to Rhyl and back, a distance of some 250 miles. However, by this time Wolseley and Austin had plans for a four-wheel 'real' car and this second tri-car was halted at prototype stage. The first four-wheel Wolseley, and Herbert Austin's third design for his employer, borrowed nothing from French ideas except perhaps the name, the 'Voiturette'. It went into limited production in 1899 with a front-mounted 3hp engine and was one of the first cars to be offered to the public that was entirely British-designed and built. Marvellously, this first Wolseley four-wheel car and the two tri-car prototypes have survived and are preserved in the BL collection.

Herbert Austin parted company with Wolseley in 1905 after a disagreement on future policy and by 1914 Austin Motors was Britain's largest motor company. This period is well documented by the museum. The first-ever Austin, a 25/30hp model, appeared in 1906 and the museum possesses a 1907 survivor. Originally supplied as a private car, this specimen has an ambulance body fitted in 1914 for the Birmingham Board of Guardians. The engine is also of historical interest as it was the basis of the Austin family of units until the outbreak of the First World War. Also surviving from 1907 is an Austin 40hp York Landaulette. This, along with a 60hp model, was Austin's venture into big-car design. It is a big car in every sense – big engine, massive body and vast headroom – but the Austin company was really making their name with handy single-cylinder small cars and they soon abandoned the higher-priced market to concentrate on the mass-production techniques that were to lead to the 10hp Tourer and the fabulous Austin 7 of which nearly 300,000 were produced. Examples of both models are on exhibition.

A contemporary and competitor of Herbert Austin was, of course, William Morris who had started his business as a bicycle and motor-cycle repairer in the 1890s and later opened a garage business at Cowley near Oxford. Here he designed and built his first car, the famous Bullnose Morris Cowley. The museum exhibits an excellent example of the more powerful and less spartan 'Oxford' version and also its immediate predecessor and prototype, the Morris Silent Six Coupé. This particular car was supplied to Mr Morris himself, which has probably been responsible for its survival. It is not a typical example and, as one distinguished observer has remarked, it has 'the most luxurious coachwork to be be found on any Bullnose with many body details reminiscent of Great Western Railway furnishings' – praise indeed!

In 1928 Morris introduced his first true small car, the Morris Minor Tourer. In appearance the Minor was almost an Oxford in miniature. The two vehicles are on display and a study of both affords a useful insight into how a major car manufacturer responded to the market forces of the period.

The initials MG stand for Morris Garages, the original garage business started by William Morris in 1904. In 1921 Cecil Kimber joined Morris and his interest in body styling, plus his appreciation that the young man of the day wanted something less staid than the Cowley or the Oxford, soon led to the introduction of the MG Marque and a long line of good-looking sports cars which have won the hearts of young and not-so-young drivers ever since. The museum has a number of historic MGs to show. 'Old Number One' of 1925 is here, not the first car to be called an MG but the first entirely purpose-built model as the earlier MGs had only been specially bodied Bullnose cars. Rescued for £15 from a Manchester scrap yard in 1932, it may be said to be the real ancestor of all MG sports cars. There is a 1930 18/80 Speed Mk I on which the now traditional MG radiator made its debut. It is a good example of late 1920s–early 1930s medium-sized fast sports-touring car design. There are many other MGs marking the progress of this remarkable company, including the poignant display of the last MGB produced which retired the MG badge in 1980, but two quite exceptional MG cars are especially note-worthy. Both are high-speed-record cars. The first is the EX135 Gardner MG. Long, low and sleek, this is the car in which Major Goldie Gardner captured a string of speed records between 1938 and 1952. In 1957 MG produced the EX181 in which Phil Hill, two years later, achieved 254·9mph – the fastest MG of all time. It was another record in the MG bag, but the last time MG went speed-record breaking.

It is one of the unique pleasures afforded by the BL Heritage Motor Museum exhibits that the histories of so many of the British car manufac-turers involved in the early days and the expansion of the motor industry can be re-searched. The story starts in the late nineteenth century and continues to the present day. It is enthralling to be able to compare Rover cars of 1906, 1931, 1956 and 1981, to observe the differences between the first Land Rover produced in 1948 and the millionth in 1976, to admire the Austin 7, the Mini and the Metro or see the Leyland Eight of 1927 next to the Jaguar XJS of 1976.

Throughout spring and summer the museum has special exhibitions that present a more detailed look at the history of a particular section of BL and the British motor industry. Past exhibitions have included 'The MG Story', which reviewed more than fifty years of this famous marque, and 'Racing, Rallying and Record-Breaking Cars', starting with the 1899 Wolseley that took part in the 1,000 miles trial of 1900 and continuing with the Austin-Healey and Jaguar exploits on road and track, the Range Rovers driven from Alaska to Cape Horn and the Maxi that competed in the London to Sydney Marathon of 1970.

HISTORIC SHIPS COLLECTION OF THE MARITIME TRUST

IN 1969 HRH THE DUKE OF EDINBURGH founded the Maritime Trust with the aim of doing for historic ships what the National Trust does for historic buildings. It had not come into being a moment too soon, and for some areas of our maritime history it was sadly too late. Over the centuries the British coastline and its rivers have spawned one of the most richly varied collections of craft anywhere in the world. As late as 1930 over 250 craft of separate design could be seen in these waters; today only a handful survive.

In spite of the dearth of material, the record of the Maritime Trust since its inception is impressive. It has established, around the country, a remarkable fleet of vessels forming an admirable representation of major sections of British maritime history. It can never be complete because so many vessels have disappeared forever and the twentieth-century aircraft-carriers, battleships, passenger liners and deep-sea traders have always been impossibly expensive to preserve.

However, in the nineteenth-century St Katharine's Dock, close to London's Tower Bridge, the Maritime Trust has brought together a number of its historic vessels to form its Historic Ship Collection. The location is a happy one. The dock provides a suitable setting and offers sheltered berths for the old ships. HMS *Belfast* is moored in the river close by and the National Maritime Museum and *Cutty Sark* are a ferry ride away. The site itself is of considerable interest and diversion. Nearly 25 acres of former docks and warehouses have been converted to a complex of shops, offices and restaurants, the new buildings blending sensibly with the architecture of the restored wharves and quays. A fine hotel and a housing development have replaced a derelict landscape, and in 1973 a yacht haven was opened, giving the visitor a chance to see a wide selection of modern cruising vessels as well as a fleet of Thames barges in all states of preservation.

But it is to the Historic Ships Collection in the old East Dock that we must steer ourselves. The pride of the fleet is undoubtedly the *Kathleen and May*, a 98-foot three-masted topsail schooner built at Connah's Quay in 1900. She was employed, like scores of other trading schooners, in taking cargoes such as cement, coal, pitch and clay anywhere between Oban, the London River, the Channel Islands and the Irish ports. In her first year she logged 3,000 miles, port to port, and continued to lead a hard and busy life in the British coastal trade for sixty years after that. In 1961 she was sold out of trade and, after numerous changes of owners and fortune, was bought and restored by the Maritime Trust. The saving of this aged schooner – the last British vessel of her kind – provides the first and perfect illustration of why the Maritime Trust was established. No drawings and few photographs existed of the vessel as she was originally rigged – changes to rigging and layout had occurred throughout her life and an engine had been installed in the early thirties – so the Trust restored her as a typical West Country schooner. Little imagination is needed, as one walks her deck and tours the holds and living quarters, to visualize the rigorous life endured by her crew (generally captain, mate, four deck hands and a boy cook) or the skill required to work such vessels in

Part of the Maritime Trust's Historic Ships Collection in the East Basin of St Katharine's Dock, London. Photo: Maritime Trust.

Britain's dangerous coastal waters.

The same imagery is inspired by boarding the other vessels. Here is the drifter *Lydia Eva*, launched at Kings Lynn in 1930 and named, as was the custom, after the owner's daughter. In the first three decades of this century, the combined English and Scottish drifter fleets of more than a thousand vessels sailed out from the East Anglian ports of Great Yarmouth and Lowestoft. Since 1970 not a single drifter has fished from Great Yarmouth and not one herring has been landed on the quays. Economic conditions, biological changes and the uncontrolled fishing of the herring spawning grounds are the main factors in this decline. The *Lydia Eva*, slightly bigger than the typical drifter of her time, is now, after thirty years of work and a decade of neglect, restored to her former working condition. Still scented by the herring catches of long ago and with her gear on deck and an exhibition in her hold, she is a fine memorial to all the other craft which used the same ancient drift-net method of fishing.

Moored next to the drifter is the Thames spiritsail barge *Cambria*. This splendid vessel, 91 feet long and 22 feet in the beam, was built in 1906 at Greenhithe with English oak frames and doubled-planked with best pitch pine. She was worked with a crew of skipper and mate and, in later years, her famous third 'hand', a small collie dog that would bark a warning in foggy weather when danger threatened. *Cambria's* first owner was William Everard, who at one time owned the biggest coasting fleet in the world. Her builder was his son William – his other son built *Hibernia* as a sister ship – and both were launched on the same day. For nearly two hundred years the Thames sailing barges were part of the maritime scene in East and South-East England. While most of them spent the greater part of their days sailing the Thames, by the latter part of the last century it was not unusual to see their red-brown sails at any point off the coast from Yorkshire to the West Country, or in any river from the Humber to the Tamar. They also traded across the English

Channel and the North Sea to the Continent. The Thames sailing barge was designed for moving bulk cargoes in soft-bedded rivers and other confined spaces. Its flat bottom and shallow draught allowed it to carry big loads in a few feet of water and to sit upright when the tide had ebbed away. In her working days *Cambria* was acknowledged as one of the 'queens of the coast' and coasting bargemen were proud to serve in her. Her preservation is a splendid achievement.

Here also is the steam coaster SS *Robin*, built at Blackwall in 1890. She was sold to a Spanish company and worked out of Bilbao for eighty-four years. Brought back to England by the Maritime Trust and restored, she is the last surviving example of the type of vessel immortalized by Masefield – she is a 'dirty British coaster with a salt-caked smoke stack'. Another steam-powered vessel on display is the tug *Challenge* which, from her launching in 1931, worked over forty years at Gravesend and Tilbury and survives as the last of the working steam tugs on the Thames. Her engines are still in fine condition, and, given the opportunity and occasion, she can still get up her steam and go as she did in 1974 to take first prize in the historic power-craft section of the annual Greenwich Barge Match – this exciting race is, incidentally, an occasion that no one fascinated by maritime history should miss.

Close to *Challenge* is another interesting craft, the lightvessel *Nore*, which was one of two such identical vessels built in 1931 of wood and iron at Cowes and operated by Trinity House in the Thames Estuary and elsewhere as a navigation aid. To join this fleet of valiant vessels in 1980 came RRS *Discovery*, built in 1901. Her importance is not only in her association with the ill-fated Captain Scott and his Antarctic expeditions, but also in that she was the last large three-masted wooden ship to be built in Great Britain – the final flower of centuries of traditional shipbuilding. The intention of the Trust is to restore *Discovery* to her square-rig form as she was in 1924 before her last two Antarctic voyages and to place her in a permanent berth in London as a museum of exploration and discovery.

The Historic Ships Collection is a noble venture in an appropriate setting. The photographs and the displays of equipment tell the tale of the sea in a vivid way and the literature available is well presented.

HMS *Belfast*

NOTHING WILL PROVIDE a greater contrast for anyone interested in ships and the sea than, after visiting the Historic Ships Collection at St Katherine's Dock, to go aboard HMS *Belfast* which is moored nearby in the Thames at the Pool of London and in the shadow of Tower Bridge. The immense difference in scale, power and purpose between the small vessels built for river and coastal work and this mighty ship of war is overwhelming. The last survivor of the Royal Navy's big ships whose main armament was guns, the cruiser HMS *Belfast* is permanently moored in the River Thames as a floating naval museum. During the Second World War the *Belfast* was one of the most powerful cruisers afloat and took part in the last battleship action in European waters. She is the first warship to be preserved for the nation since HMS *Victory*, and it is interesting to note that both vessels had a battle complement of about 850 officers and men.

HMS *Belfast* was built by Harland and Wolff

HMS Belfast, *the 11,500-ton cruiser, is the last survivor of the Royal Navy's big ships whose main armament was guns. She is moored in the River Thames opposite the Tower of London as a floating naval museum. Photo: HMS* Belfast *Trust.*

in the city from which she took her name and launched on 17 March 1938 by Mrs Neville Chamberlain. In November 1939, a few months after being commissioned, the *Belfast* was severely damaged by a German magnetic mine in the Firth of Forth. She had to be almost entirely rebuilt and did not rejoin the Home Fleet until November 1942. She then helped to cover the convoys to Russia and played a key role in the Battle of North Cape in December 1943, which ended in the sinking of the *Scharnhorst*. In June 1944 the *Belfast* led the cruiser bombardment which supported the Allied landings on D-Day. After a refit she sailed for the Far East in the summer of 1945. She was flagship at the time of the *Amethyst* incident in 1949 and provided fire support for the United Nations forces during the Korean War. She underwent extensive modernization between 1956 and 1959, before returning to the Far East to become the flagship of the station. Her active career ended in 1963, when she was placed in reserve as a floating barracks at Portsmouth. In 1967 the Imperial War Museum initiated efforts

to save *Belfast* from the scrapyard, and in 1971 she came to her mooring at the Pool of London.

Visitors may wander at will over many parts of the ship, which has been preserved in a state as near as possible to the original. The excellent guide book provides the background information to more than thirty areas within the ship which, with much climbing of ladders, can be visited. These include the navigational bridge where the captain would exercise his command of *Belfast*, the admiral's bridge from which the overall fleet operation would be directed, the operations room where there is a reconstruction of a scene which occurred during HMS *Belfast*'s participation in the Battle of North Cape and the sinking of the German battle cruiser *Scharnhorst*, the fire-control room where such complicated gunnery problems as hitting a moving target at up to 14 miles were solved, and more mundane though equally vital sections such as those dealing with engines and radio communications and the galley.

As well as providing a record of all the functions of a Second World War cruiser, HMS

An early photograph of HMS Warrior, *the first British armoured battleship built entirely of iron, which was launched in 1860, not far from where HMS* Belfast *is now moored. She is also the last British armoured battleship afloat. Photo: Imperial War Museum.*

Belfast is a naval museum and there are splendid displays devoted to ships' badges, mines, the Royal Marines, the D-Day landings and the modern Royal Navy.

Not far from where HMS *Belfast* is presently moored there was launched in 1860 what was probably the most important and influential warship to be built in the nineteenth century. HMS *Warrior* was made of iron throughout; she was bigger than any other warship and built to an entirely new concept which, at a stroke, brought to an end hundreds of years of wooden warship building. She set utterly new standards in size, strength, speed and fire power, and became the reference point for all future construction. When she was launched, her designer remarked that her hull would last for a hundred years. The claim was pessimistic, for it was still in good condition when the Maritime Trust took her in charge in 1979 and had her towed to Hartlepool where a lengthy restoration programme is now under way. The Maritime Trust's intention is to return the ship as far as possible to her 1860 state and then put her on show as a prime example of a Victorian navy vessel. If it were then possible for HMS *Warrior* and HMS *Belfast* to join HMS *Victory* at the Royal Naval Museum at Portsmouth, they would form one of the world's most dramatic maritime museums.

LONDON TRANSPORT MUSEUM

THE LONDON TRANSPORT MUSEUM, which opened in the spring of 1980, is housed in one of the most attractive buildings and urban settings one could wish for. The former Flower Market building in the revitalized Covent Garden is its new home. This splendid late nineteenth-century structure was built in the style of a large conservatory in the Crystal Palace tradition and exploited the new-found freedom of glass and iron construction that produced such many fine buildings in that period. By modern standards the lofty arched halls seem grandiose for the accommodation of flower stalls. However, the light and spacious interiors are ideal for the museum's displays.

London Transport has always taken a proper interest in its own history and over the years has built up a collection of vehicles, equipment and literature illustrating the major changes and advances in the capital's road and rail transport. The collection, as it has always been previously called, has had a number of homes but now, in what is hoped is its permanent residence, it has come together as a first-rate museum able to offer interpretative research and educational facilities in addition to displaying most of its buses, trams and trains.

The excellent guide book to the museum recommends a route for touring the exhibits. This helps the visitor not to miss anything, as some of the larger vehicles obscure smaller displays. The order of presentation is roughly chronological, but a careful reading of the guide before touring helps to make the layout clearer.

The horse buses were London's first form of popular public transport and the museum has three examples. The earliest type (although a replica built in 1929 for the London Omnibus Centenary celebrations) is George Shillibeer's omnibus which started a service from Paddington to the Bank on 4 July 1829. The earliest original vehicle is the 'Knifeboard' horse bus, a type which saw service from about 1850 onwards and in the 1870s was adapted by the replacement of the iron rungs at the back with the more convenient curved staircase to gain access to the roof. The third exhibit, the 'Garden Seat' horse bus, had the more popular forward-facing seats and was seen on London roads for nearly thirty years until the arrival of the motor bus in the early 1900s. This particular horse bus found a retirement role as a home on the banks of the River Thames until purchased and restored in the twenties.

Naturally enough, the motor bus which has served London so long is very well represented in the museum. Six years of trials with various experimental vehicles led to the introduction of the 'B' type in 1910. It is this which so often appears in those First World War photographs showing troops being ferried to the Western Front. The army commandeered over a thousand and many were shipped to France still displaying their London advertisements. A fine example starts the motor bus collection and the technical development and changes in design for passenger and driver comfort make an absorbing study as one strolls by these retired public servants. Single-deckers are well represented, including the AEC-designed 'Q' type which caused something of a sensation when it first appeared in 1932 by having the engine at an angle on the offside, to the bewilderment of many of its early passengers.

The two trolleybuses in the collection include the notable 'A1' type, which was London's very first trolleybus and was in service from 1931 until September 1948.

The museum now has an example of a horse-drawn tram on display, painstakingly restored for the purpose, but the splendid, swaying, rocking, clanging electric London tramcar is here represented by three excellent examples typical of the tram era from 1906 to 1952, including a four-wheeled West Ham Corporation vehicle. Of this an earlier catalogue says, '. . . to ride at the end of one of its balconies on a sharply curved track was an experience never to be forgotten'. Ah, the pleasures of West Ham High Street long ago!

We now come to the 'Railways in London' section. The Metropolitan Railway – the first urban passenger-carrying underground railway in the world – opened on 10 January 1863 with a service operating between Paddington and Farringdon Street, using steam locomotives owned by the Great Western Railway. The excellent displays illustrating these early days include some very graphic photographs of the 'cut and cover' method of tunnel construction used before the tube tunnelling system, which left the street surface undisturbed, was invented in 1869.

The earliest locomotive in the museum is a fine example of the Metropolitan Railway Class A 4-4-OT which replaced the GWR engines in 1864 and which was designed specifically for underground use with features to reduce steam and smoke output. This particular locomotive had eighty-two years of continuous service on a variety of duties before retirement and the reward of a restoration to its 1903 condition. Another exhibit from the same era is a very curious and diminutive locomotive bearing a

The history of public transport in London is well explained at the London Transport Museum. Here a Daimler motor bus (note the iron wheels) owned by the Motor Traction Company inaugurates their Kensington to Oxford Circus service in 1899. Photo: Veteran Car Club of Great Britain.

distinct resemblance to a traction engine, but this is perhaps not so surprising when one learns it was built by Aveling and Porter in 1872. This chain-driven locomotive replaced horse-drawn trains on the Duke of Buckingham's private railway at Wotton and later came into the ownership of the Metropolitan Railway.

The rolling stock of this period and the early twentieth century is represented by two beautifully restored passenger cars. The earliest is from the City and South London Railway which opened in 1890 as the world's first underground electric railway and is an example of their 'padded cell' car, so nicknamed because of its cushioned bench seats and 5-foot-high upholstered backs – it looks extremely comfortable. The other example is a 'Bogie' coach of 1899 – a design advance on the earlier rigid-wheelbase carriages – elegantly painted in the later livery of the Metropolitan Railway. Nearby, from the

same era, stands a railway milk van built in 1896 and with louvred sides to keep the churns of milk cool on their journey to the capital from outlying areas.

The success of electrification on the City and South London Railway gave impetus to plans to electrify the sub-surface railways, particularly the Inner Circle, and thus banish smoke and steam from these increasingly busy lines. After some experimentation with different systems, the DC system finally adopted was substantially that used throughout the underground today, with the positive rail outside the running rails and the negative rail between them. By 1905 the urban underground system was fully electrified.

A relic from these days in a section of a car built for what is now a stretch of the Piccadilly Line. This example is part of a so-called 'gate stock' which required a guard on the end platform of every car to open and close the gates

A Wotton locomotive of 1872, with Metropolitan department and District saloon carriages in the background, on display at the London Transport Museum. Photo: London Transport Museum.

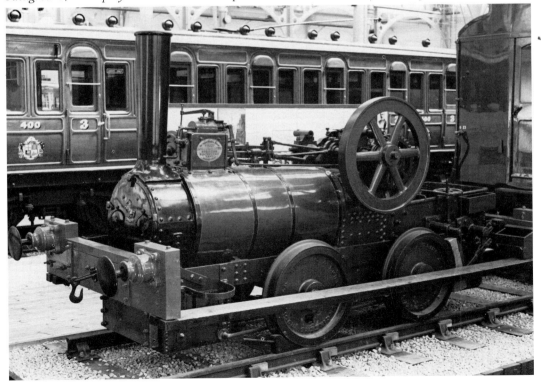

at each station. The large levers which can be seen at the end of the car section illustrate what a tedious job this must have been until the air-operated sliding doors were introduced in 1919. Two other stock cars representing later developments are a District Line car, which came into service in 1923 and had hand-operated sliding doors, and a 1938 tube stock car which, with its streamlined appearance and traction equipment mounted under the floor, is the obvious beginning of the underground car design we know today.

Interlinked with the main transport exhibits are displays using models, photographs, plans and artefacts illustrating the social, technical and environmental changes brought about by the development of London Transport in peace and war. Station architecture and poster advertising – two particular art forms in which London Transport have excelled – are not neglected. It is all excellently done. There are also items of driving and signalling equipment that can be operated by the visitor – much favoured by vigorous youths intent on re-enacting incidents from O.S. Nock's famous book *Historic Railway Disasters*!

Some visitors, forgetting that the museum is of the history of an organization now called London Transport, rather than a museum of the transport of London, might remark on the absence of many other vehicles that have been and are such a part of London street history. Particularly in relation to public or semi-public transport the hansom cab and the London taxi will be missed. For those who wish to seek them out, a number of other London museums have examples of the former and the London Cab Company in Brixton Road has a modest but interesting collection of the latter.

The London Transport Museum has a small but well-stocked souvenir shop, a cafeteria, a research library (by appointment) and a lecture theatre. On leaving the museum, visitors can indulge in a parting piece of nostalgia. If their destination is Oxford Street, Charing Cross or Piccadilly, they can board a vintage double-decker London bus to take them there. The journey will be all bustle, noise, smells and traffic jams, an experience the Londoner has enjoyed for a hundred years.

MOSQUITO AIRCRAFT MUSEUM

THE MOSQUITO AIRCRAFT MUSEUM is perhaps unique among Britain's aircraft museums in that not only is it the oldest, but it is also the only one to specialize in preserving a particular aircraft type – the classic Mosquito – and the products of one of Britain's greatest aircraft manufacturers, de Havilland. It is situated in the grounds of the seventeenth-century moated manor house of Salisbury Hall, and lies just off the A6 between Barnet and St Albans in Hertfordshire, less than 20 miles from central London. Many famous people lived in this building including King Charles II and his mistress Nell Gwynne, Warwick the Kingmaker, Sir Nigel Gresley, the locomotive designer, and Sir Winston Churchill.

When the Second World War broke out, the de Havilland company decided to move their design team away from the main factory at Hatfield to a place where they could work undisturbed and away from the danger of bombing. Salisbury Hall was chosen and in the late summer of 1939 the Chief Designer, R. E. Bishop, and his team moved in and set to work on the design of a new unarmed high-speed bomber, later to become the Mosquito. Although the project was stopped by the Government, work carried on as a private venture until in July 1940 the project was officially reinstated. In a hurriedly constructed hangar in the grounds of the hall a full-sized mock-up was assembled and shortly afterwards the prototype began to take shape, being completed less than eleven months after design work had started. It was then dismantled and taken by road to Hatfield, where it made its maiden flight on 25 November 1940. It is interesting to note how the de Havilland characteristics of original thinking, persistence and speed of work showed themselves on this occasion as they had done seven years earlier in the production of the DH88 Comet racing aircraft which was designed and built in nine months and won the England to Australia Air Race in 1934. Happily this aircraft also survives and can be seen in the adjoining county of Bedfordshire at the Shuttleworth Collection.

Three more Mosquitoes were built at Salisbury Hall, all of which were flown out from the adjacent fields, and then the design and construction work was transferred to Hatfield. The Hall was then used for a number of purposes, including the design of the Vampire jet fighter, the design and construction of the Airspeed Horsa, and the establishment of the de Havilland Technical School. At the end of the war de Havillands left and the Hall lay derelict until 1956 when it was taken over by Walter J. Goldsmith, a retired Royal Marines officer.

Meanwhile the prototype Mosquito, W4050, was lying dismantled at Hatfield, and incredible as it seems now the possibility of scrapping the aircraft was considered. By this time, however, Mr Goldsmith had become aware of the part his new home had played in the history of the Mosquito and suggested that it be returned to the Hall for permanent exhibition. De Havillands agreed, and a public appeal to raise funds to build a hangar in which to house the prototype met with a successful response. The aircraft was re-erected there by a team of volunteers from Hatfield and the Royal Air Force, and on 15 May 1959 it was displayed as a memorial to all those who had designed, built and flown the Mosquito. W4050, arguably the

W4050 – the prototype of the de Havilland Mosquito, one of the outstanding aircraft of the Second World War. Displayed at the Mosquito Aircraft Museum at London Colney, Hertfordshire. Photo: Stuart Howe.

most historic aircraft in Britain today, became the centrepiece of an impressive display of exhibits, including examples of its armament, relics, photographs and models.

It wasn't until January 1968 that the museum acquired its second aircraft, a Venom NF3 that had previously served with 23 Squadron in the Middle East and was donated by the RAF. A month later a Vampire TII joined the collection from the same source.

The museum's second Mosquito, this time a late model B35, was donated by Liverpool Corporation and was delivered to Salisbury Hall by an RAF team in October 1970. This particular aircraft was built too late to see wartime service and was used in the vital, if mundane, task of target towing. In 1963 it was used in the ground sequences of the film *633 Squadron* and in 1968 again became a film star when flown for the film *Mosquito Squadron*. On May 15 1971 this Mosquito was dedicated as a memorial to Group Captain P. C. Pickard who had been killed leading the Mosquitoes of 140 Wing on perhaps the most famous Mosquito raid of all: the daring low-level attack to breach the walls of Amiens jail and release over two hundred French Resistance fighters who were under sentence of death.

The museum began to grow rapidly, gaining a Vampire FB6 from Switzerland, a Dove from Germany, a DH125 from Rolls-Royce, a Horsa glider fuselage section rescued from a field near Banbury and other types including a Sea Vixen Chipmunk and Tiger Moth. Altogether there are eighteen aircraft, all but one of de Havilland origin.

Much of the restoration work is undertaken by skilled volunteers and a Supporters' Society is open to all who wish to help. At the time of writing a third Mosquito is being assembled from parts found in various different countries. The fuselage comes from Holland, a wing from Israel and other sections from Canada, Malta, New Zealand and Australia.

Whatever chance brought Walter Goldsmith to Salisbury Hall in the fifties, it was a happy coincidence that he turned out to be a man with a sense of history and the enterprise not to let slip away forever the evidence of its exciting past. Let Reichmarschall Hermann Goering have the final word: '. . . I turn green with envy when I see the Mosquito. The British knock together a beautiful wooden aircraft that every piano factory over there is building . . . there is nothing the British do not have.'

NATIONAL MARITIME MUSEUM

IN SUMMER, the first temptation for the maritime enthusiast on leaving St Katharine's Dock is to board one of the river launches and make the leisurely journey down the Thames to the National Maritime Museum at Greenwich (the winter journey by train from the London stations of Charing Cross, Cannon Street, Waterloo or London Bridge, or by bus has its pleasures too). On approaching Greenwich, the eye will be caught by the soaring masts of the square-rigged *Cutty Sark*, the only survivor of the British tea clippers and now preserved as a museum ship and a reminder of the great days of sail. This magnificent vessel with a length of 212 feet was launched in 1869 for the China trade and made some epic voyages in the annual race to be first home with the tea harvest and, later on in her career, with wool cargoes from Australia.

The berthing of the *Cutty Sark* in a dry dock with a stone-cobbled quay close to the Thames is perfectly reminiscent of an old sailing scene. Nearby, as evidence of how other men used the wind to cross the oceans, is Sir Francis Chichester's ketch, *Gipsy Moth IV*, in which he made his single-handed circumnavigation in 1966–7. In contrast to that of the *Cutty Sark*, the display of the *Gipsy* on an isolated concrete perch is unhappy, and its location and display will irritate most yachtsmen and patriots who may consider that the exploits of this sturdy little craft and her gallant skipper deserve to be better presented and explained.

The setting of the National Maritime Museum is however a delight. It stands at the bottom of the rounded hill in Greenwich Park, not far from the river. On the crest of the hill is the Old Royal Observatory founded by Charles II in 1675. This building, which is open to the public, houses a working planetarium and displays on nautical astronomy, time-keeping and Greenwich Mean Time. The story of the Observatory is an important part of maritime history and a visit to Greenwich should include it if only to enjoy the view, from its windows, of the river and the panorama of London.

A short and pleasant stroll down the hill brings the visitor to the main buildings of the museum. Together with the nearby Royal Naval College, built on the site of the Tudor Palace of Placentia, they form one of the most outstanding architectural compositions in the country.

The centre building of the museum is the Queen's House, designed by Inigo Jones and completed in 1635. It was the first Palladian building in England and in spite of many changes to its interior over the years remains a brilliant example of the style. It is now used by the museum to display items of its collection from the same historical period and here are many fine paintings and navigational instruments from the sixteenth and seventeenth centuries.

On either side of the Queen's House and linked to it by elegant colonnaded walks are the two wings of the museum which were built just after the Battle of Trafalgar and later extended. The principal entrance to the museum is in the East Wing, but before starting a tour (perhaps even before planning a visit) it is as well to remember that the National Maritime Museum is very large.

The collection is one of the finest in the world and embraces all aspects of maritime history with a special emphasis on that of Great Britain.

It covers many topics in considerable detail and all are fascinating. Any attempt to see the whole museum in a limited time will exhaust both body and mind: it properly requires a full day or, much better, two. The excellent guide produced by the museum and its pamphlet *25 Things to See* are well worth the study by those on a less leisurely visit.

The East Wing is devoted to the nineteenth and twentieth-century period, the time of the greatest era of British sea power and commerce. The first gallery deals in a similar evocative style to that of the Merseyside Maritime Museum with the migration between 1800 and 1875 of seven and a half million people from Britain to North America. Who they were and why they went is clearly set out. Models, dioramas, photographs and documents tell the moving story of these people inspired by a combination of hope and desperation. The hazards of the passage and their fortunes on arrival are well described.

The adjoining gallery reviews the fifty years from 1870 of the small merchant sailing vessels in the British coastal trade. It shows how they were constructed and rigged, the trades they were engaged in and the type of men who built, sailed and owned them. These vessels are particularly important in maritime history as they are the last descendants of the wooden sailing ships whose European ancestry goes back more than a thousand years. A dominant feature of this gallery is a full-size reproduction of the foredeck of a ketch of the 1880s. It is encased in high plasterboard walls and on one side steps lead up to a 'viewing' window. This enclosure is a curiously awkward contraption whose omission would benefit an otherwise clever display.

The next gallery deals with the transition from sail to steam. The parallel in land transport is the arrival of the steam locomotive to oust the canal barge and the mail coach, and by the use of some very fine models and diagrams the theme 'From Sail to Steam – the Crucial Years' is explained. Particularly well presented is the development of the screw propeller and the effect of the efficiency of the compound and triple expansion engines in sounding the death knell of the commercial sailing vessel. The historical progression is continued in the next gallery with the emphasis on the development of the passenger-carrying vessel. Large-scale models of Brunel's SS *Great Britain* of 1847 and SS *Windsor Castle* of 1970 are sectioned to illustrate the styles and standards of passenger liners at the beginning and end of this era of the grand method of sea travel. The history of merchant shipping is continued with the displays (under construction at the time of writing) in the adjoining gallery with the theme 'The Liner Trades and International Shipping Conferences 1875–1975'.

Downstairs in the East Wing, the Arctic Gallery tells the story of the search for the North-West Passage which attracted the interest of British explorers as early as the sixteenth century. It is one of the greatest adventure stories of the world. The emphasis here is on the nineteenth-century voyages of Sir John Franklin, particularly that of 1845 in which his entire expedition perished. The irony that a search party on a mission to find Franklin became the first to chart the North-West Passage is noted. Many poignant relics of the Franklin adventure brought back by the searchers are displayed.

The top floor of the East Wing contains two major galleries separated by a couple of rooms set aside to cover some aspects of sea warfare during the First and Second World Wars. As the museum admits, they are token displays, for both subjects are comprehensively covered in museums elsewhere. There are many fine photographs and paintings, particularly those relating to the Battle of the Atlantic in the Second World War and the Battle of Jutland in the First World War. Perhaps the most impressive painting is the massive canvas by Sir Arthur Cope, completed in 1921, of some of the outstanding naval officers of the time. It depicts four admirals of the fleet and many admirals and vice-admirals, numbering twenty-one in all. Close by, in stark contrast in a frame not more than 20 inches square, is a portrait of John Travers Cornwell, the sixteen-year-old gunner who was mortally wounded at Jutland and was awarded the Victoria Cross posthumously.

Of the two major galleries on this floor the first is an art gallery devoted to marine paintings of the nineteenth century, and here large and small canvases depict sea and shore scenes both violent and tranquil. Wyllie, Edward Cooke, Clarkson Stanfield, Turner and Alexander

The National Maritime Museum has an excellent section on the history of the British coastal trade, of which this vessel, the gaff-rigged schooner Stina, *is a survivor. She still sails for charter on the east coast. Photo: Basil G. Emmerson.*

Nasmyth are just some of the artists represented in this outstanding collection. The soft elegance of this gallery is in sharp contrast to the other which deals with the story of 'A Century of Naval Development 1814–1914'. Here all is dark wood and stark lighting as separate but associated displays tell of the Pax Britannica and the invincible command of the sea that the British Navy enjoyed during this period. The paddle-to-screw transition is well explained as are the developments in guns and gunnery, battle tactics, theatre of operations and the beginnings of the Royal Naval Air Service in 1914. The gallery is dominated by a magnificent model of HMS *Queen*, to illustrate the final development of the sailing battleship and a smaller model of HMS *Devastation* of 1871, the first British warship to operate without the use of sail power.

The walk by way of the colonnades from the East to the West Wing of the museum is very pleasant. To the south are views of Greenwich Park and the Old Observatory Building, to the North the Royal Naval College, designed by Wren, and the Thames.

The West Wing is much bigger than the East for it has many more stories to tell. The entrance hall includes the main bookshop, the information centre and the library of photographs of museum objects. Tucked away in a corner of this area is a small octagonal room occupied solely by a sculptured head of the Glasgow shipowner Sir James Caird, a considerable benefactor to both the National Maritime Museum and HMS *Victory*. The largest gallery here and the one generally rated the most popular is the New Neptune Hall which is devoted entirely to technical subjects and contains as its main exhibit what is probably the largest single example of industrial history under cover in any museum in Europe – the almost complete fabric of the 1907 riveted-steel steam-paddle tug *Reliant*. The visitor can go aboard her to see the machinery and will find particularly interesting her unique side-lever engines, which are very similar to those which powered early British transatlantic liners. The *Reliant* is part of a display concerned with the development of steamship propulsion from the early paddlers to the compound-engined screw. Also in this gallery are some very fine preserved steam launches and a large collection of wooden boats illustrating the use of this material from the time of the Vikings to modern yacht and dinghy designs. The New Neptune Hall is currently undergoing reroofing and rearrangement to consolidate its role as the museum's major technological gallery. To the side of the Neptune Hall is the Barge House, a long, narrow and entirely undecorated room. The splendour lies in the exhibits. They are the elegant and beautifully ornate barges used by naval officials in the eighteenth century to visit Thameside dockyards. Two royal craft here are the graceful shallop built for Queen Mary II and Prince Frederick's barge of 1732.

The history of the boat further back in time is the subject of galleries on the sub-ground floor and displayed here is the work of the museum's Archaeological Research Centre. The results of careful excavation and scientific analysis are set out in three large displays devoted to major discoveries in this field: the Ferriby boats dating from the Bronze Age and the oldest boats found anywhere in the world outside Egypt, the Sutton Hoo ship and the Graveney boat from the Viking period. The next gallery is concerned with the quite different world of the 'National Museum of Yachting' and covers three hundred years of the development of the sport from the early royal yachts to the GRP products of today. The photographs are superb. Possibly the lack of space might prevent acceptance of the suggestion that here is the proper home for *Gipsy Moth IV*.

Next door is a gallery quite removed from anything else in the museum and an excellent example of how a complex story can be simply told. The main central feature is a magnificent contemporary model of the 1813 seventy-four-

The RMS Queen Mary *on her trials off Greenock in 1935. The National Maritime Museum devotes a gallery to the liner trades. Photo: Barnaby's Picture Library.*

gun ship *Cornwallis*. To either side are three berths each dealing with a subject relevant to the vessel's time. At the touch of a button, a taped slide show explains the sailing method, mooring, stowage, signalling, navigation, and so on. Each mini-lecture is brief but brings illumination and animation to the whole subject. It is a technique that would enliven so many museums.

The size of the National Maritime Museum and its complexity have already been mentioned and at this stage, before attempting the next ten galleries, the visitor will be in need of rest and refreshment. The museum's restaurant is excellent, as are the restaurants in the town centre of Greenwich a short walk away, and on a fine day a picnic in Greenwich Park can be a pleasure. Whatever the means, some rest to the brain and nourishment to the body are recommended before the next section is attempted.

It is at the top of the great staircase leading out of the main hall that the entrance is made to the first of the series of galleries that cover a historical time sequence from the end of the seventeenth century to the first decade of the nineteenth. The galleries here present their material in a much more formal way than do those in the East Wing. Certainly the stories are well told but perhaps not with the same sense of drama that modern display techniques furnish. This observation particularly applies to the early galleries because the main features in these are contemporary oil paintings, artefacts, documents and models. Here is the museum's oldest merchant ship model (and possibly the oldest anywhere), the *Somerset* of 1738, and the splendid paintings and related dioramas of the royal dockyards at Devonport, Portsmouth, Sheerness and Chatham which began to assume their modern form in the middle 1700s.

From this point stairs descend to a gallery illustrating the work of James Cook and his exploration of the Pacific. The significance of his voyages is underlined by large wall charts that show how hazy was the European knowledge of that part of the world before Cook's discoveries and what a stupendous task of surveying his expeditions achieved. Artefacts brought back from the Pacific islands by Cook and his crew and the paintings of William Hodges who accompanied Cook on his second voyage are evidence of one of the epic feats of discovery.

The next galleries deal with the story of maritime aspects of the settlement of the United States 'from Jamestown to Yorktown' and particularly with the maritime campaign during and after the American Revolution and the long story of the war at sea with France. Maritime developments of the period covering navigation, safety at sea, rig improvements, signalling, etc, are explained. A particularly striking display in this section shows a gun position in an eighteenth-century man-of-war. It centres around a thirty-two-pounder muzzle-loading cannon and very clearly shows the mechanics of its operation, the duty and discipline required of each member of its gun crew, its fearsome power in action and something of gunnery practice of the time. The fury and devastation of a broadside from such a gun platform is vividly conveyed.

The last two galleries are a kind of national shrine to Nelson and the navy of his day. His life and times are illustrated with many relics and commemorative pieces and two massive canvasses – Turner's painting of the Battle of Trafalgar and A. W. Devis's dramatic rendering of the scene 'The Death of Nelson' in *Victory*'s cockpit. Devis's painting shows Nelson's chaplain tending the mortal wound in Nelson's right shoulder. Nearby is the vice-admiral's actual uniform coat which he was wearing on 21 October 1805 when the fatal bullet struck him – in the *left* shoulder. Artist's licence is responsible for the transposition.

The final gallery in this tour of the West Wing is the Navigation Room. The displays here illustrate the charts and instruments invented by successive generations of men to provide the means of navigating a ship. There are some fascinating fifteenth- and sixteenth-century manuscript charts, unique terrestrial and celestial globes produced by Gerardus Mercator in the mid-sixteenth century, and a quadrant invented by the English mathematician John Hadley which was a significant advance on existing instruments designed to take sights at sea when he produced it in 1731. Also here are the four marine timekeepers made by John Harrison (1693–1776). They are amongst the finest exhibits in the museum and were made

This photograph, taken through one of the two collonades connecting the Queen's House with the wings of the National Maritime Museum, shows the twin domes of the buildings designed by Sir Christopher Wren, which now form part of the Royal Naval College at Greenwich. Photo: Barnaby's Picture Library.

over a period of twenty-five years in his pursuit of the £20,000 prize offered by the Board of Longitude to encourage means of accurately determining longitude at sea. The first is a massive mechanism of brass and wood weighing 72 lbs, the last a watch of about twice the size of a pocket watch. All four have miraculously survived in working condition. The two earlier timepieces are each displayed in a glass case equipped with a button. When the button is pressed a microphone relays the steady 'tick-tock' of the mechanism, providing a sound and sight that astounded the mariners of the eighteenth century and which cannot fail to impress us now.

One final pleasure awaits visitors if they time their arrival carefully at Flamsteed House, the Wren-designed building that houses the Old Royal Observatory on the hilltop in Greenwich Park. Atop its main tower is a black pole and a large red-painted ball. This is the Greenwich time ball, the world's first visual time signal and an important navigational aid before radio time signals. In 1833 the following notice to mariners was issued:

The Lords Commissioners of the Admiralty hereby give notice, that a ball will hence forward be dropped, every day, from the top of a pole on the eastern turret of the Royal Observatory at Greenwich, at the moment of one-o'-clock pm solar time. By observing the first instant of its downward movement, all vessels in the adjacent reaches of the river as well as in most docks, will thereby have an opportunity of regulating and rating their chronometers. The ball will be hoisted half way up the pole at five minutes before one-o'-clock, as a preparatory signal, and close up at two minutes before one.

The ball still drops at precisely 1 p.m. every day.

ROYAL AIR FORCE MUSEUM AND BATTLE OF BRITAIN MUSEUM

ROYAL AIR FORCE MUSEUM

THE ROYAL AIR FORCE MUSEUM and the Battle of Britain Museum have been built on the old aerodrome at Hendon in North London. The location is indeed appropriate, for Hendon is the cradle – if not quite the birthplace – of British aviation. As far back as 1862 Henry Coxwell and James Glaisher were flying a balloon, the *Mammoth*, from the nearby heights of Mill Hill to far-distant Biggleswade, and ballooning continued to be popular in the area right up to 1910. In that year Britain's first aviator, Claude Grahame-White, purchased a French Bleriot and an English field at Hendon and established a flying school that he called the 'London Aerodrome'. By 1911 there were a number of flying schools at Hendon with instructors, mechanics and pupils of many nationalities: British, American, French, Belgian, Italian, Swiss and Russian – an international community – drawn together by the shared fascination of flying. By their enthusiasm and the immense public interest, Hendon became the venue for many spectacular events. The first Aerial Derby started and finished at Hendon after an 80-mile circuit around London, attracting 45,000 paying spectators, and was won by T. O. M. Sopwith in a 70hp Bleriot. Gustav Hamel inaugurated the airmail service, using another Bleriot to fly from Hendon to Windsor in ten minutes. Bentfield Hucks was the first English pilot to loop the loop and did it in 1913 at Hendon. In 1914 the aerodrome was taken over for war service and the Hendon area became a major centre for aircraft manufacture, producing thousands of Avro 504s and DH6s. The pilots who were trained at Hendon included three who were to win the Victoria Cross: Ball, Mannock and Warneford.

Between the wars, Hendon Aerodrome returned to racing, air display and club flying. Its annual RAF pageant rivalled Ascot, the Derby and Henley in royal favour and popular acclaim, and it was at Hendon in 1936 that the Spitfire made its first public appearance. At the outbreak of the Second World War, fighter squadrons were based at Hendon, but moved at the beginning of the blitz in 1940 when the aerodrome became a government communications base. It was from here that Churchill made his dramatic journey to France in 1940.

After the war, flying continued at Hendon until 1957 when landing on its small airfield became too risky for the modern fast aircraft. The last aircraft to land – a Blackburn Beverley destined for the new museum – flew in on 18 June 1968 and the shutting down of its engines brought to an end the flying history of Hendon.

The end of one era heralded the start of another that has proved equally popular with the public. On part of the old Hendon Aerodrome site the Royal Air Force Museum was opened by the Queen on 15 November 1972 and over 600,000 people visited it in the first year. Obviously, as its name suggests, the major part of the museum is devoted to the story of the Royal Air Force, past, present and future. However, on the approach to the first gallery, a graphic mural presents Icarus, Da Vinci, Montgolfier, Cayley and Lilienthal and ends with the dramatic picture taken at Kitty Hawk on 17

December 1903. Here then also is a developing museum concerned with aviation in all its forms. It may be that the broader interest will, at some time in the future, be reflected in the museum's name.

The building is two-floored with an exterior of brilliant white stone and smoked glass. The interior is spacious, cool and well lit. The museum is set out in a series of linked galleries: starting on the first floor, these cover the period until the end of the First World War, and continue on the ground floor from 1919 to the present day. The main halls on the ground floor accommodate the aircraft collections.

The first gallery deals with the early pioneering era and contains many relics of these days of spirited and hazardous events. The earliest surviving baskets from the Royal Engineers' Balloon Battalion, which was founded in the 1870s largely as an aid for artillery spotting, are displayed together with the scarlet uniforms of the period.

Hanging gracefully is the strangely configured military Manlifting Kite, designed by 'Colonel' S. F. Cody to take an observer in a basket up to 1,500 feet in height. This is backed by a photo-mural showing how the REs used the kite, and it is an important feature of the museum that, wherever necessary, use is made of large-scale photographs to illustrate usage and environment. Cody himself is depicted in effigy at the wheel of a full-size replica of the control-car of *Nulli Secundus*. This was the first British military airship and the first powered flying machine to take into the air the Union flag and a uniformed British serviceman. The Cody model is a poor one, as are all the others representing live figures in the museum. Modelling techniques have advanced much further than the awkwardly stiff and waxlike specimens used here, and all the displays using models would benefit in credibility if more modern methods were adopted.

Four early aero-engines, sculptural with gleaming copper and brass, are on show: a 40hp Humber which was entered in 1909 for Patrick Alexander's prize of £1,000 for an engine capable of sustaining 20hp for twenty-four hours; a 40hp Star of 1910; a 35hp Green, which as a type powered the Beta airship and early A. V. Roe and Blackburn aeroplanes; and a 50hp Gnome, a quite outstanding engine of its period that was widely used up the First World War.

To the right of the engines a showcase holds some fascinating items: a hydrogen leak detector, an important adjunct when thousands of cubic feet of that dangerous gas were overhead; lapel badges from the Lanark aviation meeting of 1910, Scotland's first; an early air-speed recorder; a fragment of the Wright brothers' immortal Flyer, authenticated by their signatures and given to C. Griffith Brewer (the son of the first Briton to be flown in an aeroplane, and whose mother was the first woman to fly to France, by balloon in 1906); and the rudders of Bristol Boxkite No. 17 inscribed with Graham Gilmour's flying log for 1911, starting with a trip over the Boat Race and concluding, '. . . Last trip to Hinton St George . . . reached 1,200 feet in height and finally smashed machine by running into fence on lawn.' The words and their placing epitomize the spirit of the early aviators.

The gallery which follows contains the first of the museum's environmental displays and is a representation of an early Royal Flying Corps (RFC) and Royal Naval Air Service (RNAS) workshop, so that the men, uniforms, engines, tools and aircraft can all be shown together in a contemporary atmosphere. This type of display is used wherever possible, and those with long memories will find many non-service items on show (e.g., cigarette packets, magazines, tobacco tins) that help to re-establish the sense of the period.

Another feature observed here is a viewing platform on to the aircraft hall, so that aeroplanes relevant to the displays may also be seen – views into the hall are provided throughout the museum so that the central theme can be related to the galleries.

In the workshop scene are four uniformed figures: an air mechanic of the RFC; a flight sergeant in the rare and splendid full dress of the RFC; and a rating and officer of the RNAS.

Dominating the display, and surrounded by a multiplicity of propellers, spare parts, tools, and engines – a 45hp Anzani and an 80hp Gnome – is the fuselage of a BE2a, an aeroplane designed in 1911 by Geoffrey de Havilland and used in France and the Dardanelles well into 1915. The display indicates something of the trade structure of the RFC, and the wall of the workshop bears a contemporary poster advertizing for recruits as blacksmiths, electricians, instrument repairers, motor fitters and riggers, all at 2 shillings (10p) per day.

Through the exit of the workshop are two cases containing memorabilia of two widely differing airmen. The first of these is Lord Brabazon of Tara, world-famous in the fields of aviation (he held the first pilot's licence in the UK), motoring (his number plate was FLY 1), sport and politics. His career ranged from pioneering flying to ministerial posts, and flanking his display case is his British Empire Michelin Trophy. This was awarded annually to the British pilot flying the greatest distance in a British machine, and he won it in 1910 with a distance of 19 miles in a Short No. 2 biplane. Close by is another of these extremely rare trophies, won by Reginald Carr – a great and very gallant Hendon colleague of Grahame-White – for a circuit flight in 1913 between Brooklands and Hendon in a Grahame-White Type 10 that covered 315 miles. The second case contains relics covering the service career of an extraordinary, yet not atypical, RAF officer – Group Captain G. I. Carmichael. The objects shown bear mute testimony to the pioneering effort, skill and bravery demanded daily from those who then chose to fly in the service of the crown.

The First World War era is introduced in the third gallery by the impression of entering a Bessoneau hangar, where a workshop scene in France is depicted. The men, shown in characteristic working informality, are using wooden formers and cams to rebuild a Morane Saulnier biplane. Among the many components, propellers and tyres shown is the rudder from an 1918 Avro 504J on which Prince Albert, later King George VI, learned to fly.

To the right of the hangar is a diorama depicting aircraft performing a trench ground attack. As with the models mentioned earlier, the museum's use of dioramas to convey atmosphere does not come off. In this example, the infantry under attack seem quite oblivious to the aircraft swooping on them.

In the centre of the gallery stand three vehicles with particular association with the RFC and RAF: a splendidly restored Crossley Tender – the standard eleven-seater personnel carrier – and two motorbikes, a Triumph and a Phelan and Moore, the standard mounts for despatch riders in the First World War. Flanking the walls are cases depicting stages in the development of engines, navigation equipment, aerial photography, signalling and cockpit layouts. By the exit is a large oil painting of the most famous of German air aces, Manfred von Richthofen. The expression is bleak and the effect chilling. His flying helmet and 'lucky dog' mascot are displayed close by.

A dominant figure of a different kind is the subject of the next gallery which is devoted to Lord Trenchard, the first Chief of the Air Staff, and leading on from here are a number of displays featuring the uniforms and decorations of many of the great leaders that the Royal Air Force produced.

The last gallery on the top floor of the museum is dedicated to all the holders of the Victoria Cross and the George Cross in the flying services. On reading the citations, one is stunned by man's capacity for bravery, devotion to duty and self-sacrifice. The posthumous awards, particularly, read like passages from Greek tragedy.

From this gallery a staircase leads to the ground floor where the chronological displays resume with the inter-war period. Technical development, engines and the airship age are the subjects of the first gallery on this floor, while the next two cover the 1939–45 war. The policy of the museum is to rotate its extensive collections, so displays will change from time to time, but here are excellent presentations on such subjects as radar, Barnes Wallis's 'bouncing bomb', Coastal Command, the RAF Regiment, the WRAF, and the escape organization. The post-war years are represented in the next two galleries which cover (again, subject to the policy of rotation) the development of the jet engine, the ejection seat, missiles, air-sea rescue and in-flight refuelling. The final gallery, entitled 'The RAF in the 1980s', presents the full scope of the Royal Air Force today.

It is worth emphasizing that a tour and study of all the galleries is the best introduction to the aircraft collection proper. Many visitors lured by the glamour of the aircraft go directly to the aircraft halls, and in doing so, unless they are

The Avro Lancaster, one of the most famous bomber aircraft of the Second World War. This particular aircraft, on display at the RAF Museum, took part in 125 bombing raids on enemy territory. Photo: RAF Museum.

knowledgeable on the background, lose the benefit of the historical information that the galleries so excellently provide.

The collection is, of course, the main attraction and rightly so, for here is a unique assembly of over forty aircraft ranging from an early Bleriot to a Mark 2 Lightning and also the astonishing Camm Collection honouring the late Sir Sydney Camm, perhaps best known as the designer of the Hurricane. The hall is of itself interesting, being formed from two Belfast-truss hangars dating back to 1915. These fine old hangars have been linked together by a handsome new building to provide a vast hall of some 40,000 square feet, giving many viewing angles and a feeling of space and air.

The earliest aircraft is a Bleriot XI monoplane similar to the aircraft in which Louis Bleriot made the first powered crossing of the English Channel in 1909. It is generally regarded as the most significant European aircraft prior to the

First World War and has a particular association with Hendon and its pioneer flying school. Other early aircraft include a Caudron Gill – the French designed two-seater trainer – and two aircraft from the Sopwith stable, the Triplane and its combat successor the F1 Camel, which was the most successful fighter aircraft of the First World War. A total of 5,500 Camels were produced, and by the time of the Armistice they were the mainstay of 32 RAF squadrons. An example (although in replica form) of larger fighter aircraft used in the First World War is the Vickers Gunbus, with its rear-mounted engine with pusher propeller to give its nose gun a free field of fire. Aircraft of considerable fame from the Second World War are the Vickers Wellington, built on the geodetic 'basket work' system pioneered by Barnes Wallis, and an Avro Lancaster, the aircraft that spearheaded the night bomber offensive. Here also is a unique reminder of the versatility and

The Camm Collection contains many examples of the work of Sir Sydney Camm, including this finely restored Hawker Hind. Photo: RAF Museum.

genius of R. J. Mitchell. In contrast to his Spitfire, of which a Mark 24 version is parked nearby, is a finely restored example of his Supermarine Stranraer flying boat which, although built to replace the earlier biplane flying boats of the twenties, served as a general reconnaissance aircraft in the early part of the war.

As with the Spitfire and R. J. Mitchell, so it is with the Hurricane and the late Sir Sydney Camm, one brilliantly successful aircraft of immense popular acclaim perhaps obscuring other achievements of outstanding merit. The Camm Collection in the centre of the Aircraft Hall honours and commemorates this genius in the field of aircraft design, who from 1923 to 1966 served variously as designer, chief designer, director and managing director of the Hawker Aircraft Company Ltd.

Sir Sydney spent his working lifetime in the British aircraft industry. An apprenticeship with Messrs Martin and Handasyde introduced him not only to full-scale aircraft construction but also to Brooklands, from which aerodrome many of his later Hawker designs flew. Camm was responsible for a wide range of highly successful aircraft, of which the Hurricane is undoubtedly the most famous in aviation history; however, he will also be remembered as the designer who, with his Hart and Fury designs, introduced into British military aviation a completely new generation of superlative aircraft with performances far in advance of their contemporaries. During his tenure the company produced nearly thirty different types which saw squadron service in the RAF and the Fleet Air Arm. Aircraft were also built for the Danish, Norwegian, Persian, Spanish, Yugoslavian and several South American air forces.

The Hawker machines in the collection range from Camm's first design, a 1924 Cygnet, a Hind and a Hart of the early days, and a Typhoon,

Tempest Sea Fury and of course the Hurricane from the war years, to a Hunter and a P1127 which led on to the vertical take-off Harrier. The collection is excellently supported by photographs and captions and is a fine tribute to a most ingenious and far-sighted man.

Post-war aircraft of the Royal Air Force end the aircraft displays and are represented by two English Electric products: the Canberra, which became the natural successor in the jet age to the de Havilland Mosquito, and the Lightning, the RAF's first truly supersonic fighter.

The Royal Air Force Museum and its associated partner the Battle of Britain Museum are two very fine establishments indeed. A Service pride is evident in all their staff, the information, lecture and research facilities are excellent, and the well-planned and well-stocked shop and the high quality of the catering facilites are of a standard rarely matched in the British museum world.

BATTLE OF BRITAIN MUSEUM

Across the car-park from the Royal Air Force Museum building is a long windowless hangar-like structure housing the Battle of Britain Museum. Unlike the RAF Museum, which is a national museum, the Battle of Britain Museum is a private concern funded from private sources and public subscription, although both establishments share the same director and staff. They also share the same problem regarding their names, for just as the Royal Air Force Museum is more than a history of the RAF, so the Battle of Britain Museum covers more than the historic events of the summer of 1940. More pointedly, it could be said that if the integrity of the name is to be kept, some readjustment of the exhibits will be necessary and aircraft such as the Short Sunderland Mark V and the Super-marine Seagull can make way for more relevant models. Unfortunately, the ravages of time and, regrettably, the lack of foresight during the immediate post-war years by all nations have dictated that some aircraft (the Dornier Do17, for example) are not represented at all and that others, more excusably, are represented by later versions. Such matters do not deflect from this intriguing, exciting and poignant exhibition.

There has, in the whole of history, been only one battle which was conducted exclusively in the air. It was, of course, the Battle of Britain, which lasted throughout the summer of 1940 and which was intended by Hitler to be the prelude to 'Operation Sealion', the invasion of Britain. The result of the battle appeared to be a foregone conclusion. The Germans had overrun Europe and established bases all along the continental coast from Norway to the Bay of Biscay. The Luftwaffe, having been blooded in the Spanish Civil War, and then its new *Blitzkrieg* style of warfare, had all the advantages – experience, strength of numbers, modern equipment, and a national leader whose territorial ambitions were rivalled only by those of Napoleon and Alexander the Great. What it did not have, and what might have been the deciding factor, was the desperation which grips those whose home and lifestyle are threatened by seemingly insuperable odds. This desperation took many forms in Britain during that summer, from the defiance of the corner shopkeeper, who refused to close despite having no shop front and no stock, and the ordinary members of the public who refused to give in, through the civil and military bureaucracy, to those whose duty it was actually to hit back, that band of young men who have been known ever since as 'the Few'.

The first thing the visitor will see on entering the museum is a cross between an aircraft exhibit and a reconstruction, being the wreckage of a Hawker Hurricane, with the figure of a member of the Local Defence Volunteers ('Dad's Army') acting as guard. This Hurricane was shot down near Clacton during the battle but in 1977 was recovered and partly restored. Other reconstructions show scenes from both military and civilian life. One depicts a London Undergound station (these were used extensively as air-raid shelters), another a bombed street with rescue workers going about their often grisly business. On the military side, two exhibits depict the chief means of warning that an air-raid was imminent. One is a Chain Home Radar hut containing equipment, primitive by today's sophisticated standards, which was able to detect the approach of enemy aircraft at sufficient range to enable interceptors to take off and get roughly in position to meet the challenge. The other is an Observer Corps post which, along with hundreds of others, relayed members' visual sightings of details of aircraft types and altitudes to the RAF Fighter Command operations rooms. Such a room is depicted in another display portraying the scene so familiar in war-time films when an enemy raid has been detected and the WAAF plotters and the Controllers work together until the order 'Scramble!' is given. The Ops Room display shows the scene at 11 Group Headquarters at RAF Uxbridge, and the actual room is preserved at Uxbridge exactly as it was at the turning point of the Battle of Britain, 11.30 a.m. on 15 September 1940, the day which has since been recognized as Battle of Britain Day.

The final tableau is to be found in the Aircraft Hall, for the Hurricane and Spitfire are exhibited in a reconstruction of a dispersal pen of the type used in the Battle of Britain and in other theatres of war as a protection against air attack. The Spitfire displayed here, a Mark I, was actually in action during the Battle of Britain and participated in the one-hundredth 'kill' of 609 Squadron. In admiring the Hurricane, the visitor should recall that it was in this aircraft type that Flight Lieutenant Nicholson of 249 Squadron won Fighter Command's only Victoria Cross of the war. The other British aircraft on display are a Boulton Paul Defiant, a type which was used in the battle but without distinction, hampered as it was by the firing limitations and additional weight of its mid-ships gun turret, and a Bristol Blenheim fighter-bomber representing the Bomber Command effort of the battle.

The German aircraft involved in the struggle are also well represented, although some are later models than actually took part in the battle. From Junkers are a JU87 'Stuka' and a JU88 which can claim to be the most adaptable and adapted aircraft of the Second World War, although devotees of the de Havilland Mosquito might disagree, but its various versions and derivatives as a day fighter, night fighter, dive-bomber, torpedo-bomber, minelayer, reconnaissance aircraft, transport, trainer and even flying bomb make a strong case. The JU88R-1 in the Battle of Britain Museum is a later version, which was a night fighter. Its nose is adorned with an array of aerials for the Lichtenstein SN2 radar which made it a very valuable prize when it was landed intact by its defecting crew at Dyce, Aberdeenshire, on 9 May 1943. Such was the value, in fact, that the two Canadian Spitfire pilots who intercepted the aircraft were recommended for a DFC each on the grounds that they did *not* shoot the Junkers down! As far as is known, this was the only time a decoration was suggested for that reason.

From Heinkel is a III.H23 bomber, one of the only two German-built machines of the type in existence, and from Messerschmitt a Bf109 fighter, which continually challenged the Spitfire for supremacy, and a Bf110E which is a later development of the type that displayed serious inferiority during the battle and suffered heavy losses. The museum's version is thought to be the only complete Bf110 in existence. The review of the Axis aircraft should not be concluded without mention of the Fiat Falco of the Italian Airforce which took part in the battle as a fighter escort to a bombing operation on English south-coast towns. The raids served only to emphasize the deficiencies of the Italian aircraft and they were soon withdrawn to the Mediterranean, leaving many behind in various states of destruction, including the museum's example which was forced down with a broken oil pipe after an engagement with a Hurricane on 11 November 1940.

Although the main thrust of the exhibition is rightly concerned with the confrontation between the fighter and the bomber, there are other exhibits to remind us of the valuable contributions made by the anti-aircraft and searchlight batteries, the fire brigade, police and ambulance services. The Battle of Britain has gone down in history as one of the most epic and vital ever fought, and this museum is a credit to its memory.

SCIENCE MUSEUM

THE SCIENCE MUSEUM, or to give it its full title the National Museum of Science and Industry, came into being as a result of the suggestion by the Prince Consort that a permanent home should be found for some of the displays from the Great Exhibition of 1851. In 1857 collections illustrating foods, animal products, examples of structures and building materials and educational apparatus were brought together on exhibition at South Kensington in London. Collections of scientific instruments and apparatus began in 1874, and subsequent years saw the addition of other collections and introduced items from the widest range of engineering, art, science and industrial sources. Up to 1899 the Art Collections, together with the Science and Engineering Collections, formed the South Kensington Museum, but in that year the name was changed to the Victoria and Albert Museum. In 1909 the arts and sciences separated, the Art Collections staying in the care of the V & A, and the Science and related Collections forming the nucleus of the new Science Museum.

At this time the Board of Education recognized the need for space and facilities to allow the Science Museum to expand and to fulfil its educational role. Plans were agreed to provide new buildings but the construction of the first phase (the East Block), which had started in 1913, was halted by the First World War and it was not opened until 1928. The economic depression of the thirties and the Second World War delayed any further development. In 1949 work was started on the second phase (the Centre Block) and it took twelve years to complete. The third phase (the

West Block), which would complete the essential plan agreed in 1913, is still an architectural drawing. These limitations and frustrations should be kept in mind when visiting the Science Museum, for they explain some of its deficiencies, but they also increase the visitor's admiration for the museum because of the way in which it has dealt with the problems since, taken in the round, it is an exciting, inspiring and rewarding place to visit.

The stated aim of the Science Museum is to aid in the study of scientific and technical development and to illustrate the application of physical science to technical industry. At the time of writing there is a superb temporary exhibition on micro-electronics which covers half the first floor of the East Block. Audio-visual equipment, lighting, models and participation techniques are used to explain a technically and socially complicated subject with equal clarity to a knowledgeable adult and an enquiring child. It is a first-rate demonstration of a museum at work.

The silicon chip, however, by reason of its small size and weight, poses fewer problems of display than the aeroplane, the locomotive or the motor vehicle. In presenting its transport collections, the Science Museum has adopted a bold but necessary policy of regrouping its larger exhibits at 'out-stations' away from London. The National Railway Museum at York, which opened in 1975, was the first, and a site at Wroughton near Swindon is earmarked for aviation, land transport, agricultural machinery and space science. A large exhibition has been created around the Concorde 002 prototype at Yeovilton in Somerset and many further items are loaned out to strengthen the displays of other museums. Thus the attractions of other locations are enhanced and material that could not be displayed at South Kensington is on public view.

All the main transport collections at the Science Museum are housed in the Centre Block with land transport on the ground floor, maritime on the second and aeronautics on the third. Agricultural machinery is found in the first-floor gallery.

From the museum entrance in Exhibition Road, the approach to the land-transport section through the high, well-lit East Hall is indeed dramatic. It is crowded with huge beam engines, turbines and hot-air, gas and oil engines. The inventions of Newcomen, Watt, Trevithick, Otto, Lenoir and Diesel abound. Some of the smaller engines are in work and their movements fascinate. The larger machinery is still, but massively impressive.

The land-transport section at the far end of this gallery is the obvious place to start a tour of the transport collections, but in the way it is presently laid out it provides a disappointing beginning, particularly after the walk through the impressive engineering hall. The main problem is not one of space – although more could usefully be employed – but rather the unimaginative presentation, particularly of the motor cars, and the lack of any obvious theme to relate one item to another. Most of the exhibits are displayed with a first-rate technical description, but little is done to explain their place or importance in the development of transport. However, a careful reconnaissance of the gallery qualifies these criticisms, for here are unique relics of the first days of road and rail transport and much else to see of exceptional interest.

We are introduced to the road-transport section by a small display of steam-propelled vehicles. The first is a Stanley Steamer motor car

Taken in 1857, this is the earliest known photograph of a mechanically propelled vehicle. It shows a Tuxford Traction engine using Boydell wheels for working on soft ground. The Science Museum has a section devoted to the traction engine. Photo: Science Museum.

of 1899 which, apart from the novelty of its propulsion, illustrates in its body design how the makers of the early automobiles adopted, with little change, the design of the horse-drawn carriage – in this case a nineteenth-century American buggy – for their horseless version. Next to the Stanley is a White steam car of 1903 whose exposed boiler and cutaway engine show the design and construction of its motive power. Both vehicles are of American manufacture – steam played a much more prominent role in early motoring in the USA than in Europe – but they serve to remind us that in the pioneer days of motoring, the steam-powered car with its quietness of operation, lack of vibration, fuel economy and the absence of a gearbox, had some useful advantages over the early petrol engines.

Across the gangway from the steam cars is a 1912 Pearson-Cox steam bicycle equipped with an engine similar in design to the earliest Serpollet steam car and the prototype Hildebrand motor cycle of 1889 which although of later design than Gottlieb Daimler's petrol-driven motor cycle of 1885, was the first power-driven bicycle to go into commercial production and over a thousand were produced. The display of steam-powered exhibits as it applies to road transport ends with an Aveling and Porter steam traction engine of 1871 and a small but fascinating collection of model steam lorries, engines and wagons.

The main display of motor cars begins with one of the Science Museum's finest possessions, the $1\frac{1}{2}$hp Benz three-wheeled car of 1888. This is claimed by the museum to be the oldest petrol-engined motor car now existing in this country. It is certainly the prototype of the world's automobile industry. In all respects it is a dramatic exhibit, having been completely restored and displayed so that its engine and body construction can be closely examined. Lest anyone think the restoration is only cosmetic, its record on the London to Brighton Run in 1958 is displayed – 56 miles at an average speed of 9mph! The collection continues with four other nineteenth-century vehicles of which three are Daimler-related but the fourth of this absorbing quartet is an 8hp two-seater phaeton built in 1897 by F. W. Lanchester who produced the first four-wheeled petrol car of

entirely British design and the first in the world to have magnetic ignition. There is an irony in the display of these four vehicles in that, after thirty years of producing quality cars, Lanchester were rescued from their 1931 financial crisis and taken over by Daimler.

The first twentieth-century car displayed in the collection is an attractive 5hp Peugeot 'baby' which played an important part in the early development of the smaller type of motor car. It is followed by three British cars, all produced in 1903, a massive Humberette, a Wolseley designed by Herbert Austin and one of the first Vauxhalls to be produced, a 5hp model with a chassis marked No. 6. This particular car's record of service is quite remarkable: it has covered 100,000 miles and been in the ownership of one family since 1904! The next car starts the Museum's introduction to the Rolls-Royce with the Manchester-built 10hp two-seater of 1905. An accompanying notice states it is the oldest original Rolls-Royce in existence and still in good running order. Next in line is a 1906 Ford Model N, a precursor of Henry Ford's famous Model T with such features as the light yet strong chassis, the simple and robust four-cylinder engine and the two-speed and reverse epicyclic gear. Strangely, there isn't a Ford T in the collection so no comparison can be made between two of the most significant designs in the development of the motor car. However, cheap, reliable motoring in the form of a small car is represented by the Austin 7 of 1922 which is displayed here. This open four-seater, with a speed of up to 50mph and covering 45 miles to the gallon, was an immediate success. Although improved versions appeared, notably in 1931 and 1935, the basic design continued in mass production until 1938 and some 350,000 Austin 7 cars were made.

In complete contrast, the next exhibit is a 1924 'Red Label' 3-litre Bentley, the supreme continental touring car. A confusing assembly of unrelated but quality machinery follows: a Connaught Grand Prix car of 1955 is parked next to a 1928 Rolls-Royce Coupé-bodied Twenty and tucked away at the back of the stand is the world's first gas-turbine motor car built by the Rover Company in 1950. Finally, two electric-powered vehicles complete the presentation of the collection, and in the light of

General view of the motor-car gallery at the Science Museum. A 1903 Peugeot is in the foreground. Photo: Science Museum.

the current oil crisis they will, as with the steamers, be studied with more than usual interest. Side by side are a Kreiger Electric Brougham and a prototype Ford electric 'Comuta' car. Both offer the advantages of reliability, ease of maintenance, simplicity of operation and freedom from noise and pollution. Their performances are similar: the Kreiger's is 20mph with a 50-mile range on a single charge, the 'Comuta' reaches 40mph but with a lesser range of about 40 miles. These electric cars would seem to represent an interesting development in the search for a new motive power, but the paradox becomes evident when the dates of manufacture of the two vehicles are noted. How much progress has been made in over sixty years between the 1904 Kreiger and the 1967 Ford?

The information and material on commercial vehicles displayed in a small area really can best be described as inadequate. The full-scale exhibits are three in number, a horse-drawn town delivery van, a coal trolley, and a Box-type tricycle of the 'Stop-me-and-buy-one' kind. Some well-made models complete the display. The adjacent display of fire-engines is more cheering; the earliest exhibit is a Newsham manual engine of 1734 accompanied by a later photograph of its 'Keystone Cop' crew demonstrating its qualities. Other engines illustrate significant technical developments and their vivid scarlet colour and polished metal give a strong impression of the efficiency that is the hallmark of this fine public service.

Impressive in a different way is the opulence in design and the craftsmanship that produced the exhibits in the coaching sections. A superb

Royal Mail coach displays all the strength and authority necessary to overcome the hazards of operating the London-to-York route in the first half of the nineteenth century. The original Brougham is here. This small, closed, one-horsed carriage created a great sensation on its introduction and led to a complete change in carriage design both here and on the continent, creating an effect similar to that of the 'Mini' a hundred years on. The Rolls-Royce of the day, a sumptuously decorated Dress chariot of 1891 used almost exclusively for civil and state occasions, stands next to it.

From here the visitor passes a small but elegant display of skates and snow sledges and enters the motor-cycle and cycle sections. Here again, the displays excite more by their content than by their presentation: the knowledge-able student will be enthralled; the schoolchild and casual visitor less so. A fine specimen of the first commercially produced machine opens the motor-cycle display. The genius Gottlieb Daimler patented and constructed the first petrol motor cycle in 1885 – his son Paul who rode it is generally recognized as the world's first motor cyclist – but it was the brothers Heinrich and Wilhelm Hildebrand and Alois Wolfmuller of Munich who built the first commercially successful motor cycle – over a thousand were produced in the two years from November 1894, one of which is displayed here. The next exhibit, a Holden motor cycle of 1897, is another example of an early commercial success, as is the De Dion Bouton tricycle of 1899. The development of the motor cycle is well marked, and the famous British names such as BSA, Douglas, Velocette, Norton, Sunbeam, and Triumph are well represented.

A slightly comic exhibit is the Avro 'Monocar' of 1926 which was designed and built by the aviation pioneer Sir Alliot Verdon-Roe and used to transport him over many journeys, totalling thousands of miles, between his aircraft factories at Southampton and Manchester. The astonishment caused by this pioneer 'bubble car' with its intrepid occupant can be imagined. The later developments of the motor cycle are less well represented, and no reference is made to motor-cycle racing which made such an important contribution to development. Significantly, the most modern exhibit is a 1978 Yamaha from Japan.

After all this display of torque and revs, performance and speed, the museum's cycle collection – and it is a very fine one – comes as a relaxation. The earliest exhibit is a hobby or dandy horse of 1818 which, the display points out, was more a recreational toy than a genuine method of travel. The first 'proper' bicycle was invented by the Scottish blacksmith Kirkpatrick Macmillan in 1837. This vehicle was constructed with a curved wooden frame and iron-tyred wheels. The pedals were connected by cranks to the rear wheel and driven by a forward-and-backward motion of the feet. Macmillan's other 'first' in cycling history was to commit the earliest-recorded cycling offence. He was fined 5s at the Glasgow court for knocking over a child at the finish of a 40-mile ride. This first bicycle has not survived, but a later copy starts the collection which shows cycle development in fascinating detail, with examples of early penny-farthings, tricycles, quadricycles and tandems through to the Rover Safety of 1885 which set the pattern for twentieth-century bicycle design. Modern 'choppers' and mini-wheeled cycles of today are also here. Separate displays on the development of gears, tyres, wheels and frames complement the main presentation.

The aeronautical collection on the top floor of the museum is arranged in a gallery which is designed to be reminiscent of an aircraft hangar and to permit aircraft to be suspended from the roof, giving the display a life and character not possible with aircraft on the ground. A raised walkway through the gallery allows good views of the aircraft fron unusual angles, and the information panels carry just sufficient text to give the visitor a quick working knowledge of the exhibits. By careful selection and imaginative display, the designers of this gallery layout have solved most of the problems of presenting a coherent history of a complex subject. Twenty-four aircraft are exhibited, ranging from a reproduction of the Wright aeroplane of 1903 to the first British jet-propelled aircraft to fly. More than 140 models cover the progress of flight from the ideas of da Vinci, through the pioneer work of Sir George Cayley and the first successful powered flight by the Wright brothers, to Concorde and the

A historic moment: Alcock and Brown take off in the Vickers Vimy at the start of the first non-stop flight across the Atlantic of 14–15 June 1919. This aircraft is on display at the Science Museum. Photo: Science Museum.

present day. The aero-engine collection is claimed to be the finest on display anywhere in the world. Over 100 engines and 40 propellers cover the history of propulsion over the last thirty years. They include a V-8 Antoinette, the first engine to power an aeroplane in the United Kingdom, the Whittle W1, the first engine to power a jet aircraft in the United Kingdom, and examples of each of the German wartime jet engines.

Probably most visitors to the aeronautical collection will begin their tour in the logical way by starting with the prehistory of flight and the dioramas showing the first balloon ascents. Others (like the author) will seek out immediately the Vickers Vimy that carried Alcock and Brown on the first direct non-stop crossing of the Atlantic in 1919. This magnificent machine is the largest exhibit in the gallery and displayed in its entirety. Because of its elevated

position it is not possible to see into the aircraft cockpit, but the museum has thoughtfully constructed a replica nearby so that visitors can see the pilot's control column and the few primitive instruments and marvel how those two brave and skilful airmen sat huddled in that freezing, noisy, vibrating and weather-exposed position for sixteen dangerous hours to capture the Atlantic prize, a place in history and the admiration of the world.

The real beginning, however, is with Montgolfier and his hot-air balloon of 1783, and the lighter-than-air section has some delightful dioramas and models to illustrate this exciting, dangerous and sometimes comical era. In the section dealing with the pioneer activity in the development of the principles of heavier-than-air flight the smallest exhibit is possibly the most significant, for here is Sir George Cayley's silver disc of 1799 on which he engraved the sketch to illustrate the principles of lift separated from thrust. It was Wilbur Wright, who when it came to practising the principles of heavier-than-air flight knew what he was talking about, who said in 1909, '. . . About a hundred years ago an Englishman, Sir George Cayley, carried the science of flying to a point which it had never reached before and which it scarcely reached again during the last century.' Cayley is now recognized as the true inventor of the modern aeroplane – in the basic sense – and the founder of the science of aerodynamics as applied to aircraft.

The one disappointment of the Cayley display is that the full-scale reproduction of his successful man-carrying glider, built with great accuracy and detail for a television film in 1973, is no longer available to the museum.* When hung in the main hall some years ago it was powerful evidence of the genius of Sir George Cayley. Its presence would also justify a more detailed description of the historic – some say legendary – first manned flight, related by Sir George's grand-daughter, Mrs Thompson, some years later: 'The coachman went into the machine and landed on the west side† at about the same level. I think it came down in rather a shorter distance than expected. The coachman got himself clear, and when the watchers had got across he shouted, "Please, Sir George, I wish to give notice. I was hired to drive and not to fly." That's all I recollect. The machine was put high away in a barn and I used to sit and hide in it (from the Governess) . . .' The anxiety of the coachman is understandable. His name is not known, but his place in the history of aviation is assured. Next to the Cayley display hangs a reproduction glider of the German engineer Otto Lilienthal who was the first man in history properly to fly a glider or, more accurately, a hang glider. Here also is a reproduction of Percy Pilcher's 'Hawk' glider – the original is in the Royal Scottish Museum in Edinburgh. Pilcher was a Scottish engineer and the first man to fly a controlled flight in the British Isles. In 1899 (like Lilienthal in 1896) he was killed in a gliding accident just a few months before he was to start experimenting with an oil-engined aircraft. We

can only surmise how near Pilcher was to being the first man in the world to fly a powered aircraft.

On 17 December 1903 the Wright Flyer, designed and built by Wilbur and Orville Wright and with the latter at the controls, became the first aeroplane in the world to make a powered sustained and controlled flight – the Everest of aviation had been conquered. Here in the aeronautical collection is an exact copy of that magnificent machine, along with photographs and other mementoes of the historic flight. The oldest original aircraft in the collection is a Roe triplane of 1909, the second aircraft to be made by that famous company. The Shuttleworth Collection in Bedfordshire has a reproduction of this aircraft with a much better flying record than the original! Two other machines of note to see are the Supermarine S6B seaplane, which won the final Schneider Trophy contest in 1931 at a speed of 340mph – the somewhat whimsically designed Schneider Trophy itself is on display nearby – and the Gipsy Moth 'Jason' in which Amy Johnson made her epic 10,000-mile solo flight to Australia in 1930. Naturally, the Royal Air Force Museum at Hendon in North London is the place to visit to see the aircraft of the Second World War, but the Hurricane and Spitfire at the Science Museum have a rare distinction: they were both in squadron service as early as 1940. In reflecting on the vital role the Spitfire played in the last war, it is sad to recall that its brilliant

*It is now displayed at the RAF Museum.
†The Vale at Brompton, near Cayley's home in Yorkshire.

designer R. J. Mitchell never lived to see the fame it achieved. He died in 1937 aged forty-two. The R. J. Mitchell Museum in Southampton is dedicated to his life and work.

One floor down from the aeronautical collection is the Maritime Gallery which, by the nature of its subject, paints on a much larger canvas.

Broadly speaking, the development of the motor vehicle, the locomotive and the aeroplane spans less than two hundred years. By comparison, the boat can mark its existence in millenia. Also, until the arrival of powered vessels, every country or region developed its own style of craft which was best suited to its trade and to local conditions of wind and water. Maritime history is the widest and deepest of transport subjects and no museum can do justice to it all. The Maritime Gallery has, therefore, used the material available to it and concentrated on a limited number of themes of which the four main ones are British coastal and river craft, foreign coastal and river craft, the history of ship-building from the Middle Ages to the nineteenth century and marine engines, of which there is a quite outstanding collection.

The gallery itself is on two levels, the main floor holding the engines and the models of the coastal and ocean steamships and naval vessels. The upper section, designed to resemble the promenade deck of a passenger liner, contains the cases illustrating the river, coastal and deep-sea sailing craft, and it is here that the student of the development of sail will want to start. Fine models, good photographs and dioramas, combined with excellent text, tell the story of sail, and it is fascinating to compare the differences and similarities in shape, rig and material of vessels that worked off the coasts of Dar-es-Salaam, Shanghai, Cornwall and the Oman or

FACING PAGE
ABOVE LEFT: *The magnificent* Cutty Sark, *the only surviving British tea clipper, which is berthed in a dry dock near the National Maritime Museum. Photo: Bill Angove.*
ABOVE RIGHT: *The Donington Collection's 1934 Maserati 8CM, one of the most original and well preserved of all historic racing cars. Photo: Geoffrey Goddard.*
BELOW: *The West Wycombe Motor Museum, Buckinghamshire. Photo: Edmund Nägele.*

traded on the Yangtse, Thames, Columbia and Fal rivers. The last days of the great age of sailing ships are poignantly recorded in a display of models of three schooners, the originals of which were all destroyed whilst in service, two with the loss of all hands.

The marine engines fascinate. An enormous number of very fine models, many of early date, present a full picture of ships' propelling machinery from the beginning. The accessories of steam and motor vessels are also fully covered, including paddle-wheels, propellers, and one of the most absorbing of working demonstrations, the steam tiller, which enabled a small wheel on the bridge to swing a great rudder at the stern to exactly the desired angle.

There are also three prime historical specimens in the marine-engine gallery: William Symington's atmospheric paddle-engine, which was really the first steam-engine to drive a boat, albeit a very small one; the engine of Henry Bell's *Comet*, the first steamer to provide a regular service in Europe; and the original turbine engine which Parsons fitted to his *Turbinia*.

Turbinia, of which a model can be seen nearby among the collection depicting various types of powered craft, was the 100-foot steam yacht and the first vessel to be propelled by turbines. It was also the fastest thing afloat, and on the occasion of Queen Victoria's Diamond Jubilee Review of the Fleet at Spithead it demonstrated, unofficially, its paces before the naval dignitaries of the world. Its appearance was dramatic, unheralded and rather upsetting, for nobody could catch up with it, but it forced the Royal Navy to take turbines seriously.

The models here also include shallow-draught river boats, warships, racy Channel steamers and a series of Atlantic liners, from the little *Sirius*, the first to reach America under steam the whole way, to the huge *Queen Elizabeth*, the largest of them all, by way of Brunel's *Great Western* and *Great Eastern*, *Britannia*, the first Cunarder, the lovely French *Normandie* and many others.

In the centre of the gallery, a superb collection of contemporary ship models from the seventeenth, eighteenth and nineteenth centuries shows the technical development in the naval and merchant ship over this period.

Dioramas illustrate the methods of construction as well as depicting lively scenes of dock and harbour workings.

Most visitors will take their leave of this gallery, and of the other dealing with transport subjects, with a sense of wonder that so much unique and remarkable material has survived the passage of time. The contents of the collections are jewels, but a criticism might be that some are badly mounted. The lack of space is a serious problem here, as at many other museums, but paradoxically it might be that there is too much on display, leaving too little room for setting or explanation. The display of the motor-car collection, for instance, has changed little in a decade and the way in which school children pass it by with obvious boredom is witness to its failings. This, in our fuel conscious age, is a great pity, for here are the vehicles and equipment on which to base entertaining thematic presentations on the development of steam and electric motor transport. No doubt such problems will be dealt with in their turn, as will the meagre selection of literature, the poor information service and the inadequate catering facilities, all of which are unfortunately not of a standard befitting a national museum of international stature.

II
THE SOUTH

BABY CARRIAGE COLLECTION

THE BABY CARRIAGE COLLECTION at Bettenham Manor, Biddenden, Kent, which now comprises some 350 prams of all types, is probably the largest and most complete collection of prams in the world. It is a private collection brought together by Mr Jack Hampshire and his wife over a period of twenty years and was started as a serious attempt to save – before it was too late – as many as possible of the old prams which were being destroyed, to preserve them as examples of a great British tradition, and to remind us of the skilled craftsmen (now fast disappearing) who built and designed them. Another reason for starting the collection was to fill a lacuna in our knowledge of the history and development of these vehicles, for, as Mr Hampshire observes, little is known about the early history of the pram, no museum has a comprehensive range of examples and his own recently published work (*Prams, Bassinets and Mail Carts*) is the first standard reference book on the subject. This is quite surprising considering that the children's carriage is of great antiquity and that the pram is the one vehicle in which we are all likely to have been a passenger.

The true perambulator in the form we recognize it today was first built in the mid-1800s, based on the design of a small three-wheeled bathchair. The Clifton Perambulator of 1845 on display in the collection is a typical example of this style and was designed, as most of the early carriages were, to transport the toddler rather than the small baby. The purchase in 1851 by Queen Victoria of several perambulators helped to stimulate sales and make the perambulation of young offspring a fashionable pastime, particularly with the rich

who enlisted the builders of the broughams and the hansom cabs to produce these small carriages as a sideline – the poor had to make do with a converted hop-cart or similar vehicle.

When the first real 'prams' appeared in the early 1880s – there are a number on display here, including a beautiful 'Winsom' built at the Silver Cross Works at Hunslet near Leeds – they immediately encountered trouble with the law, since it was illegal to use a four-wheeled vehicle on the pavement. The problem was solved by the introduction of the Bassinette (a hooded wickerwork cradle fitted with wheels), and there is in the collection a very early example in excellent original condition to illustrate this method of construction. The Mailcart (so called because it was developed from the hand-pushed or -pulled Royal Mail cart used by the Post Office) was also in demand and the collection has a number of specimens from the late nineteenth and early twentieth century showing their elaborate construction and design.

The Edwardian period could be called the heyday of the pram. By then there were many hundreds of manufacturers competing for the trade and producing between them some most attractive designs. The public needed a new status symbol – one they could afford. The baby carriage fulfilled this need. Parents vied with one another to show off their more attractively turned-out offspring. Manufacturers satisfied this requirement by producing better and more elaborate designs. The choice soon became enormous, and indeed it was highly improbable that two neighbours would own identical prams. One manufacturer alone produced a catalogue offering over a thousand variations in model, style and colour for just one season.

It so continued until the First World War, when overseas trade was lost and shortages at home caused a decline in sales. The twenties saw a revival in demand with the increasing birth rate and the trend was towards the very large, deep-bodied, low-slung prams made especially for older children. Paediatricians were advising that children as old as eight should be kept in prams, and it was not uncommon to see children being wheeled to school in a Victoria. This resulted in some very ugly and ungainly designs being produced, and the Hampshire collection has a few, but perhaps not a representative number from this period. Examples of the carriage, the Victoria and the increasingly popular folding pushchair (very suitable for the dawn of the age of mass car travel) are displayed.

After the war manufacturers returned to pre-war designs, but in the early 1950s the carriage pram staged a great revival in popularity, possibly as a result of the petrol shortage – and another increase in the birth rate. By the early 1960s one could say that the pram was having its final fling. Some very graceful designs were introduced, and I suspect it once again became a status symbol. But the car was to win in the end . . .

The Baby Carriage Collection, with its exhibits, photographs and literature, records the almost exactly hundred-year history of the British pram and it is laid out in a pleasant and chronologically instructive way. This prompted one woman visitor of liberated outlook to observe, 'Why is it that, compared to the motor car and the aeroplane, the design of the pram hardly changed during the whole if its existence?' Is the answer that it was right first time, or that it was man's design and woman's work?

C. M. BOOTH'S COLLECTION OF HISTORIC VEHICLES

MR BOOTH'S COLLECTION contains the only known 1904 Humber Tri-car, a 1929 Morris van, two or three vintage motor cycles, a penny-farthing bicycle and displays of model cars, signs and other automobilia. It also includes a dozen Morgan three-wheel cars dating from 1913 to 1935. This imbalance illustrates where Mr Booth's interest lies. He admires Morgans and has spent much time, money and energy finding and restoring them and now, behind his antique shop in the Kent village of Rolvenden, he presents them for public display.

H. F. S. Morgan, a garage owner in Malvern Links, built his first car in 1909. It was a light three-wheeler, a single-seater, powered by a 7hp Peugeot engine. The car was well received and he built a few more, but it was not until a two-seater version, shown at the 1912 Olympia Motor Cycle Show, had attracted a considerable number of orders that full-time car production began. In the following year a Morgan won the French Cyclecar Grand Prix and the name went on to become the best-known three-wheeler both in competition and as a roadcar.

An unknown Morgan and crew ready for racing in 1922. The Historic Vehicle Collection of C. M. Booth at Rolvenden, Kent, features an interesting range of restored Morgan three-wheel cars. Photo: National Motor Museum.

The earliest car in the Booth Collection is a 1913 Runabout with an air-cooled JAP engine of 964cc and a contemporary sales tag of under £100 which must have gone some way to account for its popularity. The next is the Grand Prix model of 1922 which is very similar in specification to the 1913 Grand Prix winner and was the first Morgan model not to have the engine housed under a bonnet. An Anzani engine powers the 1927 Morgan Aero, which is a good example of the Roadster model, and the 1927 Morgan Family 2+2 was advertized in the company's catalogue at the time as being constructed 'to carry 40 stone'. The fact that few of these models have survived and the one here was discovered without its engine suggests this claim might have been carelessly ambitious.

The first Morgan acquired for the collection is a 1935 Super Sports and it is in a number of ways the most significant. It has a 990cc overhead valve water-cooled Matchless engine with a three-forward-and-one-reverse-gear gearbox and a top speed of 75mph. It was the final form in which the Morgan Cyclecar was made and was produced until 1939, a few more being made from spare parts after the war. The Morgan factory was well aware that performance related to weight and was quite ingenious in solving such problems. In all models, for instance, the propshaft runs inside the main backbone tube of the car, and in many other models the two side members of the chassis act as exhaust pipes also. H. F. S. Morgan, one feels, would have designed a useful aeroplane if he had put his mind to it. The Morgan Company is one of the few independent motor manufacturers and still very much in business. Mr Booth is also a Morgan independent. May they both continue to prosper.

NATIONAL MOTOR MUSEUM

IT IS PERHAPS appropriate that the most convenient way of journeying to the National
Motor Museum at Beaulieu in Hampshire is by
motor car. Access by road is good, by rail less so.
The railway will only get the intending visitor
to Brockenhurst, some 6 miles from the museum.
The rail traveller, however, if setting out from
London, will be compensated by a glimpse of
what remains of the world's first motor-racing
track at Brooklands, as the train passes close to it
at West Byfleet some 15 miles out of the city.
Sadly, only a section of the old railway banking
survives, but with a quick sighting of that
massive, concrete curve the great names of
motor-racing history spring to mind, Campbell,
Segrave, Bira, Cobb *et al.*, and splendidly set the
scene for Beaulieu.

The National Motor Museum was founded by
the present Lord Montagu in memory of his
father, the Hon. John Scott-Montagu, later to be
the second Lord Montagu, one of the pioneers of
motoring and aviation and a great parliamentary
champion of both causes. The beginnings of the
museum date back to 1952 with a small display
of cars in the hall of the Montagu home, Palace
House, a site quickly outgrown as the collection
increased. In 1959 the cars were moved to a
building in the grounds of Beaulieu estate and
became, formally, the Montagu Motor Museum.
Eventually, with the support of the British and
European motor industry and allied businesses
and thousands of private subscribers, a completely new museum building was constructed
and this was opened by the Duke of Kent on 4
July 1972 as the National Motor Museum.

The building itself is not without interest,
being built of brick and glass on a geodesic steel
lattice and designed to give a large uncluttered
interior. By taking advantage of the sloping site,
it has provided a basement storage and maintenance area at the entrance level and, at the opposite
side of the building, an elevated gallery. The
different levels provide panoramic views across
the display area, and from the gallery the visitor
can look through observation windows on to
the repair and restoration workshops below.
The museum building covers about an acre of
ground and nearby another building accom-
modates the book, manuscript, photographic
and film libraries whose facilities are available
to all.

The stated objective of the museum is to
ensure that the exhibits are '. . . representative
of the history and development of the motor car
and motoring in Great Britain from 1895 to the
present day . . .'. The museum presentation is
divided into seven main sections. The first is the
Hall of Fame, which commemorates the great
inventive pioneers, promoters and innovators
and also the courageous and skilful drivers who
got behind the wheel, adjusted their goggles and
then put their foot down hard to prove whether
the designer was right or wrong. There follow
five other sections divided into the Veteran Age
(up to 1919), Vintage and Post-Vintage, Record-
Breaking Cars, Racing and Sports Cars, and
Commercial Vehicles. The seventh section is the
Graham Walker Gallery, containing the motor-
cycle displays. Each section will detain and
enthrall the visitor for no little effort has been
made to create a feeling of atmosphere and
period.

The entrance to the museum is pure theatre.
The doors are glazed with opaque smoked glass

and, as visitors enter, the transition from daylight to muted artificial light makes them pause, and there right in front of them is the incredible Rolls-Royce Silver Ghost of 1909, one of the world's most famous vehicles, here epitomizing the glory of the motor car and effecting a dramatic introduction to the museum.

The Alcan Hall of Fame commemorates the great pioneers. Some, like Karl Benz and Gottleib Daimler, were basic inventors; others were responsible for vital landmarks, such as Panhard and Levassor with the classic motor car configuration and Sir Alec Issigonis with his formula of an east-west engine driving the front wheels. Rolls and Royce gave their names to a new standard in luxury cars. W. O. Bentley became synonymous with the British sports car, and Henry Ford, W. R. Morris, Walter Chrysler, William Durant and Andre Citroen helped to bring the automobile within reach of the masses. Others made contributions without which the motor car would never have succeeded, such as Robert Bosch with his electrical ignition and J. B. Dunlop with the pneumatic tyre.

In a different class are the racing drivers. Some, like Lancia and Renault, were manufacturers as well, but commemorated here are twenty-one drivers of nine nationalities, from the nineteenth-century ace Fernand Charron to Britain's Jim Clark and record-breakers such as Segrave and the Campbells.

The cars on display in the hall are changed from time to time to coincide with anniversaries or events that are being recalled or celebrated, but here the visitor might see the Silver Ghost in company with an Austin 7, an 1896 Wolseley to compare with the newest prototype from Ford, BL or Lagonda, and a racing machine from the Brooklands era vying with the latest Grand Prix winner.

The veteran section which leads on from the Hall of Fame contains over thirty vehicles from the earliest days of motoring. Of particular note is the 1895 Knight, possibly the first British petrol-driven car to run on public roads and the 6hp De Dion Bouton of 1903, the first European light car, which can be compared with an American entry into the same market in the shape of the Cadillac of the same year. Moving on chronologically, the display of vintage and post-vintage automobiles ushers in the era of mass-production with models from Morris, Wolseley, Austin and Ford amongst the early arrivals, and the popular Beetle, Morris Minor and Mini representing some of the later developments. There are some oddities of this period too— the Amphicar that could cruise down a motorway and float down the Thames, and the 49cc Peel, the smallest car ever made in Great Britain, which also had the smallest production run – one unit built in 1964.

From the prosaic products of mass production, the next section introduces the ultimate 'one-off' automobiles, cars designed for one purpose only: to win the World Land Speed Record. The National Motor Museum is unique in having no less than four of these record-breaking cars: the 1920 350hp Sunbeam driven by K. Lee Guinness and Sir Malcolm Campbell, the 1927 1,000hp Sunbeam and the 1929 'Golden Arrow', both driven by Sir Henry Segrave and, finally, Donald Campbell's 'Bluebird'. The 350hp Sunbeam and 'Bluebird' were the first and last British cars respectively to hold the World Land Speed Record, and were both driven by Campbells, father and son. These four magnificent cars form the centre-piece of a dramatic tableau over 30 yards long that relates the whole history of the making and breaking of the Land Speed Record from the first official recognition of 39·24mph made by an electric-powered Jeantaud in 1899, and the epic battles in which these cars took part in the twenties and thirties, to the return to the fray by Cobb and Donald Campbell in the forties and fifties and the later attempts by the American trio of Breedlove, Arfons and Gabelich. It is a dramatic story, excitingly told with the help of contemporary photographs and a lucid text.

A different but no less exhilarating form of international competition for man and machine is covered in the sports- and racing-car section of the museum, which by the very nature of its subject makes it one of the biggest display areas. It contains nearly forty famous cars, including a 1908 Benz 120hp EP, a 1912 Hispano Suiza 'Alfonso XIII', the Bugatti Type 35, a 1931 Bentley $4\frac{1}{2}$-litre supercharged – in fact it is unfair to list any if all are not to be noted, for every car here from the early to the modern is significant in its contribution to the history and development of the sports and racing car.

The commercial vehicle section includes passenger transport vehicles of which a 1913 Thames stagecoach is perhaps the most curious: it must have been great fun to ride in or on as it trundled around the London streets on its sightseeing duties. Burrell and Aveling-Porter are, of course, in evidence and a Thornycroft steam van and a Harrods electric van represent two of the less popular forms of motive power.

The final section of the museum's presentation is concerned with motor cycles. It is shown in the gallery dedicated to the memory of Graham Walker, the TT rider and the museum's first curator of the motor-cycle collection. The gallery is arranged according to fourteen themes, each concerned with an aspect of motor cycling in Great Britain. These include 'Just Add An Engine', 'The Pioneers', 'Family Motor Cycling', 'Belt, Chain or Shaft', 'The Scooter Story', etc. 'The Post-War Years', which brings the whole story up to date, besides including a number of relatively modern imported motor cycles, attempts to show that the British motor-cycle industry is not completely dead.

Both motor cycle and light car have a common ancestor in the de Dion-type tricycle with single-cylinder engine geared direct to the back axle: the 1898 Ariel displayed here, the earliest motor cycle in the collection, was a successful British version. From the same period is an odd solution to engine accommodation in the 1899 Perks auto-wheel in which the engine lives inside the rear wheel.

Most visitors to the National Motor Museum will find that one visit is insufficient to appreciate all there is to see and study. A ride on the elevated monorail which goes right through the museum building is an unfailing temptation, as is a visit to Palace House itself. Certainly visitors interested in English and maritime history will make the short journey down to Buckler's Hard, a tiny village composed of one broad grass-verged street of small eighteenth-century houses leading down to the River Beaulieu. Here between 1745 and 1822 its shipbuilding yard produced seventy men-of-war and merchant ships – amongst them Nelson's *Agamemnon*. At the top of the street, a maritime museum has been designed around a skilful conversion of the former New Inn. Most of the exhibits concern events in the eighteenth century when Buckler's Hard was at the height of its influence and, by the use of prints, models, dioramas and drawings, recreate vivid pictures of this vanished life.

R. J. MITCHELL
AIRCRAFT MUSEUM

THERE CAN BE FEW men who have two museums in separate parts of the same country devoted to their life and work. Reginald Joseph Mitchell, CBE, FRAeS, is such a man. A tiny museum in Hanley near Stoke-on-Trent reminds us that he was born and educated there; and a slightly larger one in Southampton recalls his move to the South in 1916 at the age of twenty-one, after completing his engineering apprenticeship, to join the Supermarine Aviation Works. It tells the story of his brilliant career until his untimely death in 1937. Within three years of joining Supermarine, Mitchell was their chief designer; the year following he was appointed chief engineer. During his time there he was responsible for more than twenty types of aircraft ranging from the big Southampton flying-boats of the 1920s to the two specific aircraft with which he is most popularly identified, the Schneider Trophy seaplane and, above all, the Spitfire.

The R. J. Mitchell Museum is accommodated

The Supermarine S6 (N248) No. 8 taking off during the Schneider Trophy Competition in 1929. Photo: RAF Museum.

in a small building just off a pedestrian passage leading from Southampton's Central Station to the City's Civic Centre. It is a private venture developed with the support of local companies and the city's Air Training Corps. The museum is a modest one, bravely put together, and nothing is more surprising to the visitor than to pass from its rather nondescript exterior to the spick and span entrance and be faced immediately by examples of the world's most famous aircraft, the Supermarine S6A and the Supermarine Spitfire.

These are the only two aircraft in the museum but, with the support of an excellent photographic display, they are enough to tell the whole story. The Supermarine S6, like the S4 and S5 before it, was built to win the International Schneider Trophy which had been inaugurated in 1913. This aircraft was built in 1929 as an S6 and was entered for the eleventh Schneider Trophy contest held at Calshot in September of that year. It was flown by F/O R. L. R. Atcherley who was disqualified from the race for turning inside one of the marker pylons. However, he did set up new World Speed Records for the 50 and 100km closed circuits of 331 and 332mph respectively.

In 1931 the aircraft was modified by the addition of balancing weights on the rudder and ailerons and the stiffening of the rear fuselage, and was redesignated an S6A. In June 1931, during a practice flight, a section of the engine cowling came off and F/Lt. Hope made an emergency landing in the wake of a liner which caused the plane to overturn. The damage was not severe and it was repaired in time for the twelfth Schneider Trophy race, also held at Calshot, when it was used as the reserve aircraft. It was then put into storage until 1942 when it was used for 'The First of the Few', the film about Mitchell's life. For the filming it was painted as an S6B which had won the Schneider Trophy in perpetuity for Britain, and it was returned to storage in this state. For many years it was not realized that the markings were incorrect until it was presented by the Royal Air Force to the Southampton City Council and the Mitchell Museum who uncovered its true identity.

The Supermarine Spitfire on display is a Mark 24, an example of the last version of this famous fighter. It is fitted with a 37-litre, 2350hp, Rolls-Royce Griffon 61 engine which gave it a speed of 450mph. Armament consisted of four 20mm Hispano cannon and there was provision for the carriage of rockets and bombs.

Displayed close to the Spitfire is an example of the equally famous Rolls-Royce Merlin aircraft engine which powered the Spitfires of the Battle of Britain. The whole museum is a credit to those who worked to bring it about and a fine memorial to a brilliant and dedicated man.

TYRWHITT-DRAKE MUSEUM OF CARRIAGES

ONE OF THE OLDEST buildings in Maidstone is the fourteenth-century Archbishop's Palace, the medieval home of the Archbishops of Canterbury. It was built of material brought from a ruined monastery at Wrotham some 10 miles away. From about 1580 until 1720 it was in the ownership of the Astley family, followed by the Finches, then the Romneys. It came into public ownership in 1887 and today is used as an old peoples' day-centre. It is still in excellent repair and visitors interested in looking over the building are welcome, subject to the requirements of the centre's work.

Close by, but now separated from the palace itself by a busy road, are the stables of the same date. In its earliest days the lower part of the building was used as stabling and the upper portion for the retainers of visitors, including Henry VI and later Henry VIII when he passed through the town on his way to the Field of the Cloth of Gold in 1520. This building has particularly fine roof timbers and some early wooden winding gear in the upper part of the porch. It is 50 yards in length and scheduled as an Ancient Monument.

The palace stables now accommodate a very fine museum of carriages which is almost wholly the creation of a former Lord Mayor of Maidstone from whom it takes its name, Sir Garrard Tyrwhitt-Drake (1881–1964). He expressed his reason for founding the museum as follows: 'Thousands of fine examples of the coach builder's craft have been broken up since the end of the First World War and I am satisfied that within a few years the only examples in existence will be in museums such as this.' If only there had been more men with his vision.

The ground floor of the museum is crowded – it is the right word – with many magnificent coaches. There are landau carriages as examples of one of the most popular and useful of the fashionable carriages of the last century, including a semi-state example used by Queen Victoria. There is a travelling chariot and a dress chariot, both of exceptional splendour, the former used by King George III and the latter by the Marquess of Lansdowne. This coach is attended by full-size models of footmen dressed in their employer's livery and distinctive cocked hats and carrying staves to ward off undesirable elements; the coachman is distinguished by his tricorn.

Other coaches here which are interesting not only for their design and construction but also for their association with people or incidents in history include an ornate dress chariot owned by Count Walewski, the bastard son of Napoleon I. It is an English-built coach – by Stocken of London – and was used by the Count during his brief tenure as the French Ambassador to the Court of St James. At the fall of the Third Empire it was bought by the Earl of Dudley for use on state occasions. A coach with an even more romantic – though poignant – association is the travelling coach built for John, twelfth Earl of Moray. He was engaged to marry a daughter of the Earl of Elgin and the carriage was built in 1840 for their planned honeymoon. The wedding did not take place and the coach was not taken from the Earl's coach house in Scotland from the time it was built until it left for Maidstone in 1951. Here also is a smart-looking private hansom cab, once the property of the explorer Sir H. M. Stanley.

A semi-state landau used by Queen Victoria and now on display in the Tyrwhitt-Drake Museum of Carriages. Photo. Maidstone Museum and Art Gallery.

Striking a more domestic note is a four-wheeled Clarence cab. Popular as a hire vehicle and driven by cabmen, the Clarence was considered to be more dignified than a hansom cab. It was nicknamed the 'Growler' because of the distinctive noise it made when on the move.

The gallery on the upper floor is much less crowded and better lit than the ground-floor area, and the displays more varied in character. The oldest exhibit in the museum and probably one of the earliest carriages in existence is an Italian gig of *c.* 1675, on loan from the Victoria and Albert Museum. This lightweight single-seater is a very racy machine, capable of providing its passenger with a scintillating drive. The owners of such vehicles in seventeenth-century Milan and Rome must have regarded them with the same excitement and glee as the

modern young men of Italy do their Ferraris and Alfas. Close by, two carriages of quite contrasting character stand side by side. Whether this positioning is by accident or design the museum doesn't say, but the arrangement gives the visitor the opportunity of comparing the ornate with the plain in carriage design. The first is a four-wheeled French cabriolet of Louis XVI's reign. The stately design and elevated passenger seat are the clear requirements of a very superior person – either actual or self-appointed. The second is an Irish jaunting car of utilitarian construction. Passengers are seated back to back facing the roadside, and one can easily visualize the lurching, swaying and unceremonious transport it afforded. 'The passengers,' reads an accompanying caption, 'were easily dislodged.'

Of particular interest and charm is the

A miniature landau in the collection of the Tyrwhitt-Drake Museum of Carriages. In the background is the fifteenth-century stable building which houses the museum. Photo: Maidstone Museum and Art Gallery.

museum's collection of small carriages and children's vehicles. There is a governess cart looking safe and sedate for a matron and her charges (in practice this proved often not to be the case), a Friesland child's cart with harness for a dog, and a splendid miniature carriage designed to be pulled by a goat. Particularly noteworthy are carriages used by the children of Queen Victoria, as well as small carriages used by the Queen herself in her old age. The other children's vehicles include a four-wheeled baby carriage previously the property of the Ashburnham family. The body structure is made in the form of a scallop shell and it is sprung fore and aft. Strangely, the long pulling handle, shown in a photograph in the museum's catalogue, is missing.

There are other miscellaneous vehicles, including a traditional gypsy caravan, an Edwardian bier (formerly the property of the Hildenborough Parish Burial Board), a malt barrow, a milk churn on wheels, a baker's cart, a butcher's cart, a coster's barrow and a number of bath and invalid chairs.

Besides the vehicles, the museum has a number of related exhibits. There is a very good collection of harnesses, many models and a fine display of coach-building tools. There is also a number of veteran and vintage bicycles, tucked away in one corner of the gallery, neglected, unlabelled and in need of repair. Perhaps they are not considered grand enough for this marvellous museum of carriages.

FACING PAGE
ABOVE LEFT: *Nineteenth-century warehouses are the background to the display of some of the boats at the Exeter Maritime Museum. Photo: Exeter Maritime Museum.*
ABOVE RIGHT: *The Baker Electric 1½hp 'Stanhope' of 1902 from the collection at the Bicton Hall of Transport, Devon. Photo: Neill Bruce.*
BELOW: *The Baby Carriage Collection of Jack Hampshire at Biddenden, Kent. Photo: Jack Hampshire.*

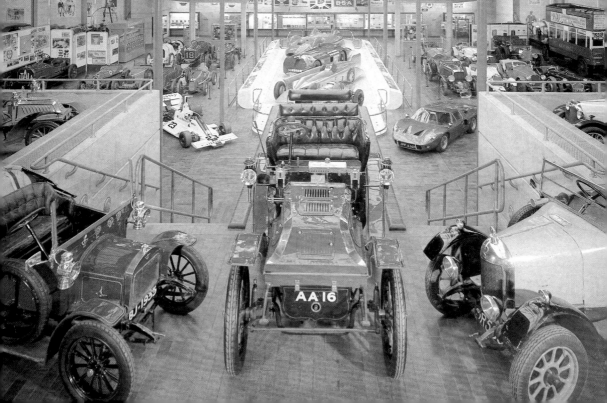

HMS *Victory* and
ROYAL NAVAL MUSEUM

HMS VICTORY

HMS *Victory* is probably the best known of all the Royal Navy's warships. She was built in Chatham as a first-rate ship of the line with a hundred guns and launched in 1765. These were peaceful times and her completion was a leisurely process. There in January 1771, at her moorings in the River Medway, she must have been seen for the first time by the young Horatio Nelson, then aged twelve, as he joined his first ship, HMS *Raisonnable*. The first commission for *Victory* was against the French in 1778 in an indecisive engagement off Ushant, but this was the start of an illustrious battle career which included the great sea battle against the Spanish at Cape St Vincent. In this engagement Commodore Nelson, in HMS *Captain*, played a most effective part in securing success for the British fleet.

In November 1797, HMS *Victory* returned to Chatham and was paid off. From 1798 to 1800 her distinguished fighting career was temporarily interrupted, and she became a hospital ship for the prison hulks. In 1801 she was docked and for the next two years she underwent a major refit. She was, in fact, almost rebuilt and her appearance altered to that she bears today.

HMS *Victory* was again commissioned in April 1803, and in July of that year she arrived in the Mediterranean as flagship of Lord Nelson, Commander-in-Chief. For the next eighteen months she took part in the blockade of Toulon, which ended with the escape of Villeneuve, the long chase to the West Indies, and the return of Villeneuve to Cadiz and her own to England.

On 15 September 1805, Nelson left England in HMS *Victory* to take over command of the fleet blockading Cadiz. Thus was the scene set for the most decisive battle ever fought at sea. On 21 October 1805, off Cape Trafalgar, the combined fleets of France and Spain were vanquished, and Napoleon was denied the use of the sea. But joy at the victory was compounded with sorrow – sorrow at the death of their great leader in the final moments of this, his greatest triumph.

HMS *Victory*, which had led Nelson's column into battle, was so severely damaged that she had to be towed to Gibraltar, where temporary repairs were hastily effected. On 3 November, with Nelson's body on board, she sailed for Portsmouth. She arrived at Spithead on 4 December, and for a week her battered sides and jury masts were reminders of the cost of the victory. On 22 December she arrived at Sheerness, and here the body of her Admiral was transferred to the Commissioner's yacht for conveyance to Greenwich, there to lie in state in the Painted Hall prior to interment in St Paul's Cathedral on 9 January 1806. Also on that day was lowered for the last time the proudest flag she was ever privileged to wear.

To heal the wounds she had sustained at

Trafalgar, HMS *Victory* underwent another extensive refit at Chatham, at the end of which she was recommissioned in March 1808. For the next five years she was constantly employed. In January 1809 she helped to bring home Sir John Moore's army from Corunna. For the greater part of the time, however, she served as flagship of Admiral Saumarez, journeying to and from the Baltic.

In November 1812 HMS *Victory* returned to Portsmouth from what was to be her last sea voyage. The following month she was paid off and once more she underwent a refit. In 1815 she was again ready for sea, but Waterloo brought an end to the Napoleonic Wars and an end, too, to the *Victory*'s long fighting career and she remained in reserve until 1824 when she became flagship of the Portsmouth Command.

Up to 1922 HMS *Victory* was berthed in Portsmouth Harbour. By this time the state of her timbers had become a matter of grave concern. In that year, however, her future safety was assured when she was removed from her somewhat hazardous berth and placed in No. 2 Dock – the site of the oldest graving dock in the world. A successful public appeal was then launched to restore Victory to the appearance she bore at Trafalgar. This was completed in 1928 and she was opened to the public, a permanent memorial to Nelson, Trafalgar and the whole of the British Navy.

To reach HMS *Victory*, which is in the Royal Navy base, the visitor walks past the massive Georgian storehouses still used by the Navy and also accommodating the Royal Naval Museum. Her masts can always be seen, but it is not until the open square is reached with the dock on the far side that *Victory* comes into full view. It is a stunning sight. The ship rests on cradles and is raised so that her normal waterline level is parallel with the top of the dock. She is 226 feet 6 inches in length, her beam is 51 feet 10 inches and the mainmast rises 175 feet above the deck; her ornate figurehead brightens the dullest day. The annual number of visitors is close to half a million and to avoid crowding they are taken on board in groups of thirty. In the summer season the waiting queue can be lengthy and the guided tour hurried. Certainly the burly marines on board firmly discourage any individual or leisurely expeditions. The reasons are understandable but the serious student will be dismayed, for there is so much to see. Most parts of the ship are open and the section of the deck where Nelson was struck down and the cockpit where he died are, of course, particular points of interest, the effect heightened by the Arthur Devis painting displayed there showing the death scene. Much has been left in the ship to illustrate shipboard life of the time. The massive guns and heavy shot hint at the murderous power of a broadside; the cramped crew quarters give an idea of the hard life at sea; and the mass of rigging illustrates the orderly complexity involved in the working of the ship.

No one who now walks the decks of *Victory* or stoops into her holds and cabins can fail to be gripped by the atmosphere of tradition and feeling of historical excitement that pervades this magnificent vessel. Nor can they feel anything but proud of her and grateful to all those responsible for her welfare.

ROYAL NAVAL MUSEUM

It had always been part of the restoration scheme to build alongside HMS *Victory* a museum of the same name. In 1929 the impetus for such a scheme was forthcoming when the Admiralty made available an old rigging house adjacent to the ship's new home for conversion into such a museum. It was not, however, until the end of the Second World War that the museum scheme really gathered momentum and began to attract public attention which resulted in many donations of Nelson relics from private sources. The collection continues to expand and is pleasantly housed in the elegantly restored rigging house.

On entering the *Victory* Collection, visitors will find their attention drawn towards the large ornate barge which occupies the major part of the central area. The craft was last publicly employed to carry the body of Lord Nelson from Greenwich Hospital, where it had been lying in state, to Whitehall Stairs prior to the ceremonial interment on 9 January 1806.

At the far end of the central area, behind the stern of the barge, is a large diorama of the Battle

One of the many very fine bone ship models on display at the Royal Naval Museum, Portsmouth. Photo: Royal Naval Museum.

of Trafalgar. It shows in model form the respective positions of each warship (seventy-three in all) at around 12.45p.m. on 21 October 1805. The whole is the work of a Thomas D. Deighton, who was model maker to the Prince Consort. When his work was completed in 1862, it was displayed in the Royal United Services London Museum for over a century, and came to the collection when that museum was disbanded. It is a remarkable construction and gives a very clear idea of the disposition of the squadrons and the course of the battle.

Throughout the ground floor and the gallieries above are displayed hundreds of items associated with Nelson and his times. Letters, diaries, furniture, miniature portraits and large canvasses, massive figureheads and delicate glassware, ships' models, tableware, ornaments, clocks and much more all help to paint a vivid picture of the life of this great Admiral and patriot.

In 1970 an American lady, Mrs J. G. McCarthy, CBE, offered her collection of Nelson memorabilia to the museum. Her particular interest in Lord Nelson was initiated by a portrait of the Admiral formerly owned by her father which he had acquired in the early 1930s. As the majority of personal relics of the Navy's greatest Admiral had already found their way into museums and private collections, Mrs McCarthy realized that what was available to any collector interested in Nelson were items of pottery, porcelain, glassware, etc., of a com- memorative nature. She decided therefore to form a collection covering examples of all media, and this is displayed in one of the old Georgian naval storehouses adjacent to the rigging house and now elegantly converted to the purpose. The painting which first prompted Mr McCarthy's interest is one of a number of Nelson portraits in this collection but, as is often the case when there are many portraits of one subject by different artists, the portrayal of physical characteristics varies considerably and one is left to wonder which is the real face of Nelson. The collection contains many fine works of art, but the majority of exhibits are examples of the quality end of the com- memorative and souvenir market with splendid items from Bilston, Wedgwood, Royal Worces- ter, William Adams and Copeland, to mention but a few. The popularity of this trade remains undiminished as the wide range of modern equivalents on sale in the museum shop illus- trates.

The McCarthy Collection and the *Victory* Collection are, of course, devoted almost en- tirely to the Nelson era, but it is the museum's aim, when more space and money is available, to tell the whole naval history story from King Alfred's time to the present age. Such an expansion will include the provision of suitable displays on board the 1860 *Ironclad* and HMS *Warrior* when she is berthed in this area on the completion of her extensive refit, currently underway in the old town docks at Hartlepool. It will also encompass the restoration of Brunel's blockmills which are situated in this naval base just north of HMS *Victory*'s stern. From 1806 onwards, and until the end of the sailing Navy, these mills with their wonderful machines, most of which are still in working order, provided hundreds of thousands of blocks and pulleys needed to maintain an efficient fighting fleet. Plans are already in hand to restore the mills to their 1806 condition and to show them to the public – they were the first example of auto- mation in Britain. In all, therefore, a most comprehensive and ambitious programme is planned for the Royal Naval Museum.

III
THE SOUTH-WEST

BICTON HALL OF TRANSPORT

BICTON LIES MIDWAY between Exmouth and Newton Poppleford, deep in the glorious countryside of East Devon, an area of outstanding natural beauty that is steeped in ancient agricultural and seafaring traditions. Sir Walter Raleigh was born and brought up a mile down the road in East Budleigh, where many Elizabethan thatched cottages can be seen today. The farm, Hayes Barton, which his father leased, is still a working concern.

Through the centuries, Bicton House was the home of the local landowners. Lying in a small valley surrounded by gently undulating land, the gardens were found to be naturally fertile because of a small underground stream draining from Woodbury Common above the nearby River Otter. Although the house is now an agricultural college, separate from Bicton itself, these superbly designed gardens have been restored to their former glory for the public to visit. Not only are they of outstanding beauty – they are also of considerable horticultural and arboricultural interest. As well as enjoying the impressive formal gardens, visitors can stroll through well-stocked conservatories, explore the fascinating collection of agricultural exhibits in the Countryside Museum, travel through the grandeur of the Pinetum aboard the unique narrow-gauge woodland railway, picnic in the woods or (best of all, of course!) visit the Hall of Transport.

The Hall of Transport is intended to illustrate the progress of transport since the turn of the century, and includes not only vintage and veteran cars, but later and more up-to-date vehicles together with a selection of motor bicycles and cycles too. The hall has been built around a collection of early vehicles assembled and restored by the late Leslie Goldsmith, who became a well-known authority on the Benz motor car and an enthusiastic steam expert. To preserve this magnificient collection, his family offered it to Bicton to house and exhibit to the public.

The oldest car on view is the 1894 Benz, which is also one of the earliest in this country. The first cars designed by Karl Benz – who is sometimes called 'the father of the motor car' – were water-cooled and chain-driven and had two belts in the gearbox for changing gear. They were originally built as three-wheelers, but Benz soon changed over to four wheels, which gave greater stability – besides becoming a commercial success!

The Locomotive on Highways Act, passed in 1896, finally made driving possible in Great Britain, and gave a tremendous boost to the industry throughout Europe. The year 1901 saw the great beginnings of today's motor car. The first flywheel magnetos were introduced, the famous Mercedes made its debut on the racing scene, and in America seven thousand cars were built. World Speed Records were set by Sharron in a Panhard and Serpollet in his own steam engine.

The 1902 Panhard Levassor in this collection is a 4-cylinder 15hp model, capable of 50mph. It illustrates the motor car's progress during the decade. Bigger engines meant faster cars, and faster cars needed padded seats and larger, tubed tyres for comfort. The angled steering wheel, windscreen and headlamps are an indication of the new speeds of these cars.

While the petrol-driven internal combustion

engine was being developed, other methods of powering cars were making their debut. The hall has fine examples of both electric and steam-driven cars. The 1901 Baker Electric is a typical early example and has taken part in the London to Brighton race without recharging its batteries.

In the history of steam cars, the Stanley Steamer must be unique. The Stanley twins were natural inventors and had already made a fortune selling their photographic inventions to Eastman-Kodak before turning to a production run of their simple steam-driven car. The Stanley was easy to drive, warmed up quickly, and in 1906 one model reached the fantastic speed of 204.16km per hour – the first time in history that man had travelled more than 3km per minute! The two Stanley Steamer cars on display here were built in 1902 and 1904.

About the same time young Henry Ford had just built his first car and started on the road that led to mass production of the motor car. Bicton has a Ford T acclaimed as 'the Car that put the World on Wheels'. It was first produced in 1908, though the model here is a 1915 example – one of 16.5 million built up to the end of production in 1927. The British involvement in mass production is represented by a Morris Bullnose tourer and an Austin four-seater tourer, both from the twenties, and the more exotic end of the market of that period exhibits a 1928 Bentley $4\frac{1}{2}$-litre tourer.

The Bicton car collection is well supported by local enthusiasts who loan their own vehicles so that the presentation will regularly change around the permanent Goldsmith display. In addition to the cars there is a small collection of early motor cycles and cycles, some model steam engines and various artefacts from the days of early motoring.

An historic picture of the man who pioneered the motor car. Karl Benz in 1894 aboard one of his early models. Photo: National Motor Museum.

CORNWALL AERO PARK

CORNWALL HAS A LONG and notable association with flying. In particular, during both World Wars Cornwall provided bases for the defence of shipping in the Western Approaches. Mullion, for example, was the site of one of the busiest airship stations in the British Isles, recording 2,845 hours of flying in 1917, the highest figure of all fifteen stations operational at the time. The primary task was submarine patrol, but convoy and troopship escorts were also carried out and flights of twelve hours' endurance were commonplace.

Since those days the task has changed little but the equipment greatly, and now it is the huge Nimrod which takes off from St Mawgan near Newquay to patrol the Western Approaches. And not far from Mullion – right next door to the Cornwall Aero Park – is the Royal Naval Air Station Culdrose where all Royal Navy helicopter pilots receive their basic training and which provides the home base for the modern anti-submarine squadrons operating the highly sophisticated Sea King helicopters. Add to this the fact that the man whose idea it was to establish the Cornwall Aero Park is a former pilot in the Royal Navy and both its subject and location become understandable.

The whole emphasis of the Aero Park – and it is set in beautifully landscaped gardens – is on family entertainment and involvement. The majority of its visitors are holidaymakers and the park has been planned to match their mood. In the main exhibition hall visitors can step into the supersonic age by climbing aboard a Concorde flight deck, they can enter the cockpits and operate the controls of a helicopter, a Hovercraft or a Shackleton bomber. The aviation enthusiast will also be entertained by the replica flying machines used in the making of the 'Flambards' television series and diverted by the well-presented thematic displays on the Dam Busters, Arnhem and the Battle of Britain.

A feature of the museum unconnected with aviation but no less interesting for that is to be found in a gallery off the main hall. It is a reconstruction of a nineteenth-century cobbled street with shop windows designed and stocked in the fashion of the period. In the 'street' a brougham carriage awaits its owner.

Motoring aficionados will be detained in another gallery showing the collection of Ford cars. What a good idea this is, to bring together the products of one manufacturer. It makes for so much more interest and enlightenment to see how one man or one company has responded to technical progress and market forces – alas, in so many museums the visitor is presented with a motley collection of developments and a long list of manufacturers. The Ford collection here is quite small but there is an early Model T, a very rare Cabriolet, which anticipated the Pilot, a Tudor and a Ford T (the Hundred-Pound Popular) and examples of the Popular, the Prefect and the Zephyr from the fifties. If gaps are filled in the historical sequence, this collection will only increase in interest.

The aircraft collection is displayed in the open air, and raised platforms and the absence of any form of barrier ensure that young and old and tall and short can have a good look around. The emphasis is on naval fighter aircraft and here, as with the Ford cars, a development sequence that makes sense is presented. One of the earliest aircraft is a Hawker Sea Hawk, of

The main exhibition hall at the Cornwall Aero Park, Helston. Photo: Cornwall Aero Park.

which over four hundred were delivered to the Fleet Air Arm between 1953 and 1958 and which took part in the Suez adventure of 1956. It was replaced in its fighter role by the Supermarine Scimitar, a single-seater twin-engined aircraft which was itself replaced by the Blackburn Buccaneer. Examples of both these aircraft are on show. Also displayed is the interesting Fairey Gannet, with its novel feature of a double contra-rotating airscrew turbine engine. Its naval use was for submarine search and attack until this role was taken over by

helicopters, and the Westland Whirlwind displayed here is a good example of that new breed of aircraft which entered service in the fifties.

A visit to the Cornwall Aero Park is both instructive and enjoyable. The exhibits are well displayed and described and the invitation to the grounds is more one of 'wander at leisure' than 'keep off the grass'. For its catering it boasts an Egon Ronay award – a rare exhibit indeed on museum premises.

EXETER MARITIME MUSEUM

TECHNICALLY, the port of Exeter reaches from Lyme Bay to Teignmouth but the town and city of Exeter serviced by the River Exe has been a port since Roman times and probably before. In 1566 a canal was dug to improve on the river facilities and this, the first pound-lock canal in Britain, was widened, deepened and lengthened in later centuries to accommodate the increase in trade. The customs house built on the quay in 1689 was one of the first brick buildings in Exeter and the quayside warehouses date from the early part of the nineteenth century. In this century the sea trade declined and the whole area fell into disuse and dereliction.

In 1964 plans were submitted to the City Council which, when fulfilled, would give Exeter a great boat museum occupying the whole of the quay, some of the buildings and much of the canal basin. The proposal received every encouragement, was vigorously pursued and in June 1969 on this most appropriate site the museum was opened by Sir Alec Rose who had just returned from sailing alone round the world in his ketch *Lively Lady*.

On opening day there were twenty-three boats on display, a large proportion of them being Arab craft, for the director of the museum had been posted to Bahrain whilst still in the army and had started to collect boats in anticipation of their being put on display. The collection was not slow to grow and the Ocean Rowers collection was opened by Chay Blyth on 1 April 1975, followed later that year by the opening by the Portuguese Ambassador of the Ellerman Collection of Portuguese working craft, including some of the most colourful and

beautiful boats to be seen anywhere. There are now nearly a hundred craft displayed afloat, ashore and under cover.

The aim of the museum, which is sponsored by the International Sailing Craft Association, is 'to preserve a cross section of the world's working boats propelled by oar and sail – and other craft of exceptional interest'. The museum is divided into three main display sections, the canal basin and its warehouse on one side of the river and, linked by chain ferry, the quay warehouse and the old fishmarket on the other.

In the canal basin is the massive steam tug *St Canute*, the largest exhibit in the museum. Built in Denmark in the thirties, she was the harbour tug of Odense where she also performed as the ice-breaker and fire-fighter. Her engine and boiler are still in good order and the museum raises steam in her from time to time. Close by is the Brunel-designed drag boat *Bertha* of 1844 from Bridgwater, the world's oldest working steamboat and still in excellent condition, and the ex-Bristol pilot cutter *Cariad*, the famous gaff-rigged cruising yacht formerly owned by Mr Frank Carr. Also here is a beautiful pearling dhow from the Persian Gulf with its tricky lateen sail and a magnificent xavega with its flat bottom and violently curved bow and stern to enable it to work from the shallow shorelines of its native Portugal.

The warehouses close to the canal basin contain a number of open boats from many ports of the world, including dhows from Bahrain, proas from Fiji and the Gilbert and Ellice Islands, and a raft-like craft made of palm fronds from the Persian Gulf. The warehouses on the other side of the river have been renovated to make them safe and weatherproof, but they still retain most of the physical characteristics present during their commercial life and this working atmosphere adds considerably to both the charm and the authenticity of the displays within their four storeys. Examples are here of Britain's most primitive craft still in use, the curraghs of Ireland and the Welsh and Severn coracles. There are also a foureen from Shetland, a skiff from the Orkneys, and a number of small vessels from the West Country, including a tub boat fitted with wheels for haulage on the inclined plane of the Bude Canal and the *Cygnet*, a tender built to resemble the shape of a swan and gracefully succeeding.

In another section are most of the one- or two-man boats that have been rowed across the Atlantic. *Britannia* looks as strong and capable as John Fairfax was when he rowed her from Grand Canary to Miami in 1969 to become the first man to row the Atlantic alone. Looking considerably less robust is Tom McClean's *Supersilver*, in which he crossed from west to east faster than Fairfax but later in the year. Both these craft and the others displayed here which have made the Atlantic crossing, as well as the circumnavigating yachts such as *Lively Lady* and *Gipsy Moth IV* on show elsewhere in the country, remind us that the oceans still offer to brave men and women the same challenge that they have made since folk first went down to the sea.

The next port of call on leaving the warehouses is the old fishmarket. To reach this the visitor walks along the old quay which in appearance has hardly been disturbed for over 150 years and which the museum had been careful to preserve. So much so that the earlier episodes of the BBC television serial 'The Onedin

A reed boat from Lake Titicaca, 12,000 feet up in the Andes. The boat is 18 feet long and made entirely of reeds, even the sail. It is in the collection of the Exeter Maritime Museum. Photo: Exeter Maritime Museum.

Line', that stirring story of nineteenth-century maritime adventure, was shot here with the need for very few cosmetic additions to the scene. The covered fishmarket holds the smaller vessels of the Ellerman Collection which is a remarkable assembly of Portuguese sail and rowed boats. The beauty of this collection is not only in the bright colours with which they are painted or the beautiful shapes in which most of the boats are fashioned, but also in that they are direct and obvious descendants of vessels that have worked the Mediterranean and North-East Atlantic coastlines for hundreds if not thousands of years. The xavega, for example, mentioned previously, beach-launched, with four oars and eleven men to each oar, has many Phoenician characteristics; and the Valboeiro, which used to bring casks of port down the Douro to the cellars in Port, is clinker-built and probably of Scandinavian origin. It is a fascinat-ing collection, and the way in which the individual items were saved and brought to Exeter is a great credit to the museum.

If an object is worthy of preservation, so, surely, is the knowledge of how it was used and, better still, the technique of actually using it. For this reason, the museum sails a number of its craft and from time to time raises steam in its tugs and dredgers. The museum is also a happy place to be in the sense that there are very few 'don'ts' for the visitor. He or she can go on board a number of the vessels, and one of the museum's pamphlets states: 'If you find a "Don't touch" notice here, you'll get your money back – you can even touch wet paint if you like!' The catalogue is well illustrated and provides first-rate background information, the staff are cheerful and helpful and the restaurant and cafes excellent. It is simply one of the best museums in the country.

Part of the Ellerman collection of working boats at the Exeter Maritime Museum. Photo: Exeter Maritime Museum.

FLEET AIR ARM MUSEUM AND CONCORDE EXHIBITION

FLEET AIR ARM MUSEUM

So many motorists passing the Royal Naval Air Station, Yeovilton, on the busy road between London and the West Country stopped to watch the flying that in 1963 a viewing enclosure was opened and three historic aircraft were placed nearby. The interest this created, together with the celebration in 1964 of the fiftieth anniversary of the formation of the Royal Naval Air Service, the predecessor of today's Fleet Air Arm, led to the decision to establish a museum where historic naval aircraft and other items associated with flying in the Royal Navy could be put on public display and all kinds of records, photographs and documents could be assembled, catalogued and made available for inspection.

The Fleet Air Arm Museum was formally opened in 1964 by His Royal Highness The Duke of Edinburgh, and over the major part of the ensuing decade a substantial collection of naval aeronautical artefacts was assembled. By 1973 the single aircraft hangar in which the museum had been established became overloaded, but following a successful programme of public appeals a phased building plan was carried through to provide covered accommodation for all the museum's possessions. In addition space was allocated for library and archive facilities and for workshops in which the refurbishing of exhibits and the construction of replicas could be undertaken. The museum buildings were completed in 1980 to accommodate all the facilities and allow for a spacious presentation of the history of the Royal Naval Air Service and the Fleet Air Arm.

The oldest aircraft in the collection forms part of the display mounted in the last gallery added to the museum, the Mountbatten Memorial Hall. This aircraft, a single-seater Sopwith Baby biplane, was developed from the version which won the Schneider Trophy race at Monaco in 1914. This type was used by the RNAS for reconnaissance and light bombing sorties. The example the museum possesses is, in fact, the only one in existence and was rebuilt in 1970 by Royal Navy apprentices from the remains of two Babies shipped to Italy in the First World War and subsequently retrieved. Close by, as a special tribute to Earl Mountbatten, is a Bleriot XI – a replica of the type in which he flew as a boy of eleven in 1911 and which was used for training by the naval wing of the Royal Flying Corps up to 1915. A less-than-complete Gloster Sea Gladiator recalls for us another historic aircraft which served with distinction the Navy and the Royal Air Force in the Second World War. The Gladiator was the RAF's last biplane fighter and it was the Sea Gladiators nicknamed 'Faith' 'Hope' and 'Charity' which were involved in the epic battle with the Luftwaffe over Malta in June 1940. The museum specimen is missing some vital engine and airframe components. What a tribute it would be to all those brave pilots who, often against the odds, flew

OPPOSITE: *The Royal Navy's 'Historic Flight'. In the foreground, the 1943 Swordfish; centre, the 1946 Sea Fury; and in the background, the 1949 Fairey Firefly. The 'Historic Flight' is often seen on Flying Days at the Fleet Air Arm Museum. Photo: Fleet Air Arm Museum.*

The interior of one of the halls at the Fleet Air Arm Museum. Photo: Fleet Air Arm Museum.

this sturdy and versatile aircraft, if this specimen could be restored to original or even flying condition.

Another aircraft in an even more incomplete state but with a quite remarkable history is represented in the damaged airframe of a Blackburn Skua. This example was in the squadron that attacked the cruiser *Konigsberg* in the Bergen Fjord, Norway, on 10 April 1940. Later in the same month it was forced down on to the frozen surface of Lake Groti. Before being taken prisoner, its crew set fire to the aircraft and it sank through the ice to the bottom of the lake where it remained until recovered by a Royal Navy sub-aqua team in 1974. It is displayed in its recovered condition.

Towards the rear of the museum is the original Yeovilton hangar which dates from 1940 and was the first part of the museum opened in 1964. Linked to it is the Caspar John Hall, opened in 1975. Together they hold the major portion of the aircraft collection, and

plenty of space has been allowed to enable the visitor to inspect closely, and at many angles, each of the exhibits.

Where possible the museum has adopted the sensible policy of displaying its aircraft chronologically and by type. This makes it so much easier for those interested in technical comparison and improvements. For example, the Douglas Skyraider and the Fairey Gannet, which replaced it as an airborne early-warning picket, are in the same viewing area. Also in line is a DH Sea Venom, and two aircraft that followed it into service, the Sea Vixen and the Supermarine Scimitar. The Scimitar is of particular interest: it was the first swept-wing single-seat twin-jet naval fighter and the first to employ the system of boundary layer control using air blown over the wing flaps to reduce landing speed. Its range of armaments and low-level high-speed capability considerably advanced naval air power when it entered service in 1958. It was superseded by the Blackburn

Buccaneer and there is an example displayed here which was one of the museum's earliest exhibits.

Another first in a different sphere is the de Havilland Sea Vampire which was the first pure jet to land on an aircraft carrier when it touched down on HMS *Ocean* on 3 December 1945. Related in a historical sense to this event is the subject of one of the many well-presented wall displays found throughout the museum. On the 2 August 1917 Squadron Commander E. H. 'Ned' Dunning, DSC, RNAS, landed his Sopwith Pup on a 200-foot-long and 50-foot-wide wooden deck built on the forepart of the heavy cruiser HMS *Furious*. This was a remarkable feat, requiring a high degree of airmanship. Sadly, during a third attempt on 8 August, a gust of wind caught his aircraft as it touched down and it crashed over the side, drowning this brave pioneer. The Sopwith Pup is one of the most significant aircraft in the history of the Fleet Air Arm. As well as performing the first landing on a ship at sea, it was also the first landplane to take off from a ship when one flew from a platform off HMS *Yarmouth* in June 1917. Earlier Pups had been in action with RNAS pilots on the Western Front and towards the end of the War and afterwards helped to pioneer arrested landings on aircraft-carriers. It is a pity, therefore, that the Fleet Air Museum hasn't a Sopwith Pup to show us. There are one or two still in private hands: perhaps their owners could be invited to help fill this important gap.

The actions and involvements of the Fleet Air Arm in the Second World War are well recorded by the museum and it exhibits many historic aircraft from that period. One of the most popular with visitors is the Swordfish or, as it was generally known, the 'Stringbag'. At the outbreak of war it was the Royal Navy's only torpedo-bomber. Its war service record is heroic. On the night of 11 November 1940 Swordfish attacked the Italian fleet in Taranto Harbour and effectively crippled the Italian Navy. In the same year their torpedoes wrecked the steering of the German battleship *Bismarck* which led to her total destruction, and amongst many other notable incidents Swordfish of HMS *Vindex* sank four U-boats in a single voyage. Another aircraft of the same period and held in similar affection is the Supermarine

Walrus known universally as the 'Shagbat'. Designed by R. J. Mitchell of Spitfire fame, this amphibian was in service throughout the Second World War as a spotter and reconnaissance aircraft and was also responsible for saving many aircrew from the sea.

The Fleet Air Arm Museum has not forgotten the contribution the United States made to the Royal Navy's air strength during the war. Here is a Harvard of which ten thousand were built for service world-wide during its eighteen-year production run and on which thousands of British pilots were trained. Other aircraft supplied under the wartime Lease-Lend Programme include a Grumman Martlet, the type which has the special distinction of being the first American-built aircraft to shoot down a German machine in the Second World War, a Grumman Hellcat fighter from the one thousand supplied to the Fleet Air Arm, and the outstanding Corsair with its distinctive inverted gull wing which, linked with a very powerful engine, gave it an excellent performance as a fighter and fighter-bomber.

Amongst all the aircraft on exhibition – and there are nearly fifty – the museum has positioned many interesting displays on particular themes or built around particular incidents connected with the history of the Fleet Air Arm. The one on early deck landings has already been mentioned; the visitor will also be intrigued by the exhibition of the history of ships carrying the name *Ark Royal*, from the *Ark Ralegh* (changed to *Ark Royal* by Elizabeth I) to the third aircraft-carrier of that name to serve the Royal Navy. Similarly fascinating are the display of photographs depicting naval flying throughout its history and the very comprehensive exhibition that pays tribute to Reginald (Rex) Warneford who, within months of volunteering for the Royal Naval Air Service in 1915, had brought down the first German Zeppelin to be destroyed in aerial combat to become the first naval aviator to be awarded the VC. Thanks to the loan of material from private collections, the museum has been able to put together a remarkable story. The Warneford Exhibition sets out to answer the question 'What made the man?' and traces the history of the Warneford family back through three generations. It is often said that the Victoria Cross is won by spontaneous acts out of character to those that carry them through. This well-researched exhibition suggests that Rex Warneford was born to make his mark, and his death shortly after being awarded the VC deprived the world of a man destined for great things.

The above are just a few of the many exhibitions and displays of photographs and paintings within the museum, all of which are a delight.

CONCORDE EXHIBITION

To the side of the Fleet Air Arm Museum's entrance hall is a door leading to a vast hangar. Before opening it, take one last look at the Bleriot then pass through. As the image of the Bleriot fades it will be replaced by that of the slim, sleek and immensely impressive aircraft that stands in front of you – the Concorde 002. The transition dramatically illustrates the progress of man's inventive genius over a period of little more than half a century.

Concorde 002 is the British-built prototype of the Anglo-French supersonic transport aircraft which entered service with British Airways and Air France on 21 January 1976. After the successful completion of her part in the Concorde flight-test programme, 002 was transferred from the Department of Industry to the Science Museum. This aircraft has been placed with the Fleet Air Arm Museum for long-term preservation and public exhibition. She now forms the centrepiece of the specially constructed Exhibition Hall which illustrates the full story of Concorde from the early project sketches of 1956 to the current airline operations.

Concorde 002 made her maiden flight from the then British Aircraft Corporation's plant at Filton, Bristol, on 9 April 1969. Basically a flying laboratory, in addition to the flight deck crew of three or four she normally carried three test observers monitoring and controlling some 12 tons of test equipment. Her research programme lasted for some seven years, during which time she flew for a total of 835 hours, 18 minutes and visited nineteen countries all over the world. She first attained supersonic speed (Mach 1.15) on 25 March 1970, and her maximum speed of Mach 2.05 on 7 October 1971.

Visitors may walk through the aircraft, entering via a specially constructed access platform. The floodlit flight deck is clearly visible, and nearly all the original internal equipment and fittings have been retained. Two of the Olympus 593 engines have been removed, and one is displayed alongside 002 herself.

Visitors should remember that Concorde 002 was a research aircraft, and the interior in no way represents the comfortable environment of the production aircraft. However, the exhibition also contains part of the original wooden engineering mock-up constructed to assist the design of seating arrangements and general cabin decor, and this is also open to the public.

Situated in echelon alongside 002 are two of the research aircraft which flew extensively in the late fifties and early sixties and provided important data to assist the final design of Concorde. The larger was originally the Fairey Delta Two, which first broke the four-figure speed record in 1956, achieving 1,132mph. With an extended fuselage and modified wingform, she became known as the BAC 221. The second is the Handley Page 115, used primarily to investigate the low-speed handling characteristics of a pure delta-wing aircraft. The beautiful lines of all three aircraft may be viewed from an observation gallery high up at the front of the large hangar.

Around two sides of the exhibition are a number of display units, conveniently arranged in seven sections. Five of these describe in colourful detail some of the problems encountered in supersonic flight and various aspects of engine and airframe design, materials and manufacture of the main structure, systems and components. The remaining sections give a glimpse of Concorde in service with British Airways and describe the role of 002 herself. The displays are augmented by three television monitors which provide appropriate 'running commentaries'.

The debate on the merits or otherwise of building Concorde is now part of aviation history. That it was not a commercial success should not detract from the fact of it being one of Britain's – and the world's – finest technological achievements.

The Sea Fury of the Royal Navy's 'Historic Flight' escorts Concorde 002 on its last flight prior to going on static display at the Fleet Air Arm Museum. Photo: Fleet Air Arm Museum.

Concorde 002 landing at Yeovilton after its last flight on 4 March 1976. This aircraft is the property of the Science Museum and is displayed in an exhibition hall connected to the Fleet Air Arm Museum. Photo: Fleet Air Arm Museum.

SS *Great Britain*

'The *Great Britain* steamship to be launched today, so asked Horrocks permission to go down to Bristol to see it.' Thus wrote Mr Snell of Swindon in his diary on Wednesday, 19 July 1843. His interest was shared by the whole population, for this great ship represented a technical development in shipbuilding of unprecedented magnitude. She was the first ocean-going, iron, propeller-driven ship in history. Designed by Isambard Kingdom Brunel, she was 322 feet in length with a displacement of over 3,000 tons and engines that developed 1500hp. She embodied new principles of construction, longitudinal framing, watertight bulkheads and a type of double bottom, which in time became normal features of naval architecture and which broke away completely from the traditional methods used by builders of wooden ships. When launched she was more than twice the size of any existing ship. On her first voyage in 1845 she covered the 3,300 miles to New York in 14 days, 21 hours at an average speed of 9.4 knots.

Great Britain's career was long and eventful – some might say chequered. She made many New York trips in her first year of operation, but on an outward passage on 22 September 1846 and as a result of a navigational error she ran aground in Dundrum Bay in County Down on the east coast of Ireland. The immense strength of her construction enabled her to survive a seven-month stranding, but when she was finally pulled off and repaired her owners were bankrupt and she was sold to a company running services to Australia who made drastic structural alterations to accommodate more passengers, more cargo and more coal for the boilers. *Great Britain* now settled down to nearly twenty-five years of steady passages between Liverpool and Melbourne, carrying the forebears of probably a quarter of a million present-day Australians. In 1861 she took out the first-ever English cricket team to visit Australia.

In 1867 the now ageing ship was put up for sale at Birkenhead. It was not until 1882 that she was bought, this time by Antony Gibbs, Sons and Company who converted her entirely to a sailing vessel. They removed her engines, the long deckhouse, and all the passenger accommodation; they cut three large hatches in her decking for easier loading, plated in the propeller aperture and placed wooden cladding right round her hull between low and high loading marks. In this form she was put on the run to San Francisco, but on 6 February 1886 she started out from Penarth, South Wales, bound for San Francisco via Cape Horn on what proved to be her last commercial voyage. Off Cape Horn a hurricane blew up, the cargo of coal shifted, parts of the masts were carried away and the crew eventually persuaded their captain to put back to the Falkland Islands. There the ship was surveyed, but repairs were considered to be too expensive to be worthwhile; in any case, few of the necessary facilities were available. A new chapter began in the life of the *Great Britain* and for fifty years she provided a service for the Falkland Islands as a hulk for storing coal and wool.

On 14 April 1937 there came one final indignity, however: the tough old lady was towed a few miles out from Port Stanley to shallow water in Sparrow Cove; holes were

A contemporary painting of Brunel's SS Great Britain *of 1843. Photo: SS* Great Britain *Project.*

Great Britain *as she is today, undergoing restoration in Bristol in the care of the* Great Britain *Trust. Photo: SS* Great Britain *Project.*

punched in her bottom and she settled comfortably down on to the seabed – beaten but unbowed.

Thirty years later, on 8 November 1967, a letter appeared in *The Times* newspaper suggesting that something be done '. . . to recover the ship and place her on display'. It inspired the formation of the SS *Great Britain* project which organized one of the most remarkable and exciting salvage operations ever, resulting in an ocean tow of 7,000 miles and her return on 19 July 1970 – the anniversary of her launch there in 1843 – to the very same dock in Bristol in which she was built.

Since 1970, work of preservation and restoration has been steadily going forward. The aims and objects are to restore the Brunel ship to its original appearance of 1843 and reconstruct enough of the interior to enable the visitor to visualize what life was like on board this famous Victorian liner. The work will include provision of six masts, funnel and deck fittings, and decorative work on the bow and stern; restoration of the public rooms for passengers in the after part of the ship; restoration of up to six cabins; construction of a full-scale model of the engines, the great driving chain and the original six-bladed Brunel propeller; and reconstruction of the officers' and crew's quarters.

In spite of the financial problems associated with nearly all such projects, the work is going on apace. Visitors can go aboard and observe the work in progress and this in itself is one of the most fascinating aspects of a visit. With a little imagination it is easy to believe that one has turned the pages of history back one hundred and thirty years, and in walking the decks or inspecting the work progressing below in cabins, saloons and engine room one might just come face to face with a small, dark-eyed, olive-complexioned man of pleasant and vigorous manner. Stand aside and let him get on with his business of building one of the most remarkable and significant vessels ever to go to sea.

TORBAY AIRCRAFT MUSEUM

THE TORBAY AIRCRAFT MUSEUM is located in one of the most popular holiday areas in Great Britain and what it has to offer is designed to appeal to the family desiring a relaxed look at aircraft and aviation. Any visitor over the age of forty-five will see many things there that will vividly recall personal memories or experiences – a gas mask, a ration book or a Hawker Hurricane. Younger visitors will become aware of how closely the civilian was involved in the military events of the Second World War compared to today's scenario where the Blackout, the ARP, the Stirrup Pump and the Home Guard have no relevance at all.

This fascinating and evocative museum has concentrated its main interest on the aviation activities of the Second World War, but photographs and relics connected with flying go back as far as 1909 with mementoes recalling such pioneers and adventures as Cody, Bleriot, von Richthofen and Amy Johnson. In the outside static display there are a number of military aircraft which were put into service after the war.

The interior displays are accommodated in buildings that were formerly stables erected about 1900 to house some of the horses of the South Devon Hunt. The buildings have been pleasantly renovated and their size and the lighting lend themselves well to the orderly display of many themes, not all of them connected with aviation. The story of Colditz and wartime escapers and of civilians at war are absorbing.

Outside in a pleasant park more than twenty aircraft are on show. The earliest in historical sequence – though not in construction, as it is a modern replica – is a copy of Manfred von Richthofen's Fokker triplane. This splendid aircraft, painted overall in the bright red colour that helped to establish the legend of the 'Red Baron', complements the display in the galleries on fighter aces of the First World War. Replicas of probably the three most famous fighter aircraft of the Second World War are also displayed and here is a copy of a Hawker Hurricane, a Supermarine Spitfire and a Messerschmitt BF109. All these aircraft were built for the film 'The Battle of Britain' and are painted in the operations colours and squadron markings of the time.

In contrast to these examples of the replica constructors' work, there is a very good specimen of the restorers' skill in the Avro Avian. Arguably one of the most important aircraft constructed during the inter-war years, the Avian was involved in many epoch-making pioneer flights. The celebrated aviator H. J. 'Bert' Hinckler, who made the first solo flight from Great Britain to Australia in February 1928, flew an Avian prototype to cover the 11,000 miles in just over two weeks. 'Hinkle, Hinkle, little star – sixteen days, and here you are' read the caption of a contemporary *Punch* cartoon. The preserved example at Torbay is a series 111A Avian which did nothing so grand as its illustrious predecessor, spending most of its flying life giving pleasure flights to holidaymakers at Southport. It was retired and put in store in 1938 where it remained until 1960 when it was found and restored for static display by a group of aviation enthusiasts.

No aircraft museum would be complete without a representation from the de Havilland stable and Torbay has five, of which two types have made their mark in the history of aviation: the DH Dove, built in greater numbers than any other British civil aircraft since the Second World War, which has carried the registration letters of over fifty countries, and the DH Vampire, which was the first pure jet to operate from an aircraft-carrier and the first jet to cross the Atlantic.

The museum also has a trio of helicopters, two of British manufacture and one American, but it is a German single-seat gyro kite that will capture the attention in this area of flight, for here is a Focke-Achgelis 'Sandpiper'. This ingenious gyro was carried by Class IX U-boats during the Second World War. Assembled in a matter of minutes, the machine would be towed behind a surface U-boat at an altitude of some 400 feet, enabling the pilot to spot Allied convoys at up to 25 miles' distance. The existence of this German secret weapon remained unknown to the Allies until 1945.

Much thought and inventiveness has gone into the content and layout of the Torbay Aircraft Museum in order to give the lay visitor (rather than the aircraft 'buff') a relaxed and entertaining hour. It is a 'holiday' museum, and all the more pleasurable for being so.

IV
THE EAST

BANHAM
INTERNATIONAL MOTOR MUSEUM

PERHAPS THE 'international' in the title of this interesting museum is somewhat ambitious, but with magnificent cars from France, Germany, Italy, America and Britain one should not quibble. As it is located some 4 miles east of the A11 between Thetford and Norwich and standing back from the B1113, a little attention to the road map is needed to find the museum, but persistence is rewarded.

It opened to the public in 1976 and houses the collection of cars and motor cycles assembled by the owner, Lord Cranworth, who started collecting in 1963 with the purchase of his first vintage car, a 1927 Bentley tourer. However, on entering the museum it is not a Bentley that first catches the eye, but a 1954 Mercedes-Benz 300SL sports car which, because of its swing-up doors hinged centrally in the roof, is aptly named the 'Gullwing'. The tubular-frame structure which imposed this form of design also necessitated an inclined engine mounting and thus only left-hand drive models could be built. The 300SL was reputed to require a good driver behind the wheel, but as the museum believes that Stirling Moss drove this particular model in the 1956 Tour de France its unmarked condition needs no comment.

Whilst passing through the small but sensibly stocked shop and reception area, it is worthwhile pausing for a few minutes to admire a remarkable collection of Victorian dolls displayed here: a rather touching feminine contrast to all the masculine machinery.

The Banham Museum has developed its presentation mainly around two particular styles and eras: the elegance of the grand cars of the twenties and thirties and the post-war sports cars of the fifties and sixties. The impression it gives is of a sort of father-and-son relationship. The atmosphere of each period is evoked by the manner in which the cars are displayed with backgrounds depicting appropriate scenes of café society, period garages, racing pits, 'flapper' picnics, and so on.

Looking at the grand cars first, an appropriate start would be the $4\frac{1}{4}$-litre-engined Bentley which began the collection. This particular model has a body built by the famous Brussels coachbuilding firm of Vanden Plas. The other Bentleys in the Banham collection are an example of the $4\frac{1}{2}$-litre 'Silent Sports Car' introduced in 1933 after Rolls-Royce bought Bentley Motors, and the Continental S1 which in 1953 was the fastest four-seater closed car of its day. This example is the later 1956 model with a 4.9-litre engine and the supremely elegant Mulliner fastback body.

After admiring the Bentleys it might be useful to seek out two other fast and elegant cars, this time from America, and make any comparisons you wish. The 1936 Cord 810, with its retractable headlights, 'alligator' bonnet and absence of running boards looks very interesting – certainly the New York Museum of Modern Art thought so in citing it as an outstanding example of industrial design. Unfortunately, the accolade didn't much help Cord who went out of business in 1937, destroyed like so many other fine companies by the Depression. The other American exhibit is a 1937 Packard 120 with a coupé body. This particular coupé has that American invention the 'rumble seat' which combines so well the elegance of a roadster with the convenience of a four-seater – although

A 1939 BMW 328 tourer from the Banham International Motor Museum. The 328 had many racing successes, including victory in the 1940 Mille Miglia. Photo: Banham International Motor Museum.

The 1950 Healey Silverstone from the Banham International Motor Museum. This marque had a particularly distinguished competition career. Photo: Banham International Motor Museum.

there must have been something more than a rumble at the car's top speed of 100mph!

Returning to British products, how can we fail to admire the two Rolls-Royce cars in the collection, a Phantom II Continental, with its low and sporty look, and its successor, a Phantom III, this one with a rare fully open touring body but a standard twelve-cylinder engine with dual ignition, requiring twenty-four sparking plugs? In comparison to all this magnificence, there are two cars parked nearby that in appearance and performance are at the other end of the motoring scale, but neverthe-less enjoy a fame all their own. First, the Austin 7 'Chummy', the touring version of the basic Austin 7 which was one of the most popular cars ever made, and then a French model of similar appeal, the Citroen 'Cloverleaf', so called because of its triangular seating arrangements and because its production colour was usually bright yellow – the Demi Citroen ('half a lemon').

Just before passing into the later era of post-war sports cars, spare a moment to examine the 1939 production model of the BMW 328 six-cylinder two-seater, a legendary sports car to which the British Motor Company paid the sincerest form of flattery by using its blueprints brought to England after the war to build their own 2-litre engine.

In the post-war section a collection of very speedy sports cars presents itself. If we exclude the Mercedes mentioned earlier, perhaps the fastest in the stable is the Jaguar XK140 which carried on the enormous reputation made by the XK120, a car whose performance and value for money astounded the world in the years following the Second World War. A Sunbeam-Talbot Alpine is here too, a roadster version of the fast good-looking saloon which won the Monte Carlo Rally in 1953. There is also a Healey Silverstone – even its name is exciting, and its competition record more so. The two best-known visual features of this car are the position of the headlamps within the radiator grille and that of the spare wheel which doubles as a rear bumper. Another interesting car in this section is the Daimler SP250 2 + 2 tourer. This is a 1963 version of the model known as the 'Dart', introduced in 1959 and reckoned by some to be a potential rival to the E-type Jaguar. The argument was never really resolved as further development was killed off when the company was bought by Jaguar. Seek out also the Aston-Martin DB2/4, which was the Company's first production coupé and with a W.O. Bentley-designed engine started the Aston-Martins on their international racing career. Other famous British sports cars include a 1953 Jowett Jupiter, a 1950 Riley Roadster and a 1958 twin-cam MGA Roadster, reckoned to be the car which, when first produced in 1946, opened American eyes to the joys of open-air motoring. A second form of open-air travelling is repre-sented at Banham by a small collection of post-war motor cycles, of which perhaps the most interesting is a 1952 Zundapp, the later develop-ment of the German army's despatch riders' famous machine and one of the very few models in this country.

The Banham International Museum is one of the latest motor museums to open to the public and will obviously develop along with the leisure complex of which it forms a part. This with its adventure playground, zoo and picnic area, offers the facilities for an enjoyable day out for the family.

EAST ANGLIA
TRANSPORT MUSEUM

SITUATED IN THE Suffolk village of Carlton Colville, 3 miles south-west of Lowestoft, is the East Anglia Transport Museum. Although its name and geographical situation – almost on the eastern tip of England – might suggest a purely local flavour, it contains exhibits from all over Britain and from abroad and is rare in the British Isles as a working museum of land transport.

The museum's beginnings, nearly twenty years ago, were very small. Four local enthusiasts discovered and purchased the body of a Lowestoft tram, and by a gradual process of making or discovering replacement parts rebuilt the tram to show condition. This activity aroused a certain amount of local interest which was increased by the arrival early in 1964 of a

A line-up of public transport and commercial vehicles from the early days of the East Anglia Transport Museum. Photo: G. M. Moon.

London Transport tramcar from Chessington Zoo, where it had been on display since 1952, and a Glasgow Coronation car. Next came an Aveling and Porter steam roller purchased from the local council. For the benefit and encouragement of other potential pioneers in this field, it should be recorded that all this process of gestation took place in one man's back garden!

The growing collection prompted two major decisions in 1965: the forming of the East Anglia Transport Museum Society, and the aim of establishing a museum of land transport. Following a successful rally held in 1966, the Historic Commercial Vehicle Club joined the venture and a large prefabricated depot building was erected to accommodate the early exhibits. Since then development has been continuous. In November 1970 a Blackpool tramcar was operated under its own power for the first time, and shortly afterwards a London Transport trolleybus made history by being the first of its kind to operate in a museum

anywhere in the country. The museum opened to the public in May 1972, and in the same year a narrow-gauge railway was constructed. It is a live, working museum where members of the public can not only see, but also travel on the vehicles of yesteryear. The museum claims to be unique in Great Britain in bringing together in a working collection a great variety of vehicles from all fields of transport, whether they be powered by petrol, diesel, steam, electricity or even horse. There are currently over forty vehicles, including cars, commercial vehicles, motor buses, trolleybuses, tramcars and municipal vehicles. The majority of these date from before the last war, and the museum's aim is to restore all of them and where possible bring them to working condition.

From the earliest days, the museum had the imaginative idea of developing its whole presentation around a street scene of the inter-war era, and the cobbled roadway, tram lines and overhead wire and many items of appropriate

The museum's Lowestoft Corporation tram No. 14, built in 1904 and still in service in the town when the system ended in 1931. Photo: G. M. Moon.

An Ashton-under-Lyne trolleybus of 1950 passes a 1939 Glasgow tramcar in the tram shed at the East Anglia Transport Museum. Photo: G. M. Moon.

street furniture convey a very realistic feeling of times past.

The largest group of vehicles numerically is the trolleybuses, twelve of which are normally at Carlton Colville. Of particular interest in this group is a splendid London trolleybus, which was the last to run in London in 1962, and the first to arrive at the museum, and a Newcastle trolley which was the last built for that town (in 1950). Another trolleybus that attracts interest is Copenhagen 5, a single-deck Garrett built locally at Leiston in 1926. It was reimported at the end of its working life.

Various ancillary vehicles for trams and trolleybuses are also on display, and worthy of note is the Ipswich solid-tyred battery tower wagon built by Ransomes in 1922 which was in use by Ipswich Corporation Transport until 1966. A bus-shunting tractor, built by Fordson for London Transport, is a reminder of the days before buses were fitted with self-starters.

Motor bus exhibits include examples from the local fleets of the erstwhile Lowestoft Corporation and the Eastern Counties Omnibus Company, represented by an AEC Regent double-decker and a Bristol single-deck bus respectively. Both carry bodies by the Lowestoft firm of Eastern Coach Works. Further examples are the famous Leyland single-deck PLSC Lion and the AEC's London RT types. A Thornycroft J-type solid-tyred lorry of 1919 exemplifies commercial vehicles of this period. Battery electric vehicles are included too: the oldest, apart from the tower wagon already mentioned, is a bread van of 1935 with a hand controller and tiller steering. A selection of motor cars illustrates private transport of the period between the wars, together with various tricycles and hand-propelled items, fire pumps and machines for white-line painting on roads.

The sound of steam is at present absent. Unfortunately, the Aveling roller referred to earlier left a few years ago, but in 1978 a replacement arrived in the form of an Armstrong Whitworth roller, once used in Ipswich Docks.

The railway mentioned above runs the length of the museum area and is a good example of the privately owned narrow-gauge type quite common in the country until recently. Most of the equipment was acquired from undertakings in the locality and includes three diesel locomotives.

This, then, is the East Anglia Transport Museum. It is the product of nearly two decades of devoted work by volunteers who, in their spare time, have built an unusual and entertaining museum that is bound to expand and progress year by year.

HISTORIC AIRCRAFT MUSEUM

THE HISTORIC AIRCRAFT MUSEUM is fittingly situated at Southend for the place has long been associated with aviation. It is believed that the first flight from Southend was in July 1910, when George A. Barnes, piloting a Bleriot, took off from Roots Hall, now the site of Southend Football Club. Not long afterwards the War Office decided upon a site at Rochford (now Southend Airport) as a potential landing ground for the Royal Flying Corps. Although the First World War records are incomplete, it is known that on 31 May 1915 F/Sub/Lt A. W. Robertson was airborne in a Bleriot reaching 6,000 feet in pursuit of the Zeppelin LZ 28. Civil aviation returned to the district on 10 May 1919 when a Handley Page 0/400 bomber, converted for peacetime use, dropped newspapers by parachute near Southend Pier. In August 1919 pleasure flying began at Rochford with the operation of two Avro 504K three-seaters of Navarro Aviation Company. After a long local campaign for proper aircraft facilities, Southend Aerodrome was officially opened on 18 September 1935.

At the beginning of the Second World War Rochford became a fighter station equipped with Mark I Spitfires and played its part in the Battle of Britain and the air defence of the United Kingdom throughout the hostilities. After the war civil aviation again re-emerged, and the air-ferrying of cars to the Continent is now one of the facilities provided by Southend Airport.

The Historic Aircraft Museum is housed within the airport complex in a purpose-built hangar which was opened to the public in May 1972, an event which marked the fulfilment of many years of voluntary work by local en-thusiasts, supported by the private company that financed the enterprise. The collection is small, totalling about twenty-five aircraft, including some replica machines. The museum does not attempt any teaching role in regard to aviation history, but presents its exhibits attractively and gives the visitor the oppor-tunity to inspect them closely and in some instances climb aboard.

The earliest-designed aircraft on display is a replica Roe triplane. This remarkable machine, of which the only original surviving example forms an important part of the Science Museum collection, was first flown by its designer, Alliott Verdon Roe, in July 1909, an event which marked the first successful flight of an all-British aeroplane and the beginning of the A. V. Roe company, which for the next half-century produced a long line of fine aircraft.

Another significant British aircraft – this time a splendidly restored original – is the de Havilland Dragon. Produced in 1933, the DH84 was the first of a new concept in small, compact, transport aircraft and was popular with many of the smaller airlines up to the beginning of the war. This particular aircraft spent most of its working life with Highland Airways ferrying passengers, freight and mail in the Western Isles of Scotland. It is still in flying condition.

From the same era is displayed a quite different aircraft in the form of the German-built Fiesler Storch. This short-take-off-and-landing monoplane was developed as a com-munications and ambulance aircraft and later extensively deployed by the Luftwaffe. The aircraft displayed by the museum was used in the North African Campaign and has now been restored and repainted in full Luftwaffe African desert colours. The Luftwaffe is further represented by a Messerschmitt Bf109, and facing it across the hangar is its historic foe, a Spitfire. Both are replica constructions but are very well made, and the menace and power so evident in the originals is amply conveyed.

The larger aircraft and the modern jet fighters are on display outside the hangar. The Blackburn Beverley is certainly the biggest and probably the most popular exhibit. In service with the Royal Air Force during the fifties and sixties as a medium-range transport, its length is 100 feet and wingspan 162 feet. Its popularity at the museum stems from the fact that it is open to the public who can walk around its vast interior and sit in the pilots' seats in the cockpit. If the Walter Mitty idea of starting up and lifting the Beverley off from some dusty runway in Kenya, Bahrain or Aden does not appeal, the young visitor (and mum or dad!) can climb into a nearby Viscount cockpit which is complete with controls and there carry out the flight-deck checks prior to taking off from Heathrow or Gatwick.

The jet fighters on display include a Sea Hawk, of which over four hundred were in service with the Fleet Air Arm in the fifties (inside the hangar is a Sea Fury which it replaced), a Gloster Meteor T1, which was the RAF's first jet trainer, and a DH Vampire TII which replaced the Harvard as its advanced trainer in 1953. Another very interesting aircraft is a Heinkel CASA 2111, which in its original form and early development was probably the best known of the Luftwaffe's twin-engined bombers. Thirty of the early production runs were delivered to Spain in 1937 and the exhibited model was in fact built in Spain on licence in 1951. The original engine was the Daimler Benz 601 but this was later changed to the Rolls-Royce Merlin Series 500. Both engine types are on exhibition. The aircraft is still in flying condition and took a villain's part in the film 'The Battle of Britain'.

The Historic Aircraft Museum presents its exhibits enterprisingly. It is not well endowed but its enthusiasm for aviation is infectious — even its publicity leaflet contains instructions on how it can be folded and flown!

IMPERIAL WAR MUSEUM
AT DUXFORD

THE AERODROME AT Duxford, 8 miles south of Cambridge, was built during the First World War and is one of the earliest Royal Air Force stations. In the first few years of its existence it played various roles. It was a training station in 1919 and for a short time a bomber unit, reverting again to a training role with Bristol fighters and Avro 504s. In 1924 Duxford became a fighter station and remained so until its closure thirty-seven years later. Its Number 19 Squadron was the first squadron to fly Gloster Gauntlets in 1935 and, on 4 August 1938, took delivery of the first Supermarine Spitfire to enter service. Perhaps the most distinguished airmen associated with Duxford have been Major H. D. Harvey-Kelley who, in August 1914, had been the first Royal Flying Corps pilot to land in France, and Group Captain Sir Douglas Bader, who flew Spitfires and Hurricanes from the base before and during the Battle of Britain.

At the end of 1940 the Air Fighting Development Unit came to Duxford to evaluate new aircraft and to test captured enemy equipment. During this period it played a major part in developing the Hawker Typhoon into a formidable low-level and ground-attack fighter. In June 1943 Duxford was handed over to the United States Army Air Forces, becoming the headquarters of the Seventy-Eighth Fighter Group, one of the units responsible for providing escorts for the daylight bombing operations of the Eighth Air Force. In December 1945 it was handed back to the Royal Air Force and remained operational until 31 July 1961 when a Gloster Meteor 14 made the last official flight from the station.

In May 1968 Duxford relived a part of its history when it was chosen as an authentic location for the making of the film 'The Battle of Britain'. A private air force of Hurricanes and Spitfires, as well as the Spanish-built versions of the Messerschmitt 109 and Heinkel III on loan from the Spanish Air Force, moved in. The buildings were painted up and the station restored to life at the cost of one hangar destroyed by 'enemy bombing'. The result was renewed public interest in the future of the aerodrome.

The following year the Ministry of Defence declared the airfield surplus to requirements, and in 1971 the Imperial War Museum, which had been seeking a suitable site for the storage, restoration and eventual display of exhibits too large for its main building in London, began to use part of one of the hangars. The first aircraft to be restored was the museum's P51D Mustang, and the first exhibit to be flown in, a Royal Navy Sea Vixen, arrived in March 1972. The public were first able to see the collection, which by then numbered ten aircraft, at an air display in October 1973. Since then a major air display at Duxford has been an annual feature.

In June 1976 Duxford was opened on a regular basis to the public, as an integral part of the Imperial War Museum. The rapid development of Duxford Airfield and its buildings as a museum and the prospects for future improvements to the premises, collections and facilities, rest upon a unique relationship between a national institution (the Imperial War Museum), a local authority (the Cambridgeshire County Council) and a voluntary society (the Duxford Aviation Society). The society, formed in 1975, assists the museum in many of the activities at

The Imperial War Museum at Duxford where this North American P51D Mustang is displayed believes it is perhaps the best single-seat piston-engined fighter of the Second World War. Photo: Imperial War Museum.

Duxford, in particular through the voluntary effort generously devoted by its members to working on exhibits in the museum's collections. In addition the society has built up an impressive collection of civil aircraft, the most important of which, the British pre-production Concorde, flew into Duxford in August 1977.

In April 1977 the Cambridgeshire County Council acquired nearly 150 acres of the airfield, including the shortened runway, and concluded an agreement with the Imperial War Museum for the joint management of this land and of other events and activities at Duxford. This made it possible both for flying to continue as an additional attraction for visitors to the airfield, and for important acquisitions such as the Boeing B-29 Superfortress, which flew in on 2 March 1980, to be delivered by air to the museum.

Duxford is more than just an aviation museum: the Imperial War Museum illustrates and records all aspects of the two World Wars and other conflicts involving Britain and the Commonwealth since 1914. Moreover, the aim of the Duxford Aviation Society is wider than its name suggests. Not only does it work to acquire, preserve, maintain and operate military and civil aircraft, but it also has a flourishing section devoted to military vehicles. The excellent working relationship between the two organizations has established a first-class museum with great potential. Although mainly a war museum, it is the large post-war civil aircraft that first catch the eye when entering the airfield, and three are particularly noteworthy: a Vickers Viscount 701, a de Havilland Comet 4 and the pre-production Concorde 101. These represent a magnificent trio of firsts, being the first turbo-prop aircraft to operate a passenger service, the world's first jet airliner and the world's first

The Gloster Javelin was the first delta-wing aircraft to serve with the Royal Air Force. It was designed as an all-weather, high-altitude interceptor. This example is at the Imperial War Museum at Duxford. Photo: Imperial War Museum.

supersonic airliner respectively. For a small extra charge the visitor can go aboard the Concorde and see the amazingly complex but well-ordered flight deck. As this particular aircraft was a pre-production test bed, some of the test equipment is still aboard, as is a typical seating arrangement. Its visit to Tangiers, Moses Lake and Nairobi in the course of its test work, its record-breaking crossing of the Atlantic and the fastest and highest flight by a Concorde are all recorded in the 'artwork' on its fuselage.

At the time of writing, the museum has been able to do very little in setting out its exhibits thematically or chronologically. This will come as planned buildings are completed and the restoration programme advances. It is ne-cessary, therefore, to go to the hangars to seek out earlier examples of civil aircraft in order to make comparisons and, generally, be astounded by the rate of progress made. Sadly, there are no survivors from the great international air service that Imperial Airways provided in the twenties and thirties, such as the Handley Page 42, the immense four-engined biplane that carried up to thirty-eight passengers at a rather ponderous 100mph, and we must content ourselves with the DH Dragon Rapide of 1935 and the DH Dove which was the first post-war aircraft produced by de Havilland.

In spite of the fact that its history dates back to the First World War, Duxford has little to show of that period in military aviation – its near neighbour, the Shuttleworth Collection, has

taken on this role. The assembly of more modern military aircraft is, however, impressive, parti-cularly the fighter aircraft which at Duxford must be led by the trio of Spitfires. Although the Spitfire is perhaps the most famous military aircraft of all time and chiefly remembered as the symbol of the Battle of Britain, it was in fact the less glamorous Hurricane which bore the brunt of the fighting.

Perhaps Duxford will be able to recruit a Hurricane to its collection in the near future or, to add a real touch of drama, a Focke-Wulf 190, the redoubtable foe of the Spitfire. The other British fighters present are all jets: the Gloster Meteor, the first jet-propelled fighter to enter service with the Royal Air Force and marking its arrival by successfully attacking the V1 flying bombs, the twin-boomed DH115 Vampire which followed the Meteor into RAF service, the graceful and versatile Hawker Hunter which served the RAF and many other Air Forces long and well, the delta-winged Gloster Javelin and, finally, the English Electric FI Lightning which ushered Britain into the era of the Mach 1 fighter. The Lightning was the pinnacle of achievement and the end of an era. It entered RAF service six years after the Hawker Hunter with more than double the speed performance and three times the thrust. It was a remarkable combination of design and engineering, but the burden of continuous research, development and production costs was not one that British industry or government could sustain. The next

The Handley Page Victor, the last of the V-bombers to be ordered for the Royal Air Force – the other two were the Valiant and the Vulcan. This example seen landing at Duxford Aerodrome is on permanent display there as part of the Imperial War Museum. Photo: Imperial War Museum.

fighter for the RAF was the American-built Phantom.

The British-manufactured bomber of 1939–45 and the post-war years is not well represented at Duxford, but scarcity of such aircraft is nation-wide. In fact, of the ten major British-designed types made during the war, only the Blenheim, Wellington, Lancaster and Mosquito survive. Gone forever are the Beaufort, Hampden, Sterling and Whitley. Duxford has a rugged DH98 Mosquito, a good example of the breed that served so well as bomber, fighter-bomber, night fighter, photo-reconnaissance aircraft and trainer, and an Avro Shackleton representing the piston-engined aircraft. The jets are repre-sented by the Canberra and the Victor. It would be apt if the Canberra could be displayed next to the Mosquito which it rivalled in versatility and the magnificent service it gave to the RAF. Designed as a high-speed bomber to replace the Lincoln, the Canberra made its maiden flight in 1949 and entered service two years later. Its performance at high altitude was exceptional, and by virtue of its low wing loading it was able to out-manoeuvre most contemporary fighters. It was supplied to many foreign air forces and fought on both sides during the India and Pakistan conflict in 1965. The Handley Page Victor is parked nearby as a striking reminder of the V-bomber fleet in service with the RAF in the fifties and early sixties. The Victor was the last of three V-bombers to be ordered for the RAF – the other two were the Valiant and the

Vulcan – and entered service in 1958. Its most striking feature was the unconventional crescent-shaped wing, which was designed to meet the conflicting requirements of high-speed operation at altitudes well above 50,000 feet and good control during approach and landing. It could fly at 640mph to deliver the atom bomb.

Duxford has not forgotten that the USAAF was its tenant during the years 1943–5. In one of the hangars there is a very good exhibition, using photographs and maps, setting out the vital part that the American Allies played and particularly the daylight escort role of their fighter units based at Duxford. In June 1943 it became the headquarters of their Seventy-Eighth Fighter Group and the operational squadrons were equipped with P47 Thunder-bolts. Sadly, an example of this fine aircraft is not in the Duxford collection but the American involvement in the air war in Europe is recalled by the presence of four historic types. There is an example of the Douglas DC3 Dakota, and nothing can be added to what has already been said by others about this immortal aircraft. A Boeing B17 Flying Fortress, the standard four-engined bomber used by the USAAF in the war, displayed here with its fighter escort, the P51 Mustang, and a B29 Superfortress, the only example of its kind in Europe which flew in on 29 March 1980, complete the wartime arsenal.

The collection of 'enemy' aircraft at Duxford is very small and contains nothing from Japan or Italy. However, the German contingent includes

One of the most famous transport aircraft in the history of aviation, the angular three-engined Junkers JU52/3M. This example came to the Imperial War Museum at Duxford after thirty years' service with the Portuguese Air Force. Photo: Imperial War Museum.

one of the most famous transport aircraft in the history of aviation in the Junkers JU52/3M. This angular, three-engined machine, with its distinctive, corrugated-metal skin, developed from the civil version which was the backbone of the giant Lufthansa fleet in the thirties and was sold to airlines all over the world. The military version gained a formidable reputation in the Spanish Civil War as both a transport aircraft and bomber and, although obsolete at the start of the Second World War, continued in its transport role throughout the war. The Duxford example served with the Portuguese Air Force from 1937 to 1965, but is shown here in its familiar German markings.

The hangars at Duxford produce all sorts of aviation delights and surprises. The restoration programme is continuous and currently includes a Short Sunderland V flying boat which, in retirement in France, suffered the ignominy of conversion to a nightclub. Engines, airframes and bomb casings abound and a collection of vintage gliders is worthy of special inspection.

In its role as a war museum Duxford, in addition to its aviation displays, has brought together relics from other spheres of combat. Here is an important and growing collection of military vehicles which at present consists of nearly fifty individual exhibits. Most of these, which range in size from motor cycles to a 65-ton Conqueror tank, form part of the permanent collections of the Imperial War Museum or are owned by members of the military vehicles group of the Duxford Aviation Society. Together they illustrate many aspects of the role and development of military transport in the twentieth century and reflect, in particular, the wide variety of soft-skinned and armoured vehicles used by the British and Allied forces during the Second World War.

The Duxford enterprise is fortunate in the working relationship that has been established between the three main bodies responsible for its operation and in the space that it has to extend its covered exhibition area and also put its exhibits through their paces out of doors. It is a fine musuem with no end to its potential.

SHUTTLEWORTH COLLECTION

RICHARD ORMONDE SHUTTLEWORTH was born in July 1909. His grandfather was Joseph Shuttleworth, an engineer and inventor and founder of the firm of Clayton and Shuttleworth of Lincoln, who built steam engines and agricultural machinery. His father, Colonel Frank Shuttleworth, was a regular soldier, big-game hunter, sportsman and landowner. Richard Shuttleworth inherited their inventive and adventurous characteristics. He became a good horseman, piloted a Comper Swift aeroplane to India and successfully competed in his Bugatti and Alfa-Romeo on the international motor-racing circuit. While still in his teens, he began to collect cars and aircraft and put together a small but interesting collection from the pioneer days. When war broke out in 1939, he volunteered for the RAF. In August 1940, whilst flying a Fairey Battle on a night sortie, he crashed and was killed.

The Shuttleworth Collection is part of a trust that Richard's mother set up in his memory. It has developed from the nucleus that this talented and adventurous man started in his youth, and has its home at a small aerodrome at Old Warden in the Bedfordshire countryside some 50 miles north of London and just off the A1, historically the Great North Road from London to York. The collection comprises aircraft, cars, motor cycles, bicycles and horse-drawn vehicles, but it is the aircraft which are its main feature and provide its unique attraction. Nearly all the aircraft are original – some dating back to 1909 – and they are kept in full flying condition. In the summer season, on special open days, they take to the air and then, for both the air enthusiast and the picnicking

family, the years roll back: the aeroplanes are standing out on the close-cut grass, a pilot appears wearing the flying kit of half a century ago – the leather jacket, goggles and helmet; a mechanic swings a propeller, nothing happens, he tries again, until on the third attempt the engine coughs into life and a flying machine from another age taxis down the field for take-off. It is all like a rather extravagant film set – indeed, many of these aircraft have become film stars of the aviation world. The pilots and technical experts at Old Warden were closely connected with the making of 'Those Magnificent Men in Their Flying Machines', and a number of the aircraft did exciting things in the film.

The collection is housed in six hangars by the side of the grass airfield. The aeroplanes on display are grouped for comparison and the earliest machines are kept together in the main exhibition hall. The oldest of these is the Bleriot Type XI of 1909, built in the same year as (and basically identical with) the machine that made the first-ever aerial crossing of the Channel. This version has a three-cylinder Anzani engine and, in keeping with other early designs, no moveable control surfaces on the wings. Turns in the air were executed by a method known as 'wing warping' and a close examination of the Bleriot structure shows how this was achieved. A year or two younger than the Bleriot is the Deperdussin, also a French design and powered by an Anzani. It is to the great credit of the management of the Shuttleworth Collection that both these aircraft, although irreplaceable if destroyed, are, when conditions allow, flown in low hops across the airfield. Nothing is more

evocative of the high excitement of the early days of flight.

The oldest British aeroplane that flies anywhere in the world is the collection's Blackburn of 1912. The three years that passed between the origin of the Bleriot and this Blackburn reveal noticeable improvements in design, this later type having cleaner lines and advanced layout and a more powerful engine. The instrument panel is, however, painfully simple. There in the centre, in solitary splendour, reposes a rev. counter. That is all: no ASI, no altimeter, not even an oil-pressure gauge.

The collection is particularly proud that its aeroplanes are genuine original veterans, often with individual histories of their own. However, two exceptions have been made to this claim. In addition to some of the original aircraft used in the 'Magnificent Men' film, two special reproductions were made. One of these was the Bristol Boxkite of 1910 design, and when the film was completed this machine was acquired by the collection. Opinions differed regarding the acceptability of reproduction machines, but two points prevailed. No genuine Boxkite existed and as the reproduction was such an accurate specimen it would usefully fill a gap in the coverage of design trends. After all, the collection's three earliest machines were all wing-warping aeroplanes, whereas here was a biplane, with a foreplane ahead of the wings as well as a conventional tailplane behind and with moveable ailerons to provide control on the wing tips. The other reproduction in the collection is the Avro Triplane IV. Although the original triplane was not produced in quantity, this exhibit serves to show the design thinking from which many Avro types developed. The famous Avro 504, the Tutors of the thirties, the Anson and Lancaster of the Second World War and the Vulcan bomber all sprang in turn from this 1910 design.

The aeroplanes in the main exhibition hall are amongst the most historically significant flying machines in existence, for without them the now-accepted pattern of development would not have started. The pioneers were great people; they taught themselves to fly in aeroplanes that were unknown quantities, with little supporting knowledge of theory of flight or weather and with engines that had very temperamental tendencies. There is a marked contrast between these machines and the next generation of aeroplanes built under the pressure of the First World War, when military demand necessitated rapid development. Certainly to realize that the British fighter, the SE5 – an example of which is in the collection – whilst only seven years younger than the 40mph Boxkite, is capable of 140mph and a high degree of manoeuvrability, brings home the rapidity with which progress in performance was achieved. Another famous type of the time is represented here by the rotary-engined Avro 504K of which over nine thousand were subsequently built. Here also is the diminutive Sopwith Pup, the first aircraft to land on the deck of a ship at sea, and a Bristol F2B two-seater fighter which was so effective that it remained in service from 1917 until 1932. The collection's specimen is fitted with the oldest Rolls-Royce aero-engine in the world. The opposition of 1914–18 is represented by the German equivalent of the Bristol in the LVG (Luft-Verkers-Gesellschaft) C-VI, an earlier example of which had the distinction of dropping six bombs on Victoria Station in London in November 1916.

Amongst the aircraft of the inter-war years are two of considerable historic merit. The Percival Gull Six flown by Jean Batten on her many record flights between 1935 and 1937 is here, as is the DH88 'Comet' racing aircraft which, flown by C. W. A. Scott and Tom Campbell-Black, won the International England-

OPPOSITE ABOVE: *The 1910 Deperdussin monoplane from the Shuttleworth Collection. A popular training aircraft prior to the First World War, it can often be seen flying during the collection's open days at Old Warden Aerodrome, Bedfordshire. Photo: Shuttleworth Collection.*
CENTRE: *The 1912 Blackburn monoplane of the Shuttleworth Collection takes off from Old Warden Aerodrome. It is the oldest British aeroplane still in flying condition. Photo: Shuttleworth Collection.*
BELOW: *A replica of the 1910 Bristol Boxkite landing at Old Warden Aerodrome. It was built in 1964 for the film 'Those Magnificent Men in their Flying Machines' and flies regularly on the Shuttleworth Collection's open days. Photo: Shuttleworth Collection.*

FAR ABOVE: *This historic photograph captures the moment when the DH88 Comet 'Grosvenor House' touches down to win the England-to-Australia Air Race of 1934. Photo: Shuttleworth Collection.*
ABOVE: *'Grosvenor House' today. This magnificent aircraft is now being restored to flying condition by the Shuttleworth Collection. Photo: Shuttleworth Collection.*
OPPOSITE: *A replica of the 1910 Avro Triplane from the Shuttleworth Collection. Although a conventional modern engine is fitted, the original early-style method of wing warping is retained. Photo: Shuttleworth Collection.*

to-Australia Air Race of 1934. The history of the DH88 is remarkable. When the race was announced, no suitable British aircraft existed, but Geoffrey de Havilland was determined that Britain should be represented and within nine months had designed and built the three 'Comets' that took part. GACSS, after only a few hours of proving flights, flew the 7,000 miles in under seventy-one hours to win the race and the gold-cup prize. As the result of an appeal launched by the Transport Trust, it is now undergoing restoration to flying condition. In spite of the hurried nature of the design and construction of the DH88, de Havilland produced more than a race winner for it led directly to the design of the Mosquito, one of the most successful fighter-bombers of the Second World War.

Another noteworthy aircraft of this period is the English Electric Wren, which in 1923 won a *Daily Mail* contest by flying 87.5 miles on 1 gallon of petrol. Whilst splendid in the air, this little aircraft has the greatest difficulty in getting off the ground. Perhaps the most successful light aeroplane of all time and certainly the one that placed private and sporting flying really on the map was the original de Havilland Moth, which appeared in 1925. This, the DH60, could do no wrong. Moths won races, broke records, flew long distances and became the standard equipment of the fast-developing flying-club scene; the Gipsy Moth followed, then the ubiquitous Tiger Moth. They are all represented in the collection, along with many other interesting but less well-known makes, including some fine examples of the efforts of amateur designers and constructors.

The late thirties and the war years are represented by, amongst others, a Hawker Hind bomber, found in Afghanistan and transported 6,000 miles overland; an example of the Gloster Gladiator, the RAF's last biplane fighter; and the popular Avro Tutor and Hawker Tomtit which replaced the Avro 504 as the RAF training aircraft. The aircraft display is completed, appropriately, by a Hurricane and Spitfire, and the whole presentation is excel-lently supported by photographic displays, engines and associated memorabilia.

The same principle of restoration and use that the Shuttleworth Collection applies to its aircraft is also adopted for its motor cars. The car collection is small, about a dozen vehicles in all, but of enormous interest and rare value, and certainly they add greatly to the charm and period atmosphere that makes Old Warden unique. The oldest is a brake-bodied Daimler, made in England in 1897, and there are three other nineteenth-century vehicles. A Panhard-Levassor, which competed in the Paris–Amsterdam Race of 1898, covering 890 miles at an average speed of 24mph, is here; it was also driven by King Edward VII to Ascot – pre-sumably at an even more sedate pace. A Benz two-seater dog cart of the same year follows, with a Mors 'Petit Duc' of 1899 completing the quartet. The earliest twentieth-century car is a 1901 Arrol-Johnston dog cart with a 12hp two-cylinder engine – 'No noise, no dirt, no smell and no vibration' was the company's sales slogan. Whether Richard Shuttleworth, who bought the car in 1931 in Dumfries and drove it the 250 miles to Old Warden, agreed is not recorded. There is a Baby Peugeot of 1902 and two fine 1903 French cars, a Richard Brasier and a De Dietrich, both from stables with a good racing record. A 1912 Crossley, a 1913 Morris Oxford and a 1935 Austin 7 complete the collection, which sadly no longer contains the Bugatti and Alfa-Romeo that were so much a part of Richard Shuttleworth's life.

The motor cycle collection is very small with but five specimens, but like all exhibits at Old Warden they repay close study. Compare, for instance, the Singer Motor Wheel of 1900 with the Cyclemaster of 1950: certainly the earlier model has the more elegant appearance. Note also the three hand brakes on the 1900 Manot-Gordon motor tricycle.

The other sections of the collection cover non-motorized transport and deal with cycling and horse-drawn vehicles. There is a quite impressive collection of cycles but here, as in so many other transport museums, they are treated as the poor relation. This is perhaps inevitable

OPPOSITE: *The Gloster Gladiator from the Shuttleworth Collection. The Gladiator was the RAF's last biplane fighter. Photo: Shuttleworth Collection.*

as, after numerous false starts in the nineteenth century, the cycle developed with a design form that changed very little for more than sixty years. Thus the variation in design and novelty of appearance of the cycles at Old Warden centres round a very early 'hobby horse', a treadle-drive Boneshaker, a Kangaroo (very aptly named) and a quadricycle. An 'Ivel' lady's cycle of 1901 made in Biggleswade some 4 miles from Old Warden pioneered the cross-frame structure, and a well preserved example is here.

Horse brasses, harnesses and about a dozen carriages and coaches form the horse-drawn section. It displays examples of the many forms of transport used by country estates during the nineteenth and early twentieth centuries, from the small gig to the park coach and private omnibus. Finally, there is a display of fire engines, including a perhaps over-restored manual engine of 1780, a Merryweather of 1906, and a veteran of local service, a Shand-Mason steam-powered engine of 1913.

In all the Shuttleworth Collection is a very pleasant place to visit. It has a well-stocked book and souvenir shop and an excellent cafeteria. Tucked away in the Bedfordshire countryside, it offers a leisurely look at most forms of Victorian and Edwardian land transport and the joys and excitements of the early days of flight.

V
THE MIDLANDS

BIRMINGHAM MUSEUM
OF SCIENCE AND INDUSTRY

ACCORDING TO ITS compact and well-illustrated guide, the Birmingham Museum of Science and Industry was founded in 1950 'to preserve the best examples of industrial machinery and products and to develop a modern Science Section and to provide exhibits and information on the latest improvements in Science and Technology'. This is a wide-ranging brief, and considering the relatively modest size of the museum it comes as a pleasant surprise to find that the transport section occupies a generous proportion of the display area.

The museum building is a converted nineteenth-century factory building to which has been added a modern section. Its location is close to the centre of the city and alongside a branch of the Birmingham Canal, and plans are in hand to enlarge the building on the present site and to allow the canal and its holiday traffic to become more a part of the museum.

Immediately on entering the museum, which starts with a Hall of Engineering, one hears the soft sound of steam at work and the low rumble of machinery in action, for it is the policy of the museum to let the machinery 'come alive' at regular intervals throughout the day, and as with a picture, a thing that moves is worth a thousand words of descriptive text. There is some grand and massive machinery here, fired originally by coal, oil, diesel, hot air, electricity or gas, and fine examples of delicate and sophisticated engines.

The Engineering Hall, which sets an appropriate scene with its cast-iron columns and roof lights characteristic of industrial buildings of the nineteenth-century, contains a number of noteworthy transport relics. The first is the model steam locomotive built in 1784 by William Murdock and which, possibly due to the jealous intervention of the designer's employer, James Watt, never progressed to full-scale production but holds its place in history as the oldest extant steam locomotive, model or full-scale, in the world, with the exception of Nicolas Cugnot's 1770 steam carriage on exhibition in Paris. The other engines are the handsome 1892 Aveling and Porter steam roller, given a good home here after a life of road building in Birmingham, and an 1898 Shand Mason horse-drawn fire engine.

With the further study of transport in mind, it might be appropriate to go first to the Locomotive Hall, which is splendidly dominated by the Pacific engine 'City of Birmingham'. This magnificent locomotive from the old London Midland and Scottish Railway was built in 1939 and originally carried the full streamlined casing; now, however, with this long removed, it is displayed in its British Railway livery that it carried when it was retired in 1964. Weighing 125 tons, it is both the heaviest exhibit in the museum and the one that moves farthest as, at every hour, it is pushed slowly along its 40-foot track by hydraulic power. The effect that this dramatic demonstration has, particularly on the very young visitors to the museum, is a pleasure to see. The route to the Transport Section is by way of a sentimental journey to visit the sole remaining City of Birmingham tramcar; she has a room of her own and stands very contentedly in her smart dark blue and cream livery, enjoying a well-earned rest after clanking over 1,000,000 miles in the city's service from her introduction in 1912 to her operational retirement in 1950. Birmingham had tramcar systems using horse trams, steam trams (there are some excellent models and photographs of these units in the Tramhouse) and cable-hauled tramcars before adopting this traditional form of electric tram.

Adjacent to the Tramhouse is the museum's Transport Section containing motor cars, motor cycles and associated equipment. A particularly exciting exhibit is the Railton Mobil Special, which held the World Land Speed Record. The problems caused by the limitation on space are evident in the presentation of the transport collection here, as in museums elsewhere. The lack of space is a good enough reason why no buses or commercial vehicles are on view, but it is difficult to see why the private cars are displayed in a random date order – a different order, but still random, is printed in the literature – or why no information except the name accompanies individual exhibits.

An 1898 Star Benz and a Benz dog cart of 1900 are the oldest cars in the collection and displayed next to them to show the origin of the phrase, is an original horse-drawn 'dog cart', featuring the box under the seat at the rear which in earlier times accommodated the master's hound and later, when the horse was dispensed with, the engine. Local manufacturers are represented by a very comfortable-looking 1912 BSA 14hp touring car, a 1914 Alldays 'midget' which in spite of its name proved to be quite a capacious two-seater, a 1935 Austin Lichfield, and the 1949 Austin A90 Atlantic which captured sixty-three class records at Indianapolis and performed the remarkable feat of running continuously for seven days and seven nights. The Lanchester experimental car of 1921 is also from a local manufacturer who produced, amongst other brilliant innovations, the prototype petrol-electric car with light wooden body and suspension. At this time Lanchester, along with many other manufacturers, were aiming to produce a cheap car for the masses, but their efforts were all eclipsed with the arrival in 1923 of the Austin 7, and here to make the point is the second Austin 7 off the production line. This was the car which provided, in the phrase of the time, 'motoring for the millions'. Improved models and variants – the Nippy, Chummy and Ulster, for example –

appeared from time to time and the Austin 7 was in continuous production until the end of 1938, during which period some 350,000 were produced at the Longbridge works in Birmingham and it was also made in large numbers under licence in Europe and in America as the 'Bantam'. It was an Austin 7 which inspired Sir William Lyons to abandon motor-cycle side-car manufacture and venture on to four wheels, which resulted in the Austin 7 Swallow – a stylish development which gained immediate popularity. The success of this model, of which, sadly, there is not an example in the museum, was the first step on the road to the creation of Jaguar cars, and one of the E-type lightweight specials that were so successful in competition racing in the sixties is on view. Other cars associated with the Midlands are a 1920 Singer coupé, a Triumph Super 7 of 1929, a Riley Imp of 1935 and a 17hp Armstrong-Siddeley saloon of the same year.

In quite another dimension of motor development is the previously mentioned Napier-engined Railton Mobil Special, in which John Cobb broke the World Land Speed Record in 1938, 1939 and, after dusting off its war-time cobwebs, again in 1947 when he became the first man to break the 400mph barrier, holding the record until 1964. The car is displayed with its aluminium body lifted to show the driving position, the engines and the S-shaped girder that did duty as a chassis. A recording of the voice of the designer, Reid Railton, laconically describing the car and the World Record attempts accompanies the display.

The motor-cycle section does not attempt to show mechanical development, but local manufacturers are well represented with models from BSA and Velocette and a rare Satley-Villiers dating from 1921. Also here is a 1921 ABC motor scooter to make the point that scooters were not simply a post-war continental phenomenon, and in the Cycle Room the emphasis is on very early models such as the Velocipede of 1860 and an 1893 Bantam. Here can be seen one or two real oddities, such as a native bike made in Nyasaland at the turn of the century and constructed entirely of wood and leather, including the driving 'chain'.

In the aircraft section the major exhibits are a Spitfire Mark X and a Hurricane Mark IV and

John Cobb's Railton Mobil Special at Brooklands in 1938. This car, the holder of the World Land Speed Record in 1938 and 1939 and from 1947 to 1964, can be seen at the Birmingham Museum of Science and Industry. Photo: National Motor Museum.

both can be inspected from elevated platforms close to their cockpits. Arranged around the aircraft are some aero-engines (the main collection is in the Transport Section), including a 1943 BMW as a reminder that the Germans were ahead of us in jet-propulsion work at that stage of the Second World War. Other engines are sectioned to show more clearly their working parts. A small demonstration wind tunnel can be used by visitors to study the effects of airflow on different shapes.

Finally shipping is represented, as in most museums, by models and there are some fine examples of the modeller's art, but good as they are there are too few to tell any maritime tale.

The Birmingham Museum of Science and Industry, as its name implies, is working to a wide brief and along an ever-increasing span of time. Its present site is cramped for space and plans to add new galleries on adjoining land will only ease rather than solve its problems. It is likely, therefore, that the transport displays will remain pretty much as they are, interesting in their individuality but lacking the facilities to link them together to form a cohesive story.

BOURTON MOTOR MUSEUM

BOURTON-ON-THE-WATER on the border of Gloucestershire and Oxfordshire is a beautiful village. The River Windrush flows under low-arched bridges alongside the main street. The houses of weathered Cotswold stone are compact and neat. Lanes open off on to small squares or byways to the fields. In summer all is tourist bustle and trade; at other times, the village returns to a rural tranquillity. It is an odd spot, perhaps, to find a motor museum, but here in an eighteenth-century mill next to his home, one man has placed his own collection and a few loaned vehicles in a setting designed to recreate the atmosphere of the motoring days of the thirties. The conversion of the mill to accommodate the museum left its exterior little changed: no signs direct you to the site and no car parks adjoin it, but in strolling along the high street you might just catch sight of a thirties trade van casually parked in the yard or hear the phonographed voice of Al Bowlley singing a romantic song from the same era – such is the style of the place.

The Bourton Motor Museum is the creation of Mike Cavanagh, who returned to England in 1977 after twenty years in South Africa. He brought with him twelve vintage and classic cars that he had collected over the years to form the nucleus of the museum which now has over thirty vehicles. The cars are not arranged in any special order, but each has a setting sympathetic to its time. The walls are hung with enamelled advertising signs, which form a collection reckoned to be one of the biggest in the country, shelves are crowded with gaskets, carburettors, plugs, piston rings, etc., and hand-operated petrol pumps carry slogans certain to provoke a sigh from any motorist for the good old days – 'Shell-Mex petrol 11d a gallon'!

The oldest vehicle in the collection is a 1903 Gamage, named after the London department store which was possibly unique in selling De Dion Boutons and Renaults under its own 'brand' name. Another French vehicle – a rare 1906 Prosper-Lambert – is next in line, and a 1906 Rover completes an interesting trio of very early vehicles, though it is the cars from the twenties and thirties that look more at home.

The smaller Austins are well represented, but in speaking of the 1931 Austin 7 Ulster displayed here, 'small' means size only, not performance. When looking at this tiny two-seater, we can be rightly amazed to learn that in a similar car S. C. H. Davis and the Earl of March won the 1930 Brooklands 500-mile race at an average speed of 83.42mph! The Nippy, the Chummy and the Swallow complete the Austin brood, with a good example of a 1923 Austin 12 looking like a mother hen surrounded by her lively chicks.

The Rileys make their presence felt with a sporting Redwing of striking polished aluminium body and uncovered engine, and an exciting 1929 two-seater British racing-green

An eighties photograph of the thirties: a corner of the Bourton Motor Museum. The car is an Austin Swallow, William Lyons' first venture on four wheels which led on to the Jaguars. Photo: Bourton Motor Museum.

Brooklands Riley of the type that Freddie Dixon and Parry Thomas drove with such panache at Brooklands long ago. A 1938 Bluestreak Adelphi and a 1950 open tourer complete the Riley stable. After viewing such machines, we can go on to other things, but remembering a quotation of Victor Riley, the company's managing director, made in 1930: 'I can only continue in business as long as it holds some promise of romance. Races, trials, round-the-world expeditions – this is the romantic side of the motor industry. When it is no more, I shall retire.' The Rileys here seem to echo that sentiment.

One of the charms of the Bourton Museum is the oddities that appear as one walks round the informal display: the collection of teapots and pottery with motoring themes; the wire models of cars made by African children; the illuminated tops from the old-style petrol pumps and the authentic garage workshop with its assembly of tools, tins and bits and pieces, where we expect the mechanics to return and take up their work at any moment. All this is part of the Cavanagh idea of creating the atmosphere of the time, plus a careful selection of cars based on the theme 'Some rare, some you desired, some you knew and loved'. Families will particularly enjoy their visit: quiz games have been prepared for the children, and the pram – and the wheelchair – are not forbidden vehicles. The sales area is not large but offers a fair choice of small motoring souvenirs and books, and the owner welcomes a chat with the enthusiast though not, he says, with the fanatic.

CAMPDEN CAR COLLECTION

CHIPPING CAMPDEN is considered by many to be the most attractive and interesting of all the towns in the Cotswold Hills. It lies in a valley in their northernmost part, close to the escarpment from which there are splendid views aross the Vale of Evesham. The long, curving high street with its medieval and later buildings has been described as one of the finest in Europe. The fourteenth-century Woolstaplers' Hall is a building of great attraction with a quite outstanding timbered roof. This building, in which the staplers once did their buying in medieval times when the town was one of the chief centres of the wool trade, now houses a remarkable museum owned by two equally remarkable people, Guy and Juliette Griffiths. No one visiting Chipping Campden should fail to go and see it and it will be referred to again in this chapter, but as this book is about transport museums, the Campden Car Collection housed close by and also owned by the Griffiths family must have our attention first.

The cars are Guy Griffiths's personal collection of twenty racing and sports cars from the period 1927–63. They are all in original condition as they might have been seen in the paddock or car park of a pre-war or early post-war race meeting. Mr Griffiths is clearly a 'Jaguar man' and the heart of the collection is a unique group of racing and sports cars from this stable. First on the grid, as it were, is a 1955 D-type, the most successful of all racing Jaguars; the journal *Road and Track* said of it, '. . . This is the best performing automobile we have ever tested and we've tested some very potent machinery. An acceleration from a standstill to 60mph in under 5 seconds, or to 100mph in just

over 12 seconds is startling enough, but this is combined with a genuine top speed of 162mph!' Like the C-type before it, the D-type was built to win Le Mans and this it did three times in succession. This particular car, driven by Captain Ian Baillie, took a number of records at Monza in April 1957, including one hour at 141mph. An earlier C-type stands next to it, the first real racing car made by Jaguar and the type that won at Le Mans first time out in 1951, averaging 93.49mph and by a clear 67 miles. The Mercedes 300SL intervened in 1952, but the C-type came back strongly in 1953 with a record of 105.85mph. The Campden car is an early model and said to be the original number one.

No Jaguar collection can call itself such without an XK120 and an E-type, and both are here. In 1948 the 120 appeared and astounded the motoring world with its combination of sporting performance, saloon-car comfort and extraordinary low price. The E-type made perhaps an even greater impression when launched in 1961 and even the non-motoring public grew to realize that a world classic had arrived. This beautiful car is well represented at Campden by the actual prototype for the production run and one of the twelve light-weight models that were produced made entirely of aluminium. This particular car was raced by Salvadori and held the Silverstone sports-car lap record in 1963 at 102.9mph.

Other Jaguars and Jaguar engines feature in the collection, but we have been spoilt by the E-type and should, perhaps, move on, and to what better than Alfa-Romeos, Bugattis and a Hotchkiss? The Alfa-Romeo is an eight-cylinder Le Mans car and one of nine built by the

A line-up of Jaguar cars from the Campden Car Collection. Photo: Guy Griffiths, Motofoto.

company between 1931 and 1934. The catalogue of the collection suggests that this particular car, driven by Nuvolari and Sommer, won the 1933 Le Mans. A Bugatti Type 44 of 1928, a magnificent and reliable touring car, and a 1930 Type 46 which has often been called the 'Baby Royale' as the design and general layout is very similar to the legendary 15-litre Royale, represent *'le pur-sang des automobiles'*. The Hotchkiss is a Grand Sport model of the type that won at Monte Carlo in the thirties, the forties and the fifties! This particular car is thought to be one of the works team cars of 1939.

From another foreign manufacturer of note come three Lancias, a 1929 Lambda with the later fabric body, an Augusta, the first Lancia small car which gained fame in 1936 by taking the first three places in the Targia Florio race and also served as a taxi in its native land (this possibly accounts for the impression given by most Italian taxi drivers of being racing drivers at heart), and a 1929 Dilambda. Finally, amongst other fine cars, the 3.4 Healey Silverstone Jaguar must be singled out for special mention.

At the 1965 Dragfest at Blackbushe it made the fastest time, driven by a lady driver – Miss Penny Griffiths.

The Campden Car Collection is what it says it is. It is not a museum but one man's devotion to the miracle of the motor car and his determination to preserve some memories of it.

On leaving, have lunch or tea, if the mood takes you, at one of the excellent restaurants or cafes in the town, but do not fail to visit the Woolstaplers' Hall Museum run by Mrs Griffiths, for here, as the saying goes, is something completely different and far from the days of the Jaguar and Bugatti. Brought together in this beautiful building is a fascinating collection of items from the past: old gramophones, apothecary bottles and containers, militaria, toby jugs, old typewriters and cameras, woodworker's tools, farmhouse equipment, country clothing, and much more. It is as though one has stepped into the crowded loft of the largest country house. It is another delight in a delightful town.

DONINGTON COLLECTION

THE DONINGTON COLLECTION is housed adjacent to the Donington Park Circuit which in the late thirties was the scene of some of the most enthralling motor racing ever staged. In 1931 motor cycles had been allowed to race round a 2-mile circuit on the park's winding rural tracks and this first meeting had attracted a large and enthusiastic crowd. On 25 March 1933 cars raced on it for the first time, making Donington the first road-racing circuit on the British mainland. By 1935 the track had been improved and extended to accommodate Grand Prix motor racing and in that year Richard Shuttleworth won the maiden race in a 2.9-litre Alfa-Romeo with Earl Howe in a Bugatti in second place. In 1936 an Alfa-Romeo won again with the brilliant but ill-fated Richard Seaman driving.

The years 1937 and 1938 saw the entry of the incredibly powerful Mercedes-Benz and Auto-Unions which swept all before them. The Second World War brought racing to an end at Donington Park and for many years afterwards its occupancy by the army prevented any revival. (Displayed in the museum is a fairly terse letter from the War Office explaining the reasons – it is signed by Field-Marshal Montgomery of Alamein.) The Field-Marshal was however, opposed by a former private in his Eighth Army, Bernard 'Tom' Wheatcroft, who had driven tanks in Europe and the Middle East and as a small boy had been amongst the 80,000 spectators at the last Donington Grand Prix in 1938. After the war he built up a successful building business and became determined to bring racing back to Donington. When the army finally vacated the land, he bought the estate

and began the long and expensive task of restoring the derelict circuit to the standard necessary for modern motor-cycle and motor-car racing. His own small collection of racing cars formed the nucleus of the magnificent display which is now on exhibition at Donington. Visitors to the collection who go on practice or meeting days will have the scene set for them most appropriately as the whine of engines at speed on the circuit is heard and the pungent aroma of methanol, rubber and oil is caught on the breeze.

Since its opening in 1973 the Donington Collection has grown, until today it exhibits over one hundred cars, engines and motor cycles, plus a mass of racing memorabilia and innumerable special displays and photographs. The cars come from a broad cross-section of the world's most famous manufacturers, such as Ferrari, Lotus, Mercedes-Benz, Auto-Union, BRM, Maserati, McLaren, Cooper, Delage – the list is immense. Broadly speaking, the cars fall into three main groups: the classical wide-cockpit racing cars of the pre-1932 period, the great front-engined true single-seat racing cars which evolved from the 'Monoposti' Alfa-Romeos of 1932, and finally the mid-engined modern racing cars built since 1959 evolving into the winged wide-tyred cars of the contemporary 3-litre Formula introduced in 1966 and still running today.

The Donington Collection is set out in three main halls in a large single-storey building. It is a wonderful surprise for anyone the least interested in fine cars and magnificent engineering to be confronted, as they enter the first hall, with the three low, sleek and powerful machines that introduce the collection. The first is the Delage formerly owned by Earl Howe and Malcolm Campbell, but which is principally associated with Richard Seamen who bought it in 1936 when it was already nine years old and drove it to many victories, including a 200-mile race at Donington Park itself. The second car is a 1951 Ferrari and the first racing car bought by Tom Wheatcroft. It is a good example of the early Ferrari EP cars. The third is also a Ferrari, a 1952–3 Tipo 500, a type of racing car that was one of the most successful ever produced. In 1952, for instance, Tipo 500s won Albert Ascari the six Grands Prix he entered, and the one he missed was won by his team-mate Tarruffi, also in a Ferrari. The presence of these three cars, one all black, one all green, one all red, quickens the pulse and sets the pace.

Amongst the other exciting cars in this hall are two that can be singled out. They are from different eras, but both remarkable in their technical innovations in the search for speed. The first is a twenties open-tourer Bentley which, after considerable modification by its owner in 1972, averaged 158·2mph over a two-way run on a Belgian motorway to become the fastest ever of its marque. Bentley purists may demure at the modifications that have been made to this car; no one will deny a remarkable engineering achievement. The other car is also controversial, or was when it entered – and won – the 1978 Swedish Grand Prix. This Alfa-Romeo-engined Brabham-built car had a high-speed fan at the rear, the function of which was the subject of considerable argument between the Brabham team and their competitors. Unluckily for Brabham, the car was subsequently banned by the international racing authorities. The technical story is well told and the car can be closely inspected.

The other two main halls are named after two racing drivers who, obviously, are heroes of Mr Wheatcroft's, as indeed they must be to anyone who saw them in action or knows of their exploits. They are the Italian Lazio Nuvolari and the German Rudolf Caracciola. Many will say, and few will disagree, that Nuvolari was the world's greatest racing driver. His early racing career was on motor cycles, and he was thirty-five before he began motor racing in earnest. During his career he won the Mille Miglia twice,

'Strewth, so that's what they're like!' – Donington Park spectators on seeing the mighty German GP cars for the first time in 1937. Manfred von Brauchitsch leaps over the hump at the top of the Melbourne Rise during the Donington Grand Prix of that year in his 600hp Mercedes-Benz. The Donington Circuit, adjacent to the Donington Collection Museum, still hosts dramatic race meetings. Photo: Doug Nye.

he came first in fourteen Grands Prix and was placed in nine. A large photograph of his lean and alert face dominates one end of the hall, and his amazing record of wins achieved in nearly thirty years of racing is on exhibition.

In front of this display stands one of the collection's most prized exhibits in the form of the Maserati 8CM. This type was an outstanding car of its era and, amongst many notable successes, brought Nuvolari victory in the 1933 Belgian Grand Prix. Other interesting Maseratis are also displayed here, including two which illustrate Tom Wheatcroft's quoted aim of the museum: 'I want to show roughly the history of all motor racing, so therefore if a car's been a failure it can still be a landmark, because you can't have success without failure.' The first is what must be one of the slimmest cars ever to take the track. This Derby-Maserati was built in 1935 as a road-racing development project. Its

Racing cars of several ages on the Donington Circuit. Photo: Geoffrey Goddard.

engine is 'about-face' and drives the front wheels. It looks an excitingly dangerous car to drive and so it was – it was not successful. The second 'failure' is the 1959 Tec-Mec which was on the Maserati drawing board when its motor-racing division was closed down and was developed independently by their former chassis designer Valerio Colotti. It was entered for the American Grand Prix in 1959 but retired after seven laps and was not seen in this standard of race again. It was a brave attempt and its demise was probably the result of lack of finance rather than anything else – a not uncommon fate in the high-cost world of motor racing.

The rest of the Nuvolari Hall is given over mainly to one man, the Australian Jack Brabham. Three times World Champion and probably the most successful driver/technician in post-war racing, he was the first driver to win a Grand Prix and a World Championship in a car bearing his own name. A whole series of Brabham-related cars are displayed here in chronological order. They are engined by Repco, Alfa-Romeo and, of course, Cosworth, whose engines have been the power plants for over one hundred Grand Prix wins. The whole presentation, comprising eight cars spanning eighteen years of Formula 1 racing, illustrates vividly the remarkable design changes that have occurred in the last two decades.

The Caracciola Hall is in honour of the famous 'Rudi', the supreme Grand Prix driver of the thirties who in that decade had twice as many major wins as any other driver. Sadly, the collection does not contain one of the peerless Mercedes cars directly associated with this formidable partnership, but one Mercedes on display is a magnificent 1927 open tourer and next to it is its British counterpart and competitor, a 1929 Bentley Speed Six. The main theme within this hall is the British-manufactured single-seater racing car and it starts with seven cars from the British Racing Motors stable to represent the greatest hope and the greatest despair of the British motoring public in the fifties and sixties. Amongst the BRMs* are the P25, fiendishly fast and devilishly unstable, the mid-engined P48 with similar

*Donington has the only complete collection of all fourteen BRM models.

Tom Wheatcroft tries one of his historic cars – a 1959 BRM P25 – for size at Donington. Photo: Doug Nye.

characteristics, and the PST V8 of the type that won Graham Hill and British Racing Motors the World Championship Grand Prix competitions. Lotus is well represented, as are the Cooper cars, including the actual T60 which won the 1962 Monaco Grand Prix. Another winner is the Vanwall which, with Stirling Moss driving, won the 1958 Portuguese and Dutch Grands Prix and took second place in the French. A year earlier Moss, in a similar car, had come first in the British Grand Prix at Aintree, thus becoming the first Britain to win a Grand Prix in a British car since Segrave had won the French one for Sunbeam in 1923.

One of the pleasures afforded by the conveniently modest area taken up by the Donington Collection and its single theme is that comparisons can easily be made. For instance, by walking a few paces, Moss's Vanwall of 1957 can be compared to the collection's Sunbeam, similar in many respects to Segrave's winning machine, and its open bonnet reveals its massive 3-litre straight-light engine to be compared with the modern 3-litre Cosworth power unit shown nearby.

Throughout the halls and wide corridors of the building are special displays reflecting the triumphs and tragedies of the sport. Mike Hailwood is remembered with a display of his hundreds of motor-cycle and motor-racing trophies and some of the Honda bikes that brought him such outstanding success in the Isle of Man races. Two single items on display are the crash helmet which saved the life of Stirling Moss in the 1962 accident at Goodwood which ended his Grand Prix career and the remains of David Purley's Tec-Cosworth F1 which hit a bank at Beckett's Corner, Silverstone, at very high speed and stopped within inches. Purley is reckoned to have experienced the most severe non-fatal impact forces ever imposed on the human frame. A particularly poignant display recalls Roger Williamson, one of the most brilliant and promising drivers, who was killed in his second Grand Prix race in 1973.

Photographs abound at Donington, showing many of the epic events and the great men who took part in them. The pictures are full of action and excitement and if copies were made available for purchase by the public they would prove more popular than the modern static and garish postcards currently offered for sale.

To conclude, a warning is offered to all visitors to Donington who travel by car. The long straight of the original circuit on which those Mercedes and Auto-Unions of old reached 160mph is, in fact, now a service road on the outside of the new circuit. Drive down its narrow track and marvel at the courage and daring of Shuttleworth, Seaman, Mays, Nuvolari, Rosemeyer and the rest, but take it easy – you'll never manage to take the bend at the end as the masters did, and the escape road was ploughed up in 1940!

MIDLAND MOTOR MUSEUM

FROM A BUGATTI in bits to one of the finest collections of sporting cars in this country is the potted history of the Midland Motor Museum. A Type 43 Bugatti four-seater Grand Sports (the full catalogue description) was bought in 1947 as a rolling chassis with the engine, gearbox and all other parts in boxes. The purchaser, T. A. (Bob) Roberts, completely rebuilt it and for over thirty years it proved itself, in true Bugatti fashion, a fast and reliable sports car, capable of racing, hill climbing, sprinting and continental touring.

Unknown at the time to its owner, this machine set the pattern for the future collection. Two more Bugattis followed in the 1950s, but it was not until a decade later that Mr Roberts and his wife conceived the idea of creating a museum and, joined by Mike Barker, an engineer and sports-car enthusiast, as partner, they set out to bring together a collection of the finest sports cars of their type in the world.

'Sports car' is a general term and different people interpret it in different ways. The Roberts/Barker criterion is a machine of good design and construction, capable of over 100mph and preferably with a racing pedigree. Not everyone will agree with this definition, but it is the one adopted by the museum and sets its style. Around this nucleus of sports cars the museum has added some of the classic cars that raced at Brooklands, cars of the *grande classe* and a posse of motor cycles. It is the museum's claim that most exhibits have been stripped down to the last nut and bolt and painstakingly rebuilt and all are capable of the performance for which they were originally designed.

The collection has now found a permanent home in the converted stable block and yard attached to a fine Victorian country house just outside the picturesque Shropshire market town of Bridgnorth (which, incidentally, amongst its other charms, has an interesting inclined railway linking Low Town on the east bank of the Severn and the High Town on the west). The grounds of the house, Stanmore Hall, are pleasantly landscaped and can be freely enjoyed as part of a visit to the museum.

The reception area of the museum is well organized and equipped. There is very little of the key-ring, tea-towel, cardboard-cut-out merchandise that clutters so many museum sales areas. The books, photographs and prints are, in the main, relevant to the museum's purpose.

The conversion of the stables to suit the needs of the museum has been attractively carried out. The exterior walls, carriage houses and loose boxes were retained and the yard roofed with a structure of slim girders and glass which allows natural light to enhance the display of more than seventy-five cars. The star of the show is the 1933 24-litre Napier Railton, the last and probably the most famous of all the legendary aero-engined 'monsters' that raced at Brooklands in the thirties. Commissioned by John Cobb and designed by Reid Railton, who installed a massive twelve-cylinder Napier 'Lion' engine (a similar engine had powered Henry Segrave's beautiful 'Golden Arrow' to a World Land Speed Record of 231·4mph at Daytona Beach in 1929), it won the Brooklands long-distance races of 1935 and 1937 and holds Brooklands' fastest-ever outer-circuit lap record of 143.44mph.

One of the oldest cars in the collection is

The interior of the Midland Motor Museum at Bridgnorth. Photo: Neill Bruce.

another famous record beater, the 1925 Sunbeam Tiger which broke the World Land Speed Record in 1926 at a speed of 152·33mph with Segrave at the wheel. Malcolm Campbell and John Cobb were amongst its other drivers. Of technical interest is that it was the first racing car to be fitted with a pre-selector gearbox. Another Campbell mount is the 1929 Mercedes-Benz 38/250 TT. The car on display is the actual one he raced in the Ulster TT and at Brooklands where for a time it held the 7-litre Mountain Circuit Record. Campbell aptly described the Mercedes as 'all go and no stop'.

One of the features of the Midland Motor Museum is the manner in which models of the same marque but from different eras are placed in line. Two particular names are well represented in this respect: Ferrari and Jaguar. The former line up with five cars amongst which are the 275GTB of 1965 and its 1972 successor, the Type 365, a dramatic car with a top speed of 175mph and the capability of achieving 150mph from a standstill in just thirty seconds.

The Jaguar stable includes an XK120 which, with its good looks, excellent performance and astonishing value for money, took the motoring world by storm when it made its appearance in 1948. Also here are a C-type and a splendid D-type, epitomizing the best in the Jaguar sports/racing tradition and considered by many to be one of the world's finest sports cars. The highly successful E-type is represented, too, and the ill-fated XJ12C of which the British public had such high hopes when the coupé version entered racing in 1976. Nearly always the fastest car on the track, it suffered various teething problems and was never to realize its true potential.

To move on from sports cars, there are a

FACING PAGE
ABOVE LEFT: *The Avro 504K from the Shuttleworth Collection. Over 8,000 Avro 504s were built during the First World War and used primarily as basic pilot trainers. Photo: Shuttleworth Collection.*
CENTRE: *One of the treasures of the Shuttleworth Collection is this replica of the Roe IV triplane built in 1964 for the film 'Those Magnificent Men in Their Flying Machines' and still flown regularly. Photo: Shuttleworth Collection.*
ABOVE RIGHT: *After over one million miles in the city's service, the sole remaining tramcar is now retired at the Birmingham Museum of Science and Industry. Photo: Birmingham Museum of Science and Industry.*
BELOW: *The 1937 Dennis fire engine from the Museum of British Road Transport, Coventry. Photo: Museum of British Road Transport.*

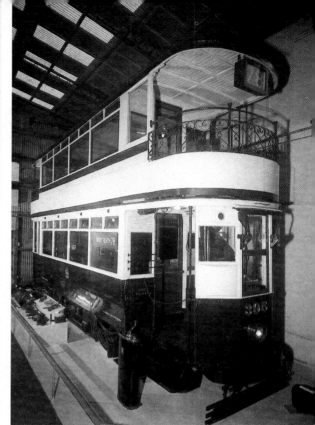

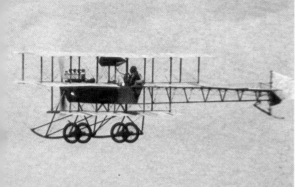

The last and most famous of all the legendary aero-engined 'monsters' that raced at Brooklands, John Cobb's Napier Railton, on display at the Midland Motor Museum. Photo: Neill Bruce.

number of *grande classe* automobiles, including a Rolls-Royce or two, but the car that catches the eye and the breath is a 1931 Type 68 V-12 Hispano Suiza. Favoured in Edwardian days by King Alfonso XIII of Spain, Hispano-Suiza always built impressive cars and this example is no exception. Superbly engineered with impeccable detail finish and endowed with the costliest coachwork, these cars were designed to satisfy the wealthiest and most demanding clients.

FACING PAGE
ABOVE LEFT: *Inside the pump house at the Boat Museum, Ellesmere Port, showing the restored steam-powered hydraulic pump. Photo: A. J. Hirst.*
ABOVE RIGHT: *The 1965 Rover BRM gas-turbine car from the Museum of British Road Transport. Driven by Graham Hill and Jackie Stewart, it competed in the 1965 Le Mans race and was the first British car to finish. Photo: Museum of British Road Transport.*
CENTRE: *A preserved Neath Canal boat at the Welsh Industrial and Maritime Museum, Cardiff. Photo: National Museum of Wales.*
BELOW: *The Lockheed T33-A 'Shooting Star' of the Newark Air Museum, an example of the finest American jet fighter to be produced in quantity. Photo: H. F. Heeley.*

An added attraction of the museum is the display of a very fine collection of motor-racing photographs from the thirties period. These prints of speedy scenes at racing tracks around the world admirably set the stage on which the dramatic machinery acts out its passive but impressive role. They are worth close study as many historic incidents are recorded.

In the museum's motor-cycle collection, many famous British names are represented: Ariel, AJS, Douglas, Matchless, Brough, Vincent, and of course Norton, and amongst the foreign contingent is an MV Augusta – sometimes termed 'the Ferrari of motorbikes' – a BMW 500 and a NSU Sport Max. It is a very good collection indeed, but it is scattered about the building which lessens its impact and increases the domination of the cars. A more cohesive presentation with additional background information would certainly enhance the total museum experience.

The owners of the Midland Motor Museum have worked hard to make a visit to Stanmore Hall pleasurable for all the family. The grounds offer idyllic picnic facilities, a bird garden housing over eight hundred birds is splendidly laid out, and the tea rooms are pleasant and homely.

MUSEUM OF
BRITISH ROAD TRANSPORT

COVENTRY'S ASSOCIATION with the transport industry goes back as far as the 1850s when a number of companies were set up to manufacture bicycles. Within twenty years Coventry had become the heart of the cycle-manufacturing industry, with more than forty separate firms making a wide range of models and involved in continuous development as improvements were made to steering, springing, gears and the tyre. This knowledge, skill and experience was readily and quickly adapted as the invention of the internal combustion engine made possible the motor cycle and the motor car and gave Coventry a head start in establishing the British motor industry which began in 1896 when H. J. Lawson formed the British Daimler Motor Company, to be quickly followed by many of the established cycle manufacturers such as Humber, Hillman, Riley, Rover, Singer and Triumph.

Considering its early history and continuous importance in transport progress, it is surprising how little the city was able to do in displaying the examples of its products. Due to the foresight of successive city councils and museum staff, much had been preserved, but it was not until 1960 when the Herbert Art Gallery and Museum opened that a limited selection could go on public display. The rest, and what was generally regarded as being the finest municipally owned transport collection in the country, remained in storage.

All this was properly put to rights, however, in October 1980 when the Museum of British Road Transport opened in Cook Street close to the city centre. Its establishment was the first phase in an ambitious programme to provide a

museum to reflect the major contribution that the Midlands area has played in the development of road transport. It has now both the material and the space to do this and should soon establish itself in the front rank of transport museums.

Although individual displays are changed from time to time the museum's general policy is to base them on a social-history theme of road transport whereby the major display items become the centrepieces but are supported by a variety of further items, such as costume, literature, models and other artefacts of the period. The positioning together of a motor car, a motor cycle and a bicycle of the same date, along with models attired in contemporary dress, is particularly useful in presenting a more rounded picture of the period, both technically and socially. The displays have also been arranged chronologically so that the visitor has the impression of walking through transport history, and each section has an information board giving the significant events of the period as well as the achievements in transport.

The first display covers the period from 1896 to 1911 and features the oldest car in the collection, a 1897 Wagonette from Daimler, which represents the first British motor car to go into large-scale production. It is in company with an 1898 Phaeton from the same firm, an 1897 Swift 'Dwarf Safety' cycle and the only surviving Payne and Bates 'Godiva' four-seater *dos-à-dos* which, although obsolescent by Daimler standards when it left the factory in 1901, still provided an interesting trip for the author on the London to Brighton run of 1976, particularly in view of the ease with which first, top and reverse gear could be simultaneously engaged! Two other vehicles of more than usual interest in this section are the 1904 Riley Tricar and the very pretty 1910 Swift light car, both products of the transition of cycle manufacturers to the building of cars.

The next grouping of vehicles covers the period from 1912 to 1925 and illustrates changes in design brought about by the war, the further development of mass production – 'motoring for the millions', as it was called – and, of course, the birth of the legendary 'Baby Austin', the Austin 7. A number of the cars produced in the early part of this period, the 1912 Crouch and the 1913 Arden, for example, are on display as evidence that cycle-construction practice still

had its influence in the design of the light car, but such companies as Morris, Rover and Humber dominate the section in the way their cars did the motoring scene at the time.

The museum is arranged on two floors, the upper section being divided into two galleries that invite visitors to divert from their chronological tour and enjoy a detailed presentation of the history of the bicycle and a display of aero

RIGHT: *An 1898 Daimler. The Museum of British Road Transport has a similar model in running order. Photo: Museum of British Road Transport.*
BELOW: *An impressive display of Daimlers outside the Daimler works, circa 1898. Daimler was the first major British car manufacturer and the Museum of British Road Transport has a number of its early products. Photo: Museum of British Road Transport.*

engines. After years of being stacked away in dusty stores, the museum's magnificent collection of cycles has now the display it deserves. The Hobby Horse, the Velocipede, the tricycle, the quadricycle, the ordinary or penny-farthing are all here with other less familiar constructions of a character ingenious, eccentric or simply hilarious. The modern cycle is represented in the main by racing models, but the side-by-side display of a 1969 Moulton and a 1903 Freak cleverly reminds us by their

ABOVE RIGHT: *The three-wheeled Crouch Carette of 1912 from the Museum of British Road Transport. The Crouch company made excellent light sporting cars during the twenties. Photo: Museum of British Transport.*
RIGHT: *The 1915 Rover 12 with doctor's coupé coachwork which is on display in the Museum of British Road Transport. The Rover company started making cars in 1904, having begun in the mid-1890s as a cycle manufacturer. Photo: Museum of British Road Transport.*
BELOW: *The interior of the Museum of British Road Transport. In the foreground is the 1910 Humber 12/20, restored to full working order in the museum's workshop. Photo: Museum of British Road Transport.*

similarities how early the bicycle came to design maturity. Is it also intended to hint that perhaps now is the time for Coventry's engineers to introduce the next development in this continuously popular form of mobility?

It may seem odd for a road transport museum to have a gallery specifically devoted to the local aircraft industry, but considering the contribution that the Coventry motor industry made to the development and production of aero engines during the Second World War, it is well justified here. At the time of writing the gallery has not established a coherent display, but the future will clearly produce a presentation of engines and components as a testament to the versatility of local industry.

To return to the chronological displays, the period up to the Second World War covers the fusion of interests whereby manufacturing was concentrated into fewer companies – General Motors taking over Vauxhall, Bentley being absorbed by Rolls-Royce, and Daimler and Lanchester merging under the control of BSA – and the enormous growth of the medium-priced, medium-powered cars from Singer, Triumph, Hillman, Austin, Morris and Ford. Many cars of this era are represented in the collection, but in the opinion of many visitors the 1933 SS One stands supreme. This delightful car is a development of the model introduced by William Lyons to an astonished and approving public in 1931 and sports the distinctive 'Lyons line' which was to be carried through all subsequent SS and Jaguar designs up to the XJ series. Coventry is rightly proud of being the home of Jaguar cars and its products are well represented in the museum, including one of the last fifty V12 E-type Series III.

The sections covering the post-war and modern years illustrate the continuing development of cars for the mass market and the moves towards the giant combines, with the demise of such companies as Lea-Francis, Jowett, Armstrong Siddeley and Lanchester followed by Riley, Singer and Alvis. The Rover company makes a spectacular appearance in this section with its T3 prototype, the more efficient development of the first practical gas-turbine-powered car which the company introduced in 1950 at the start of its long, expensive and ultimately fruitless search for a viable turbine-engined car.

Interspersed among the cars and in the appropriate eras is the motor-cycle collection of more than fifty bikes. They cover a span of eighty years from the 1897 Beeston Humber tricycle to the 1977 Triumph Bonneville. Most of the great names are here, and the tale of the rise, golden years and decline of the British motor-cycle industry is well told. The commercial-vehicle section is the one area of transport in the museum that does not yet relate a full story. There are a few buses and one or two commercial vans and lorries, but little else in the way of vehicles or historical background. This will surely come together as the museum develops and become an important part of the museum's exhibits.

The Museum of British Road Transport opened with an admirable degree of flair and enthusiasm and with the stated aim of making itself one of the best transport museums in the world. There seems no reason why this ambition should not be realized.

NATIONAL CYCLE MUSEUM

BELTON IS GENERALLY recognized as one of the most attractive country houses surviving from the Stuart period. It is situated 2 miles northeast of Grantham, just off the A1. Its location between the Midlands and the flat landscape of the Fenland is an appropriate place to find the National Cycle Museum which occupies converted stables in the grounds. It was opened in 1980 in modest style with a display of not more than twenty cycles, under the direction of its curator, Mr Ray Fixter, a lifelong cycling enthusiast and the moving spirit behind the museum's establishment. During the first six months of operation over 150,000 people visited the museum, providing a good guide to the interest in the subject and the need to expand the museum space and widen its coverage.

The aim of the museum is to present the technical and social history of the cycle and to put on riding displays to illustrate the advantages or otherwise of this mode of travel. Anyone who has seen the events organized by the various veteran cycle clubs with their members dressed in costumes of the period and vigorously pedalling their Boneshakers, Velocipedes and quadricycles will be delighted with the innovation. A workshop for restoration work is also part of the museum's brief.

As the museum is in the early stages of its development it has concentrated its presentation on the pioneer days and starts its story with replica machines: a Hobby Horse of 1820 which began the trundling history and a Kirkpatrick Macmillan bicycle which introduced pedal propulsion and gained for its constructor a place in history as the inventor of the bicycle. A lever-driven quadricycle is the oldest original cycle in the museum, but an 1864 Michaux Boneshaker is of particular interest in coming from the Michaux coachbuilding company of Paris, the first firm to produce cycles commercially. There are two other machines that make their mark but more for their oddity than their history. The first is a 1883 'Hen And Chickens' pentacycle designed for the GPO by a Mr Gibbons as an improvement on the penny-farthing, then used by postmen on their rounds. This curious cycle has one large centre wheel on which the postman perched and pedalled and one pair of smaller stabilizing wheels fore and aft. Mr Gibbons called his creation the 'Ideal', but the Post Office didn't agree and only five were made. The other curious machine is a Humber 'Eiffel Tower' cycle, popular with the young bloods of 1900 as a 'gimmick' machine. The seat is a good 12 feet from the ground! Contemporary prints show owners pedalling furiously and appearing to be thoroughly enjoying their elevated and speedy travel. Closer examination reveals the prints to be manufacturers' advertisements.

It must have been the spectacular accidents which befell these reckless riders that give rise to many manufacturers calling their product the 'Safety Cycle'. Another interesting but more practical development is the 1903 Dursley-Pedersen with its distinctive triangulated frame and unique 'hammock' saddle made of knitted and tensioned string. This light and comfortable cycle cost 19 guineas in 1899 and established itself as a 'gentleman's deluxe model'.

The National Cycle Museum has many more exhibits to illustrate the fascinating development of the cycle and others are under restoration or promised. Belton House has given the museum a good home; it has an enterprising and knowledgeable staff and it has made an excellent start in furthering its aims.

ABOVE: *The appropriately named Sociable cycle popular in the 1890s. The National Cycle Museum has well-preserved examples. Photo: Museum of British Road Transport.*
LEFT: *Ray Fixter, curator of the National Cycle Museum, mounted on a Humber High Ordinary (Penny-Farthing) of 1880 and dressed in a typical cycling club uniform of the nineties.*
BELOW: *The National Cycle Museum has possibly the only surviving example of this Post Office pentacycle. Photos: National Cycle Museum.*

NEWARK AIR MUSEUM

IN THE STEAM-RAILWAY preservation movement there are many examples of a number of enthusiasts coming together and by their own volunteer efforts building up a flourishing enterprise to save from destruction and put on public display the objects of their hobby. Such collective endeavour is not so apparent in other areas of historical transport where the establishment of museums and collections is more often the result of municipal or state enterprise or the sole commitment of an individual.

The Newark Air Museum is an exception. The air enthusiasts who pioneered it joined together in 1963 to start a movement which, ten years on, culminated in the official opening of a permanent museum on the wartime airfield at Winthorpe, 2 miles north-east of Newark. Winthorpe was an operation station during the Second World War, and it housed various different aircraft types during this period, including Fairey Battles, Handley Page Hampdens, Vickers Armstrong Wellingtons, Short Stirlings, Avro Manchesters and Avro Lancasters. There is a comprehensive photograph and model display of this period in the airfield's history in the museum's exhibition hall.

As well as being the site of the museum, the airfield is also the home of the Nottinghamshire Agricultural Society and the South Yorkshire Gliding Club. The original wartime runways are still intact and, as a result, have allowed three of the museum's aircraft to be flown in, which is the proper and most exciting way for old planes to retire. First to do so was the Percival Prentice on 8 July 1967. This was followed on 1 April 1976 by a Vickers Varsity, and the largest aircraft to land at Winthorpe since the war

arrived on 2 June 1977 in the shape of the Handley Page Hastings. A lot of the original airfield is still in existence and the actual museum site is one of the old wartime dispersals.

It is not easy for a private aircraft museum to obtain exhibits and Newark makes no claims to have an outstanding collection, nor one that shows the historical development of the aeroplane. It has collected where it could, but the inspired search and rescue operations of its members have produced some notable catches. In 1977, for instance, they dismantled a retired Avro Shackleton based at the RAF station at Fenningley and moved it by road to Winthorpe where they re-assembled it. The Shackleton is four-engined, has a wing span of 120 feet, a length of 87 feet and an all-up weight of 85,000 lbs, which gives some idea of the capability of the museum's members.

The most technically interesting aircraft on display is the Gloster Meteor acquired in 1970 from the Rolls-Royce Test Establishment where it was used for vertical lift development with a vertical-thrust engine fitted in place of its main fuel tank. It is displayed in this test-bed configuration. Another early jet fighter to see is the Supermarine Swift which, although soon eclipsed by the Hawker Hunter, was the first swept-wing jet aircraft to enter service with the RAF. Also on display is an American contemporary of the Swift in the sleek shape of the F100 Super Sabre. The development history of this aircraft type is a good illustration of the United States aviation industry at its best. The prototype was first flown on 25 May 1953 and within five months the first production aircraft took to the air. Before the end of the same year, a

A French Dassault Mystère IVA in the collection of the Newark Air Museum. Photo: H. F. Heeley.

squadron was in service with the USAAF and the F100 stayed the course in various roles into the early seventies.

In total there are some twenty aircraft on public display, with others like the curious Lee-Richards Annular biplane replica which can be viewed by prior arrangement. These will go on display as the museum area expands, but there is a large number of aviation-related items to be seen, such as engines, aircraft instruments, propellers and airfield equipment.

The Newark Air Museum is very much a voluntary organization and for this reason opens to the public only on Sundays and Bank Holidays. It also makes every effort to recruit volunteers to work on its preservation projects and the enthusiasm of its members is infectious. Many first-time visitors, who, in their Sunday best, came to look and admire, have been persuaded to return in their overalls!

ROYAL AIR FORCE
AEROSPACE MUSEUM

THIS MUSEUM IS located at the RAF station at Cosford on the A41 road between Wolverhampton and Newport in Shropshire. It is an outstation of the main Royal Air Force Museum at Hendon in London, and was opened to the public on a regular basis in 1979. Currently on display is an impressive collection of well over fifty civil and military aircraft of British, American, German and Japanese origin.

Because of their sheer size, some of the aircraft have to be exhibited out of doors. Although exterior display does not help to inhibit corrosion, the siting of these aircraft outside their hangars considerably heightens their visual effect and the line-up is impressive. Here is the oldest surviving Mark 1A de Havilland Comet of the type which provided the world's first passenger jet service in 1952. Cruising at 490mph, the Comet was able to halve the flying time of any of its competitors, but its dramatic and tragic failure due to metal fatigue is well known. Alongside the Comet are two of the famous 'V' bombers, an Avro Vulcan which was the world's first large bomber to employ a delta wing form, and a Handley Page Victor which also introduced a new concept of wing design with its crescent shape. Both these aircraft served the RAF well and many people will never forget the tremendous excitement and feeling of national pride created when they made their low passes at the Farnborough Air Shows in the fifties, particularly when on one occasion the Vulcan performed a slow roll during the course of its demonstration.

Inside the hangars are displays covering modern aviation history, including several examples of research and development aircraft which featured in the headlines not so many years ago. The Fairey Delta FD2, of which two were produced in 1956 to investigate the characteristics of flight and supersonic and transonic speed is here, as is the Bristol 188, built mainly of stainless steel to combat the enormous heat encountered in high-speed flight. The Bristol 188 never reached its design performance and the project was cancelled, but close by is another victim of a cancelled project which has been the subject of much political and technical debate ever since. The TSR2 (Tactical Strike Reconnaissance) aircraft was designed as a replacement for the Canberra. It had to be capable of carrying out strike and reconnaissance missions at supersonic speeds in any weather at high or low altitudes. The first prototype was airborne on 28 September 1964 and thirty production aircraft were ordered before the whole project was scrapped in April 1965. Whatever the merits or otherwise of this decision, the advanced navigational/attack system for low-level flying at high speeds and many other refinements put it well ahead of its competitors and were not available to the RAF until many years later when the Tornado came into service. In studying these three development aircraft, it is interesting to note how many features are incorporated in the Concorde.

OPPOSITE ABOVE: *The interior of the Aerospace Museum at RAF Cosford. Photo: RAF Cosford.* BELOW: *A museum scene the public rarely sees: 'backstage' at the Aerospace Museum. Photo: Imperial War Museum.*

In direct contrast to all this sophisticated engineering is the oldest aircraft in the museum, a Type XI Bleriot monoplane of 1909, described by one who flew it in the following terms: 'Besides being one of the most successful of present-day fliers, this machine is a comparatively simple and inexpensive one to build.' In a way it is out of place in the museum which has concentrated its efforts on collecting much later aircraft, and the Bleriot is 'waiting in the wings' until the span of the story the museum has to tell is widened. There are, as yet, no aircraft from the First World War in the museum and the Second World War is sparsely represented, but a number of the exhibits of this period are of great interest. The British line-up includes a Spitfire and a Mosquito and two types 'borrowed' from America for RAF use, a Catalina flying boat and a B24 Liberator, the latter type being developed into a useful airliner and used by BOAC on the Atlantic route immediately after the war. The world's first operational jet fighter, the Messerschmitt Me262 and the Gloster Meteor, which was the British equivalent, are also represented. Other types used by the Luftwaffe can also been seen. These include the only complete example of the Messerschmitt Me140 and the Messerschmitt Me163 rocket-propelled fighter which, with its volatile fuel, high landing speed and novel controls, claimed the lives of more Luftwaffe personnel than it did Allied.

Another rocket-powered Axis aircraft on display is the Japanese Tokosuka Okha Kamikaze aircraft. Of wood and metal construction, the Okha was designed to be launched from a specially modified Mitsubishi bomber and then make a short, piloted, rocket-engined dive on to its target. 'A very rare example', observes the museum's literature! Rarer still, as it is believed to be the oldest surviving example in the world is the Kawasaki Type 5 fighter which, in the spring of 1945 with Japan on the brink of final collapse, surprised the American B29 bombers and their fighter escorts attacking the Japanese mainland with its manoeuvrability, rate of climb and speed. Only the total destruction of the Kawasaki factory prevented it inflicting serious losses on the American squadrons. Poignantly, the aircraft is displayed in the colours of the Japanese Fifth Fighter Squadron which has special responsibility for the defence of the Japanese homeland.

Not only are aircraft on show at this museum – there is also an excellent range of aircraft engines, from the First World War rotary engine to the modern jet-power unit. The collection naturally includes the famous Rolls-Royce Merlin and the Bristol Hercules. Some of the engines are cut away to show their internal components.

The museum also exhibits a collection of rockets and missiles, probably the best in Europe. This features many of the German secret weapons, including the V1 Flying Bomb, known in Britain as the 'Doodle Bug', and the deadly V2 Rocket, against which there was no defence. Aerospace equipment includes the only example, in Britain, of the NASA-developed Moon Buggy, and there is a very fine model display which gives a comprehensive account of aviation history.

STANFORD HALL COLLECTION OF RACING AND HISTORIC MOTOR CYCLES

STANFORD, MENTIONED in the *Domesday Book*, has been the home of the Cave family, ancestors of Lord Braye, for over five hundred years. The present hall replaced the old manor house in 1690 and is a very fine example of William and Mary period architecture. The hall itself is open to the public throughout the summer and contains antique furniture, pictures, historic manuscripts and documents and an unusual family collection of antique costumes and old kitchen utensils.

The Motor Cycle Museum is housed in the stables and is claimed to be the best collection of racing motor cycles in the world. It began with an arrangement between the Seventh Lord Braye, himself a pioneer motor cyclist from First World War days, and two vintage motor-cycle enthusiasts looking for a suitable home for the many machines that they and their friends had preserved and restored. C. E. 'Titch' Allen, BEM, founder of the Vintage Motor Cycle Club and John P. Griffith, one-time president of that club, were both historians and writers and with their special knowledge were able to assemble a quite outstanding collection. Almost every machine in the collection is in running order and some are seen in action from time to time at vintage rallies and race meetings. All are on loan from owners and changes in the displays are frequent.

In order to show technical developments within a single firm, the general arrangement is to group together bikes carrying the same company name. To the casual visitor this system might be monotonous, but Stanford is in many ways a specialist museum and this serious method of presentation is very convenient to the student of motor-cycle development and racing.

The display of the Norton bikes shows this system to advantage. Norton is the only marque to have competed in every Isle of Man TT series during its production life and Stanford's oldest bike, the 6hp 1907 model, was the first Norton to appear there. Ridden by Rem Fowler, it finished first in the twin-cylinder class and made the fastest lap at 40mph. Twenty years on brings us to the next Norton specimen in the collection, the first 'camshaft' model. This 500cc bike is the type on which Alec Bennett rode to victory in the 1927 Senior TT at an average of 68.51mph after Stanley Woods had set up a new lap record at 70.90mph on a similar machine. It is a far cry from 1927 to 1960. However, the original Norton 'camshaft' design had splined couplings on the vertical driveshaft. In 1930 a change was made to the Oldham type, but after three decades, the original arrangement was reintroduced. The engine of the 1932 Norton, which is next in line, is a revamped version of the 1927 type and it was this marque which Norton developed steadily to achieve a dominance in road racing that is never likely to be equalled, let alone surpassed. Amongst the post-war models is a rare 'Beart' Norton, named after Francis L. Beart who raced and developed Nortons at Brooklands in the pre-war period and was one of the finest tuners of racing engines in the game.

The AJS stable starts with a 350cc model built for the 1914 Junior TT which, with Billy Jones aboard, averaged 43mph over $187\frac{1}{2}$ miles to finish fourth. A relatively modest performance, one might think, until the appalling state of the roads in those years is taken into account, with

Reputed to be an actual photograph of Percy Pilcher's first flight. Pilcher was the first man to fly in England, but was killed in an aerial accident on 30 September 1899 at Stanford. Exhibits connected with his flying experiments are displayed at Stanford Hall. Photo: Percy Pilcher Museum.

their rough and loose surfaces, absence of kerbs and few warning boards. At vintage motor-cycle rallies and Brookland reunions the author has met some of the veteran riders from these early days. In spite of their different personalities, shapes and sizes, one thing is common to them all: a pair of forearms and wrists of immense strength. Looking at this racing bike, typical of its age, with forks that moved only an inch or two, rigid frame and tiny tyres, it is clear that the hammering it gave to its rider was greater than that endured by any modern moto-cross king and that, apart from a good eye, some luck and more courage, a grip of steel was essential to hold the line and stay the course.

In an adjoining display is a bike which by its very name conjures up ideas of a monster model, difficult to hold and liable to buck its rider off. This is the 'Wind-Up' Bat of 1913 which possessed a powerful 770cc side-valve engine and 70mph capability. Close by are two Brough Superiors – 'fifty-one firsts in a row and then the backside torn out of my trousers' was George Brough's own terse account of the outstanding

run of success achieved by him on his 1922 1000cc sprint and hill-climb machine displayed here. Next to it is the 1930 Brough outfit built by Ted Baragwanath – another spirited racing man of the era – who took the most powerful racing engine marketed for motor-cycle use and supercharged it! At Brooklands it swept all before it, lapping the banked circuit at well over 100mph. After Baragwanath's retirement in the early thirties, the combination was sold to Noel Pope who installed a later engine and finally set the Brooklands lap record at 106mph with sidecar and 124mph solo. After an unsuccessful attempt on the world record at Bonneville it was rebuilt by C. E. Allen in the original vintage trim that it displays today.

BSA is represented by two bikes spanning forty years in a 1913 500cc and a 1954 250cc. Douglas also has two models here, a 350cc twin – 'a twin is best and Douglas is the best twin' ran the 1914 slogan, and at the time many people agreed when this lighter model of the vibration-prone 500 single appeared. Its partner is the 1928 500 twin which was very competitive at Brooklands and in a slightly modified form completely dominated speedway racing for a period. Sunbeam, Triumph, Scott, Rudge and many other famous manufacturers are represented and all have their claims to fame, but mention should be made particularly of the 1960 500cc Velocette which is classified by the museum as its best 'good old has-been'. Powered by the push-rod single-cylinder Venom engine, the machine was belted round the Montlhery track near Paris by a team of six riders to cover 2,400 miles in twenty-four hours.

The motor-cycle collection at Stanford is in its content quite magnificent. It is supplemented by an absorbing photographic display covering the whole period of motor-cycle racing history. Many visitors may feel that the exhibits are too crowded and that not enough information is given *in situ*, but it is probable that these matters will be attended to, as enthusiasm for the development of the collection is clearly evident.

Apart from its association with racing motor cycles, Stanford Hall has a direct connection with a major incident in the history of aviation. It was here on 30 September 1899 that Lieutenant Percy Pilcher, RN, crashed whilst flying his experimental glider and received his mortal injuries. Pilcher was a friend of the Sixth Lord Braye who gave him the facilities at Stanford to pursue his flying experiments which led him to become the first man to fly a controlled flight in England. At the time he had designed a triplane which was fitted with a propeller and light oil engine designed by Gordon Wilson. Percy Pilcher's death ended the possibility that he might have been the first man in the world to make powered flight. His original Hawk glider is displayed in Edinburgh, but Stanford has an excellent replica as a memorial to this brave and inventive man who, in the words of the jurymen at the inquest, 'lost his life in perfecting what, if he could have proved a success, would be some good to the world'.

STRATFORD MOTOR MUSEUM

'THE GOLDEN AGE OF MOTORING' is the theme of this motor museum, and how well it is carried through. Here is a unique collection of some of the finest motor cars in the world: opulent and lavish Rolls-Royces, Mercedes and Hispano-Suizas, glamorous sports and racing cars – Bentleys, Bugattis, Aston-Martins and Alvises. They are housed in a fine old school house and chapel whose walls have been decorated with vivid murals depicting scenes of English country-house splendour and Indian palace opulence, appropriate settings for this extravagant and extrovert machinery.

The Stratford Motor Museum was formed by the late Bill Meredith-Owens, a fighter pilot in the Second World War and a leading rally driver in post-war years. Inspired by his admiration for a period when both the designer's art and engineering excellence were pursued regardless of cost or inhibition, he brought together over a period of twenty years this quite outstanding collection of vintage and classic cars. Some of the stories of the tracking down and recovery of cars originally built for the Rajahs of India are as fascinating as the vehicles themselves. To the Meredith-Owens personal collection have been added other appropriate cars on loan from individual owners and private collections.

On entering the museum, the first period setting to be seen has a backcloth of leopards, elephants and an Indian palace and a foreground dominated by a magnificently restored French-bodied Hispano-Suiza which was specially commissioned by the Maharajah of Alwar in 1929. The car was a wedding present to the Maharajah's son and was reputedly used as a panther-hunting car. Sceptics may care to note that it carries very large adjustable spotlamps, just in front of the windscreen pillars, with extendable arms which presumably allowed them to be fixed on the prey. Most interestingly, an independent 24-volt generating system was installed to take care of the additional electrical load, a separate generator being fitted under the seats and driven by a belt from the propeller shaft! When found in India, the car was in a most neglected state both externally and mechanically. In particular its aluminium cylinder block, especially vulnerable to corrosion, was found to be irreparable. It took over a year's search through Europe and America to unearth a replacement unit.

The association with India is continued with two other cars also specially commissioned, both Rolls-Royces. The first, a 1926 Phantom I,

FACING PAGE

ABOVE LEFT: *An interior shot of part of the RAF Aerospace Museum at Cosford showing, in the foreground, a Messerschmitt Me163 Komet rocket-powered fighter which had some spectacular successes when it came into service with the Luftwaffe in 1944. Photo: RAF Aerospace Museum.*
ABOVE RIGHT: *Two rare exhibits at the RAF Aerospace Museum at Cosford: the only surviving Kawasaki Type 5 Japanese fighter of the Second World War and, in the background, a Catalina flying boat. Photo: RAF Aerospace Museum.*
BELOW: *The restored warehouse by the Trent and Mersey Canal at Shardlow, Derbyshire, where the story of the history of canals, their building and the people who worked and lived on them is excellently told. Photo: E. P. Wannamaker.*

was ordered by HE Nawab Wali-ud Dowla Bahadur, the Prime Minister of Hyderabad State, India. The body is an outstanding example of the work of Barkers, who specialized in barrel-sided open tourers at that time. The whole body is finished in highly polished natural aluminium and it is a tribute to the craftsmen of the time that every area is free of imperfection. One can easily imagine how its brilliantly polished surface reflected the bright sun of India and, coupled with the colourful clothes of the Nawab and his entourage, made a most spectacular scene. The car was used on many state occasions by the Viceroys of India and many other distinguished visitors, including King Edward VIII. After the partition of India in 1948, its state duties ended, and it was left neglected in the palace garage until discovered by Bill Meredith-Owens.

The other Rolls is a 1934 Phantom II commissioned by the Maharajah of Rajkot to replace his previous car, a 1908 Silver Ghost, which had given twenty-eight years of faithful service. The flamboyant torpedo cabriolet was specially constructed by Thrupp and Maberley Ltd, the outstanding coach builders of that time, and has highly polished aluminium wings and bonnet, and saffron paintwork, a colour chosen for its religious significance in the Hindu world. Technically, the car is very interesting as it is fitted with one of a small series of high-lift camshaft engines. These were introduced short-

ly after the death of Sir Henry Royce and were subsequently discontinued when it was realized that Rolls-Royce customers preferred the traditional Rolls-Royce silkiness and smoothness as opposed to higher output and loss of flexibility. A surprising feature of this car is the auxiliary headlamps connected to the steering so that the beams follow winding roads. Another novel lighting feature is the pair of yellow-glassed sidelights on the scuttle which were only lit when the Maharajah himself entered the car, so that his subjects might know the the royal presence was within.

The elegance of the Golden Age is captured in another setting which presents a Lagonda V12 Roadster Rapide in a thirties picnic scene in the English countryside. The Lagonda V12, whose illustrious career was cut short all too soon by the outbreak of war in 1939, was most certainly the culmination of the preceding two decades of grand sports tourers. To appreciate the significance of this car in the context of its time, its origins must briefly be considered. For the Lagonda Company, who were on the brink of folding in the early thirties, it was a lucky day when Rolls-Royce took over their rival Bentley, for W. O. Bentley, the brilliant designer of the cars that bore his name through the twenties and thirties, found himself unable to realize his desire for high-performance design beneath the more restrained control of his new masters. Thus when the opportunity arose to move to the Lagonda Company as chief designer in an attempt to revive their ailing fortunes, he seized the chance wholeheartedly. Immediately his modifications to the existing $4\frac{1}{2}$-litre Meadows-engined Lagonda made dramatic improvement; the company's fortunes revived and the opportunity was created for W. O. Bentley to realize his long-considered dream of mechanical perfection – a wholly original $4\frac{1}{2}$-litre V12. This car reached the show stands in 1937. Its innovative design, extensive use of light alloys and superb workmanship soon established its reputation as the finest luxurious high-performance car of its day. W. O. Bentley himself regarded it as the pinnacle of his achievement. The example of this marque seen in the museum carries Bentley's favourite coachwork, the company-designed 'Rapide Coupé'. The outstanding elegance of the bodywork speaks for itself:

compared to the perfection of its sweeping line, even the Rolls-Royce might appear a little vulgar!

Another car representing a classic compromise between the twin demands of high performance on the one hand, and comfort and manageability on the other, is the museum's 1937 Aston-Martin 2-litre Speed model. Although the Aston-Martin racing buffs were, at the time, not impressed by this concession to comfort in a marque of such fierce sporting pedigree, it was very popular with the public – at least with those members who could afford one.

The panache and excitement of the racing days of the Golden Era are recalled by the pack of Bugattis in the displays: a Type 35, undoubtedly the classic Grand Prix racing car, heads this stable, as the Speed Six and the Supercharged $4\frac{1}{2}$-litre lead the Bentleys. 'The fastest lorries in the world', Ettore Bugatti called them, and here, given the opportunity of comparing them with his own elegant products, we can see what he was getting at.

The Stratford Museum has a congenial arrangement with private owners of other exotic and interesting cars that enable it to change its displays from time to time and show vehicles that would not normally be seen by the public. The trouble which it has taken to evoke the atmosphere of the time, its splendidly reconstructed 'vintage' garage, its collection of advertising signs and paintings, its well-stocked bookshop and the sheer raciness of the whole show will excite any motoring fan. 'The spirit of the time shall teach me speed,' said the bard born not more than 200 yards away, possibly anticipating this Golden Age of Motoring.

TRAMWAY MUSEUM

THE TRAMWAY MUSEUM at Crich, near Matlock in Derbyshire, was set up to keep alive a form of urban transport which has almost disappeared from British streets but which played a major part in the development of the Victorian and Edwardian city. The origins of the museum go back to 1948, when a group of tramway enthusiasts paid a farewell visit to Southampton Tramways and decided to purchase one of the old open-top trams on which they had toured the system. From this pioneering act in the field of transport preservation developed the Tramway Museum Society, recognized as an educational charity, whose volunteer members have built and operate the open-air museum at Crich.

The museum collection, which totals over forty trams, has been chosen to depict the development of the British tram from its beginnings in the horse-car era to the final prototypes built for an extensive modernization programme in Leeds in the 1950s which was never implemented. The earliest cars in the collection are two horse trams, both over one hundred years old, one of which, built in Birkenhead in 1873 for export to Portugal, resembles very closely the trams with which the American pioneer, George Francis Train, had opened his tramways in Birkenhead and London in the 1860s.

The steam tram era, which overlapped that of the horse tram, is represented at Crich by a Beyer Peacock steam tram locomotive, built in 1885 for experimental use in Australia. It then returned to Britain, and after many years as a works shunter, came to Crich in 1962. A double-deck passenger trailer, originally in service in Dundee, is in with the locomotive.

It was, however the electric tram which made the greatest impact on the Victorian city, and the museum collection spans a period of development of nearly seventy years from 1884 to 1953. The earliest tram of this type on display at Crich carried its first passengers in Blackpool in the Victorian era and served Blackpool tramways in various guises before being restored for the seventy-fifth anniversary of the system. This early tram originally drew its current from an underground conduit – a system which remained in use in central London until the closure of the London tramways in 1952. The familiar overhead wire first appeared in Leeds in 1891 and this method of current collection soon spread to other British systems as they replaced their steam and horse cars with electricity at the turn of the century. One alternative method of current collection is on display at Crich – a series of metal studs fixed in the road surface which were energized only when a tram passed over them.

The electric tram continued to expand in Britain until the 1920s and the Crich collection includes double- and single-deck cars, cars with open top decks or open balconies, as well as early closed cars which all date from this period. By the end of the 1920s the overall number of trams and tramways in Britain had begun to decline, although some cities continued to extend their systems and modernize their trams. Prominent among these were Glasgow, Sheffield and Leeds and examples of their designs are to be seen at Crich. The prototype of what was to have been the new standard tram of the London County Council is also here – a lone survivor, since policy changed before any more trams of this type were built. The three post-war cars on display – again from Glasgow, Sheffield and Leeds – demonstrate how far the tramways had contracted and served their native cities only briefly before being pensioned off in favour of the all-conquering diesel bus.

From its early beginnings, however, the Tramway Museum was intended to be a living demonstration of the tramway and not merely a static memorial to the past. After many years of search, the infant Tramway Museum Society located in 1959 what was then a disused quarry in which it could not only assemble its collection, but also construct an operating tramway line. Using track recovered from depots due for redevelopment and from long-forgotten sidings, the slow process of building a new tramway began. Part of its route lay along the line of a mineral railway built by the great railway pioneer, George Stephenson, to link the Crich limestone quarry with the North Midland Railway which he was building through Ambergate, and some of Stephenson's buildings were adapted to museum use.

It soon became clear that the museum would have to provide extensive covered accommodation to protect its precious relics from the extremes of the Derbyshire weather, and over the years a complex of depots and workshops has been erected. These workshops were to prove their value when the Government announced its Job Creation Programme, for they gave the museum the opportunity to provide much-needed temporary employment as some of its collection was painstakingly restored to its original condition. It was the Job Creation Programme, too, which enabled the museum to add the most spectacular section of its tramway – a 500-yard extension which took the trams round the side of the hill, giving visitors new and spectacular views over the Derwent Valley.

This extension won for the museum a British Tourist Authority 'Come to Britain' Award – a far cry from the early pioneering days when a handful of enthusiasts toiled against the odds in a derelict and unsightly quarry.

While the chief purpose of the museum was, and is, to demonstrate the tramway, it has adopted a programme of development which involved creating the type of townscape through which the trams used to run. Over the years, therefore, the museum has collected not only trams and tramway equipment, but also stone sets and flagstones, gas lamps and other street furniture, and even buildings. The most striking of these is the façade of the original Assembly Rooms from Derby, a scheduled Ancient Monument, donated by the municipality when it was found to be in the way of a modern development. It not only forms the impressive centre of the museum street scene but also houses, in new buildings at the rear, a library devoted to the history of the tram. The street project has also included a bandstand from a park in Stretford, Greater Manchester, while at the Wakebridge stop of the tramway visitors can leave the tram to see the museum's power station. At the same point the Peak District Mines Historical Society has built a display relating to the local lead-mining industry, of which Crich was once an important centre.

The Tramway Museum is a living museum in two senses: first, it demonstrates its exhibits in motion, doing the task for which they were designed; second, it continues to develop – plans for the street scene are still being realized, and the tram fleet is subject to continual change as newly restored trams enter service while others, which have carried thousands of Museum visitors – many on their first tram ride – are withdrawn for overhaul and restoration.

OPPOSITE ABOVE: *Third Avenue streetcar which ran in New York before being acquired by the Vienna transport undertaking as part of Marshall Aid after the war. It is now at the Tramway Museum. Photo: David Frodsham.*
BELOW: *Former Glasgow and Blackpool trams in service at the Tramway Museum. Photo: David Frodsham.*

WATERWAYS MUSEUM

HARDLY A MORE appropriate or attractive site could be found for a museum than that of the Waterway Museum at Stoke Bruerne in Northamptonshire. It is housed in a converted warehouse at the head of a series of six locks on the Grand Union Canal and just south of the Blisworth Tunnel* which, at 3,075 yards, is now the longest tunnel on the British Waterways system. With its towpath cottages and flower gardens, the thatched Boat Inn, the hump-backed bridge and the church on a wooded hill just above, Stoke Bruerne is one of the prettiest places in the Midlands. The section of canal on which it stands was originally the Grand Junction Canal, and later, as the Grand Union, linked Birmingham and the Potteries with the distant Thames and the London docks. Construction started in 1793 and great problems were encountered before the canal's completion in 1800. Blisworth Tunnel was opened five years later, and until the whole route was opened, goods were transhipped at Stoke Bruerne, taken over the hill by a horse tramway and reloaded into boats on the completed section of the canal on the other side.

Relics from almost every part of the canal system in England, Wales and Scotland, augmented by many gifts and loans from private collectors, went to the making of this instructive and entertaining museum, which was opened in 1963. The indoor displays in the converted grain warehouse are arranged on three floors, and the showing of the relics is supplemented by photographs, prints and drawings to illustrate the construction of the canals and the part they played in the economic life of the country, and to relate something of the people who lived and found their livelihood on the waterways.

OPPOSITE ABOVE: *The Waterways Museum at Stoke Bruerne reviews the history of two hundred years of British canals. Photo: British Waterways Board.*
OPPOSITE BELOW: *The* Sunny Valley *narrowboat at the Waterways Museum. Splendidly restored both inside and out, her picturesque appearance may give a false impression of the hard life of the boat people. Photo: British Waterways Board.*
BELOW: *The Measham Teapot in the collection of the Waterways Museum. This kind of highly decorated ware was greatly prized by narrowboat folk. Photo: British Waterways Board.*

*In 1981 Blisworth Tunnel was closed indefinitely because of roof falls.

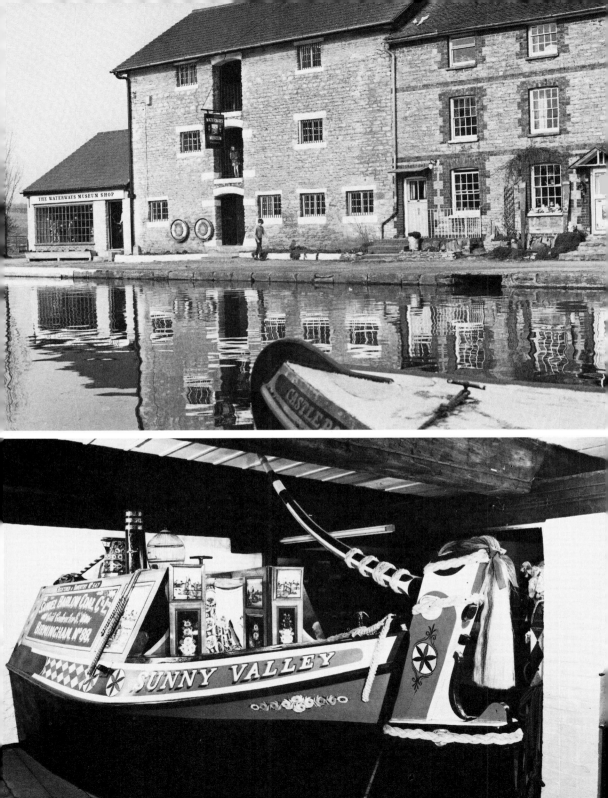

This latter aspect is one of the most fascinating subjects in the museum. There is a full-sized model of a typical narrow-boat cabin which was 'home' to a boatman, his wife and family. Visitors will marvel at the black iron cooking range, the ingenious joinery that makes use of the smallest space and the cheerful atmosphere created by the polished utensils and the 'roses and castles' painting that traditionally decorated boats and equipment. They may also be appalled at the cramped conditions that allowed no privacy and that sickness would make almost unbearable. The boat people were an insular group and formed a very close community. Their style of dress, their customs and their unique way of life are well recorded at Stoke Bruerne; so, too, are the tools of their trade such as 'legging' boards used by boatmen to propel their craft through tunnels where no towpaths ran. While the horse was walked on over the hill by his wife, the boatman and his mate would lie flat on these boards which were placed across the boat cabin top and so 'walk' the craft through the darkness by pushing with their feet against the sides of the tunnel. The length of Blisworth Tunnel justified the use of registered 'leggers' to take the boats through. These men used to await jobs in a little hut outside the Boat Inn at Stoke Bruerne. Leaving the craft on the far side of the tunnel, where the horse rejoined it, they would join another about to go through in the opposite direction.

The founders of the British canal system are well represented in the museum by portraits and documents, beginning with Frances Egerton, third Duke of Bridgewater. About 1760 the Duke commissioned James Brindley, a millwright and self-taught engineer, to construct the first industrial canal for carrying coal from his mines at Worsley to Manchester, 8 miles away. We are reminded too of how Brindley achieved something of an engineering miracle at that time by carrying his canal on a high-level aqueduct, now much altered, over the River Irwell. Other canal builders and their achievements are also recalled: for example, Thomas Telford, who spanned Scotland from east to west with the Caledonian Canal and raised spectacular monuments like the Pontcysyllte and Chirk aqueducts to carry the Llangollen Canal across the Dee and Ceriog valleys.

One corner of the museum is devoted to historical documents, plans and maps concerned with the formation of early canal companies. There were a surprisingly large number of these enterprises. The oldest of several parchment subscription lists of the first canal 'proprietors', or shareholders, is one relating to the Warwick and Braunston Canal, dated 1793.

In a disused lock alongside the canal are two fully restored traditional narrow boats. The first is *President*, one of the thirty-two steam-propelled narrow boats operated by Fellows Morton and Clayton Limited. She was built by the company at their Saltley Boatyard, Birmingham, for £600 and launched in June 1909. Most of her working life as a steamer was spent carrying manufactured goods and imported commodities on the 'fly' service between London, Birmingham, Leicester and Nottingham. This was an express run, where boats operated almost non-stop, night and day, completing, for example, the run from London to Birmingham in fifty-four hours. The second boat, the *Northwich*, was built as a horse-drawn boat for the same company and first registered in 1898 in Birmingham. She later worked as a 'butty', the non-powered half of a working pair, and in the 1940s again worked as a horse-drawn boat for the Cadbury's chocolate trade on the Shropshire Union Canal. *Northwich* was sold to the British Transport Commission when Fellows Morton and Clayton ceased trading in 1948, and continued cargo carrying in the north-west until the 1960s. She was selected for preservation as the oldest boat still in work and along with *President* was restored to her original condition.

The last steam narrow boat finished trading around 1930 and so it was that considerable delight was given to canal-boat enthusiasts when, in May 1980, *President* towed *Northwich* from the Walsall boatyard where they were restored to Stoke Bruerne in the traditional pairing manner that had not been seen on the canals for fifty years. Indeed, the museum's policy is to ensure that these beautiful boats from time to time journey to other parts of the canal system and such a plan is just one example of how this attractive and instructive museum tells its story.

VI
WALES

TOM NORTON COLLECTION
OF OLD CYCLES AND TRICYCLES

TOM NORTON WAS born at Newtown in 1870 and lived to be eight-five. Apprenticed at the age of sixteen, he earned a shilling a week while learning the ironmongery business. A keen cyclist, Norton would frequently ride the 27 miles to the then fashionable spa of Llandrindod Wells, grew to like the town and in 1898 set up in business there as a cycle retailer. He was one of the first Raleigh agents and by 1904 guaranteed all the bicycles he sold for three years, repaired punctures free for the first season and allowed the return rail fare to purchasers living within a 100-mile radius. Such commercial acumen ensured his success and he went on to develop a large motor agency which still flourishes under the long-established and splendid title of the Automobile Palace. It still retains the Raleigh cycle agency.

Throughout his life Tom Norton remained interested in cycling and cycles and the collection he built up is now on display at the company's premises in the centre of Llandrindod Wells. It is made up of some twenty machines dating from 1867 to 1938. The earliest are three examples of the Velocipede, also known as a 'Pickering', Michaudine' or 'Boneshaker', and when looking at the sturdy but unsprung design it is easy to imagine which name was the most popular! Another early cycle is the Coventry-manufactured 'Ariel' or 'Spider' of 1870, which was considered by most historians to be the first real bicycle and represented the first attempt to produce a light all-metal machine. It was also the first bicycle to be fitted with tyres of solid rubber. Some three years elapsed before the appearance of the 'Ordinary' or 'Penny-farthing', which is most people's idea

of an old cycle, but at the time this, in spite of its grotesque appearance, was considered to be an advance on its predecessors the Velocipede and the Ariel. There are two good examples of the Penny-farthing in the collection and also an example of the first safety cycle (c. 1886) designed by J. K. Starley, one of four well-known Coventry brothers. Originally catalogued as a 'Rover', it has since been confirmed as a clever contemporary copy, known as the 'Juno'. 'Safety' is an apt description, for it has direct steering, wheels of equal diameter and chain wheel drive and was offered with cushion tyres. Gone were the hazards of mounting, dismounting, or actually riding an 'Ordinary'.

An ingenious 'Quadrant' tandem tricycle (c. 1879) creates much interest. The riders are seated one behind the other. Steering is effected through a small (front) wheel and, like the brake on the rear axle, can be operated by either or both riders. Democratic though this system may be, one cannot help but wonder how it functioned in practice – particularly when two equally firm-minded riders were aboard!

The collection also contains two Dursley-Pedersen cycles (1897–1902) designed by a Dane and manufactured by R. A. Lister & Co. Ltd., of Dursley. Their light triangulated frames are quite intriguing in any study of the cycle.

There are three cycle exhibits from the first decade of the twentieth century – two lady's Raleighs of 1902 and 1905 and a gentleman's Lea Francis (1908). They demonstrate the evolution of the earlier 'modern' bicycle.

A Kendrick tricycle made in 1938 to special order for Tom Norton is regarded as a family treasure by his son. It has twin front wheels and

Ackerman steering. Unlike the conventional tricycle with twin rear wheels, it will not readily overturn and Tom Norton rode it half a mile to and from his office until just before his death in 1955. During the Second World War the Kendrick Cycle Company made many of these machines for the government at their Reading factory as substitutes for the 'Invacar'.

The Tom Norton Collection is not a complete history of cycling, nor it is an outstanding exhibition of bicycles. Its charm is that it represents one man's interest in, and admiration for, the humble bicycle. The pleasure he gained in building it up can be shared by those who go to see it.

WELSH INDUSTRIAL
AND MARITIME MUSEUM

DURING THE 1950s and 1960s there were many major changes in industry in Wales, both in the machines and engines used and in the social and economic backgrounds of the people who worked them. There were also changes in maritime activities around the coast of Wales but the major changes here had already taken place some years before. There was thus a need to preserve and record these industrial and maritime changes and this resulted in a proposal to establish the Welsh Industrial and Maritime Museum. A suitable site was found in Cardiff Docks and the present purpose-built building was erected and duly opened in 1977. This building was intended as the first stage of a long-term development and the major exhibits in it were deliberately restricted to examples of the engines or prime-movers used in or having an association with industry in Wales.

The principal exhibits within the building are various types of steam, gas and oil engines, some of which are always operated in keeping with the museum's policy of having, as far as is possible, all its exhibits in working order.

The transport items on display include examples from road, rail, sea, canal and air. Starting with road transport, the oldest vehicle in the collection is a horse-drawn bus which was operated by the Andrews Star Omnibus Company in London from 1892 until 1909. The Andrews Company was a Cardiff-based organization with widespread commercial and transport interests and it is still in existence today. After seeing service with different companies, the bus finally failed its annual licence inspection in 1949 and finished up in use with Bertram Mills Circus as a bandstand. It was then acquired by a member of the Andrew family who restored it to its present fine condition.

The motoring era followed closely behind the horse bus and the first really successful mass producer of cars was Karl Benz. In the collection is an example of one of Benz's larger and rarer cars, a 1900 Ideal. It is interesting to note that this car, as with Benz's other models, had features such as face-to-face seating, a rear-mounted, horizontal, single-cylinder engine with an open crank, 'handle' steering and belt transmission – features which were already becoming obsolete in 1900. It illustrates well why the sales of Benz cars fell off sharply and it was the amalgamation to form Daimler-Benz, later known as Mercedes-Benz, which ensured the survival of the company. This particular car was in store from 1910 until 1978 and, after a mechanical overhaul in the museum workshop, has twice successfully participated in the London-Brighton Veteran Car Rally.

At the other end of the motor-car spectrum is a Gilbern Mk II which is a representative of the only car manufactured in Wales in significant numbers. Regarded very much as a car for the connoisseur, this model has a fibre-glass body and a 3-litre V6 engine. An example of another Welsh manufacturer was Bown of Llwynypia, which produced large numbers of autocycles over the years, until this type of vehicle fell into disfavour and was replaced by the moped. One of the Bown autocycles has recently been restored and is now on display.

Passenger transport is represented by a trolleybus and a Crossley oil-engined bus, both of Cardiff Corporation Transport. Trolleybuses disappeared from the streets of Cardiff in 1970 and, although their silent and pollution-free electric motors prompt many people today to advocate their return, the inflexibility of the overhead wire system is likely to prevent their reintroduction in this form. The narrow valleys in parts of South Wales resulted in roads frequently having to pass under railway lines with very limited height clearance for double-deck buses. One way of overcoming this problem was to locate the top-deck gangway to one side of the bus and to lower it below floor level, thereby allowing the roof to be made lower. The Crossley is an example of a bus with this type of body and is also one of a handful of vehicles of the make still in existence. There were many small municipal bus operators in South Wales, one of which was Gelligaer UDC. This authority has now disappeared, but a single-deck AEC Regent from its fleet is now in the collection.

Steam vehicles always have a fascination of their own, and while many visitors will remember steam rollers working on the roads, few will remember traction engines at work. The museum has an example of each type and one of the two is operated on the monthly 'Steam Days' (see below). The traction engine was made by Ransomes. Simms and Jeffries in 1921 and spent the whole of its working life on the estate of Lord Mostyn in Flintshire. It was used almost entirely for driving threshing machines and saw-benches and travelled very few miles on the road, so that the road gears are still in almost-new condition. The steam roller was made in 1948 by Aveling Barford and was one of the last to be made in this country, most of them being exported to the Far East. This model is unusual in that the rolls are hollow and can, if necessary, be filled with water to provide additional ballast. It has recently had a complete overhaul and has been repainted in its original Borough of Rhondda livery.

The museum owns a number of railway locomotives but only one is displayed on the site, the others, including a former Taff Vale Railway tank locomotive, being maintained and operated at Caerphilly by members of the local railway society. The locomotive on display in the museum is a six-coupled saddle tank by Hudswell Clarke and is typical of the multitude of similar locomotives used by industry throughout Wales. This particular engine was purchased new by Powell Duffryn in 1900 and spent its life working in collieries in Glamorgan owned by that company. As a contrast in scale, a railway ganger's tricycle, dating from about 1890, from the Barry Port and Gwendraeth Valley Railway can also be seen. This was used for track inspection and for checking the line in the event of a signal failure. Although the GWR was much in evidence in Wales, the only rolling-stock on display is a 1-ton hand crane complete with match-truck, but there is a GWR footbridge from Aberdare.

Water-borne transport is represented by three items starting with a canal boat from the Neath Canal. This was built by the canal staff in 1934 as a maintenance rather than as a cargo-carrying boat and, after lying submerged in the canal for many years, was lifted out on a special cradle and has now been restored. A very different vessel is a particularly fine sailing pilot cutter, appropriately called the *Kindly Light*, one of the last of its type to be built for use in the Bristol Channel, in 1912. These vessels would often sail as far as Lands End in search of ships needing a pilot and it is salutary to remember that, once the pilot had been transferred, they would have to be sailed back to port single-handed in any weather by a crew consisting only of a man and a boy: compare this with the crew of ten or more used on a modern racing yacht. A reminder of the vanished era of steamships is the tug *Sea Alarm* whose working life was initially in the Clyde but latterly was in the Bristol Channel when she coaled regularly at Barry. The cabins, boiler room and engine room, with its triple-expansion engine, can be visited and give some idea of what life on board a tugboat could be like.

Air transport is represented by two aircraft engines, both of which were overhauled at British Airways major overhaul base at Treforest, near Cardiff. One is a Pratt and Whitney Wasp twenty-one-cylinder engine, typical of the ultimate in aircraft piston engines, while the other is a Rolls-Royce Conway jet engine from a VC-10 aircraft. This has been sectioned by apprentices at the base so that the interior workings of the engine are visible.

Visitors should note that part of the transport collection is contained in a separate building only open to the general public on 'Steam Days', which are held on the first Saturday of every month, and to organized groups at other times by prior arrangement.

VII
THE NORTH-WEST

BOAT MUSEUM

In the height of the canal age and late into the time of the railways Ellesmere Port was one of the principal ports of the country, linking by water such important industrial areas as Birmingham, the Black Country and the Potteries with the sea and thence the rest of the world.

The beginnings of the port were conceived in the last decade of the eighteenth century with the proposals for a canal linking the Mersey with the Dee at Chester and one linking the Wrexham and Ruabon industrial areas with the sea. Ellesmere Port was born in 1 July 1795 with the opening of the Wirral line of the Ellesmere and Chester Canal. The original port was no more than a few buildings and three broad locks down to the tidal basin into the estuary. A map of 1802 shows only five buildings, a lock keeper's cottage, stables, a row of cottages, an inn and a building containing a steam-driven pump to bring water up to the canal, augmenting the supply from the Chester Canal. There was a large basin at the upper level running parallel for the full length of the locks. None of these buildings exists today, although the present toll house, stables and lighthouse at the river entrance must have been built shortly afterwards, and it is possible that the toll house, which is on the site of the original stables, was converted from that building.

The real expansion of the port to its current size was being planned in the 1820s and was the result of two new lengths of canal. One of these was a link between the Ellesmere and Chester and the Trent and Mersey Canals at Middlewich, enabling the Potteries traffic to use the port not only for the export of finished products, but also for the import of flints and china clay from Cornwall. Even more important was the link between the end of the canal at Nantwich and the Staffordshire and Worcester Canal at Autherley near Wolverhampton. This, called the Birmingham and Liverpool Junction Canal, provided a direct route between these towns through Ellesmere Port, opening up the industrial Midlands to the sea and avoiding the climb up to and the congestion through the Harecastle Tunnel.

As this new canal and those in Birmingham were narrow (taking boats whose beam was up to a maximum of 7 feet), all the cargoes had to be transhipped before going into the estuary or to sea. This new traffic required a massive increase in basins, warehouses and general facilities. Thomas Telford, who had been involved with the original developments, was asked to draw up plans for the expanded docks in 1828, his proposals being the foundation of the layout of the area as we know it today, even though many of the major buildings have subsequently been destroyed. Not only did the canal company build its extensive dock complex, but it also constructed a town for its employees to live in, and from 1816 onwards help with the financing of churches and other buildings that go to make a community was provided as well as houses. Some housing still remains, notably four houses from Porter's Row, built in 1833, and a fine Georgian terrace in Lower Mersey Street which was used for senior employees. In 1863 a gasworks was built by the company, probably to provide lighting to enable work to carry on at night. Later the system was extended to supply the town, and the pipe used for this still crosses the canal.

A gathering of narrowboats at the Boat Museum. Photo: A. J. Hirst.

The middle of the nineteenth century saw the coming of the railways that provided fierce competition to the waterways, but Ellesmere continued to prosper, particularly when the Manchester Ship Canal was opened as far as Ellesmere Port in 1891 and completed to Manchester in 1894. This enabled much larger craft to reach the port – previously, craft entering the dock had been limited by the 110×30-foot dimensions of the sea lock. Wharves were built alongside the canal, as well as another grain warehouse. Slowly, however, the railways began to assert themselves and there was a dramatic drop in trade, particularly after the First World War, and the main operating company finally gave up carrying in 1921, selling off their canal fleet and leaving just a few independent operators to continue in business.

After the Second World War traffic slumped even further, and in 1958 the docks were officially closed, though the Ship Canal Company continued to use the workshops and there still are many ships using their canal. The area quickly became derelict; many of the historic buildings have been destroyed and the land occupied by much of the old housing is now the site of the container port.

In 1974 a society that had been active in the area preserving boats and canal equipment reached agreement with the borough council to establish a boat museum on the site of the old Shropshire Union Docks, and the massive task began of reclaiming and restoring the abandoned buildings and clearing the docks and locks. The site consisted of a large basin capable of holding about thirty boats, the early nineteenth-century toll house mentioned above, a dual flight of locks and a mid-nineteenth-century island warehouse and pump house containing four steam engines and their boilers. A nucleus of a boat collection had already been built up, and restoration had been carried on from towpaths at the side of various canals by the type of hardy volunteers of all ages that are at the heart of most transport preservation projects. Amongst the early boats acquired were a 72-foot-long wooden Mersey flat now over a hundred years old and the only one of its type still afloat, the ex-Thomas Clayton tar boat, again the only one of its type in its original form, a 45-foot tunnel tug which was lying derelict on the Macclesfield Canal and a wooden Leeds and Liverpool dumb barge.

From these beginnings has grown a lively and comprehensive presentation of the history of the working of our canal system and the people who found their living on it. The collection of boats now numbers nearly thirty; the large warehouse has been completely renovated and houses the exhibition area, workshops and archives; the pump house has been restored to its previous role as the power centre of the estate and the barges and boats, with slow grace, move out into the canal system.

Much of this section has been taken up with an historical account of Ellesmere Port for the site of the museum is as much a part of the history of the town as the exhibits are of canal life and times. The founding and development of the museum is also a case history of what can be done when sympathetic local authorities respond to the enthusiasm and skill of well-organized volunteers, as is the way in which the society has gone about recruiting the public to membership and raising funds by such diverse methods as selling limited editions of Wedgwood plates and making representations to the EEC. A published account of this remarkable campaign would be a useful reference for future preservationists.

MANX MOTOR MUSEUM

THE MANX MOTOR MUSEUM is a private venture owned by Richard Evans, a Manx businessman. It was established in the early sixties at Crosby, 4 miles west of the island's capital, Douglas. Most car collections built up by one man reveal a preference for a favourite type of car or period and are properly described as a collection, but here is something more in content and wider in scope and with a better right to the title of museum. Much effort has gone into the presentation of the car in a historical sequence but no private museum has the resources or the space to cover the subject adequately, and the Manx Museum has placed its emphasis on areas not often dealt with in any detail by other museums.

Particularly interesting is the group of cars made in the United States. The earliest car is the 1904 Stanley Steamer acquired by Mr Evans in a very dilapidated condition and with many parts missing which required a tour of North America and meetings with many steam buffs to replace. In the first decade of the twentieth century, the Stanley Steamer, with its quiet engine and vibration-free movement, was a popular vehicle, but soon to be eclipsed by motor cars powered with the internal combustion engine. A look at its performance parameters reveals the reason: an hour to raise steam from cold, petrol consumption 5mpg, water consumption 1mpg and, while travelling, the need to watch boiler level, main steam pressure, main and pilot fuel pressures, oil sight glass, tank water level and – if you have time – the road.

Another technically interesting car is the 1920 Briggs & Stratton open two-seater of basic construction and claimed by the museum to be the only type of five-wheeled vehicle ever made. The fifth wheel is behind the two rear wheels and driven directly from a $\frac{1}{2}$hp motor mounted in a frame around it. The performance was unexceptional.

Much more serious – and powerful – contenders in the American car market on display are the Oldsmobile tiller-steering 'Curved Dash' and a Model T Ford. By 1905 the Oldsmobile held the volume production record for cars in the United States and was only eclipsed when the Model T Ford 'Lizzie' – its detractors called it the 'Tin Lizzie' – appeared in 1908. The 'T' on view is a 1913 version, representing what is probably the most famous car of all time.

Before leaving the American collection, a very dainty light car in the shape of the 1916 Detroit Electric should be inspected. The museum imported the car from Salt Lake City in 1978 and must be considered lucky to have found such an example in almost original condition. The Detroit Electric's advertising brochure claimed a range of 85 to 100 miles in between charges, although with the latest traction batteries kindly provided by Exide, Mr Evans is getting an average 'run' of 35 miles – mainly because of the hilly nature of the local countryside. It seems that this figure is similar to the mileage obtained by the Electricity Council with their relatively modern batch of Enfield Electrics which can get up to around 35mph, whereas the Detroit's maximum is 22mph.

A similarity in body styling to the Detroit is noticed in the elegant 1912 Napier displayed close by: this example was found in pieces in Eire and rebuilt at the museum. A car with no body at all that will attract the visiting motor historian is the chassis and 2hp engine assembly of a Way cycle car. Nothing is known about this little car; it is thought to be the only one in existence and in fact its complicated design, much of it based on motor-cycle practice, suggests that it might be a prototype that was never put into production. A Bullnose Morris and the Austin 7 are finely preserved examples of British cars that went into production in a very big way, and a pride of Rolls-Royces and Bentleys elegantly and powerfully represent the upper end of the market.

The museum has a number of other interesting and fine cars, of course, but space must be left to mention the Peel three-wheel 'Bubble Car' made in 1965, the only car ever to be manufactured in the Isle of Man. It is an attractive little thing, but the visitor who knows something of aviation history might be struck by the similarity in appearance – and possibly safety – it has to the Flying Flea.

The museum's policy is, wherever possible, to restore its cars to running order and to their original condition. Its record of rescuing and renovating complete wrecks, that others might have given up as hopeless, is admirable. 'Deplorable!' is the reaction of the owner when he hears of some abandoned or neglected machinery – and we know what he means.

MERSEYSIDE COUNTY MUSEUMS

THE TRANSPORT COLLECTION of the Merseyside County Museums is housed within walking distance of Lime Street Station and the former North Western Hotel. Both are magnificent structures and worthy of inspection by the transport enthusiast. The nearby St George's Hall is a massive and impressive building in the Greek style and, to quote Queen Victoria at its opening, 'worthy of ancient Athens'. The transport collection is found to the north of this building in the William Brown Library and Museum. This elegant structure is too small to accommodate a comprehensive transport collection and the museum has wisely confined its displays to presenting the history of Liverpool as a port and to the land transport for the Merseyside region.

The collections are housed in the basement of the museum building and the horse-drawn section is seen first. It includes three fine coaches from the 1850s, a barouche, a dress coach and a chariot; and dating from the latter end of the same century, a rare glass-enclosed wagonette. Accompanying photographs show such vehicles in local use.

Two horse-drawn commercial wagons lead to an entertaining display titled 'The Decorated Horse' which details the history of horse brasses from their origins in very early times, when horses were thought to be particularly susceptible to witchcraft and the glitter and jangle of the brasses were used to divert malign influences, to their general use after the Napoleonic Wars when they were employed mainly to decorate horses on special occasions such as fair days and, locally, May Day parades. It is interesting to note that the brasses were the property of the carters rather than the employers and were often handed down as family heirlooms.

The fire service, so important to a dock city, is represented by a Merryweather hand pump of 1888, a Shand-Mason steam pump of 1901 and a Leyland motor pump escape of 1929, all excellently preserved.

Later commercial vehicles are represented by a trio of steam wagons and a 1940 Atkinson flat wagon, and the private car by examples from opposite ends of the designer's range. Close to the former mayoral Rolls-Royce Silver Wraith stands a humble Ford Anglia but with a greater claim to fame by being the first car made on Merseyside when the Hale Wood plant opened in 1963.

The railway section covers the largest display area and with pictures and text gives an interesting history of the Liverpool Overhead Railway. It is proper that this subject should be fully covered as the Liverpool system pioneered elevated railways for urban transport. An 1892 coach from the railway forms part of the display. There is also a 1904 saddle-tank locomotive used on the Mersey docks for many years, but the pride of the transport collection is the splendidly restored steam locomotive *Lion* from the Liverpool and Manchester Railway, built in 1838. It is one of the oldest surviving steam locomotives in the world and is displayed here with replica tender and first- and second-class carriages. It was restored to steam in 1979 and took part in the 150th anniversary of the L & MR in the following year. It is a most impressive relic from Liverpool's past.

The history of the city as a port is not

neglected by the museum, but limitations of space prevent any full development of the subject and very few examples from the city's magnificent collection of ship's models are on display. No doubt the future will see arrangements between this museum and the developing Merseyside Maritime Museum for the very many marine artefacts not on view to be put on public display. Meanwhile the Port of Liverpool Gallery on the ground floor of the museum tells its story very well with pictures, photographs, models and text, and city's involvement in the slave trade in peace and war is explained. Two other items are most noteworthy: a large-scale model of the buoyage scheme of the River Mersey and an amazing 50-foot-long panorama of the Liverpool waterfront drawn by a nineteenth-century balloonist from a height of 2,000 feet.

The ambitious plan for the Maritime Museum in the city dockland is certainly a challenge to this established museum's ability to attract the public to its transport – and certainly its maritime – displays. The complementary arrangement that will have to be worked out will be interesting to witness.

MERSEYSIDE MARITIME MUSEUM

A FASCINATION for the story of man and the sea is deeply rooted in these islands and nowhere more so than in Liverpool, the city whose ships traded with every port throughout the world during the nineteenth and early twentieth centuries. As far back as 1884 a proposal for a museum specifically about Liverpool's maritime past was made by the curator of the Mayer Museum who stated that 'a marine collection would be of great local interest in Liverpool and a source of considerable attraction to visitors'. Nothing came of it, however. Perhaps the city was too busy with its current and future trade to pay much attention to its history and nearly a hundred years passed before the idea became a reality.

In 1980 a start was made to refurbish part of the neglected and derelict site and buildings that had once been the busy quays and warehouses on Liverpool's world-famous waterfront. This was the beginning of an imaginative, ambitious plan – and a brave one – by the County Council to bring about the Merseyside Maritime Museum. The location of this new museum is both ideal and appropriate. It is situated in the heart of Liverpool's nineteenth-century dockland around the two Canning Graving Docks (dry docks originally built in 1765) and the Canning Half-Tide Basin. The now restored and cobbled quaysides have many of the original dock fittings, such as cast-iron bollards, capstans and dock-gate winches, which establish an immediate link with the sailing-ship era. The massive Albert Dock warehouses (Britain's largest Grade I Listed Buildings) stand to the south, whilst immediately to the north are the internationally famous Royal Liver, Cunard and Mersey Docks and the Harbour Company buildings at Pier Head.

Because of the richness of Liverpool's maritime past and the comprehensiveness of the County Museums' collections (close to 900 ship's models and over 500 marine paintings, for instance, are in store for want of display space) the Maritime Museum is conceived on a large scale. The story it has to tell is wide-ranging and packed with detail, and rather than setting out the history of Merseyside chronologically and demanding that visitors see the whole museum to gain a complete picture, the presentation is sensibly divided into self-contained themes. Currently there are four: 'The Port of Liverpool', dealing with the docks, the Mersey estuary, social history and the experience of wars; 'Liverpool's World-Wide Links', covering emigration, the great lines and liners, the deep-sea tramps and tankers, and the slave trade; 'Ships and the Sea', presenting the development of the ship and ship-building,

OPPOSITE ABOVE: SS Aquitania *at Princes Landing Stage in 1919 preparing to leave for the United States. 'The Great Liners and the Atlantic Trade' is a section in 'Liverpool's World-Wide Links', one of the display themes of the Merseyside Maritime Museum. Photo: Merseyside County Museums.*
BELOW: *The Canning Graving Dock at the Merseyside Maritime Museum. Sir Alec Rose's* Lively Lady, *in which he circumnavigated the world in 1967–8, is among the vessels anchored there. Photo: Merseyside County Museums.*

navigation, fishing and pleasure sailing; and finally a 'Maritime Park' designed to recreate the industry and atmosphere of a real seaport with preserved vessels in the docks and traditional and sail-training ships visiting. Thus visitors intending to spend a whole day at the museum will be able to see all the themes; those with less time, however, may choose between looking at one theme in depth, or making a complete tour of the displays at a less intensive level.

At the moment economic circumstances have held back the full implementation of the grand design. What has gone ahead with vigour and imagination is a pilot scheme which is a 'mini' museum in itself and gives an exciting vision of how the whole plan will evolve.

The present arrangement starts with an illustrated quayside trail which tells the history of the docklands and buildings surrounding the museum and explains how capstans, pitch boilers and other dock machinery worked. The old pilotage building has a River Room overlooking the Mersey where the complexities of cargo-handling, past and present, are explained and the numerous activities on the river itself can be observed. A Boat Hall provides a large open display area for a growing collection of full-sized local craft and the visitor can observe the repair and restoration of them by traditional methods.

The economic climate of recent years has not been kind to Merseyside and today's disappointments should not be allowed to obscure the triumphs of yesterday. The aim of this project is to develop a Maritime Museum and Maritime Park which will create local and international interest, improve the environment of an historic seaport and raise the morale of an area which for some years has suffered a decline in its fortune.

On the day the museum opened its first phase, the chairman of the Merseyside Council said, 'This new riverside window will show the world what sorts we are and from whence we come. It is a drawing on our past for encouragement and a promise for the future.' As he spoke, a flotilla of 70-foot ketches under sail, crewed by young people of the Ocean Youth Club, tacked up the Mersey with a skill and style that the gaffers of old would have admired. It was a good omen.

WINDERMERE
STEAMBOAT MUSEUM

It is appropriate and fortuitous that Windermere should possess a unique and historical collection of boats. Throughout history the lake has witnessed the imprint of almost every generation. The Romans used it from their camp, Galava, at Waterhead; and in the Middle Ages monks found sanctuary on the small island of St Mary's Holme. Like the monks, the communities near Windermere used the lake as a source of food and means of transport, and created around the largest natural stretch of inland water in England a picturesque and fascinating world which is today renowned as one of Britain's premier tourist attractions.

With the advent of the Industrial Revolution, many enterprising engineers in the north-west were quick to take advantage of a large freshwater lake for their experiments and recreation. Their ingenuity was soon followed by an enthusiasm amongst the local gentry, and a world of elegant fashion centred on the yacht racing and weekend steamer and tea parties. The ladies competed as much with their dresses and parasols as the gentlemen with their steamboats.

The rich and varied history of boating on Windermere might easily have become just a memory, however, were it not for the foresight of largely one person, George Pattinson, and his love for Windermere and its tradition of boating. As a boy he watched and admired the fine yachts and magnificent steamlaunches and made it his life's interest to record and preserve as much as he could. He acquired a collection of historic craft, one by one, cared for them, and watched over others in the sure knowledge that one day they would be appreciated. Gradually,

the germ of an idea began to grow for a museum on the lake shore of Windermere to house and display this collection. The Maritime Trust in London and Ocean Fleets Ltd of Liverpool lent their support to develop the proposal, until in 1977 a fine new museum was built on the site of the former Windermere sandwharf which had been acquired by George Pattinson and his family.

The Windermere Steamboat Museum created interest from the start, particularly when visitors found that the boats themselves told a remarkable story spanning two centuries. For example, a sailing yacht of 1780 is preserved there, having been discovered in an abandoned boathouse in 1934. This sturdy but graceful vessel allows the visitor a glimpse of the nature of the great Georgian and Victorian regattas. Records still exist of yacht races on Windermere in 1793 between her and the *Peggy*, which had been especially sailed from the Isle of Man for the event. Like so many others in the Maritime Trust's collection, this old yacht had her own salvage story: after her discovery in 1934 she was subsequently lost again until George Pattinson tracked her down in a field on the outskirts of Southport, where she was being used as a hen house.

The most remarkable salvage story, however, surrounds the discovery and raising of the steamlaunch *Dolly* in 1962. Built on Windermere around 1850, she had been taken to Ullswater towards the end of the last century and sank during the great frost of 1895, lying forgotten until discovered by divers in 1960. Incredibly, after sixty-seven years on the bed of Ullswater and after a painstaking restoration, she was relaunched with her original timbers, boiler and engine, and proudly remains in use today – the oldest working mechanically powered boat in the world.

This little steamer is a fine example of craftsmen's work in the early days of steam and provides a living picture of a facet of life about the time of the Great Exhibition of 1851. It was just prior to this time that Windermere as a popular tourist attraction had been born with the coming of the railway in 1847, and the first of the great public steamers, the *Lady of the Lake*, launched amidst great celebrations and controversy in 1846. Photographic displays at the museum provide fascinating tableaux of these fine steamers, the commercial warfare that existed between steamer companies and the colourful characters, events and disasters over the years.

It was not just the tourists who flocked to Windermere: the aura of the lake and its surroundings so popularized by the Lake Poets also held great prestige for the wealthy industrialists of the North-West who established their fine houses and estates around the lake and who, of course, threw themselves enthusiastically into the pleasures of boating. In 1869 one Henry Schneider, a local industrialist who lived in fine style in Bowness on Windermere, had a great iron twin-screw steamyacht, *Esperance*, built on the Clyde and transported to Windermere. *Esperance* was designed to commute daily from Bowness to Lakeside at the southern tip of Windermere, a distance of about 6 miles, from where Schneider – having eaten his breakfast on board – caught his special train to Barrow. As her owner sailed in all weathers, *Esperance*'s bow was heavily raked to break light ice. Her beautiful lines were almost lost forever when she sank in 1941, but she was successfully salvaged at the time by George Pattinson's father, and is now preserved at the museum, bearing the distinction of being the oldest boat on Lloyd's Register of Yachts.

The gentlemen with their large houses around the lake and the growing number of hotels compelled the directors of the Furness Railway Company in 1871 to commission the largest of the museum's vessels, the steamship *Raven*, for use as a cargo boat to serve all the scattered

The steamlaunch Dolly. *Built at Windermere around 1850, she sank in Ullswater in 1895 and lay forgotten until discovered by divers in 1960. Rescued and restored, she is the oldest working mechanically powered boat in the world. Now at the Windermere Steamboat Museum. Photo: Windermere Steamboat Trust.*

settlements around the lake. *Raven* provided an efficient alternative to the laborious journey by horse and cart over very poor roads, and carried everything from coal and timber to farm produce – and even the constituents of gunpowder to service the gunpowder works at Elterwater. During her active career, the vessel became an integral part of the local life around Windermere and commanded enormous affection for over fifty years as she tirelessly served the community and broke ice for the passenger steamers in winter. She, too, happily survived and was restored and refloated in her original Furness Railway colours.

The steamyacht was perhaps the ultimate status symbol in Victorian times and, although of more modest scale, the steamlaunch on Windermere was no less prestigious. The wealthy industrialists and men of commerce competed with each other to build better, faster, and finer steamlaunches. The 1880s and '90s saw the golden era of these incomparable craft. The Thames could boast many similar craft, but few could compete with the refinement of line developed on Windermere, no doubt in response

to their setting on wide-open water and backdrop of rolling foothills and mountains.

The Steamboat Museum is fortunate in having a representative collection of these launches. The steamlaunch *Branksome*, built for the wealthy Mrs Howarth in 1896, represents the ultimate in Victorian elegance. Built from teak and walnut with embossed velvet upholstery, carpet, leather seats, and original white rubber mats, she is one of the finest launches ever built with beautiful clipper bow and counter stern, fitted with every convenience and comfort. In the galley is a solid white marble wash-hand basin with beer-pump handle to provide water; and the original 1896 WC is still operational. Like most Windermere steamboats, *Branksome* is equipped with the ever-popular copper steam tea urn or 'Windermere kettle' which boils a gallon of water in ten seconds. The launch still possesses her silver tea service engraved with the boat's name, together with tablecloths and maids' lace aprons. At the heart of the vessel amidships is her powerful Sissons compound steam engine which enables her to glide across the lake swiftly and silently – every

The Clyde-built steamyacht Esperance *of 1869, the oldest boat on Lloyd's Register of yachts, is now part of the Windermere Steamboat Museum's collection. Photo: Windermere Steamboat Trust.*

The Swallow, *a classic Windermere steamlaunch of 1911 in the collection of the Windermere Steamboat Museum. Photo: Windermere Steamboat Trust.*

inch a lady of grace and style. It is the policy of the Steamboat Museum to keep the launches in regular use so that visitors to Windermere are able to see boats in their element and fully appreciate their elegance.

Swallow, Osprey, and *Water Viper,* although slightly smaller than *Branksome,* represent the classic Windermere steamlaunch, the product of years of refinement and development.

After the First World War excitement centred upon the new generation of motor speed boats, like *Canfly,* which is preserved in the museum, with her Rolls-Royce Hawk aero engine. During her occasional races up the lake, visitors are given a rare glimpse of the great pre-war age of speed racing on Windermere which so captured the public imagination at the time, culminating in the tragic death of Sir Henry Segrave whilst attempting the World Water Speed Record in *Miss England II* in 1930.

Although the main purpose of the museum is to celebrate the steamboat, it also has a fine collection of motor boats, including early examples of 1898 and 1903, a Canadian Dispro (Disappearing Propeller) Boat of *c.* 1924, a Chris Craft Special Race Boat of 1936, and even a hydroplane speed boat, *Cookie,* of 1962 – already an interesting museum piece. More

humble boats also find their place: an original Rob Roy canoe, Beatrix Potter's rowing boat, and even a collapsible canvas coracle that can be carried on the back when hiking.

So long as people enjoy messing about in boats or just dreaming about them, there will be people who will enjoy the Windermere Steamboat Museum whose significance lies perhaps in the bridge that has been built between the traditional concept of a museum, a boatyard and the weekend boating scene. The Windermere Steamboat Museum has shown that museums can be places of activity without prejudice to the important ethics of preservation. The active preservation of the boats here has also maintained and developed the skills required to repair and restore the hulls and machinery.

The museum is strict in its policy of only acquiring and displaying boats either used or built on Windermere, because it is essentially concerned as much with Windermere as with the steamboats. The boats and the fine collection of historic photographs and artefacts remind us what a beautiful place Windermere is and what remarkable, ingenious, sporting and sensible people our forbears were – and how they must have enjoyed themselves.

VIII
THE NORTH-EAST

KINGSTON-UPON-HULL
TOWN DOCKS MUSEUM

HULL'S MARITIME MUSEUM is housed in the city's best-known and most distinctive building, the Docks Offices, completed in 1871. Designed by Christopher Wray, the building is of triangular shape with drum towers at each corner, topped by cupolas which are still a landmark in Hull. The two principal rooms, the former Wharfage Office on the ground floor and the original Directors' Court Room on the first, are situated behind the long, curving façade facing the site of Queen's Dock (now filled in and occupied by Queen's Gardens), the origin of the company's prosperity. The Court Room, 70 feet long, 29 feet wide and 21 feet high with its imitation marble columns and decorated ceiling, a monument to Victorian optimism, is now finely restored and used by the museum for its temporary exhibitions.

The museum is a very good example of how a city can tell its own story. The prosperity of Hull in the eighteenth and nineteenth centuries came from her skills in ship-building, fishing and whaling and the Town Docks Museum, which was opened in 1975, has used an extremely effective blend of artefacts and graphics to present these histories.

The main entrance to the museum, from Queen Victoria Square, with its twin globe lamps, leads to the foot of the main staircase; to the left is the entrance to the Fishing and Trawling Galleries, prefaced by the Silver Cod Trophy, an award given between 1954 and 1968 to the captain of the trawler with the largest catch of the year.

The first room, with its mural depicting types of fish caught and the depths at which they are found, illustrates traditional inshore fishing and the historic fishing gear of Yorkshire. There are models of typical local vessels, few of which survive today: a Paull shrimper, a North Sea herring drifter and Yorkshire cobles.

The second room, which is round in shape, contains a larger model of a sailing trawler, the *Specimen*, built in 1879 at Goole, and the displays show the working methods which the West Country fishermen brought to the North Sea and to Hull.

The next section is devoted to the steam trawlers introduced in the 1880s, many of them built in Hull shipyards. The first display shows the working methods of the boxing fleet which allowed greater exploitation of the Dogger Bank. Smacks stayed at sea for six to eight weeks at a time and transferred their catches to a steam cutter which rushed the fish to markets in Hull and London.

The Whaling Galleries complete the tour of the ground floor. The displays occupy the former Wharfage Office with an upper deck over the skeleton of a whale and a room for the important collection of scrimshaw. The species of whale and their life cycle and feeding habits are described. These creatures used to be valuable for their blubber, which was rendered into oil lamps, and for their whalebone which was made into brushes, umbrella ribs, corset stays, etc. Examples of these pathetic products, for which the giant creatures were hunted at such risk, are shown.

It was not until the latter half of the eighteenth century that Sir Samuel Standidge equipped the first Hull ships for the Arctic Fishery. His portrait and pictures of his fleet are to be found next to the illustrated map which shows the routes they sailed in that icy region. As the whale population off east Greenland diminished, the ships sailed further west and then northwards up into the Davis Straits and Baffin Bay. Vessels usually left Hull in March with a crew of twenty men and stopped off at Lerwick to take on thirty or so Shetlanders before sailing for the fishing grounds. They were merchant ships converted for sailing in ice by strengthening their hulls with extra planking and stout internal buttresses. Models of these ships are shown in cases on the ramp leading to the upper deck.

Only when a portion of open water was found could the boats be launched from these ships in pursuit of their quarry. On the opposite side of the ramp are models of these boats and a full-scale reproduction is visible from the upper deck, equipped with the tools of the trade. On the ramp, leading down from the reconstructed crow's nest, are examples of objects made by the crews during their long voyages and records of the catches they made.

The exploits of some of the famous Hull whalers are illustrated in paintings by John Ward, the leader of the Hull School of maritime painting. Mementoes of the famous *Truelove*, which made seventy-two voyages from Hull to the Arctic between 1784 and 1868, are displayed on the lower deck together with the surgeon's log and medicine chest of the *Diana*, the last of the Hull whaleships, which was trapped in the ice through the winter of 1866-7. She was eventually wrecked on the Lincolnshire coast on her way up the Humber in 1869, marking the end of the trade from Hull.

The whaler's contact with the Eskimos created a great deal of interest in Hull and elsewhere in the country. Captain Parker of the *Truelove* brought back an Eskimo couple in 1847 and exhibited them in the Mechanics Institute, attracting five thousand curious visitors. Plaster casts of their heads were made and these are shown with the *Truelove* souvenirs. There are many items of Eskimo origin, and particularly of note is the kayak or one-man canoe with the figure wearing a sealskin tunic. Other Eskimo exhibits include clothing, weapons and delightful miniature toys and animals carved in bone or stone, such as the sled dogs and an igloo which opens to reveal an Eskimo family inside.

Next to the Eskimo case is a skeleton of a polar bear cub and a mounted specimen of an adult bear, lent by the Dundee Museum. These creatures were also treated as curiosities and hunted and brought back for exhibition in zoos.

Beyond the polar bears, a door leads to the small round room containing Hull's collection of scrimshaw which is one of the most important in the world. The origin of this word is obscure, but in particular it is used to describe the carving of whalebone, particularly sperm whale teeth, with illustrative patterns to produce decorative or utilitarian objects. Ships and scenes of the whale hunt predominate as subjects, and scrimshander provides an important source of knowledge of the methods of the whalers and their vision of the polar landscape.

Conventional designs were also popular, patriotic emblems and lovers' designs, even well-dressed ladies and gentlemen from contemporary fashion plates. It is strange to think of a hardy old salt laboriously scratching pictures of Victorian ladies in crinolines or bustles, and gentlemen in frock coats and top hats. But it must be admitted that the more elaborate designs may have been made by full-time craftsmen and women back home, particularly in the United States. The Eskimos also incised bones with scenes of Arctic life – igloos, sleds and hunting – presented with a simple and revealing directness.

The list of articles which come under the heading of scrimshander is enormous and includes such useful things as belaying pins, fids, bodkins, sewing boxes, clothes pegs, pastry crimpers and napkin rings as well as purely decorative ornaments. The Hull collection is superbly displayed.

On the first floor the rooms that were formerly the director's offices display the history of the development of Hull as a port. We see the importance of the Humber as a trade route and the problems it presents to mariners. Five major rivers drain into the estuary, together with a great many minor ones; the Humber itself starts at Trent Falls, the junction of the Trent and the Ouse. The waters are difficult to navigate owing to the vast amount of silt brought down by the rivers and spread by the ebb tide, forming constantly shifting patterns of shoals and channels. Thus conservancy, or making the estuary safe for ships, has been

A boxing-fleet trawler of the Great Northern Steamship Fishing Company of Hull, in about 1903. The history of the Hull fishing fleets and their methods of operation are well covered by the Town Docks Museum, Hull. Photo: City of Kingston-upon-Hull Museums.

the constant preoccupation of the port of Hull since the Middle Ages. In this section the displays show how the conservancy battle is fought: they explain the need for continual surveys to correct the charts and for the repositioning of buoys and light floats; the setting-up of shore lights and beacons; and the mooring of lightships.

A further display illustrates the other side of Hull's trade: the navigation of the Humber and its tributaries to the markets and manufacturing towns of inland Yorkshire. The history of that distinctive local vessel, the square-rigged Humber keel, and her sister, the sloop, is set out here. Both types traded in large numbers to the West Riding, to York, Lincoln and Nottingham, whilst the smaller keels even crossed the Pennines by way of the Rochdale Canal to reach Manchester and Liverpool.

The final display of this section has paintings by John Ward and his school, showing the steam packets of the early nineteenth century which made Hull the junction for passenger and freight services from Doncaster, Leeds, York and Gainsborough, with connections for the coastal and short sea services. As an introduction to the galleries of merchant shipping, a section is devoted to the men who sail from Hull, with displays of their uniforms and badges of rank, including the famous uniform of Trinity House Navigation School, a conspicuous feature of Hull's street scene. The panels around describe the missions and the churches which operate in Hull, looking after seamen and their orphans. There is also a case of seamen's art and hobbies – ships in bottles, ropework, and so on.

The story of Humberside shipping starts with the Ferriby boat which was found in the Humber mud in 1937 and shows the earliest-known type of ship construction in the region. Medieval trade is illustrated in the museum displays by representations of the seals of the Hanseatic League, the trading confederation of North European towns established in the thirteenth century. These seals are fair evidence of what the ships of the period looked like, single-masted at first, with a second and third mast added during the fifteenth century.

Moving past the reconstructed saloon of a topsail schooner, typical of the many which worked out of Hull in the years before 1914, the visitor reaches displays of famous ships: the *Bounty* of mutiny fame, built in Hull; HMS *St George*, a one-hundred-gun warship; the *Southampton*, which continued as a training ship in the Humber until the 1900s; and ship models which were made by French prisoners-of-war during the struggle against Napoleon.

An adjoining display deals with the cargoes most frequent in Hull, the methods of handling them and the work of the dockers, their conditions and the development of trade unions.

Steam services to London were first introduced in 1821 and soon covered the continent as Hull became the centre for a great fan of routes – coastal, north and south, to the Low Countries, Scandinavia, the Baltic and the Mediterranean. Ocean steamships came later, when problems of fuel consumption had been solved by the latter half of the nineteenth century, but most local owners stuck to the short sea routes whose purpose and nature are illustrated by the model of the SS *Ouse* unloading produce from the Low Countries at Riverside Quay *c.* 1912. The sole exception was the celebrated Wilson Line, founded in 1825 with one sailing ship. Expansion was rapid and by the 1900s Wilson's had services to the United States, India, the Black Sea and the Mediterranean, as well as the traditional routes to the Baltic which brought not only timber and other products, but also countless Jewish emigrants who passed through Hull to Leeds and Liverpool and across to New York. The Wilson Line became the largest privately owned shipping company in the world and the Wilson family leading members of fashionable Edwardian society. There are detailed displays of the development of the line, including a model of the *Eskimo* and water-line models of other vessels. This section includes details of other Hull shipping companies of the period, too.

Hull also became the headquarters of Britain's major towage company, United Towing, founded in 1920 by amalgamation of several competing owners. The company maintained their harbour work, ocean towage and salvage and, since 1974, have participated in the development of the North Sea oil field. The displays include illustrations of their methods of handling ships and a model of one of the company's ocean tugs, the *Englishman*.

The story is brought up to date with details of the deep-sea ships using the port today, including the roll-on, roll-off ferries and the vast increase in container traffic which has revolutionized dock work and installations.

SANDTOFT
TRANSPORT CENTRE

AS FAR BACK AS 1882 Doctor Werner von Siemens designed and built a railless electric vehicle drawing power from overhead wires, and the first trolleybus service began in 1901 at Bielethal in Saxony. The idea did not develop quickly in Germany or elsewhere in Europe, although several trolleybus systems were operating on the continent before the First World War. By 1903 there were proposals to run trolleybuses in Britain, but it was not until 1909 that the newly formed Railless Electric Traction Company gave a demonstration. The year 1911 saw Bradford and Leeds open a trolleybus route in their cities. Between then and 1922 over a dozen trolleybus systems were inaugurated, and by 1950, when the trolleybus

service had reached its peak, over four thousand vehicles were running on thirty-six systems. As late as 1952, when the trams were finally retired in London, a new fleet of trolleys was ordered, but the end of the trolleybus was in sight, and within ten years it too had disappeared from London streets. The city of Bradford, which had pioneered the system proudly, continued to operate what became the last trolleybus system in Great Britain until 1972 when it was replaced by the all-conquering diesel bus to end a remarkable record of sixty-one years of service.

A number of continental cities still operate trolleybus systems, and in Britain there are frequent calls for the return of this mode of transport. The protagonists cite the fact that it

Trolleybuses from Maidstone, Walsall, Teeside and Bradford await visitors at the Sandtoft Transport Centre. Photo: D. Tate.

Restored trolleybuses from Huddersfield and Nottingham and the Sandtoft Transport Centre. Photo: D. Tate.

was fast, quiet and pollution-free, while the more pragmatic emphasize the reasons for its decline: the inflexibility of routeing and the cost, both of maintaining the overhead equipment and the electric power.

'Gone but not forgotten' could be the motto of the Sandtoft Transport Centre, for here in spite of its general-sounding title is a museum devoted almost entirely to the preservation and operation of trolleybuses. It occupies a 5-acre site on a former RAF aerodrome near Doncaster and is run by volunteers from a number of national and local transport societies. Between them they have built a covered depot, workshops and an overhead supply system so that some of the trolleybuses can be seen in motion and visitors can enjoy the experience of a gentle trolley ride on summer Sundays and Bank Holidays.

The centre has a collection of over seventy vehicles from many parts of Britain and some fine examples from the continent, including a massive one-and-half-deck trolleybus from Aachen, a small early Liège vehicle and a London-type trolley that spent nearly twenty years in Spain. Visitors can see a Mexborough-Swinton trolleybus dating from 1928, a Bourne-

mouth vehicle of 1935, a Derby, a Glasgow, a Maidstone and a Teesider.

By a neat piece of historical transition, the first time a trolleybus ran at the Sandtoft Centre was in the same year that they were taken out of public service. This link between public decline and private preservation has ensured that many of the later types have survived in good condition, although a number of complete rebuilds are under way in the Sandtoft workshop.

The oldest trolleybus in the collection is the 1928 Swinton vehicle which, of course, dates from some seventeen years after trolleybuses were put into service in Britain. This problem of the dearth of early material is one that faces all museums, particularly those attempting to relate the whole history of an era. Might one suggest that the building by the skilled tradesmen at Sandtoft of a replica of the earliest model could be a valuable contribution to the story it is telling? Currently they are planning the construction of a 1930s street scene with all the appropriate street furniture so that the vehicles can swish along and create for their visitors the feeling of how it was to 'travel on a trolley'.

IX
SCOTLAND

EAST FORTUNE
MUSEUM OF FLIGHT

THE EAST FORTUNE MUSEUM of Flight is an outstation of the Royal Scottish Museum. It occupies part of a former RAF wartime station at East Fortune in North Berwick, also the departure point of the airship R34 which made the first east to west crossing of the Atlantic in July 1919 – only a few weeks after Alcock and Brown's historic flight. The museum is housed in two large hangars, and although the collection of aircraft and other aviation items is by no means large, there are some interesting and important relics.

The earliest aircraft on display is a 1934 Weir Autogiro, the sole survivor of the early involvement of the Scottish firm of G. & J. Weir in the building of helicopters and autogiros. Apart from its historical importance, its presence gives the museum the opportunity of pointing out the intriguing technical differences by which the autogiro and the helicopter obtain their lift.

Here also is what is thought to be the oldest surviving de Havilland 'Dragon Rapide' in the UK. More than seven hundred Rapides were built in the thirties and forties in response to its popularity as a short-range passenger aircraft and this particular example operated for many years from Dyce Airport on the Orkney and Shetland routes. This classic biplane is regarded with affection by most aviation enthusiasts and there are a number in the UK and around the world still in airworthy condition.

Displayed close by is another aircraft that in later years served the Islands and Highlands in a similar capacity to the 'Rapide'. This is the Beech E185, built by the Beechcraft Corp. in the United States. The example preserved in the museum was built in 1956 and originally used by business corporations in the US. It was acquired by the Scottish company Loganair in 1968 and opened their first international service, Abbotsinch-Dyce-Stavanger (Norway) in July 1969. Later it was used for charter and air-ambulance duties to the Scottish islands. The museum makes the point that, from the first Beech being built in 1937, the aircraft was in production until 1969, which gives it a claim to have had the longest continuous production run of any aircraft.

At the other end of the scale of style and reliability is the Mignet 'Pou du Ciel' or 'Flying Flea', probably one of the most notorious aircraft ever to fly and as ugly as it was dangerous. The 'Pou du Ciel' was a small 'do-it-yourself' aeroplane designed by the Frenchman Henri Mignet. He published instructions on how to build and fly it, and in late 1935 about a thousand 'Fleas' were begun. Although Mignet flew his over the Alps, many other 'Fleas' crashed through being under-powered, or through a design fault of the wings which made it possible to put the aircraft into a dive from which recovery could not be made. As a result of such accidents, the 'Flying Flea' was banned from flying in the UK until it was redesigned to correct its fatal flaws.

The military aircraft of the Second World War are represented by perhaps the two most famous protagonists, the Spitfire and the Messerschmitt. The former is an LF Mark XIVE type and one of the last Spitfires to be built during the war. The latter is an example of the formidable Me163B 'Komet'. The 'Komet' was a very fast, rocket-powered aircraft, used by Germany in the Second World War to intercept the Flying Fortresses of the United States Air Force on their high-altitude daylight bombing raids over Germany. This marque could reach its service ceiling of 12,100 metres (39,690 feet) in 3 minutes but its maximum powered endurance was only 8 minutes. It took off on a wheeled undercarriage which was jettisoned when the aircraft was airborne. Landings were made on a simple skid undercarriage and were fraught with danger as the shock of touch-down could cause any residual fuel to explode. Part of the testing programme for the 'Komet' was carried out by the famous woman pilot Hanna Reitsch. This machine was captured in Germany in May 1945, and is on loan from the Cranfield College of Aeronautics.

Later military aircraft on show include a Gloster Meteor as an example of the first and only jet-powered aircraft type to be used by the RAF in the Second World War and a Hawker Sea Hawk and a de Havilland Sea Venom, both with Scottish associations, having operated out of the Royal Naval Station at Lossiemouth on the north-east coast.

Representing lighter-than-air aircraft is a Slingsly 'Gull' Glider, one of the most successful pre-war British high-performance gliders. This example is made up from a number of original parts: the fuselage came from another 'Gull', while the tailplane, rudder and wing-struts came from Geoffrey Stephenson's 'Gull' in which he made the first cross-Channel glider flight in April 1939.

There is here a modern hang-glider. This is a Rogallo type; that is, it has a triangular or delta-shaped wing and is controlled entirely by the movement of the pilot's weight. Weight movement is achieved by the pilot's sitting on the swing-seat and pushing or pulling on the control bar in front. In fact, the Museum of Flight's major exhibits start with an early hang-glider (the historic Pilcher 'Hawk' of 1896, currently displayed in the Royal Scottish Museum) and end with this modern product of 1975. Within that time span it is developing its collection and extending the displays of its excellent assembly of research rockets, and its engines, equipment and photographs. It will not be easy to build up a presentation truly to justify the name 'Museum of Flight', but the progress made in its early years is encouraging.

GLASGOW
MUSEUM OF TRANSPORT

PRIOR TO 1 November 1979 one of the more perverse pleasures to be enjoyed by the transport enthusiast visiting Glasgow was a ride on its underground railway. On that date a modern, fast, comfortable service replaced the old subway system which is now the museum piece it had already come to resemble while still in use.

The original Glasgow District Subway was opened to the public on 14 December 1896. Twin 11-foot tunnels, each $6\frac{1}{2}$ miles long, carried cable-drawn subway cars on a 4-foot gauge track. The Outer Circle trains ran in a clockwise direction and the Inner Circle ran anti-clockwise. However, no sooner had the subway opened than it had to close again: a derailment on the Inner Circle and a collision on the Outer meant that, before the end of its first day, the subway was out of action. It did not open again until 21 January 1897.

The original system was cable-drawn and powered by two massive 2,000hp steam engines. It was not until 1934 that it was converted to electricity and the semi-automatic block system of signalling replaced by the fully automatic system as used on the London Underground. A train on the new system takes twenty-two minutes to complete a circle journey, taking in fifteen stations. Travellers destined for the Museum of Transport should alight at West Street Station.

It was the announcement in 1958 that the last of the Glasgow trams would be replaced by motor buses that stimulated the first moves towards the formation of a transport museum and this, together with the Glaswegians' legendary love of the 'caurs', makes it most appropriate that the museum is housed in the old tramway depot and works where for many years the city's trams were built and serviced. Visitors who remember the period atmosphere created at the old British Transport Collection at Clapham in London, which was also accommodated in a former tramshed, will be struck by the similarity here.

The Transport Museum was opened in April 1964 and to begin with it was established to house a small collection of vintage motor cars, tramcars and bicycles. Since that time the museum has been extended every year or so, until now it houses a large and representative collection of all forms of land transport. In fact, Glasgow's Transport Museum has become one of the most comprehensive of its type.

On entering the museum it is, of course, the trams that first capture the attention. Big, bright and bold, they form a collection that is one of the most admired and popular in the museum. The exhibits are arranged in two rows in order of date which makes it possible for the visitor to follow the chronological development of the tram through a period of about sixty years. The vehicles cannot be boarded, but the interiors are well lit and a good view of the inside of the saloons may be seen from the ground and from a raised catwalk which affords a view into the upper decks. Starting with early horse-drawn trams of the nineteenth century, the collection includes examples to show nearly all the stages of technical development. Of particular interest are two single-deckers, one the 'Room and Kitchen' tram of 1898, so called because of its centre doorway dividing the body into a small and a large compartment, and the other an experimental car of 1926 intended for inter-urban service which, because of its small stature and smooth top, was soon nicknamed 'Wee Baldie' by its affectionate passengers. The final era of the tram in Glasgow is represented by a splendid example of the 1938 Mark I 'Coronation' type tram and by the last double-decker tram ever built in Britain, the 1952 Cunarder.

Although the first motor omnibuses date back to the beginning of this century, their appearance in Glasgow was comparatively late. This was because Glasgow had a large fleet of tramcars, and even when buses were introduced – the first single-deckers in 1924 and the first double-deckers three years later – they were looked upon simply as an addition to the tramway fleet, to help out at busy times and

perhaps to provide a feeder service.

Unfortunately, few if any of the really early buses have survived. However, two of particular importance have been preserved for the museum. First there is a 1949 Albion No. B92 complete with bodywork by Croft and fitted with India tyres. It was the last completely Scottish-built bus to join the fleet. The other preserved bus is a Leyland Atlantean which dates from 1958 and illustrates what was to become the mainstay of the corporation fleet for about twenty years.

There is one trolleybus in the museum to represent the years when these swift and silent servants glided through the streets of Glasgow between 1949 and 1967. It is not one of the more numerous double-deckers, but a 1958 fifty-seater single-deck example of the later stage of

OPPOSITE: *In the early days of motoring many fine cars were manufactured in Scotland. The Glasgow Museum of Transport has an excellent collection of home-built vehicles, including a number of Arrol-Johnstons. The photograph above is a contemporary shot of a 1901 model in private ownership; that below shows an Arrol-Johnston 24/30hp Six of 1911. Photos: above, Veteran Car Club of Great Britain; below, National Motor Museum.*

BELOW: *The 1952 Cunarder, the last double-deck tram to be built in Britain, forms part of the admirable tram collection at the Glasgow Museum of Transport. Photo: Glasgow Museum of Transport.*

this most agreeable form of public transport.

At the side of the main hall is displayed the museum's car collection and it is a fascinating one. It is often not realized that at the beginning of this century Scotland was in the vanguard of the motor industry or that over forty Scottish-based makes of cars have been produced. Examples of the products of many of these companies do not now exist and many indeed made a comparatively small impact on the industry. Properly, the Glasgow Museum of Transport has concentrated on the Scottish car, and the main firms, Argyll, Albion and Arrol-Johnston, which made international re-putations, are well represented. A brace of 1900 Argyll voiturettes starts the Scottish display, one with a 5hp MMC engine, the other with a lower-powered De Dion. A very rare Argyll four-seater car follows and alongside is a 1907 tourer from the same company with a wheelbase almost double that of the models produced seven years earlier. A 1901 dog cart and a 1912 Paisley-built tourer, which shows some French influence in design, particularly in the Renault-like radiator, are two fine examples from the Arrol-Johnston stable and the Albion company is represented by a very well-preserved 12hp model of 1904 vintage. There are later models on display of all these famous Scottish firms, and an associated photographic exhibition recalls less well-known companies, such as Skeoch, Drum-mond, Tod and Madelvic, whose products have gone forever.

Most of the more recent cars displayed are of British rather than Scottish manufacture. Such classic cars as a Rolls-Royce Phantom II Lan-daulette of 1931 and a most original 4½-litre Bentley tourer of 1929 can be seen. The excellent display of post-war cars includes an early Morris Minor, possibly the oldest Mini in Scotland and the first Scottish-built Hillman Imp as well as a Standard Vanguard and a Triumph Mayflower.

The Museum continues to acquire cars all the time, so the collection is by no means complete and hopefully never will be. Meantime, there can be no doubt that it has the finest collection of Scottish-built cars anywhere – which is as it should be.

The motor-cycle collection will excite interest because of its technical and historical coverage.

In the first few years of this century motor tricycles, forecars or quadricycles were in vogue. An example of one of these machines to be seen in the collection is the 1905 Lagonda tricar. It is a forerunner of the heavy motor-cycle combination which provided family transport for those who could not afford a car. The 1913 AJS 800cc vee-twin and the 1914 Scott water-cooled two-stroke demonstrate how ad-vanced machines were prior to the First World War, and the BSA single-cylinder model of 1925 and the powerful Zenith vee-twin of 1921 are examples of models that were very popular in the twenties. Norton, Brough, Douglas, Sun-beam, Matchless and Vincent are all represented for the later years, but without saying it publicly the museum seems to have decided that the motor-cycle age came to an end when British dominance in the industry was eclipsed, for the contemporary scene is hardly mentioned and the near-monopoly of Japanese bikes ignored except for the display of a solitary Honda.

Leading off from the main hall are a number of small halls in which the railway locomotives, the fire engines, the bicycles and the commercial vehicles are displayed. After seeing the motor cycles it is worth going to the commercials first if only to view a rather nondescript little exhibit typical of the kind of popular vehicle that in its time is so commonplace that its passing is unremarkable and it just disappears, yet which has served a better purpose and had a greater effect than many of its grander contemporaries. Such a vehicle is the 1950 Empolini Tricar, in reality a motor scooter with a covered driving position and an open truck back of a type familiar to all who have visited Greece, Spain or Italy – it is the little 'work-donkey' of many countries with a rural-based economy. It looks lost and timid surrounded by the Sentinel steam lorry, the Rushton & Hornby traction engine, the Albion coal lorry and the Aveling and Porter engine which are some of the exhibits that boldly present themselves as its neighbours, but in its own ant-like way it has, in all probability, made a more significant contribution to the world's distribution system than any of them. It is an unusual item for a museum to preserve, but its presence here shows inspiration.

The museum's bicycle display covers all the important developments from the beginnings to the present highly efficient lightweight road racer and the small-wheeled Moultons and Choppers. One of the most important exhibits is a contemporary example of the first pedal-operated bicycle invented in 1839 by Kirkpatrick Macmillan – this is probably the oldest surviving pedal cycle in the world. Fine examples of the early High or Ordinary – popularly known as the Penny-farthing – and tandems, tricycles and many other developments such as the Quadrant, all of which enjoyed brief periods of popularity, are displayed here too, as are many models from the period when Hans Renold invented his new type of link chain which introduced the gearing for the Safety Cycle with two wheels of equal size. In spite of claims by competitors offering bicycles with more elevated seated positions that the Safety Cycle 'incurred a disagreeable affinity with muddy earth,' it soon became the popular model and was only superseded when designs from T. K. Stanley, from Rover and the diamond-framed machines from Raleigh became more popular because of their superior comfort and ease of steering. This historical development is well illustrated.

The horse-drawn vehicles display, which occupies another small hall, is dominated by a Glasgow and London Royal Mail Coach of 1840 – and quite rightly. It shows the height of perfection in carriage-building art when coaches were at their zenith before the railway age and at the start of the penny post.

Other public-transport carriages include a station omnibus which belonged to Lawsons of Kirkintilloch and was used to convey passengers from the railway station to the hotel. The 'Ardrishaig Belle' represents the char-à-banc and was used to carry groups on local outings, while the highly decorated gipsy caravan shows the type of vehicle used by the travelling people in former times. The collection also includes a governess car and a typical country gig of the type once common in Scotland. By way of contrast, a cabriolet, for fashionable town use, can be seen too. One of the few horse-drawn vehicles still in fairly common use in Ireland is the jaunting car, and an excellent example is on show. Two four-wheeled phaetons are on display, a show version for demonstration rides and a lightweight spider phaeton, the horse-

drawn sports model – the Jaguar XK120 of the late nineteenth century. Many closed carriages are exhibited, the brougham being a representative type. A large private coach can also be seen which competes with the Royal Mail coach in style and opulence.

In vibrant contrast to pedal and real horse-power are the railway locomotive displays which occupy the adjoining halls. Almost immediately after the opening of the museum, consideration was given to extending the display to show railway as well as road transport. Full development of the idea became possible as a result of the offer of five historic locomotives by the British Railways Board. These, together with one on loan from the Scottish Locomotive Preservation Fund and one presented by the South of Scotland Electricity Board, form a good selection not only of the work of the Glasgow locomotive manufacturers but also of the different types of locomotive used by each of the main Scottish railway companies.

Pride of place in the display must surely go to Caledonian Railway No. 123, a 4-2-2 locomotive built in 1886 at Hydepark Works to the design of the Locomotive Superintendent Dugald Drummond. This locomotive took part in the famous London to Edinburgh race of 1888 and reached speeds in excess of 70mph. The engine was withdrawn from special duties in 1935 and restored to its 1922 (pre-grouping) livery. It was again overhauled in 1957 and was the last single-driver to be run in the United Kingdom.

The other Caledonian Railway locomotive on display was lent to the museum in 1966 and is No. 828, one of a class of 79 built for mixed traffic duties. It was built in 1899 by the Caledonian Railway at St Rollox Works, Glasgow.

In 1980 the museum acquired a most interesting little industrial loco, built by Alex Chaplin & Co. in Glasgow in 1888. This 0-4-0 TG type was built for service in the Northampton gas works but has now returned, in retirement, to its native land.

Representing the Glasgow and South Western Railway is their 0-6-0 side-tank locomotive No. 9 built in 1917 by the North British Locomotive Company at Hydepark Works, Glasgow, for dockyard shunting duties. After many years of

The Locomotive Hall in the Glasgow Museum of Transport. Photo: Glasgow Museum of Transport.

hard service, this engine, the sole survivor of the Sou'West was presented to the museum by the British Railways Board.

Glen Douglas, locomotive No. 256 of the North British Railway Company, was built in 1913 and is a 4-4-0 type of the Glen Class of thirty-two. While most of these were used on the whole of the NB system, it is for their work on the old West Highland line that they are best remembered. *Glen Douglas* can be seen in her 1922 livery, except for a few minor details.

Operating over some of the most rugged and beautiful scenery in Scotland, the Highland Railway, founded in 1865 and working largely on single-line track, is represented in the museum by its locomotive No. 103, a 4-6-0 type built in Glasgow in 1894. this was the first British 4-6-0 class in service, a notable feature being the flangeless centre-driving wheels. The engine is displayed in an unusual shade of straw yellow known as Stroudley's improved engine green, the colour long being the subject of controversy among railway enthusiasts.

A more recent addition to the locomotive display is an unusual type with no boiler or firebox, known as a fireless locomotive. It was built in 1917 in Kilmarnock, and was supplied with steam sufficient for a few hours' work from a stationary boiler.

These locomotives, together with many associated pieces of railwayana and a fine collection of models, help to illustrate the rich railway history of Scotland. For those who appreciate the skills of model railway engineering there is, adjacent to the main railway display, a 00-gauge model depicting the Citadel Station, Carlisle, which is an interesting layout although numerous inaccuracies in its content are acknowledged by the museum.

The underground railway mentioned in the opening of this chapter, such an important feature in Glasgow's transport history, is well recorded in the museum by a reconstruction of one of the stations, with one track carrying an 1895 cable-era trailer car. The other car illustrates the days of the electric-powered subway and shows the type of carriage best remembered by the Glaswegians who travelled in this long-lived product of Victorian engineering.

The final display concerns itself not with how the Glaswegians travelled but with what they built for others to travel in. The Clyde Room, opened by the Prince of Wales in 1978 and housing the museum's collection of models, is a remarkable tribute to the Clydeside shipbuilders. The models represent the products of most of the major Clyde yards and illustrate vessels of a great many types. There are rivercraft and ocean-going passenger liners. The collection includes also warships, yachts, dredgers and other specialized craft; it is outstanding for its quality and includes fine examples of many famous ships built on the Clyde.

The largest models – not surprisingly – are the 'Queens': the passenger liners *Queen Mary* and *Queen Elizabeth* are each about 17 feet long. Other passenger liners covering the past hundred years include the famous *Empress of Britain* and the ill-fated *Athenia*. Small passenger steamers include the beautiful *Columba*, the Clyde pleasure steamer of 1878. Also to be found is a model of the pioneer turbine steamer *King Edward*. Along with these Clyde vessels are the cross-Channel steamers, including those which sailed the Irish Sea and the English Channel.

Warships always make superb models and the builder's model of HMS *Hood* must surely be one of the finest. There are also battleships, cruisers and destroyers of both World Wars, as well as one or two ships built for foreign navies. Sailing ships are numerically among the smallest groups but those on exhibition are quite remarkable in the detail of fine workmanship. The *Cutty Sark* is especially worthy of note, but perhaps the ultimate will be a choice between HMS *Oxford*, with its contemporary rigging of 1727, and HMS *Howe*, which was rigged in the museum by the chief technician a few years ago. There are also some magnificent models of yachts, both sail and steam. Then there are the dredgers and the tankers and the humble tug. A floating dock and a shallow-draft hospital ship for the Dardenelles are all included in the near two hundred models in the Clyde Room.

The last twenty years or so have been difficult times for Glasgow and it is greatly to its credit that during them this fine museum has been established and developed. It serves Glasgow and Scotland well.

MYRETON MOTOR MUSEUM

TUCKED AWAY OFF a winding country lane in rolling farm land between the small East Lothian town of Aberlady and the village of Drem, the Myreton Motor Museum is a no-nonsense, matter-of-fact, down-to-earth type of place. The building is an unremarkable barn-like structure, the cars are not of exotic or expensive breeds and there has been no attempt to restore them to 'showroom' condition. The exhibits are bunched together in a historical jumble; an antique pair of wheeled crutches casually hangs near a rather crumpled-looking tourer (we are not told if there is a connection); and petrol cans, tools and accessories crowd into odd corners. To the purists or those of orderly mind it will all come as a shock, but for those who like their motor cars *'au naturel'* it is a delight.

This museum is owned by Mr W. P. Dale and was opened by him in August 1966. Since then the collection has grown more than fourfold and now claims to be the largest collection of road transport in Scotland. Most of the cars were purchased in derelict condition and have been saved from almost certain destruction. They are not static museum pieces; the majority are used during the year, and some of them cover large distances. Every car in the collection is in running order and only about two of the motor cycles are non-runners; the bicycles are another matter – many of them would have to be respoked, etc., before they could be used with safety and it has been decided that they are better left in original condition as restoration would destroy their patina.

In addition to the vehicles there are collections and displays of other items connected with motoring. In the motor-cycle hall is a collection of advertising posters – mostly reproduction, though some are originals in fine condition. Upon the walls are nearly three hundred enamel and tin signs which adorned garages in the past.

The museum catalogue presents its contents in no particular date or make order. This can be irritating to the fastidious but it does help to increase the pleasure of suddenly discovering, for instance, that the 1920 Armstrong-Siddeley 30hp tourer is probably the earliest example of the make to survive, or that the 17/50 Arrol/Aster of 1928 is the last in the world, or that the 1-litre Singer is one of the infamous quartet built by the works for the 1935 Tourist Trophy race of which three crashed at the same point on the circuit – one even finishing up rolling down a bank and coming to rest on top of the one which had crashed on the previous lap! This particular model survived, cured its steering problems and was competing at Silverstone as late as the mid-fifties.

The two oldest vehicles on display are on loan from the Royal Scottish Museum and both are nineteenth-century. The elder is an 1897 Arnold-Benz built by Walter Arnold and Sons of Kent and one of the earliest British-built cars. Just one year younger is a Leon Bollée motor tricycle originally owned by the Hon C. S. Rolls. The intrepid passenger rode in front of the driver in a wickerwork bathchair with the driver in tandem busily occupied with the hand-operated steering, gears, clutch and brakes.

Although the Scottish motor industry produced over forty different makes of car in its time, the total production was relatively small

A superb example of the Alvis 'Duck's Back' two-seater from the Myreton Motor Museum. Manufactured in 1924, this car is still capable of its original performance. Photo: Myreton Motor Museum.

A 1926 two-seater version of the Morris Oxford, one of the best types of light car of its day. This one can be seen in the Myreton Motor Museum. The driver is the actor Noel Purcell. Photo: Myreton Motor Museum.

and all the names have gone forever. Here is an D-type Arrol-Johnston tourer and a 1927 12hp Galloway saloon. This latter vehicle, although not very exciting in its mechanical performance, has compensated itself with a rather entertaining screen career, appearing in 'Dr Finlay's Casebook' and in the unlikely role of a police car in an Ian Carmichael film. Indeed, if the Myreton Museum wished to develop a theme of 'cars in films', it has some useful sources, for apart from the many vehicles in the museum that featured in the 'Dr Finlay' series, including the Buick Regent hearse that helped dispose of his mistakes, there is a superb 1930 'Speed Six' Bentley of Le Mans fame that made motor buffs take an even greater interest in the film 'Five Red Herrings' and a very pretty 1912 De Dion two-seater that was the extra heroine in 'The Thirty-Nine Steps'.

In transport museums there are often motor

RIGHT: *This small OHV 1935 Triumph motor cycle is a good example of the popular bike of the thirties. It is in the collection of the Myreton Motor Museum. Photo: Myreton Motor Museum.*

BELOW: *Found in a barn in 1953 with the statutory chickens roosting in it, this 1927 Rolls-Royce Phantom was restored to excellent order and has made an extensive tour of the Continent. It is now in the possession of the Myreton Motor Museum. Photo: Myreton Motor Museum.*

cars whose own claims in history are relatively modest but whose owners' reputation has elevated them to special notice: a king's car, for instance, a field-marshal's staff car, or a gangster's bullet-proof automobile. Such a vehicle for its own special reason is Myreton's 1937 Wolseley 10hp saloon. This car was left to the museum by Mr W. Ward who purchased it new and used it until his death in 1972. He kept a very full record of *every* penny spent on the car: petrol, oil, road tax, insurance, repairs and maintenance, even down to the cost of polishing rags and the taxi fare home the one time it let him down. An analysis of this record reveals that it cost him 6·51d (about $2\frac{1}{2}$p) per mile to run. Petrol went from 1s 7d to 6s 11d per gallon, oil from 1s $0\frac{1}{2}$d to 4s 5d a pint,

On a tricycle made for two – a Coventry-built Léon Bollée of 1897. A number of motor museums have similar machines. Photo: National Motor Museum.

insurance from £10 12s 8d to £16 2s 6d, road tax from £7 10s to £25. Over his total mileage of 127,971, the car returned a figure of 28·52 miles to the gallon.

The commercial vehicle display is very small but certainly entertaining. The 1917 Maudslay lorry started life as an army vehicle, converted to a travelling caravan and finished up as a static home. Its rescue and reverse conversion is a triumph as it is the earliest Maudslay to survive. The 1928 Austin started work as a private car and was successively a hire car, a hearse and finally a lorry in which role it appears here, and the third major commercial exhibit is a horse-drawn fish-and-chip wagon, complete with original frying equipment, that provided a meals-on-wheels service in Dunfermline from 1900 to 1939. Its restoration to full working condition is the wish of every transport enthusiast – and gastronome.

The motor-cycle collection is in a separate hall and contains many of the famous names from the earliest days. As with the cars, the museum's policy with the motor cycles is one of repair and renovation rather than wholesale restoration and this gives the visitor the opportunity of seeing bikes in working rather than exhibition condition. In fact some have not been touched at all, as with the earliest exhibit, a 1903 Beeston-Humber in a highly corroded 'as found' condition, vividly illustrating the amount of work needed to bring such vehicles back to life. The progression of this policy is shown by a 1915 new Hudson 'Big Six' which was purchased in the 1970s as 5 cwt of assorted ferrous scrap and restored to a fine condition. A contemporary advertisement for the model displayed nearby features a satisfied South African owner stating, after a 700-mile trip to Natal, that 'the machine took to the hills around Majuba splendidly'. Exciting racing names include Martinsyde, AJS, and of course Norton, but one particular bike that will excite attention is the ordinary 1924 BSA 250cc 'Roundtank' which was purchased in Norfolk in 1942 for one journey only when the present owner discovered it would be cheaper to buy it and ride home to North Berwick than go by train!

The museum also has a small cycle collection and although it does not attempt to be an historical survey of the machine, it has, nevertheless, a number of very interesting exhibits. Of particular note, especially as some other museums featuring bicycles are without one, is an example of the unusual Hammock saddle which is tensioned by string rather than steel: 'favoured', the catalogue says, 'by the clergy.' Small assemblies of horse-drawn and farm vehicles and a developing collection of military vehicles complete the museum's presentation.

ROYAL SCOTTISH MUSEUM

THE VICTORIANS' EAGERNESS for education, combined with the general interest in the applied arts which had been aroused by the Great Exhibition of 1851, led to the building of many museums and art galleries in Britain during the second half of the nineteenth century. The Industrial Museum of Scotland, the forerunner of the present museum, was founded in 1854. Ten years later it was renamed the Museum of Science and Art. In 1904 it became the Royal Scottish Museum.

The building was designed by Captain Francis Fowke, RE (1823–65). Fowke was an experienced exhibition designer and was familiar with the latest architectural practices of the day, such as the use of cast iron, plate glass and terracotta. He had already designed the Sheepshanks Gallery, now part of the Victoria and Albert Museum in London, and the National Gallery in Dublin. His design for the Industrial Museum of Scotland, as it was, illustrates several characteristic features of Victorian architecture, particularly revivalism, cast-iron construction and overhead lighting. Its massive sandstone façade is in the Venetian Renaissance style and contrasts strongly with the graceful modernity and airy lightness of the interior, which was clearly influenced by Sir Joseph Paxton's Crystal Palace and earlier cast-iron and glass structures.

By the early twentieth century the growth of the museum's collections made further extensions necessary, and between 1911 and 1937 an administrative block, a staircase and a series of galleries were erected on the south side of the Victorian building. The last major extension to the museum was the construction of a lecture theatre, library and galleries on the Lothian Street frontage, built between 1959 and 1961. Since then the north-west and north-east wings have undergone a complete internal reconstruction. The north-east wing was opened in 1975.

The transport exhibits, with the exception of the aeronautical section which is located at the museum's outstation at the East Fortune airfield and is described earlier in this book, are displayed as part of the Department of Technology's aim of illustrating technical development and how things work as well as showing items of historical value. In the section dealing with railways there is an excellent illustration of this policy in action. Here is the *Wylam Dilly* locomotive built by William Hedley in 1813 and vying with the Science Museum's *Puffing Billy* as the oldest locomotive in existence. At the touch of a button the visitor can hear a recording of its history (including its short time afloat as a keel boat engine) and close by is a very fine model of the engine to demonstrate its mode of working. With this concise arrangement an instructive and interesting story is told. There are a number of other locomotive models, particularly of engines that worked the Scottish routes and also some American locomotive models – and how comfortable the cabs of these giants seem to be compared to British designs.

OPPOSITE: *The* Wylam Dilly *locomotive of 1813 at the Royal Scottish Museum has a claim to be the oldest locomotive in the world. Photo: Royal Scottish Museum.*

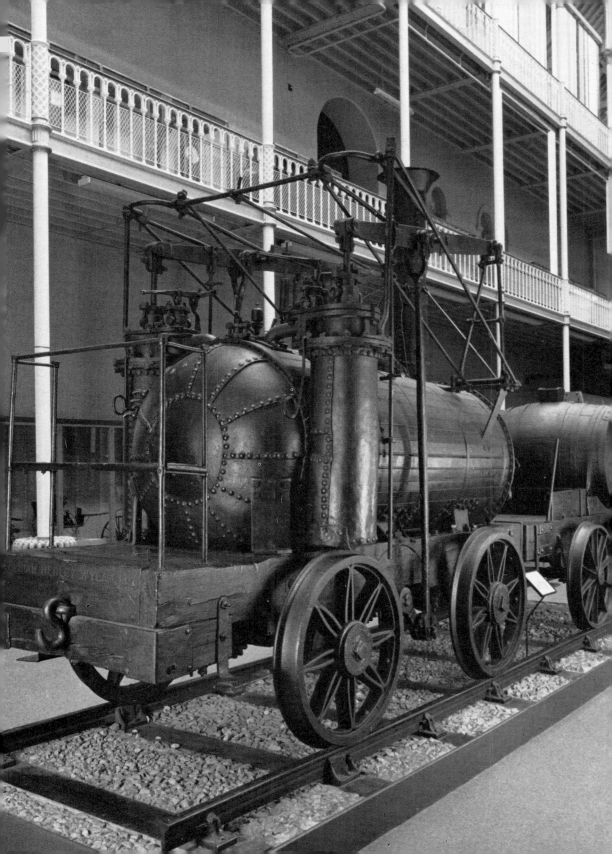

Another vehicle of notable antiquity is the horse-drawn Bolton hearse which is claimed to be the oldest surviving road vehicle in Scotland. This item makes no technical point except perhaps to suggest that eighteenth-century travel was just as uncomfortable in death as it was in life, but exhibits on display from transport of a later age illustrate important milestones. The first is an Albion 8hp dog cart of 1900, one of the earliest examples of a Scottish-built car. A study of it shows well enough that its design was at least the equal of its English and European competitors at the turn of the century and the fact that this car's first owner drove it from Edinburgh to London and back says something about the quality of its construction. Here also is a Stanley Locomobile steam car showing a form of propulsion that equalled and in some conditions surpassed the early internal combustion engines. A chassis of an A40 with the differential gear exposed and accompanied by another excellent push-button commentary, and a rare and original example of the ABC motor cycle, which pioneered the 'flat-twin' engine, four-speed gearbox and drum brakes on both wheels, are other examples, as is the front wheel from the first bicycle to be fitted with an inflatable tyre.

Among the maritime exhibits is a notable collection of ships' models which show the development of small sailing craft and examples of Scottish fishing vessels, as well as paddle- and screw-driven steamships.

As mentioned earlier, the museum's aeronautical collection is, with one exception, housed at the East Fortune airfield some 20 miles from Edinburgh. The exception is the 'Hawk' glider of Percy Pilcher. This is the very glider in which Pilcher crashed and was killed on 30 September 1899, shortly after becoming the first man to fly a controlled flight in England and within sight of being the first in the world to make a powered flight. The Hawk has remained in Edinburgh, protected by the better circumstances of environment and security. It is proper that this historic aircraft should be well cared for, but its isolated display here is not a happy one and perhaps when conditions allow it can join the museum's main aviation displays at East Fortune.

The transport collection at the Royal Scottish Museum is not a large one and there is no reason why it should change its policy of illustrating and explaining fundamentals. This collection and those in the Glasgow Museum of Transport complement each other and together tell a very full story of the history of transport and Scotland's place in it.

X
NORTHERN IRELAND

ULSTER TRANSPORT MUSEUM

THE ULSTER TRANSPORT MUSEUM originated from a collection of vehicles brought together by the former Belfast Museum and Art Gallery during the latter part of the 1950s. In 1967 the Belfast Transport Museum was merged with the Ulster Folk Museum with the joint title of the Ulster Folk and Transport Museum. It now occupies a magnificent estate at Cultra, some 7 miles east of Belfast on the Bangor road. Although administratively the two museums have become one, they have kept their separate identities and function independently. The museum estate lies on either side of the main Belfast-Bangor road and railway line. On the south side is the Folk Museum, occupying the old Manor House and its grounds; to the north is the 40-acre estate of the Transport Museum. It is here that the Ulster Transport Museum has that precious commodity of which practically every other transport museum in the United Kingdom will be jealous – room to expand. The new split-level main building is not large, but the temptation to crowd it with all the exhibits that the museum owns has been resisted. Those that remain in store or currently on display in the old museum premises in Belfast (described later in this section) will have to wait until future development and building plans are realized. Meanwhile this modern, well-lit and scrupulously clean building uses its open-plan design and linked display areas to present a well-balanced story of the history of transport in Ireland and the important role that Belfast herself plays in it.

The history of land transport in Ireland, while illustrating progress towards the complex technology of modern vehicles, is also character-ized by the fact that archaic forms of rural transport survived in certain areas until the mid-twentieth century. Their persistence reflected their ability to provide adequate answers to transport problems in difficult environmental conditions ranging from human haulage through wheelless slide carts to the spoked-wheel cart; they not only give a latter-day glimpse of Ireland's remote past, but they also represent in principle the pre-history of land transport in general. The display in the first gallery, subtitled 'In the Beginning', exhibits examples of the basic horse-drawn sledges and slide carts and a set of Irish block wheels. This type of wheel pattern made of three components dovetailed together and fixed on an axle of wood, so that axle and wheel revolved together as a unit, is known to have been used in the third millenium BC in the Near East. It was also in use in parts of rural Ireland in the 1950s. Also here are pannier creels which were borne by horses, ponies or donkeys and widely used in Ireland for the carriage of all kinds of loads – the stuffed donkey in the display is showing signs of wear caused by the fond patting by visiting children! There are a number of fine Scotch carts of the type introduced to Ireland from Scotland in the early nineteenth century. With their large independently-revolving spoked wheels and big load-carrying capability they were a great improvement on the cruder native carts and widely adopted and adapted.

The photographs in this gallery are first-rate. Students of Ulster folk life in general and of local transport history in particular are fortunate in having at their disposal substantial photo-

graphic records made on location in the early decades of the present century by the Ulster photographers R. J. Welch and W. A. Green. The Green collection is held by the museum and vividly portrays the use of the transport artefacts displayed, as well as showing a life style now gone but that hardly changed over hundreds of years. Perhaps the outstanding exhibit in this section is a finely restored side or jaunting car. Generally regarded as a peculiarly Irish vehicle, it represents in Irish transport history a point at which the dual-purpose farm cart and the passenger vehicle part company and go their separate ways. The model horse, harnessed and standing between the shafts, and the background of a large blow-up of a Green photograph of an identical combination outside a nineteenth-century thatched cottage complete a very striking display.

The jaunting car leads on to the next gallery where many types of horse-drawn passenger-carrying vehicles are assembled. The centre-piece of the display is the mid-nineteenth-century dress chariot of the Marquess of Abercorn. Splendidly restored in its original crimson and black livery and sumptuously upholstered in fine cloths and heavy braid, it is one of the finest examples of the coachworker's art. Close by are a brougham, a Victoria, a mail phaeton, a stage coach, an American buggy – used, it is said, by the donor's great-grandfather, an army surgeon, at the Battle of Gettysburg in 1863 – and a private omnibus used in its day for conveying passengers and luggage to house parties, holiday resorts, railway stations and the races. Its large closed carriage, with accommodation for six people on cushioned benches either side of a centre table, seems to carry still the echoes of the talk and laughter of occupants long ago. Nearby is a more

OPPOSITE ABOVE: *The Ulster Transport Museum's Fergus motor car. Built in Belfast in 1915, it was used in America for twenty-eight years before being returned to Northern Ireland in 1971. Photo: Ulster Transport Museum.*
OPPOSITE BELOW: *Chassis and engine of the prototype OD (owner driver) car at the Ulster Transport Museum. The OD was designed by James A. McKee and Frank Eves about 1916 and the prototype manufactured in 1918. Successful mechanically, it failed to attract financial support for a production run. Photo: Ulster Transport Museum.*
BELOW: *W. A. Green's photograph of an Irish jaunting car. There is a well-restored example of this type of vehicle in the Ulster Transport Museum. Photo: Ulster Transport Museum.*

The Aviation Gallery at the Ulster Transport Museum, Cultra. In the foreground is the Ferguson replica; in the background, the SC1 VTOL experimental aircraft. Photo: Ulster Folk and Transport Museum.

modest vehicle, a pony trap, probably the best known of all the two-wheeled conveyances, having been built in large numbers throughout the country until recent times. A simple, easily maintained vehicle, the pony trap is still quite common on the quieter roads of Ireland today.

In contrast to the informal arrangements of the carriages, the adjacent display under the title of 'Development of the Bicycle' is much stricter and one of the best museum displays of its type. It has the minimum amount of text and dating and the number of bicycles is not more than twenty. They range from the Dandy of the early nineteenth century through to the Bone-shaker, the Penny-farthing and the first Safety Cycles of the 1900s – the general-purpose roadsters whose basic design hardly changed over fifty years – and on to the modern models on sale today. Of particular interest are an 1887 Dublin tricycle with a large chain-driven wheel at the rear and the passenger seated between the two front wheels; an American Star of 1886, really a 'Farthing-penny', the smaller wheel being placed at the front to assist downhill

stability; and the comparison to be made between a Dursley-Pedersen of 1902, which, with its cantilever forks and lightweight tri-angulated frame, was one of the most successful of Edwardian luxury cycles, and the Ulster-manufactured Viking Debutante cycle of 1981 which incorporates similar principles to modern engineering.

The plan for the display of the motor cars and motor cycles at the museum is to concentrate on the common rather than the exotic. At the moment the museum exhibits a mixture of both, but with its Peugeot Bebe light car of 1913, its Ford T of 1922 and its Austin Chummy of 1925, it has started to develop the agreed theme. Two locally built cars are the 1915 Fergus and 1918 OD (owner driver) designed to meet the need of the newly emergent class of car owners in-terested in driving and servicing their own vehicle. Neither model succeeded commercially but both have interesting technical features. Another aspect of the Ulster car scene is the staging of Tourist Trophy races on the splendid Ards circuit outside Belfast in the twenties and thirties. These popular races are recalled by the museum with a display of photographs from the time and an Austin sports model of the period.

As yet there are no public service or commercial vehicles displayed at Cultra, but a fine collection presently in store awaits the construction of new buildings in which they can be placed on show.

Two other subjects, ship-building and aircraft construction, are covered on a modest scale, again because of the museum being in its early stages of development. The ship-building industry was firmly established in Belfast as far back as 1790 with the construction of wooden ships, but it was not until the second half of the nineteenth century that the city became world-renowned for the construction of iron and later steel ships. The Harland and Wolff company was formed in 1861 and was later to build the world's largest passenger liners of their time, *Olympic*, *Britannic* and the ill-fated *Titanic*, as well as introducing many magnificent advances in cargo-ship and steam-engine design. With photographs, drawings and models, the story of this period of Belfast's pre-eminence is briefly told. The museum has over twenty sea craft in store, and as its estate runs down to the shores of the Belfast Lough, one must hope that in the fullness of time they can be displayed in their natural element in spite of the increased preservation costs that such a policy would incur. Meanwhile, trestled high and dry close to the museum building is the three-masted topsail merchant schooner *Result*. Built at nearby Carrickfergus in 1892 to a length of 102 feet, *Result* was the final development in a series of wooden- and metal-hulled schooners and proved one of the fastest and most successful schooners ever to sail in home waters. She is one of the few remaining nineteenth-century Irish-built merchant ships and is certainly the only surviving merchant vessel built at the Carrickfergus shipyard. Maritime enthusiasts will await with impatience the re-masting, re-rigging and more dignified display of this graceful and historic vessel.

The final gallery in the museum has aviation as its subject and the emphasis is on two projects separated by nearly a half-century of flying history. The first is the Bleriot-style monoplane built at Hillsborough in 1909 by Harry Ferguson. Inspired by the success of the Wright brothers at Kitty Hawk in North America, many adventurous spirits embarked on the building and flying of these rudimentary machines. The principles of heavier-than-air flight were as yet only vaguely understood and the machines produced at this stage were cranky, underpowered and dangerous when not lethal. Nonetheless, Harry Ferguson pressed on with his experiments and was officially confirmed in 1910 as the first man to fly in Ireland. Suspended from the roof of the gallery is a full-scale replica of the Ferguson monoplane built by Captain Kelly Rogers. There is also a display of contemporary photographs, most of which clearly indicate that Mr Ferguson led a charmed life.

At the other end of the time scale is the SC1 VTOL aircraft built by Short Bros and Harland Ltd as a result of a research contract for the development of a turbo-jet-powered aircraft capable of landing and taking off vertically. The machine on display is one of two aircraft built to this specification which resulted from initial tests in 1953 with the Rolls-Royce Thrust Measuring Rig, better known as the 'Flying Bedstead' or 'Bedspread', as the museum's pamphlet has it. Also here is the story of the Skyvan – again from Short Bros and Harland Ltd – of which over a hundred have been sold and are in service in more than twenty countries. The success of this aircraft and, at the time of writing, the great interest being shown in the Belfast-made DeLorean luxury sports car, is evidence enough that the Ulsterman's prowess in engineering design and manufacture has not declined. Sadly, what has decreased are the opportunities to demonstrate it.

Mention has been made previously that a large section of the transport collection is still on display at the old Belfast Transport Museum building and it is to this that the visitor should go either before the visit to Cultra or after. For the non-motorist, the bus or train provides a service to Witham Street, some 2 miles east of the city centre off the Newtownards Road. Compared to the well-lit and spacious environment of Cultra these premises are distinctly gloomy and very crowded. As they are now really just a storage facility, improvements would not be justified, but the visitor is compensated by the splendid material within. At the entrance to the building is a wooden ramp leading up to a platform alongside which stand two railway carriages and three locomotives. The first carriage is from the Dublin to Kingston Railway, the first railway in Ireland, which opened in 1834. The carriage dates from about 1840 and, with its wooden seats, open windowless sides and tiny oil lamp for illumination, gives a fair illustration of the discomforts of the railway passenger in that age. The next carriage is an early twentieth-century first- and second-class composite. The first-class section, looking opulently comfortable, is not far removed from the upholstered quality of the best gentleman's horse-drawn carriage and it was a quality that lasted, for the carriage was only withdrawn from service in 1951. Next are two tank engines, one a 4-4-2 from Beyer Peacock and at work on the Belfast and County Down Railway for over fifty years, the other a 2-4-2 of the Great Northern Railway (Ireland) which was built at the Dundalk works in 1895, rebuilt in 1917 and retired when the Dundalk to Greenore Line closed in 1951.

At the far end of the platform stands *Dunluce Castle*, built in Glasgow in 1928 for the Belfast-Larne Line to the 5ft 3in. Irish gauge. She was retired in 1961, having covered more than a million miles in steam. Close by is *Maeve*, the Great Southern Railways 800, the first and only survivor of a class of three built in Dublin in 1939 for the Dublin-Cork line on which she pulled 400-ton passenger trains non-stop and unassisted. She is viewed at ground level, giving full effect to her weight of 84 tons, wheel height of 6 feet 7 inches and tractive effort of 35,000 lbs. It also adds piquancy to the story of her disappearance for several days in 1947. She ran out of coal *en route* for Cork, the engine was detached from the train and shunted into a wayside shed. Her crew went off duty and it was some days later that Dublin realized that *Maeve* was lost. Enquiries up and down the line produced her from a small shed at a wayside station. All steam enthusiasts will hope that it won't happen again on her way from Witham Street to Cultra!

At the opposite end of the scale from *Maeve* is one of the 2ft narrow-gauge engines which for fifty-one years until 1956 performed the enviable task of hauling barrels of Guinness at the Dublin brewery. Narrow-gauge railways played an important part in the economy of Ireland, particularly in opening up the western part of the country, but it was the omnibus with its route flexibility and superior cost efficiency that defeated them in the end. An example of the compromise stock that was tried in an attempt to hold off the omnibus proper is here in the shape of the tiny rail bus from the County Donegal Railways. Purchased by them in 1906 as a petrol-driven inspection car and later modified for passenger-carrying, it was in use, with a trailer coach, from 1926 to about 1952 between Stranorbar and Strabane. It is one of the oldest and smallest of such vehicles to be seen anywhere and, with its red and yellow paintwork brighly restored, is one of the gems of the collection. Close by the rail bus is what is certainly the smallest permanent-way vehicle. It is a Belfast-made pedal-and-chain-driven inspector's trolley with side-by-side seating. Being light in weight and readily portable, it could be quite easily lifted off the track so as not to disturb train schedules. The inspector and his foreman must have enjoyed, on a summer's day, their sedate cycle along the permanent way. Similar machines were used by railways throughout the world, some being equipped with auxiliary sails.

As well as the railway collection, the Witham Street depot houses the museum's trams. There are three double-deckers from the city of Belfast, a horse-drawn tramcar in use from about 1885 to 1905, an ex-horse tramcar converted to electric traction about 1905 and in use until 1948 and a modern car in service from 1929 to 1954, the year the service ended. All these vehicles are to the English standard gauge 4ft 8½in.* There are other tramcars on show that operated on the larger gauge of 5 feet 3 inches, such as the double-decker on the Great Northern Railway (Ireland) on its Fintona line in County Tyrone which, throughout its entire life, from 1883 to when the line closed in 1957, was pulled by horses. Representatives of the 3ft narrow-gauge operation are here too: the Bessbrook-Newry tram of 1885 and the single-

---

*Strangely, the track reconstruction contracts of the 1920s quote 4ft 9in as the required gauge!

The interior of the museum at Witham Street, Belfast, where the public-service vehicle, railway and part of the motor-vehicle collections of the Ulster Transport Museum are displayed pending their move to the new museum site at Cultra. Photo: Ulster Folk and Transport Museum.

A photograph of a tram and trailer of the Giant's Causeway Tramway taken at Dunluce in 1875. The empty front section is for first-class passengers. At the Witham Street depot of the Ulster Transport Museum there is a well-preserved trailer car from this tramway which is claimed to be the oldest hydro-electric system in the world. Photo: Ulster Transport Museum.

deck trailer car of the Giant's Causeway system, said to be the oldest hydro-electric system in the world.

Witham Street also contains many motor cars (mainly from the twenties and the majority on loan from private owners) and a fine assembly of over fifty motor cycles with famous British names such as Velocette, Sunbeam, Ariel, Triumph, Scott and Norton. It also has horse-drawn carriages and coaches, veteran cycles and vintage scooters, but as all these items are part of the reserve stock for the established displays at Cultra any detailed description would quite soon be out of context.

It is this depth and breadth of material that makes the Ulster Transport Museum so exciting in both its present state and its potential. By its move to Cultra it has the opportunity, over the years, to develop into one of the premier transport museums in Europe.

GAZETTEER

The following pages list and briefly describe all the transport museums in the main text plus fifty-four others.

Each entry includes:
Name of museum
Address
Telephone number if available
Details of access by public transport where possible
Brief description of exhibits
Opening times
Facilities

Symbols used for facilities are:
P parking
R refreshments
S shop

Each entry is numbered. Italic numbers (e.g. *26*, used for museums not in the main text) refer to the endpaper map. Museums with main-text entries have bold numbers (e.g. **168**) which are page references as well as being on the map.

I LONDON

13 BL Heritage Motor Museum
Syon Park, Brentford, London.
TEL. 01-560 1378
By rail from Waterloo to Kew Bridge, then bus; or by Underground or North London Railway to Gunnersbury, then bus.

BL Heritage is a subsidiary of BL Limited and preserves a collection of over three hundred historic vehicles originally built by the constituent companies of BL. Only a proportion of the collection is displayed at any one time within the programme of frequently changing presentations. Every craft in the motor business from coach building to foundry work, from Grand Prix engines to double-deck buses is represented.

Open Tuesday to Sunday inclusive, including bank holidays except Christmas Day and Boxing Day.

P   R   S

17 Historic Ships Collection of the Maritime Trust
St Katharine's by the Tower, London E1 9LB.
TEL. 01-481 0043
By Underground to Tower Hill.

The Maritime Trust's Historic Ships Collection features a range of British coastal vessels, both sail and steam. Most can be boarded and some have exhibitions in their hold which present an excellent review of the coastal trade in the eighteenth and nineteenth centuries, particularly the fishing industry.

Open daily throughout the year.

P   R   S

20 HMS *Belfast*
Symons Wharf, Vine Lane, London SE1 2JH.
TEL. 01-407 6434
By rail to London Bridge; or Underground to London Bridge or Tower Hill. A ferry operates daily from Tower Pier throughout the summer and at weekends in winter.

The last survivor of the Royal Navy's big ships whose main armament was guns, the 11,500-ton cruiser HMS *Belfast* is permanently moored in the River Thames opposite the Tower of London as a floating naval museum. During the Second World War *Belfast* played a key role in the sinking of the German battleship *Scharnhorst*. The greater part of the ship is open to the public.

Open daily. Closed most bank holidays.

P   R   S

1 Imperial War Museum
Lambeth Road, London SE1 6HZ.
TEL. 01-735 8922
By Underground to Lambeth North or Elephant and Castle.

The Imperial War Museum illustrates and records all aspects of the two World Wars and other military operations involving Britain and the Commonwealth since 1914. Exhibits with transport connections includes aircraft and armoured fighting vehicles.

Open daily. Closed most bank holidays.

P   R   S

23 London Transport Museum
Covent Garden, London WC2E 7BB.
TEL 01-379 6344
By Underground to Covent Garden (closed Sundays), Charing Cross, Leicester Square or Holborn; or by bus to Aldwych or Strand.

Horse buses, motor buses, trams, trolleybuses and railway vehicles illustrate the story and growth of London's transport systems. Special displays allowing the visitor to operate the controls of an Underground train or operate points or signals give added interest. The Old Flower Market building in which the museum is housed is of special interest.

Open daily except Christmas Day and Boxing Day.

P   R   S

2 London Cab Company Museum
1–3 Brixton Road, London SW9 6DJ.
TEL. 01-735 7777
By Underground to the Oval.

A modest display of London taxicabs from the turn of the century to the present day.

Open Monday to Friday and Saturday morning.

P

27 Mosquito Aircraft Museum
Salisbury Hall, London Colney, Nr St Albans, Herts.
TEL. Bowmansgreen 23274

By rail to St Albans, then bus; or by Underground to High Barnet, then bus.

It was here that the prototype of the historic de Havilland Mosquito aircraft was designed and built. The original aircraft survived and is on display along with other examples of de Havilland fighters, including the Venom and the Vampire as well as earlier types from the same stable such as the Chipmunk and the Tiger Moth.

Open Sundays from Easter to end of September and Thursdays from July to September.

P

3   Museum of London
London Wall, London EC2Y 5HN.
TEL. 01-600 3699
By rail to Cannon Street, Holborn Viaduct or Liverpool Street; or by Underground to Barbican, Moorgate or St Paul's.

There are a number of items in the Museum of London related to the history of transport: the remains of a boat from Roman times, an eighteenth-century sedan chair, a hansom cab, a Model T Ford car and a number of early fire engines make up an interesting collection. The premier transport exhibit is the Lord Mayor's state coach which has been the much-treasured centrepiece of the Lord Mayor's Show since it was built in 1757.

Open Tuesday to Sunday.

R   S

29   National Maritime Museum
Romney Road, Greenwich, London SE10 9NF.
TEL. 01-858 4422
By rail to Maze Hill; or by ferry (in summer) from Charing Cross Pier.

The National Maritime Museum is by far the largest and most complex museum in the world. It is concerned with every aspect of mankind's encounter with the sea and its displays and presentations will delight both the child and the scholar. The library, reference section and information service are excellent.

Open every day except bank holidays.

P   R   S

35   Royal Air Force Museum and Battle of Britain Museum
Aerodrome Road, Hendon, London NW9 5LL.
TEL. 01-205 2266
By Underground to Colindale.

Two quite separate museums on one site. The Royal Air Force Museum is the only British national museum devoted solely to the history of aviation and to the complete story of the Royal Air Force. The Battle of Britain Museum exhibits both Allied and Axis aircraft connected with this historic event and realistically portrays events in the air and on the ground.

Open every day except bank holidays.

P   R   S

4   Royal Mews
Buckingham Palace, London SW1.
By rail or Underground to Victoria.

The royal carriages, horses, harnesses and related equipment are on display.

Open Wednesday and Thursday afternoons (not Ascot Week in June).

42   Science Museum
Exhibition Road, London SW7 2SS.
TEL. 01-589 3456
By Underground to South Kensington.

Contains one of the most comprehensive transport collections in the world, covering road, rail, air and sea. The emphasis is on technical and historical development but the displays lack the imaginative presentation in evidence elsewhere in the museum.

Open daily except most bank holidays.

P   R   S

II THE SOUTH

53   Baby Carriage Collection
Bettenham Manor, Biddenden, Kent TN27 8LT.
TEL. Biddenden 291343
By rail to Headcorn or Staplehurst (6 miles).

One of the largest collections of prams and baby carriages in the world with some three hundred exhibits dating from 1750 to the present time, together with much related ephemera.

Open by appointment.

P

55   C. M. Booth's Collection of Historic Vehicles

63 High Street, Rolvenden, Kent.
TEL. Rolvenden 234
By bus to Tenterden Ashford.

This rather general title covers the specific interest of Mr Booth in the Morgan three-wheeler car and the main feature of the museum is a unique collection of Morgans dating from 1913, plus the only known Humber tri-car of 1904.

Opening times vary – check by telephone.

P   S

5   Breamore Carriage Museum

Breamore House, Nr Fordingbridge, Hants.
TEL. Breamore 233 and 468
By rail to Salisbury, then bus.

A small collection of horse-drawn vehicles and coaches, mainly nineteenth-century and displayed in the old stables of Breamore House which afford a very appropriate setting.

Open every afternoon except Monday and Friday from April to end of September.

P   R

6   Buckler's Hard Maritime Museum

Buckler's Hard, Beaulieu, Brockenhurst, Hants S04 7XB.
TEL. Buckler's Hard 203
By rail to Brockenhurst (7 miles).

This museum traces the history of Buckler's Hard on the banks of the Beaulieu river. It was a flourishing shipbuilding hamlet which built a number of Nelson's ships. The museum contains some fine models and a number of Nelson relics.

Open daily all year round.

7   Cobham Bus Museum

Redhill Road, Cobham, Surrey KT11 1EF.
TEL. Cobham 4078
By rail to Weybridge (2 miles).

Here under one roof is a motley collection of privately owned buses belonging to members of the London Bus Preservation Group. There are some forty buses, mainly from the period between the wars, and a collection of street furniture and associated relics.

Open on the last Sunday of each month.

P

8   Cowes Maritime Museum

Cowes Library, Beckford Road, Cowes, Isle of Wight PO31 7SE.
By ferry from the mainland; by bus from other parts of the island.

Based upon the archives of a local shipbuilding firm and including a magnificient photograph collection of the construction, launching and trials of the ships, boats and yachts built by the firm, the scope of the museum is being widened to embrace the maritime history of Cowes and the Isle of Wight generally.

Open Monday to Saturday. Closed Sundays and bank holidays.

P

9   Dolphin Sailing Barge Museum

Dolphin Yard, Crown Quay Lane, Sittingbourne, Kent.
TEL. Sittingbourne 24132
By rail to Sittingbourne.

This folk museum is based at one of the old East Coast shipyards and places particular emphasis on the history of the Thames sailing barge. It has a particularly fine collection of barge-building equipment and visitors can observe the work of restoring and re-rigging sailing barges still in commission.

Open Sundays and bank holidays.

P   R   S

10   Gangbridge Collection

Gangbridge House, St Mary Bourne, Hants.
By rail to Whitchurch.

A private collection of about sixty motor cycles dating from 1909 to 1965. Most have been restored to running order.

Open by prior arrangement in writing.

P

11   Museum of Airborne Forces

Browning Barracks, Queens Avenue, Aldershot, Hants GU11 2DS.
TEL. 0252 24431
By rail to Aldershot, then bus (5 minutes).

The museum depicts the history of the British Airborne Forces from their inception in 1940 to the present day. The presentation is mainly in model and photographic form but just outside the museum is a DC3 Dakota, one of the most famous aircraft of all time, which took part in all the major airborne operations in the Second World War.

Open every day except Christmas Day.

P S

57 National Motor Museum
Beaulieu, Hants SO4 7ZN.
TEL. 0590 612345
By rail to Brockenhurst (7 miles); or by bus from Lymington or Hythe.

The National Motor Museum is one of the world's finest motor museums with over two hundred historic vehicles presenting the story of motoring and the motor car from its nineteenth-century beginning to the present day. It includes four Land Speed Record cars and excellent presentations of commercial vehicles and motor cycles. The purpose-built building is of considerable interest.

Open daily all year round.

P R S

12 **Poole Maritime Museum**
Paradise Street, Poole, Dorset.
TEL. Poole 5323
By rail to Poole.

The museum is appropriately housed in a fifteenth-century building on the quayside which has been the focal point of the port's activities for many centuries. It is a very small museum but contains many fascinating maritime relics and a number of preserved local boats.

Open every day except Christmas Day, Boxing Day and Good Friday.

P S

60 R. J. Mitchell Aircraft Museum
Kingsbridge Lane, Southampton, Hants SO1 0EB.
TEL. Southampton 25830
By rail to Southampton.

This museum is a memorial to R. J. Mitchell, the designer of the Spitfire and many other famous aircraft. A Spitfire and the Supermarine S6A, which competed in the 1929 Schneider Trophy race, are the main exhibits.

Open Tuesday to Sunday.

S

13 **Ramsgate Motor Museum**
West Cliff Hall, Ramsgate, Kent.
TEL. 0843 581948

By rail to Ramsgate.

This is the second motor museum venture set up by Lord Cranworth and it follows the style of his first enterprise, the Banham International Motor Museum in Norfolk. Over forty cars and motor cycles from the early days to the post-war period are presented on backcloths relevant to their history. There is also a marine archaeological exhibition.

Open daily during the summer season.

R P

14 **Southampton Maritime Museum**
Wool House, Bugle Street, Southampton, Hants.
TEL. 0703 23941
By rail to Southampton, then bus.

This small museum is accommodated in the fourteenth-century Wool House which was originally a warehouse, but was used in the eighteenth century to house French and Spanish prisoners-of-war. Photographic displays illustrate the development of the port and there is an interesting collection of model ships.

Open Tuesday to Sunday. Closed most bank holidays.

62 Tyrwhitt-Drake Museum of Carriages
Archbishop's Stables, Mill Street, Maidstone, Kent.
TEL. 0622 54497
By rail to Maidstone East or Maidstone West.

This famous collection of horse-drawn vehicles, including most types of state, official and private carriage and more modest conveyances totalling over fifty in all, is almost wholly the creation of the man from whom it takes its name, the late Sir Garrard Tyrwhitt-Drake. It is housed in a fifteenth-century stable block which is a scheduled Ancient Monument.

Open every weekday. Closed Sundays and bank holidays.

65 HMS *Victory* and the Royal Naval Museum
HM Naval Base, Portsmouth, Hants PO1 3LR.
TEL. 0705 22351
By rail to Portsmouth Harbour.

HMS *Victory*, Lord Nelson's flagship at the Battle of Trafalgar, is still in commission with the Royal Navy and now rests in a permanent berth at Portsmouth dockyard. Adjacent to *Victory* and housed in the restored Georgian dockyard buildings, the Royal Naval Museum contains many relics of Nelson and Trafalgar but has as its main aim the presentation of naval history from King Alfred's time to the nuclear age.

Open every day except Christmas Day, Boxing Day and New Year's Day.

15   Warnham War Museum
Durford Hill, Warnham, Nr Horsham, West Sussex.
TEL. 0403 65607

By rail to Horsham (3 miles).

A very large collection of vehicles and equipment from both World Wars and from British, American and German sources. The displays are enlivened by appropriate backgrounds and spoken commentaries.

Open every day of the year.

III THE SOUTH-WEST

16   Arlington Court Carriage Museum
Arlington, Nr Barnstaple, Devon.
TEL. 039 288 681
By rail to Barnstaple.

Arlington Court was donated to the National Trust by its last owner, Miss Rosalie Chichester, who had many interests including a very fine collection of ship models which are now displayed. The collection of carriages in the stables is of great interest.

Open Tuesday to Sunday from 1 April to 31 October.

P

17   Bath Carriage Museum
Circus Mews, Bath BA1 2PW.
TEL. 0225 25175

By rail to Bath, then bus.

An interesting collection of over thirty horse-drawn vehicles and coaches with a display of harness, liveries and whips together with many mementoes of the coaching era including prints and documents. The coaches are all housed in an eighteenth-century mews and the state coach loaned by the Duke of Somerset is splendidly presented.

Open daily except Christmas Day.

P

71   Bicton Hall of Transport
East Budleigh, Budleigh Salterton, Devon EX9 7DP.
TEL. 1395 68465
By rail to Exmouth, then bus.

The Hall of Transport is part of the many attractions of the Bicton estate which include a countryside museum, magnificent gardens and a woodland railway. The hall has been built around

a private collection of Benz and steam cars and includes an interesting collection of early motor vehicles, motor cyles, cycles and related transport accessories.

Open daily from 1 April to 31 October.

P   R   S

18   Camborne Carriage Collection
Lower Grilles Farm, Treskillard, Nr Camborne, Cornwall.
TEL. Camborne 3606
By rail to Camborne, then bus.

A private collection of horse-drawn conveyances including carriage, trade and agricultural vehicles and a number of Shire, carriage and riding horses. There is also a large collection of harness and horse brasses.

Open daily during the summer.

P   R

73   Cornwall Aero Park
Culdrose Manor, Helston, Cornwall TR13 0GA.
TEL. Helston 3404
By rail to Redruth (10 miles), then bus.

A relaxed and entertaining exhibition which ranges from the setting of coaches and Edwardian cars in appropriate street scenes to allowing the visitor to board a Concorde flight deck and sit at the controls of hovercraft, helicopters and Second World War bombers.

Open Easter to November.

P   R   S

19   Dodington Carriage Museum
Dodington, Chipping Sodbury, Avon BS17 6SF.
TEL. 0454 318899

A Ford GPW 'Jeep' which saw service with the British Army in North Africa, now part of the large display at the Warnham War Museum. This vehicle is an example of the type adapted for use by the SAS for long-range penetration behind enemy lines. Photo: Warnham War Museum.

By rail to Bristol or Bath, then bus.

The carriage museum housed in the stables of this splendid house and park is both interesting and instructive. There are over forty vehicles which include specimens of almost every well-known type of carriage. There is also a fine collection of sporting and coaching prints, harness and livery.

Open April to September – days vary.

P R S

75   Exeter Maritime Museum
The Quay, Exeter EX2 4AN.
TEL. 0392 36031
By rail to Exeter.

One of the most interesting and exciting museums to be opened in recent times. The world's largest collection of British and foreign boats displayed in and around the quay buildings and basin of the old ship canal and dock area.

Open every day of the year except Christmas Day and Boxing Day.

P R S

78   Fleet Air Arm Museum and Concorde Exhibition
RN Air Station, Yeovilton, Somerset BA22 8HT.
TEL. 0935 840551
By rail to Yeovil, then bus.

A unique collection of over forty historic naval aircraft. Many ship and aircraft models, paintings and photographs present a full history of the Fleet Air Arm and Royal Naval Air Service. Flying can be seen most weekdays and Concorde 002, the first British prototype, is preserved in a separate exhibition hall.

Open every day except Christmas Eve and Christmas Day.

P   R   S

84   SS *Great Britain*
Great Western Dock, Gas Ferry Road, Bristol, Avon BS1 6TY.
TEL. 0272 20680
By rail to Temple Meads, Bristol.

The SS *Great Britain*, launched in Bristol in 1843, was the first iron, propeller-driven ship in history and one of Isambard Kingdom Brunel's finest achievements. Her recovery and return from the Falkland Islands and her restoration is one of the most remarkable preservation projects of all time.

Open daily.

P   R   S

20   **Guernsey Motor Museum**
La Charroterie, St Peter Port, Guernsey, Channel Islands.
TEL. 0481 28313
By bus.

Here displayed is one man's vehicle collection. It has no theme or story to tell but is a combination of motoring nostalgia and exotica and includes, amongst many Rolls-Royces, a 1908 Silver Ghost in addition to a 1932 Hispano-Suiza, a rare 1913 Buick two-seater and fire engines, motor cycles and cycles.

Open every day during the summer season.

P   R   S

21   **Jersey Motor Museum**
St Peter's Village, Jersey, Channel Islands.
TEL. 0534 82966
By bus from St Helier.

A small collection of mainly vintage cars, with a particular emphasis on the preservation of transport relics and photographic records related to the history of the island.

Open daily from March to November.

P   R   S

22   **North Devon Maritime Museum**
Odun House, Appledore, Devon.
TEL. Bideford 6042
By train to Barnstaple, then bus.

A range of presentations on aspects of Devon's maritime history with good use of models and photographs to illustrate fishing, shipbuilding, pilotage and navigation.

Open daily from Easter to end of September.

P

23   **National Lifeboat Museum**
Princes Wharf, Wapping Road, Bristol, Avon BS1 4RN.
TEL. 0272 213389
By rail to Bristol.

Slowly developing in a disused warehouse in the Bristol City Docks and adjacent to the Bristol Industrial Museum and SS *Great Britain*, this museum displays an increasing range of traditionally built lifeboats together with old equipment and examples of today's life-saving technology.

Open Saturday and Sunday from 1 April to end of September.

87   Torbay Aircraft Museum
Higher Blagdon, Nr Paignton, Devon.
TEL. 0803 553540
By rail to Totnes or Paignton.

Organized to offer something for all the family, this museum relies heavily on nostalgia. It has on display more than twenty aircraft and operates a policy of frequently changing exhibitions on various aeronautical subjects that are both interesting and instructive.

Open daily except Christmas Day and Boxing Day.

P   R   S

24   **Totnes Motor Museum**
Totnes, Devon.
TEL. 0803 862777
By rail to Totnes.

A private collection of motor cars ranging across fifty years and including the modest Austin 7 as well as such exotic machinery as an Alfa-Romeo Super Sport and a Talbot Lago $4\frac{1}{2}$-litre. There is also a fascinating collection of racing photographs. The museum is housed in one of the early warehouses of the port of Totnes.

Open daily from Easter to October.

P   S

IV THE EAST

91   Banham International Motor Museum
Banham, Norfolk.
TEL. 0473 35 202
By rail to Attleborough or Diss (6 miles).

A very interesting private collection owned by
Lord Cranworth and covering the great years of
motoring from the elegance of the 1920s to the
excitement of the sports cars of the 1950s. The cars
are placed in imaginative settings of the period in
which they were built.

Open every day during the summer season.

P   R   S

25   **Caister Castle Motor Museum**
Caister-on-Sea, Nr Great Yarmouth, Norfolk.
TEL. 057 284 251
By rail to Great Yarmouth (4 miles).

One of the few museums that the author has not
visited. Reputed to contain many veteran and
vintage cars and some interesting steam-driven
vehicles.

Open every day except Saturday from May to
September.

P   R

26   **East Anglia Maritime Museum**
Marine Parade, Great Yarmouth, Norfolk.
TEL. Great Yarmouth 2267
By rail to Great Yarmouth.

The museum is housed in a large Victorian building
which was formerly the shipwrecked sailors' home.
The displays are on three floors and centre on the
history and activities of the port of Yarmouth and
the Norfolk Broads. They include the history of the
herring fisheries, local shipbuilding and coastal
trading, and there is an outstanding collection of
models and photographs.

Open every day from June to September and
Monday to Friday from October to May; closed
most bank holidays.

P

94   East Anglia Transport Museum
Chapel Road, Carlton Colville, Lowestoft, Suffolk.
TEL. Ubberston 398
By rail to Lowestoft, then bus.

A working museum on a 3-acre site that has

brought together a great variety of vehicles from all
fields of transport. They include motor cars,
commercial vehicles, motor buses, trolleybuses,
tramcars and steam rollers. Rides are given on a
tram service and a narrow-gauge railway.

Open weekends and bank holidays from April to
September and from Tuesday to Friday during
August.

P   R

98   Historic Aircraft Museum
Aviation Way, Southend, Essex.
TEL. 0702 545881
By rail to Southend.

The museum displays over thirty aircraft of various
types from de Havillands of the twenties to modern
British and American fighters, plus many other
aeronautical exhibits.

Open daily from May to September and at
weekends from October to April.

P   R   S

100   Imperial War Museum at Duxford
Duxford, Cambs CB2 4QR.
TEL. 0223 833963
By rail to Cambridge, then bus.

The location of this museum is itself historic. It was
a military airfield in the First World War and a
Battle of Britain station in the Second World War.
British civil aircraft are very well represented and
include Concorde 001. The main exhibition is of the
Imperial War Museum's collection of military
aircraft, tanks, patrol boats, etc., and the purpose of
the enterprise is to demonstrate military transport
in all its aspects.

Open daily from March to end of October.

P   R   S

27   **Lincolnshire Aviation Museum**
Old Station Yard, Tattershall, Lincs.
TEL. 0526 42249
By rail to Boston (14 miles).

A small but interesting aircraft collection brought
together by a group of aviation enthusiasts. Among
the exhibits is a Ward P45 Gnome which is the
UK's smallest piloted aircraft.

A heavily laden wherry working on the Broads. The story of the Norfolk wherries is told by the East Anglia Maritime Museum and the wherry Albion *still sails in the care of the Norfolk Wherry Trust. Photo: Norfolk Wherry Trust.*

Open on Sundays and bank holidays, Easter to October.

P

28 Norfolk and Suffolk Aviation Museum
Flixton, Nr Bungay, Suffolk.
TEL. 050845 444
By rail to Beccles (5 miles).

A handful of British and American fighter aircraft from the Second World War, aircraft engines and equipment and a number of displays present a useful history of the development of flying.

Open afternoons on Thursday, Saturday and Sunday from Easter to end of September.

P

29 Sandringham Museum
Sandringham Estate, Norfolk.
TEL. King's Lynn 2675
By rail to King's Lynn, then bus

Sandringham will generally be visited for reasons other than its transport collection but it is not one that should be missed. It is small, consisting mostly of vehicles that have been associated with the estate, but contains the first car owned by the royal family – a 1900 Daimler Tonneau delivered to the Prince of Wales (later Edward VII) in that year.

Open various days throughout the year.

P R

105 Shuttleworth Collection
Old Warden Aerodrome, Nr Biggleswade, Beds.
TEL. 0767 27 288
By rail to Biggleswade (3 miles) or Bedford (10 miles); or fly in!

The collection contains a unique range of airworthy historic aircraft dating from 1909 onwards and has many flying days throughout the summer. There is also an interesting display of veteran and vintage motor cars, motor cycles and fire engines

Open every day of the year except Christmas period.

P R S

30 Thursford Collection
Thursford, Nr Fakenham, Norfolk NR21 0AS.
TEL. Fakenham 3836
By rail to King's Lynn (30 miles).

Not really a transport collection but a delightful display of steam road locomotives, showman's traction engines and steam wagons and barn oil engines presented with the sound of the music of Wurlitzer organs and a gondola ride.

Open daily from Easter to end of October. Sunday only from November to Easter.

P R S

V THE MIDLANDS

115 Birmingham Museum of Science and Industry
Newhall Street, Birmingham B3 1RZ.
TEL. 021 236 1022
By rail to Birmingham (New Street).

As its name suggests, the museum's interests are wide-ranging but transport plays a very important part and railway, public and private transport, aviation and their associated engineering developments are well covered.

Open daily except for Christmas Day, Boxing Day and Good Friday.

P S

31 Black Country Museum
Tilton Road, Dudley, West Midlands DY1 4SQ.
TEL. 021 537 9643
By rail to Wolverhampton (6 miles), then bus.

An open-air museum illustrating the social and industrial history of the region. The development of the canal system is well presented and the influence of the horse-drawn vehicle, the tramcar and the trolleybus as well as that of the private car is covered.

Open every day except Saturday from 1 May to 31 October.

P R S

118   Bourton Motor Museum
The Old Mill, Bourton-on-the-Water,
Nr Cheltenham, Gloucs.
TEL. 0451 21255
By rail to Cheltenham Spa or Moreton-in-Marsh,
then bus.

The owners of this private museum have taken
some care to recreate the atmosphere of the
motoring age between the wars. There are some
early veteran cars but the emphasis is on the
twenties and thirties, and some thirty vehicles plus a
collection of more than two hundred old motoring
and garage signs convey the style of the period
with effect.

Open every day.

P   S

32   **'Canal Story' Exhibition**
Clock Warehouse, London Road, Shardlow,
Derbys DE7 2GL.
TEL. 0332 792844
By rail to Long Eaton, then bus.

Housed in a restored eighteenth-century canal
warehouse, this exhibition tells the story of the
building of the canal system and, by the use of
photographs, dioramas and models, illustrates the
sort of life the boat people led and the work they
did. It is not a museum, in that very few original
articles are displayed, but presents the rise and the
reasons for the decline of the canal system in a
straightforward and interesting way.

Open every day.

P   R   S

121   Campden Car Collection
High Street, Chipping Campden, Gloucs GL55 6HB.
TEL. 0386 840289
By rail to Moreton-in-Marsh (8 miles) or Evesham (9
miles), then bus.

A unique collection of Jaguar production and
racing cars plus a range of sports cars all in original
condition, and an outstanding library of black and
white and colour photographs of motor racing in
the twenties and thirties.

Open daily, except Mondays and Fridays, from
Easter to September.

P

123   Donington Collection
Donington Park, Castle Donington, Derby DE7 5RP.
TEL. 0332 810048

By rail to Derby (8 miles), then bus.

This, the largest single-seater racing-car collection
in the world, is located adjacent to the historic
racing circuit at Castle Donington which is still in
use. It traces the history of motor sport from the
pre-war period to the present day.

Open every day except during Christmas week.

P   R   S

33   **Leicester Museum of Transport**
Corporation Road, Leicester LE5 4PX.
TEL. 0533 554100
By rail to Leicester, then bus.

A section of this museum has a transport collection
which covers motor vehicles, motor cycles, horse-
drawn vehicles, fire appliances and cycles. It also
has a large collection of battery electric vehicles.

Open every day except Christmas and bank
holidays.

P

34   **Midland Air Museum**
Coventry Airport, Baginton, Warks CV3 4FR.
By rail to Coventry (7 miles), then bus.

Here is a collection brought together by air
enthusiasts which includes some very interesting
aircraft: the Gloster Meteor, for example, and the
de Havilland Vampire, as well as the less well-
known Boulton Paul P111A, the single-engined
delta-wing research aircraft. The collection has a
span of over sixty years of military and civil
aircraft types.

Open on Sundays

P

127   Midland Motor Museum
Stourbridge Road, Bridgnorth, Salop.
TEL. 074 62 61761
By rail to Wolverhampton (14 miles), then bus.

A remarkable collection of international sports cars,
all of which have been fully restored and are
capable of the performance for which they were
originally designed. The motor cycles and the
collection of photographs and paintings are
outstanding.

Open every day except Christmas Day.

P   R   S

130   Museum of British Road Transport
Cook Street, Coventry.

TEL. 0203 25555
By rail to Coventry.

Here, in the home of the British motor industry, is a museum devoted to the contribution that the Midlands has made to the development of road transport. The museum has over a hundred cars and commercial vehicles, fifty motor cycles, two hundred and fifty cycles and a wide variety of transport artefacts and literature. The technical development of transport and its social influence are well presented.

Open every day except Monday.

134   National Cycle Museum
Belton House, Grantham, Lincs NG32 2LW.
TEL. 0476 67719
By rail to Grantham.

One of the latest museums to appear on the scene and certainly one of the most interesting, its purpose is to show the technical development of the cycle and its social effects. Photographs and period costumes give added atmosphere to the wide range of cycles displayed.

Open every day March to October. Other times by appointment.

P   R   S

136   Newark Air Museum
Winthorpe Airfield, Newark, Notts.
TEL. 0636 76302
By rail to Newark, then bus.

This museum is a fine example of what a group of enthusiastic amateurs can do. It is a small collection of a variety of aircraft, engines and other relics. The volunteer members work on the restoration of the aircraft and run the museum.

Open Sundays and bank holidays, April to October.

P   S

138   Royal Air Force Aerospace Museum
RAF Cosford, Wolverhampton, West Midlands WV7 3EX.
TEL. Albrighton 4872
By rail to Cosford or Wolverhampton, then bus.

This splendid museum displays an impressive collection of more than fifty military and civil aircraft from the Bleriot to the de Havilland Comet and several examples of R & D aircraft. Within the hangars space equipment, engines and rockets are exhibited and there are excellent displays portraying the history of aviation.

Open Saturday, Sunday and bank holidays from Easter to end of October. School parties during the week by appointment.

P   R   S

141   Stanford Hall Collection of Racing and Historic Motor Cycles
Stanford Hall, Lutterworth, Leics LE17 6DM.
TEL. Swinford 250
By rail to Rugby, then bus.

It was in the grounds of Stanford Hall that the aviation pioneer Percy Pilcher was killed in 1899 and his life and work is recorded at Stanford. It is, however, the motor cycles that dominate and this collection must rate as one of the best in the world. All the famous racing and production names are here and the display of contemporary photographs is excellent.

Open Thursday, Saturday, Sunday and bank holidays from Easter to September.

P   R   S

144   Stratford Motor Museum
Shakespeare Street, Stratford-upon-Avon, Warwicks.
TEL. 0789 69413
By rail to Stratford-upon-Avon.

This museum takes as its theme 'The Golden Age of Motoring' and presents examples of some of the finest grand touring cars of the twenties and thirties, including some very exotic examples owned formerly by Indian maharajahs.

Open every day except Christmas Day.

P   S

147   Tramway Museum
Crich, Nr Matlock, Derbys DE4 5DP.
TEL. 077385 2565
By rail to Matlock.

Sited in a former quarry, the museum has a fascinating collection of more than forty horse, steam and electric trams, both British and foreign, covering the period 1873–1953. Visitors can ride on an operating tramway and see the depots and workshops.

Open Saturday, Sunday and bank holidays from Easter to end of October, and Tuesday, Wednesday and Thursday from 1 June to end of August.

P   R   S

150   Waterways Museum
Stoke Bruerne, Northants.
TEL. 0604 862229
By rail to Northampton, then bus.

At Stoke Bruerne – a Northamptonshire beauty spot which, with its hump-back bridge, canalside inn and picturesque lock, is itself a bit of canal history – the Waterways Museum records the fascinating canal story of over two centuries. Canal boats, prints, models, photographs, maps, documents and a display of the dress and costumes of the boat people tell a vivid tale.

Open daily from Easter to mid-October and from Tuesday to Sunday from October to March.

P   R   S

35   **West Wycombe Motor Museum**
Cockshoot Farm, West Wycombe, Nr High Wycombe, Bucks HP14 3AR.
TEL. 0494 443329
By rail to High Wycombe, then bus.

A recent arrival on the motor museum scene and including some very exotic machinery from the stables of Bugatti, BRM, Aston-Martin and Fraser Nash, plus the famous MG Magnette K3 once owned by Dick Seaman. Space is limited in the eighteenth-century barn in which they are shown and the fourteen cars on display at any one time are changed frequently.

Open daily from spring until November.

VI WALES

36   **Canal Exhibition Centre**
The Wharf, Llangollen, North Wales.
TEL. Llangollen 860702
By rail to Ruabon, then bus.

This canal museum was built especially with schoolchildren in mind. It presents the Canal Era in a most interesting way by using projected slides, photographs, narration display and working and static models. A trip on a horse-drawn boat is part of the fun.

Open every day from Easter to end of September.

C   R   S

37   **Pembrokeshire Motor Museum**
Pembroke Dock, Dyfed, South Wales.
TEL. Pembroke 3279
By rail to Pembroke.

A number of vintage and veteran cars and some early motor cycles and cycles are displayed. A replica garage of the twenties and an exhibition of period motoring costumes add to the atmosphere.

Open June to September daily except Saturdays.

155   Tom Norton Collection of Old Cycles and Tricycles
The Automobile Palace, Llandrindod Wells, Powys LD1 5HL.
TEL. Llandrindod Wells 2214
By rail to Llandrindod Wells.

A splendid collection of vintage cycles and tricycles, including some very rare models dating from 1867. Most were collected by the present owner's father and some were used by him for racing in the 1880s.

Open weekdays throughout the year. Closed Sundays and bank holidays.

P   R   S

38   **Wales Aircraft Museum**
Cardiff (Wales) Airport.
TEL. Cardiff 29880
By rail to Cardiff.

A privately run museum with a small collection of aircraft including the first production Auster, fighter aircraft, helicopters and a Viscount airliner.

Open every Sunday from April to end of October.

P   R

157   Welsh Industrial and Maritime Museum
Bute Street, Cardiff DF1 6AN.
TEL. 0222 371805
By rail to Cardiff.

Part of the National Museum of Wales, this tells the story of motive power in the history of the industrial development of the country. The transport displays include examples from road, rail, sea, canal and air with some very fine early motor cars, a horse-drawn bus, a trolleybus, canal boats and a magnificent pilot cutter.

Open every day except Mondays and most bank holidays.

P   R   S

VII THE NORTH-WEST

161   Boat Museum
Dock Yard Road, Ellesmere Port, Cheshire L65 4EF.
TEL. 051 355 1876
By rail to Birkenhead, then bus.

Situated in the old docks at the junction of the
Shropshire Union and Manchester Ship Canals, this
museum has brought together more then thirty
historic wide and narrow boats. There is an
exhibition illustrating the development of canals
and the life of the people who lived and worked on
them. Trips are available by horse-drawn narrow
boat.

Open daily from Easter to third week in October.

P   R   S

39   **Castletown Nautical Museum**
Bridge Street, Castletown, Isle of Man.
TEL. Douglas 5522
By bus from Douglas.

This tiny museum is based at the eighteenth-
century boathouse constructed to house the
clinker-built schooner *Peggy* which was built
locally in 1791. She still survives and is the main
exhibit along with excellent displays on the fishing
industry of the island and its ships.

Open every day from mid-May to late September.

P   R

40   **Gilbey Horses**
Ballacallin Bee, Crosby, Marown, Isle of Man.
TEL. 0624 851450
By bus from Douglas.

A very fine collection of more than twenty horse-
drawn coaches, carriages, wagons and carts. The
magnificent horses that pull them are stabled
nearby and can also be seen along with mares and
foals of the associated riding school. One of the few
bloodhound packs also is kennelled here.

Open daily over Easter and from 1 May to
30 September.

41   **Greater Manchester Museum of Transport**
c/o Greater Manchester Passenger Transport
Executive, Boyle Street, Manchester.
TEL. 061 273 3322
By rail to Manchester, then bus.

No area better deserves or requires a
comprehensive transport museum, but until such
time as one is established we must make do with

this commendable effort that has brought together
one of the largest collections of preserved buses in
the country. Housed in a former bus garage are
nearly fifty buses and coaches and a number of
displays of related material such as ticket and fare-
collection equipment, uniforms, models, stop-signs.

Open Sundays and bank holidays from early April
to late October.

P

42   **Heaton Park Tramway**
Heaton Park, Manchester.
TEL. 0706 43918
By bus from Manchester; or by electric train to
Bowker Vale or Heaton Park stations.

This tramway is a surviving section of the
Manchester Corporation Tramways and was
originally opened in 1905. A former Manchester
Corporation 'California' type car built in 1914 and a
former Blackpool and Fleetwood Car of similar
vintage provide rides and there is an exhibition of
the history of the Manchester Tramways. There is
also a vintage omnibus service in the park.

Open Sundays and bank holidays from late April to
the end of October and Wednesdays from May to
the end of July.

P   R

43   **Lakeland Motor Museum**
Cark-in-Cartmel, Cumbria.
TEL. 044 853 328
By rail to Windermere, then bus.

Set in the peaceful surroundings of the stately
Holker Hall, the Lakeland Motor Museum houses
over a hundred vehicles including a fine collection
of cars, many of vintage quality, and some excellent
racing and sports marques. There are also motor
cycles from the twenties and thirties and some
nineteenth-century bicycles. A special exhibition is
a full-sized replica of Sir Malcolm Campbell's
world-record-breaking car *Bluebird* which has a
particular association with the area.

Open daily except Saturdays from Easter Sunday to
30 September.

P   R   S

164   Manx Motor Museum
Crosby, Isle of Man.
TEL. Marown 236

A display of some of the buses on show at the Greater Manchester Museum of Transport. Photo: NW Museum of Science and Industry.

By rail or bus from Douglas.

The exhibits are small in number but have been sensibly selected to illustrate three main aspects in the history of the car: first, the early technology; second, a few design oddities; and third, some of the exotic American designs. There is also an example of a Peel, the only car manufactured in the Isle of Man.

Open daily except Sundays from May until mid-September.

P   R   S

166   Merseyside County Museums

William Brown Street, Liverpool,
Merseyside L3 8EN.
TEL. 051 207 0001
By rail to Liverpool (Lime Street).

The transport section in this wide-ranging museum concentrates on the land transport of the Merseyside area and the history of Liverpool as a port. The *Lion* locomotive of 1838 is splendidly displayed and there are horse-drawn vehicles from local estates and a Ford Anglia – the first car made

A former Manchester Corporation 'California' type tramcar built in 1914, now operating at the Heaton Park Tramway. Photo: Manchester Transport Museum Society.

The replica of 'Bluebird', Sir Malcolm Campbell's World Land Speed Record car. The Campbell association with the Lake District is very strong and the car is on show at the Lakeland Motor Museum. Photo: Lakeland Motor Museum.

on Merseyside. A gallery devoted to the story of the Port of Liverpool is well set out.

Open every day except Christmas Day, Boxing Day, New Year's Day and Good Friday.

P   R   S

168   Merseyside Maritime Museum
Pier Head, Liverpool, Merseyside L3 1DN.
TEL. 051 236 1492
By rail to Liverpool, then by Underground to James Street station (closed Sundays) or by bus.

This new museum is one of the most ambitious of recent times. The site is the quays and buildings of the South Docks area on Liverpool's world-famous waterfront. A start has been made on a long-term project to present the history of the Port of Liverpool in all its aspects, to tell the story of ships and the sea and to develop a collection of historic ships of all types. It has started very well.

Open every day from late May to November.

P   R   S

44   Murrays Motor Cycle Museum
Bungalow Corner, Snaefell, Isle of Man.
TEL. Laxey 719
By rail to Snaefell.

Here is a remarkable collection of more then eighty veteran and vintage motor cycles displayed in a building adjacent to the TT track. Photographs and relics of the racing abound and there are also some nineteenth-century cycles.

Open every day.

P

45   Port Erin Motor Museum
High Street, Port Erin, Isle of Man.
TEL. 0624 8329 64
By bus to Port Erin.

This museum, surprisingly located in a shopping precinct in Port Erin, has on display a splendid private collection of about twenty veteran and vintage cars including an 1899 Star, a French Vemorel and a 1919 Secqueville-Hoyau claimed to be the only one in the world in running condition.

Open daily in the summer season.

171   Windermere Steamboat Museum
Rayrigg Road, Windermere, Cumbria.
TEL. 09662 5565
By rail to Windermere.

This museum has a unique collection of Victorian and Edwardian steamlaunches, yachts and working boats and most are preserved in working order and frequently displayed on Lake Windermere itself. The museum building contains displays and exhibitions which tell the story of the Windermere district and its people.

Open daily from Easter to end of October.

P   R   S

VIII THE NORTH-EAST

46   Army Transport Museum
Normandy Barracks, Leconsfield,
North Humberside HU17 7LX.
TEL. 0401 50386
By rail to Beverley, then bus.

This museum is the Royal Corps of Transport collection of Army road, rail, sea and air transport, but space restrictions oblige it to concentrate on road and rail. The road-transport section consists of about twenty-seven vehicles and includes the wagon used by Lord Roberts in the South African War, the Rolls-Royce used by Montgomery in the Second World War and the only serviceable Comet tank in Europe. Other subjects are well covered pictorially.

Open Saturdays, Sundays and bank holidays from the last weekend in June to the last weekend in September.

P   R   S

47   Bradford Industrial Museum
Moorside Mills, Moorside Road, Eccleshill,
Bradford, West Yorks.
TEL. 0274 631756
By rail to Bradford Exchange.

The emphasis in this museum is properly placed on the history of the wool industry, but in the transport galleries are early cycles, a 1901 Foster steam car, Bradford-built Gowett cars, motor cycles

A lantern from the original lighthouse erected on the Heugh at Hartlepool in 1847 and now at the Hartlepool Maritime Museum. To the right is a simulated fisherman's cottage. Photo: Hartlepool Maritime Museum.

Part of the interior of the Army Transport Museum. Photo: Army Transport Museum.

and horse-drawn transport used for the local textile trade. The only surviving Bradford tram and a trolleybus are housed in an adjacent building.

Open daily except Christmas Day, Boxing Day and Good Friday.

P   R   S

48   Hartlepool Maritime Museum
Worthgate, Hartlepool, Cleveland.
TEL. 0429 66522
By rail to Hartlepool.

The purpose of this museum is to illustrate the maritime history of the town, and with models and displays it covers the principal subjects of fishing, shipbuilding and marine engineering in some detail and traces the rise of Hartlepool from a humble fishing port to an important maritime port. The presence of HMS *Warrior*, built in 1860 as the first all-iron armoured ship and being restored in the nearby Coal Dock, is an added – although temporary – attraction.

Open Monday to Saturday. Closed Christmas and bank holidays.

P   S

177   Kingston-upon-Hull Town Docks Museum
Queen Victoria Square, Kingston-upon-Hull, Humberside.
TEL. 0482 222737
By rail to Kingston-upon-Hull.

Housed in the fine old Dock Offices which overlooked the Town Docks when they existed, this museum contains what must be the finest collection in the country of arctic whaling artefacts including a superb scrimshaw collection. It tells the whaling story well. Other galleries deal with the Hull fishing and trawling industry and there is a fine collection of marine paintings by local artists.

Open every day except Christmas Day, Boxing Day and Good Friday.

49   Kingston-upon-Hull Transport Museum
36 High Street, Kingston-upon-Hull, Humberside.
TEL. 0482 222737
By rail to Kingston-upon-Hull (Paragon).

A formal presentation of horse-drawn vehicles, motor vehicles (mainly 1890 to 1910), bicycles and motor cycles. Prize exhibits are the Ryde Pier tram – Britain's oldest surviving tramcar – and the

Kitson steam tram locomotive of 1882.

Open every day except Christmas Day, Boxing Day and Good Friday.

P S

181   Sandtoft Transport Centre
Sandtoft, Nr Doncaster, South Yorks.
By rail to Doncaster, then bus.

Here is where Britain's largest single collection of preserved trolleybuses resides – almost fifty in all – together with associated ancillary vehicles and a handful of preserved motor buses. Restored trolleybuses operate public rides on the centre's own overhead circuits at various weekends throughout the year.

Open every other Sunday and every bank holiday from Easter to the end of September.

P   R   S

50   Yorkshire Museum of Carriages and Horse-Drawn Vehicles
Aysgarth Falls, Nr Hawes, North Yorks.
TEL. 0748 3325
By rail to Darlington, then bus.

This private collection of carriages, brought together from all over the United Kingdom, is one of the largest in the country. It contains a splendid road coach, a Windermere charabanc and an Irish jaunting car, plus a display of privately owned vehicles including a pony Victoria, a gig, a George IV phaeton, a remarkable 'Whiskey' (a two-wheeled sporting vehicle) and many more. There is also a large collection of harness and coach and carriage equipment.

Open every day from Easter to end of October.

IX SCOTLAND

51   Doune Motor Museum
Doune, Perthshire FK16 8HD.
TEL. 0786 84 203
By rail to Stirling, then bus.

This is one man's personal collection and there is no attempt to present a motoring theme or any particular aspect of motoring development. The interest is in the cars themselves and they are magnificent. The collection contains some thirty-five vintage and post-vintage thoroughbreds ranging from Alfa-Romeos, Hispano-Suizas, Bentleys, Aston-Martins and Bugattis to the second oldest Rolls-Royce in the world.

Open daily from April to October.

P   R   S

185   East Fortune Museum of Flight
East Fortune Airfield, North Berwick, East Lothian.
TEL. 062 088 308
By bus from Edinburgh

This museum is an outstation of the Royal Scottish museum. East Fortune was the departure point of the airship R34 which made the first east to west air crossing of the Atlantic. It is a developing museum and has brought together a small variety of aircraft

and aircraft equipment, with a particular emphasis on rocket development.

Open at various days during the year and by appointment.

P

187   Glasgow Museum of Transport
25 Albert Drive, Glasgow G41 2PE.
TEL. 041 423 8000
By rail to Pollokshields East; or Underground to West Street; or bus.

Nearly all aspects of transport history are represented here. The car collection includes an important group of Scottish-built vehicles; the oldest surviving pedal cycle in the world is exhibited, and there is an excellent horse-drawn vehicle collection. The tram, bus, train, traction engine and commercial vehicle are well represented and their histories are fully explained.

Open daily except Sundays, Christmas Day and New Year's Day.

P   R   S

52   Grampian Transport Museum
Old Station Yard, Alford, Aberdeenshire.

TEL. 0336 2045

By rail to Aberdeen (25 miles), then bus.

This contains a wide range of transport vehicles including a 1903 Silver Ghost, a rare 1926 Cluley car, a horse-drawn tram, a Ford Model A lorry and a number of interesting stationary engines. There is also a narrow-gauge (2ft) railway line with 1 mile of track.

Open every day from 1 April to 30 September.

53   Linlithgow Canal Museum

Manse Road Basin, Linlithgow, West Lothian.
TEL. 050 684 4730
By rail to Linlithgow; by bus from Stirling.

A tiny museum in a beautiful setting. Housed in a former stable for the barge horses, it presents by audio-visual displays and models a history of the 30-mile waterway and of the Scottish canal system as a whole. The replica steam packet *Victoria* operates regular trips on the restored canal.

Open Saturdays and Sundays from Easter to September.

194   Myreton Motor Museum

Aberlady, East Lothian.
TEL. Aberlady 288
By rail to Drewn; or by bus from Edinburgh.

An interesting collection of some seventy cars, motor cycles, cycles and commercial and military vehicles. A particularly enjoyable feature is that most of the vehicles are unrestored and have a 'still in use' feeling. No historical or theme displays are attempted, but questions on particular items are readily answered by the curator.

Open daily from May to October and winter weekends.

P   S

198   Royal Scottish Museum

Chambers Street, Edinburgh EH1 1JF.
TEL. 031 225 7534
By rail to Edinburgh.

The Royal Scottish Museum is a national museum and transport comes under its Department of Technology whose aim is to illustrate technical development and how things work. The transport collection is not a large one but has some early Scottish horse-drawn vehicles and motor cars and a notable collection of ship models. The technical 'how and why' is well presented.

Open every day except Christmas and New Year period.

P   R   S

54   Strathallan Aircraft Collection

Auchterarder, Perthshire PH3 1LA.
TEL. 07646 2545

A collection of small historic aircraft including a Lancaster bomber and fighter aircraft from the Second World War. A de Havilland Comet airliner museum is in a separate hangar and there is a programme of flying days in the summer.

Open every day.

P   R   S

X NORTHERN IRELAND

203   Ulster Transport Museum

Cultra Manor, Holywood BT18 0EU.
TEL. Holywood 5411
By rail to Cultra; or by bus from Belfast.

The Ulster Transport Museum is at present divided between the new building at Cultra and the former museum building at Witham Street, Belfast. When completed, the new Transport Museum will provide for the adequate exhibition of all Irish transport history. Meanwhile, the displays are limited but well presented.

Open every day.

INDEX